THE
BLACK ROSE
OF
FLORENCE

THE
BLACK ROSE
OF
FLORENCE

MICHELE GIUTTARI

Translated by Howard Curtis

Little, Brown

LITTLE BROWN

First published in Italy in 2010 by Biblioteca Universale Rizzoli
First published in Great Britain in 2012 by Little, Brown

A CIP catalogue record for this book
is available from the British Library.

Hardback ISBN 978-1-4087-0360-1
Trade Paperback ISBN 978-1-4087-0361-8

Papers used by Little, Brown are from well-managed forests
and other responsible sources.

MIX
Paper from
responsible sources
FSC
www.fsc.org   FSC® C104740

Typeset in Horley by M Rules
Printed and bound in Great Britain by
Clays Ltd, St Ives plc

Little, Brown
An imprint of
Little, Brown Book Group
100 Victoria Embankment
London EC4Y 0DY

An Hachette UK Company
www.hachette.co.uk

www.littlebrown.co.uk

To Christa

He who fights with monsters might take care lest he thereby become a monster. And if you gaze for long into an abyss, the abyss gazes also into you.

Friedrich Nietzsche, *Beyond Good and Evil*

Prologue

'I'm Italian . . . You're in the Emergency Department . . . Can you hear me?'

The wounded man on the stretcher nodded weakly. He was pale, his eyes staring straight ahead.

'I'm Doctor Torrisi. I need to know if you can breathe.'

The man half closed his eyes and nodded. He was conscious!

'Don't fall asleep! Hold on!'

Silence.

The man gave a long sigh. 'Did they get him?' he asked in a thin voice.

'I don't know. Just calm down, don't worry about a thing.'

In the meantime, a brisk, pretty nurse had inserted a butterfly needle, connected to a drip, into a vein in his left arm.

'The oxygen mask, now,' the doctor ordered. Then he bent over the patient and whispered, 'We'll get through this, you'll see.'

'Pe . . .'

But the wounded man could not complete the word. He closed his eyes and drifted off.

He had just come through the toughest two weeks of his life.

Two weeks that had begun one morning in June.

PART ONE

MESSAGES

1

Tuesday, 22 June 2004

Silence hung heavy in the air.

A long, deathly silence.

The uncovered coffin was in the middle of the mortuary chapel, beneath a dim fluorescent light. The body, small and thin, was wearing a black dress and immaculate black shoes. The hair was short, smooth and white as snow. The hands, joined on the stomach, held a mother-of-pearl crucifix. It was the body of a woman of about eighty, who must once have been beautiful.

Now, though, a scar disfigured her ashen face. In the middle of her forehead, just between her eyes.

The police officers had been standing looking at her incredulously for some minutes. They were waiting impatiently for the pathologist to arrive. From time to time, one or other of them muttered a few words, to the effect that this was awful and that they had never seen anything like it before.

'Poor woman,' a tall, thin young man with fair hair and a freckled nose said out loud. This was Inspector Marco Cioni of the mobile unit, who had been the first to arrive on the scene.

'This city ...' Chief Superintendent Michele Ferrara started to say, then let the phrase fade away and went back to chomping on the Toscano cigar clamped between his lips, still unlit. He was wearing a blue linen suit, sky-blue shirt and matching tie. At nine that morning he was supposed to be seeing the Commissioner to update him on the narcotics operation currently in progress. Instead of which, here he was, in the New Chapels of Rest at the Careggi Hospital.

He moved closer to the coffin and stared down at the body for a while. Suddenly nauseous, he closed his eyes. He took a deep breath and opened them again. He glanced at his watch: 8.46.

At that moment he heard a voice behind him.

'Good morning, Chief Superintendent, sorry I'm late.'

He turned. It was Francesco Leone, the pathologist. They shook hands.

'The usual morning traffic ...' Leone said, with a shrug.

He was a rather thickset man, with a bald, egg-shaped head. Ferrara trusted him implicitly. His post-mortem reports were meticulous, and the suggestions he made about the modus operandi of different homicides had frequently proved to be spot on.

Leone unbuttoned his jacket, which was a bit tight on him, put on his glasses with their thin gold frames and began his examination, while the others looked on in silence. After a few minutes, he straightened up and said, 'Whoever did this did a good job. Highly professional, in fact. Your men can check the inside of the coffin now, Chief Superintendent.'

He walked out into the corridor.

Ferrara gave the order, although he advised them to wait until the forensics team arrived so that the various phases of the operation could be photographed. 'I'll send some men from the *Squadra Mobile*,' he said, then followed the doctor out.

Yet another mystery.

A Florentine mystery.

Florence seemed to be doing everything it could to put him off staying.

2

'So tell me,' Ferrara asked when they were face to face, 'how long did such a . . . *highly professional* job take?'

It had not been a simple operation, Leone explained, but one that had been carried out with great skill and with the appropriate instruments. It was highly unlikely to have been the work of anyone untrained in the surgical field or acting on the spur of the moment.

'What kind of instruments?'

'A scalpel, forceps and surgical scissors. In other words, the kind that doctors and paramedics can easily get hold of, but that you wouldn't find in a pharmacy.'

'I see. But how long did it all take?'

'Not too long. Ten, fifteen minutes. Closer to fifteen than ten, I'd say, considering how clean the cut is. But I'll be able to tell you more after I've had a proper look at the body.'

'Thanks.'

They walked together to the exit, shook hands at the door and parted.

Ferrara hurried across the courtyard. It was raining hard. By the time he got to his car, he was drenched from head to foot. The driver quickly opened the door and Ferrara got in.

'To Headquarters,' he ordered.

He was late.

The day had got off to a bad start. He had known that as soon as he'd got the call from the operations room telling him that the Commissioner wanted him to proceed immediately to the New Chapels of Rest. That was at 7.20, just as he had been having breakfast with his wife in the kitchen, which was imbued with the pleasant aromas of coffee and freshly baked bread from the nearby bakery.

'Make it quick,' he had said to the driver, getting into the metallic grey Alfa 156 a mere ten minutes later. 'Use the siren and the flashing light if you have to.'

Now Ferrara glanced at his watch again: 9.36.

He didn't know it yet, but this Tuesday would turn out to be a day he wouldn't forget in a hurry. If ever.

3

Police Headquarters was in the Via Zara.

It was a building with an eighteenth-century colonnade, to the north of the historic centre. It stood on the site of a lunatic asylum, the famous Spedale di Messer Bonifazio, which had become, between the end of the eighteenth century and the beginning of the nineteenth, the first psychiatric hospital in the modern sense. The offices of the Flying Squad were in a wing of the first floor. The chief superintendent's office had two wide windows in adjoining walls, which filled it with light on sunny days. Today, though, wasn't a sunny day.

The driver parked the car in the courtyard, and Ferrara got out, entered the building and ran up the stairs to the second floor, where the Commissioner had his office.

Filippo Adinolfi, who had been transferred to Florence during the time that Ferrara had been in Rome, had, paradoxically, spent most of his own career in the capital, first in various departments at Police Headquarters, then in different sections of the Ministry of the Interior. A solid bureaucrat, no doubt, but with no real experience as an investigator.

As he got to the top of the stairs, Ferrara took a handkerchief from one of his trouser pockets and dabbed his wet hair.

Then he pressed the button to the left of the door and the green light immediately came on. He went in.

'Ah, Chief Superintendent, please come in and sit down.'

As red-faced as a beetroot, Adinolfi was sitting behind the solid walnut desk, which was immaculately tidy. He was writing something on a sheet of paper, but as Ferrara advanced he slowly moved his pudgy right hand and put down his Mont Blanc fountain pen.

He had only just turned sixty, but, perhaps because of his weight, he looked every one of those years, or even older.

Ferrara sat down in one of the armchairs for visitors. Looking closely at the Commissioner's face, he thought he detected, as well as his impatience to hear the latest news, a certain anxiety, a touch of nervousness. Had the day got off to a bad start for him, too? It was very likely.

'Chief Superintendent,' Adinolfi began in that baritone voice of his, 'I'd like you to tell me exactly what happened in those mortuary chapels. The mayor has already been on to me a couple of times, and you know what a pain in the arse he can be. He sounded quite worried, but then people here in Florence seem to get worked up about not very much, or even nothing at all. Strange city! Be that as it may, tell me all about it.'

Calmly, Ferrara filled him in on the details.

'Could it have been an animal, do you think?' the Commissioner asked when Ferrara had finished. 'A rat, perhaps?'

'I very much doubt it,' Ferrara replied, unruffled. 'The edges of the cuts seemed quite clean. It could only have been a human being. Someone who knew what he was doing, according to the pathologist, and used specific instruments, like a scalpel.'

Silence fell in the room. The Commissioner looked more anxious than ever.

'But why would anyone do something like that?' he asked, looking Ferrara straight in the eyes.

Ferrara was in no hurry to answer. He wasn't in the habit of speculating about motives at the start of an investigation. Within weeks, days, or even hours, such speculation often turned out to be entirely unfounded.

'That's a complete mystery at the moment, Commissioner,' he said at last.

'Well, it's a mystery that needs to be solved as quickly as possible, my dear Ferrara. We don't want the wider population to be alarmed, which is what I assume the mayor is worried about.'

'My dear Ferrara'! None of his previous superiors had ever called him that.

'I can assure you, Commissioner, we'll work flat out on this. I'm already in touch with the pathologist, and you should get the first results as soon as possible.'

'All right. As you can imagine, even the Head of the State Police will want to be kept up to date, and I can't disappoint him. In the meantime, let's hope the news doesn't leak out, or the press will be all over this. You can imagine the kind of stories the crime reporters would come up with.'

Ferrara nodded, then changed the subject and gave Adinolfi a summary of the latest developments in the narcotics operation. It was clear, though, from Adinolfi's attitude, that his mind was elsewhere.

Finally, they both stood up and shook hands, and Ferrara left.

Once alone, the Commissioner hitched up his trousers and sat down again. He picked up his pen and resumed his writing. At least now he had more details to send to the office of the Head of the State Police.

Before anything else, the bureaucratic niceties had to be respected.

4

By the time their chief, Gianni Fuschi, joined them, the forensics team, who had arrived at the chapels with their heavy cases, had been hard at work for almost half an hour.

Fuschi had received the request to intervene as soon as he had set foot in his office.

'There's something you should see, chief,' the oldest of the technicians had said over the phone. 'It's inside the coffin.' Fuschi had hung up and come running.

He was wearing a brown suit and a cream-coloured shirt, without a tie. He rarely wore a tie, except on official occasions. His informal manner of dressing was matched by his longish hair. Anyone who did not know him might have taken him for a university professor, certainly not a police official who worked with microscopes, test tubes, lasers, luminol and all the cutting-edge technology pathologists used these days.

'Well?' he said as he entered.

'Look here, chief,' replied the same technician who had called him, pointing to the inside of the coffin, which was now empty: the body had been transferred to the morgue at the Institute of Forensic Medicine.

Fuschi approached the coffin, bent slightly and peered down into it, holding that position for quite some time.

'Did you use a video camera?' he asked, straightening up.

'No. We took lots of photographs.'

'Film it, too. And make sure we get some close-ups. Then put this stuff carefully in a bag.'

Then he walked back out into the corridor.

In the coffin, where the dead woman's feet had lain, he had seen something that should not have been there, something that had clearly been put there intentionally. But God alone knew why. It was a substance that had been burnt at some point, apparently tobacco.

He took out his mobile phone and dialled Ferrara's number.

'Michele?'

'What is it, Gianni?'

'We've finished here, but there's something I should tell you before anything else.'

'What is it?'

'I can't be sure of this yet, so this is purely a provisional assessment. In the coffin, under the dead woman's feet, was a substance that, in my opinion, could be burnt tobacco.'

'Tobacco?'

'That's right. Leaves of tobacco.'

Ferrara did not reply.

'Michele, are you still there?'

'Yes.'

'Do you still smoke cigars?'

'Yes.'

'Well, it could be leaves of cigar tobacco, but it's best to wait for the results.'

'You mean lab tests?'

'Yes, I'll personally drop the stuff at the Institute of Forensic Medicine and ask for it to be looked at urgently, but in the meantime I think you should take all due precautions. Do you understand what I'm saying?'

'Yes.'

'It might be a message —'

'Let me know what you find, Gianni,' Ferrara cut in.

'Of course. You'll be the first to be informed.'

Ferrara hung up bad-temperedly.

He stared at the wall facing him. It was covered with commendations and photographs showing him with colleagues and with various holders of the post of Head of the State Police. He shifted his gaze to the framed photograph on the desk, showing him and his wife on the occasion of their twenty-fifth wedding anniversary. Then he took a cigar from his black leather case and looked at it as if for the first time.

He tried to imagine the length of the leaf before it was rolled. He suddenly remembered a visit he had made years before to the tobacco factory in Lucca, where leaves from Kentucky were turned into cigars, left to age for periods ranging from six months to more than a year in special rooms. Like a fine wine, to be savoured slowly. From his jacket pocket, he took his cigar cutter, and moved it halfway along the cigar. A sharp click echoed in the air. There were the two pieces. Exactly equal. As always.

He recalled that he had been smoking this kind of cigar for more than twenty years now, ever since he had thrown a still-full packet of cigarettes in the rubbish bin. And his wife had soon become accustomed to the smell of tobacco on his clothes and to tolerating a bit of passive smoking, convinced that cigars probably did less harm than cigarettes. Deep down, though, she still hoped that he would quit one day. He was about to light it when he stopped. He picked up his notebook and pen and jotted down the information gathered so far, underlining some details in red ink:

Night of Monday 21 to Tuesday 22 June
Expert job.
Special instruments: a scalpel, forceps and surgical
    scissors.
Time: 10–15 minutes.
Material burnt inside coffin. Perhaps tobacco leaves!
Toscano cigar?

Finally he updated the deputy prosecutor. A brief call, which the deputy prosecutor concluded with the words: 'If that stuff is confirmed as tobacco, let's keep it to ourselves. We don't want the press finding out.'

Should that tobacco be understood as a threat? Yet another? Was his past catching up with him?

It was still too soon to be sure.

5

It looked like a large warehouse, standing there on the hills outside Florence, next to the Careggi Hospital. Surrounded on three sides by open country, it was protected by high iron railings. Those who did not know its true purpose would never have imagined that it was a place where the bodies of those who had died in hospitals and in nursing homes were displayed before being buried.

This was the New Chapels of Rest, so called to distinguish it from the dilapidated old chapels that had been replaced at the beginning of the 1990s.

The two officers were in an unmarked Fiat Punto. The car was more than five years old, and at the very least the tyres needed changing and the brakes inspecting. Ideally, the Motor Vehicles Office at the Ministry of the Interior should long ago have decommissioned it. But, despite repeated requests, they refused, pleading 'lack of funds'. That was the excuse they always used, and nobody was very convinced by it, especially when there were senior civil servants and politicians in Rome driving around in expensive new cars.

The rain was beating insistently on the roof of the car, and the windscreen wipers were working overtime. A real storm that perhaps presaged the start of summer.

Officer Pino Ricci was driving, with Inspector Antonio Sergi in the seat next to him.

Once they had entered the courtyard, Ricci switched off the engine, lowered the sun shield and stuck the signal paddle with the words STATE POLICE under it. They got out and ran towards the building in silence.

It was Sergi and Ricci who had been assigned the task of investigating the desecration of the body in the New Chapels of Rest.

Both men had athletic builds. Sergi's distinguishing feature, though, was his thick beard. He had grown it to cover an old scar left by a shoot-out with members of the Sacra Corona Unita, the Apulian Mafia, almost ten years previously in a disreputable neighbourhood of Bari, where he had worked before Florence. Because of his strong resemblance to the character played by Al Pacino, his nickname was 'Serpico'.

The two men had been a team for some years. When they were after drug traffickers, they usually played good cop, bad cop with the junkies and small-time pushers they pulled in. Sergi, naturally, was the bad cop. He acted tough, like a volcano ready to explode, while his broad-shouldered, barrel-chested colleague was the 'gentle giant', the one who tried to calm him and cajole the prisoners into telling the truth. It was an old ploy, but an effective one, except when they were dealing with hardened gangsters, who weren't taken in by it.

Having finished their inspection, they were shown to the director's office, An intense, stagnant smell of mildew and disinfectant hung in the air. A fluorescent light glared coldly from the ceiling on to the white walls and linoleum floor. The furniture was basic: a worn wooden desk and a couple of metal chairs. The director was a short, squat man named

Alessandro Vannucci. It had been at seven this morning, he told them, that he had discovered the scar on the woman, who had died the previous day in the cancer ward of the hospital. The gates had been closed at six the previous evening, by which point the relatives of the dead people currently housed there had all left. During the night, the building had been watched by security guards until he arrived in the morning.

Sergi noted down the dead woman's details, the name of the security firm that provided the guards and the company responsible for cleaning the premises. Before leaving, he asked to check the TV camera he had noticed during the inspection, it was over the door separating the office area from the chapels. But it was a pointless request. The camera was not working: it had been out of order for months and nobody had bothered to repair it.

The two officers left, carrying the foul smell of the air in their nostrils.

The other thing they carried away with them was the thought that these days not even the dead could find peace in Florence.

Meanwhile, Inspector Riccardo Venturi had been busy at the computer. Even though he was only thirty-two, he could recall every crime ever committed in the city, every case the *Squadra Mobile* had worked on. He was an IT expert, a real genius, nicknamed 'the wizard' by his colleagues. It was a name he may have laughed off, but deep down he seemed proud of it, except when he wasn't in the mood for joking.

When Ferrara told him about the incident in the chapels, the first thing that came to mind was the summer solstice.

A brief search confirmed that this year it had fallen at exactly 00.57 on 21 June.

A coincidence? He knew that it was an important moment of the year, one that age-old popular tradition invested with a magical significance.

He printed a few pages and went back to his search.

6

It was 11.06 by the clock on the desk.

Ferrara had finished reading Sergi's latest report and countersigned it, ready for it to be sent off to the Prosecutor's Department. He took off his glasses and put them in the breast pocket of his jacket.

One less walking the streets, he said to himself, lifting a hand to his dark hair, which was greying slightly at the sides.

The report concerned the arrest of an Albanian suspected of pimping and drug trafficking. After keeping him under surveillance for a month, they had finally arrested him late last night as he was getting off his bicycle outside a bar in the Piazza Santa Maria Novella. In the course of the search they had found him in possession of a semiautomatic pistol with the serial number erased and more than 200 grams of pure heroin.

It was Sergi and his team who had brought the operation to a conclusion. The investigation had begun, as so often happened, with a tip-off. A young junkie and dealer – the report did not mention his name, or anything that might help to identify him – had ratted on him in the hope of getting a few favours from the inspector in return.

'Excellent work!' Ferrara commented. Then, turning to

Venturi, who had just sat down in front of him, he added with a bitter smile, 'These Albanians are making their mark in the drug trade. Seems pimping isn't enough for them.'

'Well, Chief Superintendent,' Venturi replied, 'it's only to be expected: money attracts money. Let's just hope we don't see this guy out on the streets again tomorrow or the day after.'

Ferrara simply nodded.

The rise of Albanian and similar criminal groups in Florence and other cities in Northern and Central Italy was indeed predictable, given the lack of a Mafia-style organisation in such places to stop them moving in. It was hardly surprising that regions like Sicily and Calabria were immune to their incursions.

'Chief,' the inspector went on, 'I've brought you some material I collected from the web.' With one hand he put down on the desk the pages he had printed and with the other he held out a sheaf of press cuttings. 'These are articles I found in the Headquarters collection covering the past few years.'

Ferrara took them and slid them to a corner of the desk. 'I'll read them later. Just tell me for now if you found anything interesting.'

'Nothing specific on our case. There are no exact matches, at least not in the records. But I wanted you to see these things because some of them are quite unusual. And one interesting point is that quite a few of these incidents took place during the summer solstice . . .'

He went on to list some of them.

'Good work, Venturi. But now let's focus on the present. When Sergi brings you the lists of people who have some connection with the chapels, I want you to make it your top priority. We need to know everything about them, and about the dead woman's family. We can't yet rule anything out.'

'Of course, chief,' the inspector replied, barely concealing his impatience to get back to work.

Left alone, Ferrara devoted himself to a pile of paperwork. The usual office routine. Some of it concerned his men: requests for leave, conduct reports, evaluations, and so on. It was a bureaucratic chore he was finding increasingly burdensome, a job that had nothing to do with any of the cases they were investigating, but which still fell to him, as head of the *Squadra Mobile*. Of course, his secretary, Sergeant Nestore Fanti, had prepared every document for him with his usual care, according to his instructions, especially when it came to the evaluations of the men's conduct, but it was up to Ferrara to go through it all, state the reasons for the scores given each man, and sign.

He settled down to his task, resolving not to move from his chair for the rest of the morning.

7

Thanks to heavy traffic it had taken them nearly an hour to get to the Campo di Marte area, not far from the football stadium.

Sergi dashed in the rain towards a three-storey block, followed by Ricci. He rang the bell and the lock of the front door clicked immediately. They were clearly expected.

In the doorway of the apartment, they were greeted by the dead woman's daughter. She was in her early forties, short and thin, without make-up. She looked startled: she had clearly not expected to see two big, casually dressed men, one of them with a beard so dishevelled it made him look like a villain. Sergi realised he had scared the woman. To calm her, he brought out his badge: the accompanying photograph, showing him in an impeccable uniform, was much more reassuring. She led them into the living room, where her husband was sitting. He was about the same age as her, a plump-faced man with a thin moustache and a twitch that kept closing his right eye.

Sergi wasted no time in explaining the reason for their visit. Then he took his notebook and pen from the pocket of his leather jacket and asked for the full name of the dead woman and some details about her. She had been retired for years, he was told, having previously taught Italian literature and history at a secondary school in the city. He went on to more direct questions.

'Yes, we were at the chapels yesterday afternoon, until just before closing time,' the wife said. 'It must have been about half past five when we left.'

'Did you notice the scar?'

'There wasn't one. Otherwise we would have seen it, wouldn't we?'

'Did you notice anything suspicious?'

'No,' the woman replied.

The husband spoke now for the first time, his eyelid twitching. 'Don't you think we ought to tell them about those people, darling?'

'Which people?' Sergi asked.

The man explained that, just as they were leaving, they had seen a couple wandering the corridors as if they didn't know where to go.

'A couple?'

'Yes. A man and a woman.'

'Can you describe them?'

'We weren't really paying much attention, but what I did notice was that the man was holding a big bag. You know, like a doctor's bag. My brother-in-law may be able to tell you more, because he stayed a bit longer than we did.'

His wife nodded.

'What's your brother-in-law's name?'

'Ferdinando Berti,' the woman replied. 'He's my only brother.'

'Perhaps you could tell him to come to see us at Headquarters, signora.'

'Would it be all right if he came after the funeral?'

'Of course. No problem.'

'Talking of which, Inspector,' the husband said, 'when will the body be returned?'

'That'll have to be authorised by the Prosecutor's Department. Deputy Prosecutor Vinci is the one dealing with the case. If they don't need to do any more tests, I think you should be able to get it back today.'

'I'll phone the Prosecutor's Department straight away,' the man said, as he saw the two officers to the door.

'A couple with a doctor's bag, who didn't know where to go ...' Sergi said, as soon as they climbed back inside the Fiat Punto.

8

In the meantime, Ferrara had received confirmation of the substance found inside the coffin.

The result had been unequivocal: burnt leaves of cigar tobacco, of the very kind he had been smoking for years. Unfortunately, no fingerprints or biological traces had been found: the fire had burnt them all away.

The information raised a lot of questions in Ferrara's mind.

Was Gianni Fuschi right to interpret this as a message for him? Should he start taking precautions? And who could be behind it? What twisted mind had dreamt this up?

He still had a vivid memory of the attempt on his life in October 2001, which he had miraculously escaped but which had been used as a pretext to get him away from Florence for his own safety and transfer him to the Anti-Mafia Investigation Department in Rome. Would his superiors force him to move again? What would he tell his wife?

He was still ruminating on these questions when he heard a knock at the door.

Teresa Micalizi was a new superintendent, just out of gradu-ate training at the Police Academy.

Ferrara explained to her the workings of the *Squadra*

Mobile, its various sections and what each dealt with, and the hours, both the regular ones and the overtime.

She listened attentively. It was her first real introduction to the world of day-to-day detective work, and it was all the more impressive coming from the head of the most important department in Headquarters. She was wearing a dark grey suit, white blouse and high-heeled shoes. She did not look like a policewoman. Were it not for the gun in her shoulder holster bulging beneath her jacket, she might be taken for a young female executive.

She was of medium height, with dark hair cut in a bob and a pleasant face. But what was most striking were her deep black eyes. They were remarkably lively and intelligent, darting everywhere, anxious not to miss anything. She was clearly an interesting young woman. But she was just as clearly embarrassed and kept brushing her fringe back from her forehead with her right hand. Ferrara went to her and put a hand on her shoulder. 'I know you're from Naples,' he said, 'but you don't have an Neapolitan accent.'

'I was born in Naples,' she replied, 'but I lived in Milan for eighteen years.' She was about to tell him that her father had been a police officer until he was killed in a shoot-out with robbers who had raided a bank in the centre of the city, not far from the famous Galleria Vittorio Emanuele. She was also about to tell him that her mother, who was from South America, was a painter, but she held back. Most likely the chief superintendent already knew these things, she thought.

'Even though you're the only woman superintendent in this department at the moment,' Ferrara continued, 'you shouldn't feel uncomfortable. I'm certain you're the first in a long line. The role of women in the police force is becoming increasingly important, especially when dealing with certain types of crime.'

She smiled. Was he telling her the truth, or only what he thought he was expected to say? And what did he mean by 'certain types of crime'? Child abuse? Rape and sexual assault? For the moment, she told herself, these questions were pointless: only time would tell. But one thing was certain: she had made the right choice, this job was going to give her a lot of satisfaction.

At this point Ferrara took a cigar from his case, lit it and puffed at it for a while, watching the smoke as it drifted up towards the ceiling. It was his second cigar of the day. Realising that the introduction was over, Teresa stood up and said goodbye. She was anxious now to meet her colleagues.

Ferrara plunged back into his own thoughts.

9

It was just before six in the evening when a thin girl with short dark hair entered Sergi's office. She worked for the firm that handled the cleaning at the New Chapels of Rest.

Sergi and Ricci had been back in Headquarters for little more than half an hour and were putting their notes in order. They had also questioned the two security guards who had worked, respectively, the six p.m. to midnight shift of the day before and the midnight to six a.m. shift this morning, and had learned nothing of any significance. Both men had stated categorically that they had not seen anything unusual. Neither of the two, though, had gone inside the individual chapels: that wasn't in their remit. They had limited themselves, as per company instructions, to making sure the outside gates were closed and staying in the guard box situated in the courtyard between the main gate and the entrance to the chapels. Every two hours they had walked along the internal corridors, making sure that the night lights were on in the chapels, but had not been aware of any suspicious presences or noises.

Sergi's questioning of the young cleaning woman, however, was to prove more useful.

Her name was Rosaria Pizzimenti and she was twenty-four. Originally from Lecce, she had been working in Florence for nearly two years, always for the same company, which, apart from the New Chapels of Rest, also had the contract to clean other parts of the Careggi Hospital.

'What time did you get to work this morning?' Sergi asked. Ricci had already sat down at the computer to write up the statement.

'Six o'clock, same as every day. I do two hours, six to eight. There are always two of us. The other girl's outside in the waiting room.'

'Was she also at the chapels this morning?'

'Yes.'

'Could you please tell us what you did?'

The young woman explained that their daily work consisted of emptying the wastepaper baskets in the offices and in the corridors of the chapels, then sweeping the floors and dusting the desks. On alternate days they also had to wash the floors. That morning, she had worked just in the chapels.

'Did you notice anything suspicious?'

'No, I just picked up a few pieces of paper from the floor and . . . ' She broke off for a few moments, with a frown. The two officers stared at her. 'I don't know if this is important, but in one corner of the corridor I found a wrapper . . . ' She stopped again.

'A wrapper?'

'Yes, Inspector. I might be wrong, but it looked like a wrapper from a disposable camera. My first thought was that maybe someone had wanted to take a last picture of a relative.'

'What did you do?'

'What was I supposed to do? I threw it in the bag we use for collecting the rubbish and before I left I put the bag in one of the dustbins outside the building.'

'Have you ever found a wrapper like that before?'

'No, never.'

'Did you know that something had happened in the chapels?'

'No. Nobody told me anything, though I did notice a couple of police cars in the courtyard on my way out. And when I finished my shift and my boss told me I had to come here and see you this afternoon, I assumed something must have happened.'

'So you have no idea what this is all about?'

'No. Can you tell me?'

Without going into details, Sergi simply told her that one of the bodies had been desecrated.

'Oh, my God! I can't believe it!'

He thanked the young woman and walked her to the door, then asked for the other girl to be brought in. This second interview was very short: she had not seen or noticed anything suspicious in the various offices she had cleaned.

Once the second girl had gone, Sergi and Ricci rushed back to the chapels to see if they could retrieve that wrapper from the dustbin.

It wasn't much of a clue, but at the beginning of an investigation nothing could be left to chance.

10

It was just after eight in the evening.

Ferrara opened the front door of the small apartment block where he lived with his wife. Their renovated top-floor apartment enjoyed a sweeping view all the way from the Arno to the Piazzale Michelangelo, the famous observation point above the city, and even beyond.

Between the first and second floors, he took the key from his trouser pocket, although he knew there was no point: Petra always recognised his footsteps on the stairs.

'Look! Look at this! We've only just got back and they're already starting!' These were the words with which he was greeted as soon as he had crossed the threshold.

Petra was visibly upset. Her lower lip was trembling, and he could almost hear her heart thumping. She was waving a piece of paper in the air. Ferrara looked at her questioningly.

The lighting in the apartment was, as usual, warm and intimate, but the atmosphere was one of imminent catastrophe.

'You know what I think, Michele?' Petra said. 'I think we should go back to Rome! I want to get out of here, once and for all! I can't stand it any more ... *Wir müssen weggehen* ... We have to go ...'

His eyes kept moving from her face to the sheet of paper

and back again. He did not know what was on that paper, but he could imagine.

'Read this, Michele!' she said, holding the paper up in front of him.

He knew what his wife was feeling. He could see it in her eyes, those expressive green eyes of hers. He took his glasses from the breast pocket of his jacket and looked closely at the paper, taking care not to touch it.

It was a typed note, probably printed off a computer.

We're getting closer. It's not long now.
We're coming for you and your . . .

His jaws stiffened and a shiver ran down his spine. He completed the sentence mentally. *Your wife.*

The note said *we*. It wasn't a single person who had it in for him this time.

Who could it be? Why were they threatening him? Was the past really catching up with him? And was his wife really in danger?

'It was in a white envelope without a stamp,' Petra went on, a little calmer now. 'Someone came to the front door and put it in our letterbox, after the postman had been. I found it when I got back from the laundrette.'

'And the envelope?'

'It's on your desk. I touched it when I picked it up, but then when I realised it didn't have a stamp or a postmark, I put this on.' She raised her hand to show him the rubber glove she was wearing, a slight smile hovering over her lips.

'You did well, darling.'

Petra rarely asked him questions, but this time it was something that had happened in their home. 'Why, Michele?' she asked. 'What do they want from you? Who are they?'

Ferrara thought about it for a moment. 'Don't worry, Petra, we'll find them,' he said, trying to hide the anxiety in his voice, although he knew perfectly well how unlikely it was that they would get any prints off that piece of paper. He went to her and hugged her tight. He could feel the anger rising in him.

He kissed her on the cheek, then gave her a long kiss on the lips. She was still shaking and her eyes were watery.

'Michele, if you're starting to get threats again, either they transfer you to Rome, or I go back to Germany.' She had raised her voice again, and the note of anxiety had returned. 'Hold me close. Don't leave me alone.'

'Don't worry,' he said reassuringly, still holding her tenderly in his arms. Gradually the colour came back into her face.

After a few minutes, she said gently, 'Let's eat now. The dinner's ready. I made you lamb cutlets with potatoes, those potatoes from Bologna that you like so much.'

She carefully put the paper down on the desk, beside the envelope, close to the white orchid that always stood there, and headed for the kitchen. Ferrara went into the bedroom.

A lovely smell wafted out from the kitchen, whetting his appetite.

Over dinner, they did not speak again about the message and Ferrara ate the lamb with gusto. His mind, though, continued to buzz. He remembered the scar on the thin face of the dead woman and imagined those burnt tobacco leaves in the coffin ... And now here was this threatening letter, received the same day, even before the news of what had happened in the New Chapels of Rest had appeared in the media.

A coincidence?

It was possible, although everything seemed to point to a single source, as if the writer of the anonymous letter was trying to tell him: *It was us at the chapels.*

He looked at his wife with a mixture of tenderness and

anxiety. He knew how much she loved him and that, whatever happened, she would stay by his side and support him.

They drank a glass of Brunello di Montalcino, raising their glasses in a toast. Then he went and sat down in the black leather armchair and put his feet up on a stool. It was his favourite place at the end of a day, a place where he could savour the joy of being within his own four walls.

Not that it would be easy to overcome the tension of this strange day.

11

He went through all the cases he had dealt with over the past few years.

His operation against the Sicilian Mafia in 2001?

No, he didn't think so. That was water under the bridge.

There had also been two bomb attacks in 2001: the one he had survived and the one that had killed his friend Deputy Prosecutor Anna Giulietti, along with her driver, as she was on her way to the Prosecutor's Department.

But the Sicilians had other problems to deal with these days: internal rifts, the arrest and conviction of some major bosses, the defection from their ranks of a number of members who had turned State's evidence. In the world of organised crime, Cosa Nostra wasn't the force it had once been.

There was also the Calabrian Mafia, the 'Ndrangheta. Only a few months earlier, he had broken up a ring channelling cocaine from the Colombians and had helped to unmask the perpetrators behind the slaughter of a Calabrian family in an apartment in Manhattan.

But that was another hypothesis he thought had to be ruled out. In those cases, he had simply acted as a liaison between police forces in America and Italy, in his role as head of the

Anti-Mafia Investigation Department in Rome. And besides, the 'Ndrangheta weren't usually so sophisticated. They settled scores with their enemies directly and immediately, because they wanted their message to be clear and unequivocal, both to their enemies and to their own members.

He went even further back in time, until he came to the one case that might provide a plausible explanation for what was happening: the crimes of the so-called 'Monster of Florence'. That was a case in which he had speculated that somebody highly placed had been pulling the strings, and in which he had been forced to desist from further investigation.

Was somebody still threatening him over that accursed business?

It was nearly midnight by the time he went to bed.

Around the city, though, in discos, private clubs and high-class drawing rooms frequented by the aristocracy and the nouveau riche, the night was only just beginning.

The secret face of Florence, which showed no sign of going away.

12

It was a clear night, and the cypresses that lined the drive leading to the villa stood out in the moonlight. Only the barking of dogs in some of the houses on the hills broke the magic spell of the countryside.

Enrico Costanza was sitting behind a massive desk in the semi-darkness, his back towards the door. He was wearing a made-to-measure suit. His pencil-thin moustache was white, as was his hair.

He was waiting impatiently.

The room was very large, with three windows covered in heavy maroon-coloured curtains. It was lit by two elegant antique silver six-armed candelabra, each placed on a period cabinet at opposite ends of the room. The ceiling was more than twelve feet high and was covered with a religious painting.

On one wall hung the portrait of one of his forebears: a man with a thick grey beard, an austere uniform and a long black cloak over his shoulders.

'At last!' he murmured, turning, as soon as he heard footsteps. A liveried butler admitted the visitor, who was holding a package in his hand.

He waited until they were alone, then resumed his previous position. 'Why are you late?' he asked.

'Something came up,' the other man replied curtly. 'Nothing of importance, though.'

He wasn't used to having to justify himself to anybody. He stood there, his long arms down at the sides of his well-shaped body, his grey eyes fixed on Costanza. Then he walked to the desk and put the package down on it.

'As long as you haven't had any problems . . .' Costanza said.

'No, everything's fine.'

'Good!' He sounded pleased. 'Good,' he repeated in a lower voice, almost as if he didn't want to be heard even by the walls or the sacred figures that seemed to look down at him from the ceiling.

'It's always been a great honour for me to come and see you,' the visitor replied with a slightly forced smile, emphasising the word *honour*. He put his hand in his trouser pocket, took out a key and placed it on the desk.

'Thank you,' the old man said.

'I'm the one who should thank you for the favour,' the guest replied ceremoniously.

'Oh, it's nothing. Remember, son, I love you and you'll always be able to rely on me.'

He stood up, and his visitor went to him and embraced him.

'I'm your godfather and you're the son I wish I'd had,' the old man whispered in his ear. 'You'll have news soon, but for now you can go. You know the way.'

The visitor broke free of the embrace. As he turned, he admired, as he always did, the big display case with its collection of pipes, including the one he had himself given the old man on his last birthday. He walked towards the door, his footsteps barely audible on the time-worn tile floor.

He was pleased with himself.

*

Alone again, Enrico Costanza opened the package. Inside it was a cellophane bag. He mopped his forehead with his hand-kerchief, then picked up the phone and dialled a number.

'Friday night, same time,' was all he said. He listened for a few moments, then hung up.

Then he put two fingers in the bag, took out a little white powder, placed it on the back of his left hand and sniffed it in, once, twice. He sat back in his armchair and closed his eyes. The pain of his lung cancer had become almost unbearable lately, and this was the only way he could alleviate it.

Outside, his visitor walked towards his car, which he had parked close to a small chapel that had lost its roof and a large part of its walls and was now used as a tool shed. Before getting in his car, he looked back at the villa. It was an impressive stone building, situated on a beautiful hill from which, by day, there was a breathtaking view of Florence, with Brunelleschi's majestic dome and the Arno clearly visible. A donjon with a loggia occupied the central part of the villa. Against the facade, a wide colonnade. The garden, surrounded by box-wood hedges, was very well tended, as were the extensive grounds, part of which was an olive grove.

He noticed that the windows, protected by black bars, were completely dark, but that the wrought-iron lantern with its coloured panes of glass above the main entrance had been left on.

Maybe the old man was expecting someone else, he thought to himself. He knew that on occasion meetings were held here, very private meetings to which he was not yet admitted. He sat down behind the wheel of his shiny black Mercedes SLK. In a little more than fifteen minutes he would be back in the sub-urbs of Florence.

But he wouldn't be going straight home.

Someone else was waiting for him.

13

He was parked where he shouldn't be. But he didn't care.

On the Ponte Vespucci, he had to manoeuvre to wedge the Mercedes in between two other cars. He got out, turned on to the Lungarno Corsini, walked along it and then along the Lungarno degli Acciaioli, then turned left, towards the pedestrian area. Left again, another hundred yards or so. He stopped and looked behind him. There wasn't a soul about. He rang the bell. The door was opened by a weary-looking young man, to whom he showed his card. He entered, walking past the sign that said PRIVATE CLUB – MEMBERS ONLY. There were many private clubs in the city, catering to all classes. But this was the most elegant and the most exclusive. Busy every night, often until the small hours of the morning, and sometimes even later. As it was tonight.

The subdued lighting and low music made for a soft, silky atmosphere. Gorgeously tanned girls in leather miniskirts sat on tall stools at the bar counter. They were all young, probably no more than twenty, and most of them were not Italian. The glances they cast the members were provocative, greedy for pleasure and above all for money. Other girls were navigating their way between the tables, topless, holding expensive bottles of champagne.

He wandered through the room, looking around. He recognised a few people, but ignored them. As he passed a small velvet sofa, he winked at a tall, beautiful, dark-skinned, black-haired young woman who was sitting there talking to two rather elderly men. She gave him a forced smile back. Or so he thought. Then he climbed the stairs to the first floor. Here, he walked along a peony-scented corridor with rooms on either side. The doors, each of which bore a number painted in red, were closed. As he passed, he heard moans of pleasure. He smiled. He reached a private area, demarcated by a red curtain hanging in front of the mahogany door. He moved the curtain aside, stared for a moment at the spy hole, then rang the bell with a confident air, three times. As he waited, he imagined an eye scrutinising him through the hole. There was the clink of a chain, the lock turned twice, and the door opened.

The woman stood there with a warm, inviting smile on her face. 'Come in,' she said, in a voice so low as to be almost inaudible.

Although pushing forty, she didn't look a day over thirty. She was the owner of the club. She also ran a high-class prostitution ring, one of the most sophisticated in the whole of Tuscany. Not all the girls who worked for her were professionals. Some were aspiring models or actresses looking for the right contacts to bring them fame and fortune.

The man entered and the door immediately closed behind him.

'Did you bring it?' she asked, her voice soft and melodious.

He nodded. 'Of course.'

The living room was as welcoming as the woman's smile. Magazines and items of underwear were scattered over the chairs. On a small table in the corner lay a pack of tarot cards. It wasn't just a pastime, she really believed in the cards, and always had. The scent of fresh flowers hung in the air, coming from a bouquet of splendid long-stemmed red roses in a crystal vase.

The man took a small plastic bag from one of his jacket pockets. It contained heroin. He lifted it with his right hand and shook it slightly. He felt a quiver on his skin and his blood pressure rose abruptly. How beautiful she was in her pink silk dressing gown, which allowed a glimpse of her shapely curves and the delicate outline of her breasts with their prominent nipples. Her long black hair was gathered in a ponytail, leaving her face free. Her eyes were large and dark. Her feet were bare and her nails were painted bright red. The first time he had met her she had reminded him of Madonna, and she still did.

The woman placed a wad of hundred-euro notes on the small table and picked up the transparent bag. He put the money in his pocket, gave her a broad smile, and said, 'I'd like you to come with me again this weekend. You'll like it, I'm sure.'

'Like last Saturday?'

'You mustn't worry about last time. It's all right. Nobody even noticed, not even him.'

'We'll see,' was all she said in reply. She gave a wave of her hand, making it clear to him that he could go. She was a moody person who did not always give herself away. Besides, something had happened the previous Saturday that she hadn't liked, that had scared her. She walked him to the door and closed it behind him. Then she went to her bedroom, where she opened the bag and took out a small quantity of powder. Letting her dressing gown slip to the floor, she slid into bed and lay there on her back. She switched on the CD player. The voice of Ornella Vanoni singing *'La voglia, la pazzia'* spread through the room.

The music seemed to relax her.

Let's just enjoy
the beauty of the day
any moment now
it may fade and die away.

On the bedside table, a hypodermic syringe, a silver spoon and a match lay ready. She prepared her little cocktail, then loaded the syringe, lifted it and expelled the air. Cautiously, she injected it into a vein of her left arm. A few seconds later, the first effects began to be felt. Her head started moving backwards and forwards spasmodically. This was followed by shudders that went through her whole body. She moaned and at last entered a state of artificial ecstasy.

She was in another world and would remain there for the rest of the night at least.

In the meantime, on the ground floor and in the other rooms on the first floor, people were still enjoying themselves.

Nobody would ever deprive them of their pleasures.

Nobody.

14

Wednesday, 23 June

Ferrara had a restless night.

He did not have just one dream but several, one after the other, interspersed by moments of being half awake and even quite lucid, yet still in a state of nervous tension.

At about seven, he heard his wife getting up, trying not to make a noise, and tiptoeing to the door. Then he heard the click of the light switch in the corridor and saw a band of light on the tiled floor. But he had not woken up completely and he gradually went back to sleep. He felt exhausted, the way he had felt at the beginning of his career after spending an entire night in the operations room. His mind was in a ferment, his eyes swollen and his face drawn. His first thought was of the words uttered by his wife the previous evening, that threat to go back to Germany.

Then he remembered how, at about three in the morning, Petra had shaken him and said in a trembling voice, 'I'm scared, Michele. I heard a noise . . .' He had got out of bed, rubbing his eyes, and inspected the rooms. Everything had been normal. Then he had gone out on the terrace, wrapped in his smoking jacket. The cool air had caressed his face. Cries, curses and coarse laughter had drifted up from the street, along with the noise of bottles being smashed on the pavements. You often heard that kind of thing in the middle of the night when young drunks roamed the streets on their way to their homes or their hotels.

'It must have been a cat,' he had said as he stumbled back to bed. 'Don't worry, darling.' Then he had lightly touched her face with one hand and hugged her to him for a long time. In the end they had both fallen asleep, Petra with her head on his chest. He had wished he could always see her smiling and happy, the way she'd been those last months in Rome.

Now he heard her moving almost furtively between the corridor and the kitchen, but he stayed in bed for a while longer. As he usually did, he aimed the remote at the TV and switched it on. There was nothing on the eight o'clock news about the incident in the chapels. He switched it off and got out of bed.

'Breakfast is ready,' Petra said as soon as he entered the kitchen. On the table there was yoghurt, butter, jam, ham, a boiled egg, coffee, and the French loaves delivered a little earlier by the assistant from the bakery near their building. A copious breakfast that would allow them to get through to the evening, dinner being their one true meal of the day.

Before going out, Ferrara advised her not to open the door to anybody – he emphasised the word *anybody* – and told her that he would leave his private mobile phone – *their* phone – on, in case of emergency. That was a mistake. It merely helped to make Petra even more scared and tense.

Petra had been planning to tidy the apartment. They had been away from Florence for quite some time, and their clothes were spread all over the place because the wardrobe was completely full. She had decided that she would go through them and throw out those she was unlikely to wear again. She had also planned to tidy the part of the terrace that she hoped she could use again as a greenhouse. The hours she spent tending to her flowers and plants had always been a great joy to her, and she was hoping she could recover that.

But what had happened the previous day, and above all her husband's words as he said goodbye to her, turned everything upside down. In her agitation, she resolved to make a phone call.

15

The streets, still silent, were filled with sunlight and the air was mild. Perhaps, after the last storm, summer had finally arrived. The pavements were almost deserted. It was not yet nine.

Florence, with its squares and streets, its alleys and tightly packed houses, once again seemed immaculate. It was like something out of a picture postcard, the kind you saw displayed on every stall. In those images, Florence gave the impression of being one of the most harmonious cities on earth: a city where tragedy was unthinkable.

Ferrara had often wished that reality conformed to the tourists' view of Florence. But he of all people could not delude himself. He was constantly being forced to look beyond appearances, to penetrate the hidden side that almost all the city's inhabitants insisted on denying, claiming it was a journalistic invention.

During the ride to Headquarters, he was lost in thought. He couldn't get the image of Petra waving that threatening letter out of his mind, or rid himself of the feeling that he was missing something important.

When he reached the Via Zara, he looked at his watch. It was 9.10. A strange time for him: he was normally the first, or at least one of the first, to arrive. As usual he entered his secretary's office, and found Nestore Fanti behind his desk, with his usual colourless expression, busy tapping away at his computer keyboard. He was a man who never smiled, not even when his colleagues tried to provoke a reaction by telling him a joke.

'Morning, Fanti.'

The secretary leapt to his feet and returned his greeting. It only took a quick glance for him to see that the chief was not looking very well. It might just be tiredness, he thought, but he suspected there was something else: he seemed to be brooding. Fanti sat back down and resumed his work in silence, with the air of someone who has a lot of things to get through. It was typical of him to do that when he realised no contribution was required from him. He knew he was only a very small part of the investigative machine, and nobody owed him any explanations. Pointless, then, to ask any questions. He had never done so, especially of the chief.

The first thing Ferrara did once he was in his office was to look through the newspapers. He found them on his desk as usual, next to the computer.

Not much space had been given over to the episode at the chapels of rest. The press did not seem interested in the case.

There was some speculation that it had been the act of a sick person, and that the police believed it was someone who had visited the place.

His eyes were then caught by a headline in the *Corriere della Sera*:

THE GHOST OF JACK THE RIPPER HAS RETURNED

His curiosity aroused, he read the article:

Male, between 20 and 35, agile build, above average physical strength. The description of the typical serial killer. It sounds very ordinary, which is what makes it all the more frightening. He could be our mild-mannered next-door neighbour … Another recurring factor, say criminologists and police officers, is his profession: usually he has no regular job, but when he does have one he is often a doctor or a nurse. 'One day men will look back and say I gave birth to the twentieth century.' These prophetic words have been attributed to Jack the Ripper, the first of this sad species, the dark face of late nineteenth-century London. More than a century later, his legend, far from fading into oblivion, continues to attract proselytes and imitators. In reality and in fiction …

Often a doctor or a nurse …

He noted the phrase on a piece of paper. You never knew, it might lead to something.

Then he read the morning report from the operations room on what had been happening in the past twenty-four hours. He did not find much of interest. A few drunks arrested for breaches of the peace, some youths getting into a fight outside a pub in the city centre, the usual events that made up a day's work for the police. What did attract his attention, though, was the brief mention of an attempted robbery in a small villa in San Domenico, near Fiesole. The criminals had fled after the owner of the house, a well-known shopkeeper, had fired a few gunshots into the air to scare them off. Carabinieri from the local barracks had been informed.

Probably the usual gang, he thought, convinced that sooner or later someone was going to get killed. For some months now, dangerous criminals had been carrying out a series of robberies in isolated areas near Florence, sometimes using strong-arm methods. It was a new phenomenon, most likely the work of criminals from Eastern Europe. It certainly didn't seem to be the local gangs, who had 'rules' against attacking defenceless old people, even women and children, invading houses and beating up the owners for a handful of euros, or even for nothing. The world was changing. Crime was changing. Florence was changing. Everything was changing. Most of the locals stayed at home in the evening, or avoided the more dubious parts of the city. Now it looked as though those who had abandoned the historic centre to go and live on the splendid hills would soon come scurrying back.

He had just summoned his men to his office for their usual morning briefing when the telephone rang.

Once, twice, three times . . .

For a moment Ferrara sat staring at the phone, as if reluctant to answer. Then, almost irritably, he lifted the receiver. He listened, not saying much. Before hanging up, he said, 'I'll drop by later.'

The call had been from Massimo Verga.

16

He found Massimo sitting at a little desk in his office, lighting his pipe. The room, which was not large to start with, was made to seem even more cramped by the piles of books on the desk, the shelves filled with binders, and the chairs cluttering the space.

When Ferrara had entered the shop, the assistant, Rita Senesi, who had been working here for ever, and had probably been secretly in love with her employer for ever, too, had looked up from the pile of books she was arranging on the counter near the cash desk and smiled at him.

'I'm not here to buy the latest thriller, Rita,' Ferrara had said. 'Massimo phoned me. Isn't he here?'

'Yes, he's here. He's in his office.' She motioned with her head, meaning he could go up.

Massimo Verga was his best friend. They had known each other since their schooldays. A Sicilian like Ferrara, Massimo was the owner of a prosperous bookshop in the Via Tornabuoni, bang in the centre of town. The two of them, after not seeing each other or being in touch for a long time, had met again by chance here in Florence, the city that had adopted both of them, though for different reasons. Massimo for his broad culture and his knowledge of the literary world, Ferrara for his skill as a detective.

The bookshop covered three floors.

On the ground floor, the latest books and a section for newspapers, magazines and luxury stationery. On the first floor, the art books, including antiquarian volumes, as well as Massimo's office. In the basement, the storeroom, the paperback department, and a meeting room, where members of the local intelligentsia, almost all of them socialists or ex-Communists, met from time to time to discuss the latest bestsellers or local and national politics. Book launches were also held in this room.

'Ah, at last!' Massimo exclaimed with a smile as soon as he saw Ferrara in the doorway. He stood up and embraced him. Then, when they had sat down again, he put his pipe down on the crystal ashtray and without further ado – he knew that his friend was always in a hurry on the rare occasions when he dropped by – asked, 'Michele, is Petra all right?'

At this question, Ferrara frowned. 'Why do you ask that?'

Massimo hesitated for a moment, as if debating with himself whether to tell the truth or avoid it. He chose the second solution.

'No particular reason. Maybe it's just a premonition.'

'Don't talk rubbish, Massimo. A premonition? Whose leg are you trying to pull? Mine? I know you better than the streets of Florence.'

His tone was so tense and irritable, it surprised even Massimo.

'Calm down, there's no need to get upset. I spoke to her on the phone and she sounded worried. She wasn't the same old Petra. I know her well enough to sense the difference. I thought I knew you well, too, but maybe I was wrong, seeing the way you reacted.'

Ferrara was on the verge of telling him about the threatening letter, but then it occurred to him that now was not the right moment. He still had to have tests carried out on it, and besides, he hadn't even told his colleagues.

'I'm sorry, Massimo, I didn't mean to react like that. It's just that I've been under a lot of pressure lately.'

'Nothing new about that. You're always under pressure. So, Michele, are you going to answer my question honestly?'

'Petra's fine. She's probably just tired after the move from Rome. There's still so much to do in the apartment. That's all.'

'Maybe . . . '

'That's all it is, don't worry.'

'All right. I see I was wrong.' And with these words, the subject was closed. He picked up his pipe and resumed lighting it.

'What are the two of you doing on Sunday?' he asked. 'We could go for a meal at Beccaccino's in Forte dei Marmi. I'll bring a friend with me.'

'A girlfriend?'

'Yes.'

'Another girlfriend, eh? How many more are you going to introduce me to? Massimo, it's time you got your act together. You should be in a stable relationship at your age.'

'Don't let's get into that. You know what I think about women . . . '

Ferrara did not insist. Massimo was still the same old Peter Pan.

'We should be able to make it, Massimo. But let me pay.'

'Don't tell me you're looking for forgiveness!'

Ferrara smiled.

Before saying goodbye, he invited Massimo to his apartment

the following evening. The next day was the feast of San Giovanni, and they could watch the firework display from the terrace.

Next stop: the forensics lab.

17

'What *is* this, Michele?'

No sooner had he entered Fuschi's office than he had taken the anonymous letter from his jacket pocket.

'Well, it certainly isn't a love letter, Gianni.'

'So I see,' Fuschi replied.

Taking a pair of latex gloves from a drawer and slipping them on, he held out a hand for the letter, turned it over, then held it up to the light. He decided he would use a laser on it. They moved into a large room full of apparatus.

'I'm going to use ninhydrin, Michele,' Fuschi said. 'It has the advantage of being fast and practical.'

'Go ahead, Gianni.' He had complete faith in his colleague's skill and discretion. He knew that ninhydrin reacted to amino acids and the other components of sweat and that it was used to lift fingerprints from porous surfaces such as paper and wood. Applied before the laser, it helped to increase its luminescence.

Unfortunately the result of the test was negative. No prints. No biological traces.

Fuschi then examined the envelope. Here, he found a few fragmentary prints, not enough to make a match possible. There had to be at least seventeen points of comparison for a print to be usable as evidence, and there was nowhere near that number here.

'Petra may have left these prints when she took it from the letterbox,' Ferrara said.

Fuschi did another test, after which he said, 'There aren't even any traces of saliva. It was a self-seal envelope. A common brand, too, the kind you find in every stationer's. I'm going to try one last thing, Michele.'

'What?'

'I'm going to use the Electrostatic Detection Apparatus. As you know, it can spot any impression, however shallow, that's been left on a piece of paper by pressure put on pages laid over it, even through ten sheets. If there are any words there, it'll show them, even if they're completely invisible to the naked eye.'

But here, too, the results were negative.

'Is it at least possible to find out the make and model of printer?' Ferrara asked.

'We can try. I'll let you know.'

'Thanks, Gianni.'

Whoever had handled the paper and the envelope had covered his tracks very well, like a true professional. Which meant that tracing him was going to be very, very difficult.

18

The funeral had already taken place.

In the afternoon, the dead woman's son, Ferdinando Berti, a distinguished-looking man in his early forties, presented himself at Headquarters, as agreed with his sister and brother-in-law, and asked to see Inspector Sergi. After sitting down in front of the desk, he forestalled any questions by saying, 'I saw that couple, too.'

Opening his notebook, Sergi wondered if they were on the right track.

'Where exactly did you see them?' he asked.

'They were sitting in the corridor next to my mother's chapel. To be more specific, they were in a stretch of the corridor between my mother's chapel and the next one, which was empty at the time.'

'Empty in the sense that there was nobody there? Not even a dead body?'

'Precisely.'

'Can you describe this couple?'

Ferdinando Berti paused for a moment, clearly attempting to focus on the image. 'I'm trying,' he said.

'Let's start with their age. How old do you think they were?'

'They weren't all that young, but they weren't old either. No, they definitely weren't old.'

'You mean they were middle-aged?'

'About thirty-five, forty, I'd say.'

'Both of them?'

'Yes.'

'Any distinguishing features? Beard, moustache, long hair, piercings, things like that?'

'I really don't know. Don't forget, I saw them only in passing. And you have to remember my state of mind . . . All the same, I had the impression he was a professional. I remember one thing: he had what looked like a doctor's bag on his lap. In fact, I thought he might actually be a doctor and that he was there waiting for a body to be brought in.'

'What about his hair? Fair? Black? Brown?'

'I couldn't say. All I can say is that it didn't seem dark.'

'Height?'

'At first sight, like me or a bit taller. I'm five-seven. But don't forget he was sitting down when I saw him, so I might be wrong.'

'What kind of build?'

'Fairly average. He certainly wasn't fat.'

'How was he dressed?'

'Light-coloured clothes, I think. I didn't really pay that much attention.'

'A suit?'

'I think so.'

'What about the woman? Do you remember anything about her?'

'She didn't really strike me, I don't know what to tell you.'

'Was she tall? Short? Fat? Thin?'

'Give me a moment . . .'

'Please try to remember. Anything might turn out to be important.'

'I had the impression she was anorexic. I mean, she seemed very thin, bony, like some models. That's really the one thing that struck me, the fact that she was thin. Oh, and she was short, too, especially next to the man.'

'What about her hair?'

'Maybe reddish, long anyway. Wavy at the ends, I think.'

'Did you see anybody else? Men on their own, looking suspicious? A family?'

Berti thought about it for a moment, then shook his head. 'No, I really don't think so. In fact, I'm sure of it. The only people I saw were that couple.'

'Do you feel up to doing an identikit?'

'I really don't think so. As I explained, I only saw them in passing.'

They had got precisely nowhere.

19

It was seven in the evening by the time Ferrara put the last file away in the top drawer of his desk. He switched off the light and, as usual, turned the key twice in the lock.

As he left the building, a gust of wind struck him like a fist. It was the Sirocco, the hot wind so common in his native Sicily. For a few moments, he seemed to smell the strong iodine smell of the sea and hear the rhythmic sound of the waves breaking clear white on the shore and see the seagulls outlined against the sky ... How he missed that blue sea here in Florence! Having been born and brought up in Catania, the sea held so many memories for him, all of them beautiful. Memories of other times, when he had been young and in love with life, and had not yet seen evil at close quarters.

He turned back and took shelter in the doorway. He lit a cigar and began inhaling it slowly to savour the taste and avoid it burning down too quickly. He felt tired, weighed down with thoughts. To unwind, he decided to walk home. Walking in the open air often helped him to relax and clarify his ideas. He ordered the driver to follow him at a distance in the car, and set off at an unhurried pace.

Like a tourist visiting the city for the first time.

*

The Via Cavour. The Via Panzani. The Cathedral.

As he crossed the street, he was overwhelmed by exhaust fumes from a coach and had a coughing fit. Every day, hundreds of coaches passed through this part of the historic centre, polluting the air and the monuments. The smog level was increasing alarmingly year by year.

Ferrara left Brunelleschi's dome behind him on his left. On the opposite side, a couple of pavement artists sat at their easels doing quick portraits of tourists. He turned on to the Via dei Calzaiuoli, a pedestrian street on which the only vehicles allowed were police cars and ambulances answering emergency calls.

The place was as animated as always, with streams of tourists, most of them Japanese, heading in both directions. Some lingered for a few moments in front of the illuminated shop windows. There was the same din, the same chatter as there was every evening. Drawn by the heaped trays in the window of an ice-cream parlour, Ferrara went in and bought a hazelnut-and-pistachio cup.

He continued on his way, overtaken for a moment by a large, rowdy group of American students whose teachers had their work cut out keeping them together and making sure they did not stray. At the corner of the Via Orsanmichele he stopped to watch a scene taking place around a small table on which a candle stood, its flame flickering in the wind. On one side of the table, a young woman, thirty at the most, sat on a stool. She was wearing a dark miniskirt that left her tanned thighs half uncovered, and a flimsy blouse, also dark, unbuttoned just enough to emphasise her prominent breasts. Her copper-coloured hair was gathered in a long plait. She was attractive, if somewhat vulgar. On the other side of the table, on a director-style chair, sat a man with long hair and a wide-brimmed white hat, reading tarot cards. Ferrara saw him turn over another card. The young woman was staring at the man, anxious to know her own future, to have solutions to her money worries or her difficulties in love.

In a niche at the corner of the church stood St Peter, with a book held tight in his left hand and two iron keys in his right, apparently reminding humanity of the Day of Judgement.

The sacred and the profane, juxtaposed.

He continued walking.

In the Piazza della Signoria, he was struck by the number of cameras flashing. As always, the tables outside the cafés and restaurants were full of people, regardless of the wind. On one side, a group of tourists were applauding a street musician. On the other, a mime was pretending to be a marble statue, only moving his lips slightly whenever somebody threw him a coin.

He turned right, in the direction of the Ponte Vecchio, which was only dimly lit at this hour. All the goldsmiths' shops were closed by now, their windows protected by wooden shutters. He was forced to walk in the middle of the street. Street vendors, all foreigners and unauthorised, occupied both pavements. With one eye on the passers-by and the other darting in every direction to make sure the police weren't around, they displayed their fake designer products: women's handbags, purses, travelling bags. This parallel trade was constantly growing, despite the efforts of the Commissioner and the mayor to fight it and the almost daily protests of the shopkeepers. All to no avail. These vendors passed through so quickly, often in Florence today and in another city, or in another region altogether, by tomorrow.

If they spotted a police officer, they hurriedly lifted the four corners of the sheets on which they displayed their goods and ran to hide in the dimly lit side streets and alleys. There was something ridiculous about such scenes, which might draw an instinctive smile from passers-by, but they demonstrated, if you stopped to think about it, the way the city was declining.

Ferrara began walking faster. Within a few minutes, he was home. He waved to the driver, who was still following him from a distance, went in through the front door and closed it immediately behind him.

20

Thursday, 24 June

There she was, in San Lorenzo, standing by the first line of pews with a shopping bag in her hand, waiting for him.

Inspector Venturi had telephoned her two evenings earlier, catching her as she was on her way home, stopped at a traffic light, and had given her the gist of what he was after. She was an old friend of his, someone he turned to whenever he wanted to know what the word was in those circles involved in the occult and the esoteric, especially after something unusual had happened. Venturi considered her almost a colleague, and she was proud of the fact.

Now here she was.

He was the one who had chosen this place, to make it look as if they had met by chance.

She was wearing a knee-length black dress and carrying a shoulder bag of the same colour. As he walked towards her, Venturi had time to notice that she had grown thinner in the face since the last time he had seen her. She had lost her husband in a road accident the year before and, despite the affection of her family, she had been unable to come to terms with such a sudden loss.

'Been shopping?' he asked, nodding towards the bag as he joined her.

'A couple of little gifts for my grandchildren.'

'So, Silvia,' he said next, getting straight to the point, 'what can you tell me?'

'In my opinion,' she said, in a low voice, looking around cautiously, 'the scar on that poor woman's face definitely has an esoteric significance.'

'What kind of significance?'

'The third eye.'

'The third eye?'

'Obviously, it's hard for someone who doesn't know much about the subject to understand ...'

'Try me.'

A cut on the forehead, she explained, symbolised the opening of the third eye. In Eastern esoteric traditions, the third eye was the centre of energy that gave the person who had it access to the so-called sixth sense, to intuitions, or, more generally, to the perception of extrasensory phenomena.

'It's also called the sixth chakra,' she said.

The inspector gave her a puzzled look.

'You see, Riccardo? You don't understand.'

'But in this particular case, what were they trying to tell us?'

'I don't know,' she replied with a slight smile. 'I can only speculate.'

'Then go ahead, speculate.'

'Perhaps whoever did it – an initiate, most likely – was trying to send a message.'

'A message? Who to?'

'To someone who hasn't developed the sixth sense, to make that person understand something important. Something he will have to sense intuitively, because obviously whoever made the scar must think the person he's sending the message to is capable of understanding the symbolic value of his gesture.'

'You said an initiate. Why?'

'Don't forget what we've talked about before. Right here in Florence, some people hold séances in their houses, many people read tarot cards, and there are even some, so it's said, who celebrate black masses in deconsecrated churches ... There are black magicians here, wizards.' She smiled again, this time with a touch of irony. 'Not computer wizards like you.'

'Where do these black masses take place?'

'In deconsecrated churches, like I said, but I don't know where exactly. You need to give me a bit more time. But I think it must have been the initiate of a secret society who make that cut.'

He did not insist. 'Get in touch when you have any information.'

They said goodbye and she walked away confidently, like someone who knew where she was going.

She was a real expert. Not everyone took her seriously, but Venturi, the computer wizard, certainly did.

21

'Sit down, Inspector.'

Don Gino belonged to the Capuchin Fathers, who managed the chapels of rest. Up until a few months earlier, he had held religious services there.

He was not surprised to find Sergi at the door when he went to open up. He had been informed of his visit by a parishioner. He admitted him to a small room furnished with bamboo chairs covered in plain maroon cotton cushions. There was a small window in one wall and a small bookcase opposite. In a corner were some large bags filled with used clothes to be distributed to the poorest in the parish. Don Gino indicated one of the two chairs with his hand.

'At this hour, I usually have a nice cup of coffee,' he said. 'Would you care to join me?'

Sergi accepted.

Don Gino left the room and returned after a few minutes carrying a tray with two cups and a sugar bowl. His hands trembled slightly as he put it down on a little table. Then he sat down on the other chair. Sergi guessed his age as seventy-plus. He had a pale, lined face, and he was wearing thick glasses.

They drank in silence.

It was Don Gino who spoke first. 'Well now, Inspector, what can I do for you?'

'I understand there was an incident in the chapels some time ago similar to the one the day before yesterday? I assume you've heard about the latest one?'

'My parishioner, the man you contacted, informed me. I don't always read the newspapers.'

'What do you remember about that other incident?'

'I still remember it very well. There are some things it isn't easy to forget. That image ... ' He broke off to make the sign of the cross. 'I was just about to bless a dead person when I noticed a scar on his face.'

'What was your reaction?'

'I was shocked at first. Then, when I'd recovered sufficiently, I went to see the director, the one who retired a few years ago. I wasn't very convinced by his explanation.'

'What did he tell you exactly?'

The priest smiled. 'That it must have been a rat bite.'

'Do you remember when it happened?'

'No, I'd have to check my old diaries. I'm sure I wrote it down. But it must have been before 1993, because that was the year I first started working at the New Chapels of Rest. The old chapels were really dilapidated and it's quite possible there were rats there, but for a rat to make such a clean cut ... no, I don't think so. You didn't need to be a surgeon to realise that.'

'So you'd describe it as a clean cut?'

'Yes.'

'I see. Well, if you could look at your diaries and let me know.' He handed the priest a business card with his contact details.

Another clean cut, he was thinking. Hardly the work of a rat!

22

Unusually for this hour, the Caffè Gilli in the Piazza della Repubblica was almost full.

In the evening, of course, it was impossible to find a free table, especially outside, under the white awnings, with the band playing golden oldies, but in the mornings it was usually less crowded. Not today, though. The city was preparing to celebrate its patron saint, St John the Baptist, and many people had come flooding in from all over Tuscany.

A regular customer sat down at one of the tables.

He was tall, with light brown hair, worn rather long and combed back. His eyes were hidden behind very dark sunglasses. His general appearance was quite distinguished, and his contagious smile drew admiring glances from women of all ages. A handsome man, in other words. Someone who knew how to take care of himself.

This café was one of his favourites.

He could get a bite to eat here, while at the same watching passers-by, especially attractive female tourists.

He had spent a fairly restless night, haunted by memories of the past. Several times he had got up and gone into the kitchen for a drink, but still he had been unable to get rid of the knot in his throat or to stop his brain from endlessly churning things over. In the end he had made himself a cup of coffee, switched on the TV, and channel-hopped with the remote control. He had also repeatedly checked the news on teletext, going from page to page without finding anything to interest him. Then he had shaved, taken a shower, and come outside. For a long time he had strolled with his hands in the pockets of his jeans. On his feet, he was wearing the comfortable trainers he had bought the day before.

Now he ordered a portion of cod *alla livornese* with a side order of beans *all'uccellina*, a typical Tuscan speciality, and to drink, white wine, Pinot Grigio.

While waiting, he began wearily leafing through *La Nazione*. He had just bought it from the Edison bookshop, where he usually picked up the latest bestsellers. Reading had been his great passion ever since his teenage years. He had thousands of books in his house. He was fond of thrillers – he preferred those by English and American authors – autobiographies of great composers – he had all of Richard Wagner's writings – and epic poetry. He was particularly drawn to medieval tales of chivalry.

Not finding anything of interest in the newspaper, he closed it with a sigh and put it down on one of the free seats. As he bent forward to do so, his glasses fell off. He leaned down, picked them up from the ground and hurriedly put them back on again.

Meanwhile a young couple, dressed in jeans and T-shirts with the slogan *I love Firenze*, had sat down at the next table. Their combined ages probably didn't even add up to forty. They were holding hands and kept looking tenderly into each other's eyes and kissing. From time to time, the girl moved her sinuous body closer to her companion. They were laughing, oozing joy through every pore.

He looked at them for a long time. Then, to his right, he

noticed a group of Japanese tourists, equipped with cameras and camcorders, coming out of the Hotel Savoy on the other side of the street. Some were in short sleeves, as if it was already the height of summer. He smiled as he watched them walk off in single file behind a young woman – clearly their guide – holding up a sign. By now the square was flooded with sunlight, and filling up with humanity in all its guises.

It was 2.30 in the afternoon and the Piazza della Repubblica was now completely packed. People were flooding in to witness the historic procession that would set off at exactly four o'clock from the Piazza Santa Maria Novella, winding its way to the Piazza Santa Croce, its participants all in period costumes, some waving banners.

It was an exciting spectacle that took place every year on 24 June.

The waiter approached with his food. He set to it with gusto: it would be his only meal of the day. When he had finished, he paid the bill, left his usual tip – ten euros – on the table, and set off for home.

Looking like a perfect tourist.

23

He was sitting in his favourite armchair.

Everything in the room was impeccably tidy. All the objects on the desk were arranged in perfect symmetry. In his right hand, he held a glass of Scotch and soda, which he took a sip from. Then, slowly, he stood up and looked around the room, eventually letting his gaze come to rest on a framed photograph that stood on a period cabinet. It showed him in a coach drawn by two wonderful horses, the kind that are used to take visitors around tourist spots.

What a happy day that had been!

He closed his eyes and the past returned: a series of images in rapid succession. In one, two women's faces were superimposed, both very clear. One was round and chubby, the other thin, with perfect features. She was reading him the legend of Parsifal: the hunter killing the swan with an arrow and then being captured, the knights gathering around the altar, the sign of the cross traced in the air with the sacred spear, the white dove descending from the dome.

A shudder went through him.

Those ghosts were still pursuing him.

Just then, he heard yelling from outside, followed by a loud cry of 'Long live Florence!' It was five in the afternoon on the day the city celebrated its patron saint, and out on the square the traditional football match between the blues of Santa Croce and the reds of Santa Maria Novella was starting. He went to the window and leaned out. The players, in their fifteenth-century costumes, fought hard to gain control of the ball, just as if they were playing rugby. He watched for a while, following the progress of their attacks, scuffles, scrums, each move ending in a tangle of bodies.

At ten that evening came the high point of the festivities: the spectacular firework display.

The best place to watch it was the Ponte Santa Trinita, from where you could see the Ponte Vecchio and the fireworks lighting up the sky behind. The bridge, the others nearby and all the streets along the river were packed, and people who lived in buildings with a view facing the Piazzale Michelangelo invited friends and relatives to watch the spectacle with them.

Even Ferrara and his wife had a few friends over this evening, to watch the display from their terrace. Among them was Massimo.

The atmosphere was very lively. At last, a moment of genuine distraction.

There was no hint of the drama that was about to unfold.

24

She was very pleased with her day.

She was wearing a close-fitting two-piece suit of black silk crêpe, which made a nice contrast with her short blonde hair. On her feet she had high-heeled gold sandals and in her hand she was holding a rectangular gold-coloured clutch bag. She had been celebrating both her birthday and her saint's day. In the evening, she had stood on the Ponte Vespucci watching the firework display.

It was a few minutes to midnight and she had reached the front door of her building.

As she was slipping the key into the lock, she gave a start, thinking she heard steps close behind her. She had been quite nervous recently, jumping at any sudden noise. Instinctively, she turned. She did not see anyone, but a chill went through her all the same. A few yards to her right stood two dustbins, side by side. Someone had left some broken chairs and an old gas cooker beside them, to be picked up by the dustmen when they came.

Maybe the noise had been caused by a cat or a mouse. She slipped the key in the lock, opened the door and immediately closed it behind her. She let out a deep sigh of relief. At last she was safe within the walls of her own building, her kingdom. She switched on the light and began climbing the stairs.

For some time now, she had had the feeling that she was being followed, even though, like just now, she had never actually seen anything suspicious. She put it down to the nervous state she had been in ever since the accident, six months earlier. She had been riding her Vespa down a side street when she went straight into a car that had jumped a light. She had been sent flying, hit the ground and, as she had learned later, briefly lost consciousness. She had escaped with a few small fractures, but luckily nothing serious.

Reaching the last landing, she gave another start, a bigger one this time. It was dark on the landing, because the light was off. Her anxiety returned. When she had gone out, just before midday, it had been working perfectly well.

Her anxiety turned to terror. She looked behind her. She searched for the right key in the bunch she had in her hand. It was easy to distinguish by touch because it was the longest.

But she did not have time to turn it in the lock.

A hand covered her mouth. In the darkness, her eyes searched for help.

It wasn't just her nervous state this time.

It was really happening.

25

Friday, 25 June

It was a few minutes to eight.

Olivia opened the door and went in, as she did every morning.

No sound.

The 'signora' was probably still asleep.

The lights were on in the corridor, but she didn't find that suspicious. She kept going and saw that the lights were on in the bedroom, too, and the door ajar.

'Signora Giovanna?' she whispered.

No answer.

Then she called a second time, a little louder.

'Signora Giovanna?'

A third call had the same effect. That really was unusual. Something was wrong.

Discreetly, she put her head in the room, and then, however reluctantly, reached her arm out and pushed open the door. She tiptoed in. After a few steps, she stiffened. A shiver ran down her spine. A moment later, she let out a piercing scream. She stood completely still, as if rooted to the spot. Petrified.

Her signora lay motionless on the bed. She was on her back.

Her arms were outspread, bound to the wrought-iron bedhead with handcuffs on the wrists, her head tilted to the left, eyes open, hair stuck to her temples and forehead. A linen sheet covered half her body, from the abdomen down.

Olivia wanted to go closer, but her feet refused to move. They were like stone. She managed to take a few steps. She had to get out of the room as quickly as possible, she couldn't bear it any longer. She avoided looking at the body again. She staggered to the bathroom and vomited into the wash basin. Then she slid down on to the white marble floor. She lay there for a few minutes, then came to her senses and dialled, first 112, then the number of her signora's parents.

26

The first patrol was on the spot in a few minutes.

They found the woman standing, pale-faced, with her back against the main door. She was clutching a handkerchief and sobbing.

The victim's name was Giovanna Innocenti.

It was a high-profile surname that belonged to one of the oldest and most prestigious families in Florence. Her parents owned a vast estate in the countryside near Pontassieve, where they ran a flourishing wine business.

Their wine was on sale, not only in Italy, but in a number of European countries and the United States. Giovanna, their only daughter, was unmarried. She had just turned thirty-six and had been living for a long time in this apartment where the smell of death now hovered.

Before long, other Carabinieri arrived from the Carlo Corsi barracks in Borgo Ognissanti, the headquarters of the provincial command. With them, the chief of the Criminal Investigation Squad, Marshal Edoardo Gori.

Tall and thin, with thick dark hair, slightly greying at the temples, and prominent cheekbones, Gori, at the age of forty-one, was quite accustomed to the sight of death. He had seen it in many forms in the course of his career. He had encountered many homicide victims, some horribly mutilated. But the one lying before him now seemed different. He sensed a carefully studied brutality to this murder.

Giovanna Innocenti appeared to have been crucified in her bed. As he looked at her, the first thing the marshal wondered was whether, at the moment she had been handcuffed to the head of the bed, she had realised what was about to happen to her and had remained lucid but powerless to do anything to avoid death, or whether the shock had made her lose consciousness.

It was a particularly gruesome scene.

The first hypothesis that he formulated, however, was that it had been an accident, perhaps a sex game that had gone wrong, as wrong as it possibly could. Could it be that her partner had squeezed her neck too hard in trying to intensify the pleasure of the orgasm?

But what if it really was a murder? Perhaps the work of someone she had rejected? In other words, a crime of passion?

As an experienced detective, Gori filed these questions away in his mind, remembering the proverb he often repeated to his men: a cat in a hurry produces blind kittens. There was no point jumping to conclusions, however attractive they might seem, until they could be verified. Better to take a good look at the scene of the crime.

He stared at the exposed part of the body and did not see any blood. He was tempted to lift the sheet, but preferred to wait for the pathologist and the forensics team to arrive. He tried instead to think like the killer – assuming this really was a murder – to identify with him in order to reconstruct the sequence of his actions. He wondered if, after having committed the crime, the killer had lingered to look at her, to contemplate her body, or if he had run away immediately. He also wondered whether the killer had cleaned up after himself, removing anything that might lead them to him: fibres, hair, prints.

He ordered his men not to touch anything and began looking through the rooms.

The apartment was very large.

Eight rooms in all, spread over two floors. From the top floor there was access to a well-tended terrace, where various species of evergreen plant stood in large terracotta vases. The marshal noticed that the lock on the main door of the apartment, a solid, reinforced door, did not appear to have been forced. He also glanced down into the inner courtyard, which was adorned with flower beds and slender trees, their leaves shiny from the fine rain that had started falling again. The courtyard was silent and secluded, far from the crowds and the traffic.

He walked quickly through the other rooms. The only one in which he lingered was the living room, which had a door through to the bedroom. It was large and sumptuously furnished. From the ceiling, which was distempered in a floral pattern, hung two crystal chandeliers. There were thick Persian rugs in warm colours on the Carrara marble floor. Two sofas, one of them in the corner, and three armchairs, all of white leather, made for a very welcoming atmosphere. Some of the furniture was antique. In a corner stood a sophisticated modern stereo unit, which suggested that music had been one of the victim's passions. A glance at the vast collection of CDs revealed that she had been particularly fond of classical music. The two windows showed no signs of a break-in. At this point it was clear, either the killer had entered with a key or it had been the victim herself who had opened the door for him. Did that mean they knew each other? The presence of a video entryphone, in full working order, beside the main door seemed to confirm this hypothesis.

Gori turned his gaze to the white walls. There were a large number of paintings hanging on them, some in black frames, many of them old. The pattern of the curtains incorporated the traditional fleur-de-lis of Florence. Overall, the style of furnishing was a blend of old and new.

All at once he heard voices in the corridor. 'Things never stop in this city!' someone was saying.

The pathologist and the deputy prosecutor had arrived at last.

Meanwhile in the kitchen, Sergeant Domenico Surace, a young man of well over fifteen stone, was sitting at a table beneath ceiling spotlights, questioning the woman who had discovered the body.

Her name was Olivia and she was from the Philippines. She was twenty-five years old, although she looked much younger. Her thin dark face, which had turned ashen, was framed by long smooth hair. Her eyes, also dark, were still watery from all the tears she had shed. From time to time, she took a sip of water from a glass.

She told him she had been working here for nearly three years, ever since she had arrived in Italy. This morning, as usual, she had let herself into the apartment: she had her own keys.

'Did you touch anything?'

'No. I know you're not supposed to. I watch a lot of crime series on TV. And anyway I was afraid someone was still here, maybe hiding in a corner, and might jump out and attack me.'

'Was it you who turned on the lights?'

'No. That's how I found them.' At this point her voice faltered, her hands started shaking, and she lowered her eyes as if about to start crying again.

'Have some more water. Please try to calm down. See if you can remember anything else.'

Almost as if she had not heard these words, the woman continued singing the praises of her signora. How beautiful she was, the most beautiful and kindest woman in the world. Such a good person. She did a lot of charitable work: she couldn't remember the name of the charity, but she knew it helped children in India.

'Did you notice any changes in Signora Innocenti lately?'

'No. She was always the same, always cheerful.'

'Any enemies?'

'No.'

'Had she quarrelled with anyone?'

'No.'

'Can you tell me anything about the people who came to the apartment?'

'Nobody ever came while I was here. I only work for three hours. But one morning I found cigarette ash on the floor next to an armchair in the living room. And I thought that was strange . . .'

'Why?'

'The signora didn't smoke.'

'Are you sure?'

'Yes. I never saw her smoke.'

'When was it you saw this ash?'

She thought about this for a moment, then said, 'About ten days ago.'

'Do you remember anything else?'

'No. That's all.'

'As far as you know, did the signora use drugs?'

'No!'

She sat there for a moment, staring into the distance.

At this point, Surace thought it best to conclude the

interview. He asked her where she could be reached, and learned that she lived with a sister, who had come from Manila ten years earlier.

'The body's cold,' the pathologist said.

Piero Franceschini had been working at the Institute in Florence for just over two years. Pushing forty, tall and thin, with smooth fair hair that was starting to recede, he had quickly become a star pupil of the director, Gustavo Lassotti.

He moved aside to allow the photographer from forensics, who had just arrived with his colleagues, to process the scene before lifting the sheet and removing the handcuffs from the victim's wrists. Once that had been done a technician removed the sheet.

They were surprised to see, not only that the woman was completely naked, but that between her slightly parted legs, on the pubic area, lay a long-stemmed artificial black rose. Gori looked at the deputy prosecutor, who said, 'Take it away, but carefully. The handcuffs, too.'

Only then was Franceschini finally able to begin to examine the corpse. He turned it over several times, helped by two Carabinieri, then said, 'Death occurred several hours ago, perhaps late last night or in the early hours of this morning.'

'Cause of death?' Marshal Gori asked.

'Strangulation. There's no doubt about it. Look.' He pointed to the continuous horizontal furrow in the middle of the neck. 'Not to mention the discoloration of the face and the conjunctival bruising.' His voice was loud, as if he was addressing unruly young medical students at their first autopsy.

The marshal went closer to the bed and leaned over the dead woman's face. The skin was smooth and tanned, but with that pallor typical of the dead. He noticed a pair of valuable-looking earrings. He nodded and turned to the deputy prosecutor. 'What about the murder weapon? It's not here.'

The deputy prosecutor had been thinking the same thing. He shook his head and turned to look at the pathologist. They both wanted an answer.

'No, it's not here,' Franceschini said. 'The killer must have taken it with him, unless you find it somewhere in the apartment. It might have been a piece of rope, a wire, or even a strap. He could even have used her bra.'

'And what happened to the bra?' Gori asked. 'And the rest of her underwear? Where is it?'

'It's up to you to find it,' the deputy prosecutor said. He turned back to Franceschini. 'Any signs of a struggle?'

'None whatsoever.'

How could the victim have struggled with both her wrists handcuffed? Gori thought. Something else struck him: if a wire or a strap or something like that had been used, then his first hypothesis of an accident during an erotic game seemed unlikely. If the killer had not throttled her with his bare hands, the crime must have been premeditated.

But what was the motive? That was the crucial question, and the hardest to answer. Knowing the killer's motive might point the investigation in the right direction. To discover it, they needed to find out as much as they could about the victim's life, habits and friends. Especially in this case, where the fact that the lights were still on suggested that the murder had taken place at night and that the victim had admitted the killer of her own free will. They needed to go beyond appearances, dig deep into the life of Giovanna Innocenti, uncover whatever there was to uncover. The witnesses they found would have to be questioned closely, caught out in any lies or evasions. Anyone who knew the victim would have to be probed and made to give up their secrets.

Marshal Gori was well aware of this. Just as he was aware that, until the motive had been identified, he would have to follow every possible lead, building up the picture piece by piece until everything fitted.

There were two diamond rings on the victim's right hand. That definitely ruled out robbery as a motive. A crime of passion was still possible.

But why the black rose?

'There are no other lesions visible to the naked eye, apart from the one caused by the strangulation,' Franceschini was saying. 'Nor are there any marks on the legs and arms to suggest the use of drugs.'

'Was there any sexual violence?' asked Gori.

'An initial examination suggests not, but I'll be able to confirm that after the post-mortem.'

'When are you thinking of performing it?'

'This afternoon. But I can tell you right now that there are no signs of sexual activity either on or near the body.'

The doctor walked away from the bed, took off his latex gloves and threw them to one of the Carabinieri, as if divesting himself of a theatrical costume after a show. Then he said to the deputy prosecutor, 'My work here is done, so if you don't mind, I'd like to go. I'm sure the Carabinieri still have a lot to do.'

'Thank you. Keep me informed of any developments.'

'Of course. You'll have my preliminary report by this evening. I'll phone you anyway.'

He said goodbye and shambled towards the door. The deputy prosecutor left soon afterwards.

At last the Carabinieri could get down to work.

27

The search was a meticulous one and lasted several hours. For all their efforts, they did not find any clues that might suggest someone had ransacked the rooms. No traces of blood or biological material.

Nothing at all.

The killer had been diligent and meticulous. He had not left anything at the crime scene, apart from the artificial black rose, the handcuffs, and perhaps the wrapper of a disposable Kodak camera, found on the floor between the bedside table and the edge of the bed.

An unusual object, which suggested that photographs had been taken of the woman – but why?

It seemed the only element, apart from the handcuffs, that might link the culprit to the crime scene, unless they found his prints, of course. A killer usually left something of himself at the scene of his crime, just as something of the scene remained on him. Sometimes, however, the traces were so tiny as to be overlooked, and only the skill and intuition of the crime-scene investigators could reveal them. At other times, they were visible but proved to be of no use.

Gori and his men knew all this, which was why they had been so thorough in their search. They had lifted some fingerprints, to be cross-checked with the victim's and Olivia's. They had emptied all the drawers and cabinets, stripped the bookshelves of books. They had looked in every nook and cranny. Particular attention had been paid to the wardrobe: a large one, in solid walnut, with various drawers and shelves. Inside it, dresses hanging neatly on hangers, handbags, shoes, hats, and other accessories. Everything was expensive and bore witness to a certain kind of lifestyle. They had taken out every item, every object, and inspected it, hoping perhaps to find something forgotten in a pocket or a bag. They found nothing. But under one of the drawers they discovered a hidden compartment, about twenty inches by twelve, filled with designer watches, cash, and a small quantity of jewellery: a couple of diamond bracelets, and some rings and earrings.

They had not found any personal letters: the victim seemed neither to have written nor received correspondence. Only bills, invitations to cocktail parties and dinners, magazines and newspapers advertising holidays, especially holidays abroad. In a box, they found some photographs seemingly thrown in at random. Most looked like holiday snaps. Some showed the victim in a swimsuit, others wrapped up for skiing. She was either alone or with other women. Men were conspicuous by their absence, except in a few group photographs.

So far, no member of the victim's family had appeared, even though they had been informed by Olivia. That was really strange. Usually, as soon as they were informed of a tragedy, the members of the family were the first to come running. Some wept uncontrollably, some became voluble and blurted out things that could prove helpful to an investigation. Dealing with relatives was one of the most thankless tasks, because they usually wanted straight answers – who had killed their loved one, and why? – and demanded immediate justice.

In the case of Giovanna Innocenti none of that happened.

The woman had lived alone and even in death she was still alone.

Has she been on bad terms with her family? So bad that they were keeping their distance even after her death?

And what had happened to the victim's underwear? Had the killer taken it away with him? If so, why? Did it indicate they were dealing with a psychopath?

Anything was possible at this stage.

The marshal ordered his men to take away the two computers – one laptop, one desktop – the diaries, various documents, including bank statements, notebooks, and the box of photographs. They would examine them carefully at the barracks. Finally, they left the apartment.

Before they went downstairs Gori said, 'Check the light on the landing, Petrucci.' He had only just noticed that it was off.

The sergeant got up on a chair.

'It's only unscrewed, Marshal.'

The light came back on. Both wondered whether it was the killer who had unscrewed it. Gori ordered him to carefully remove the bulb.

'But I've touched it, Marshal!'

'We'll eliminate your prints when we run the test.'

They might find usable prints. You never knew.

As usually happened, a crowd of onlookers had gathered outside. Gori wondered if the killer was among them. Inevitably, there was a small group of reporters. He recognised those from the local press, among them a young reporter from the NSA agency, well known for his scrupulous accuracy.

They were waiting for him impatiently, desperate to know something about the crime.

It was just after one.

As soon as he saw them, the marshal started walking more quickly, with his head down. A young woman ran after him, crying, 'Do you have a minute for us?' A cameraman from a private TV channel had started filming him.

'No comment,' Gori said curtly. He had no intention of making any statement: he always let the public relations office handle these people.

'Just one question, Marshal,' the young woman insisted, thrusting her microphone – it had a TV logo on it – into his face. 'Is it true that this was an unusually savage killing?'

Gori stiffened. 'The investigation has only just begun,' he said, 'and as you know, we don't release details while inquiries are in progress.' Then he got into his duty car and ordered the driver to head back to the barracks.

For the journalist it was a confirmation of what everybody had been saying.

The neighbourhood was gone over with a fine-tooth comb. House by house. Street by street.

All available Carabinieri were put on the case. No stone was to be left unturned.

Even the dustbins were searched. But not a trace was found of either the victim's underwear or the murder weapon. The tenants of the neighbouring buildings were questioned, as were the local shopkeepers and artisans. Nothing useful was discovered. Nobody had noticed anything unusual, or else nobody had had the courage to come forward out of fear for themselves or their own families. They all confirmed that the victim, who was shy by nature, had never been the subject of gossip. Almost all of them, on the other hand, made the usual complaints about the drug dealers, junkies and bag snatchers who were infesting the area, attracted by all the tourists visiting the nearby Palazzo Pitti. The taxi drivers who had been in the area during the previous evening and night were questioned, too, but nothing came of that either.

So far there were no leads, no clues, no tip-offs.

This was not shaping up to be an easy case.

28

In the meantime, there was a great deal of upheaval in the offices of the *Squadra Mobile*.

Just before midday, two criminals riding a large motorcycle in the Via di Novoli had robbed a jewellery salesman who was crossing the street on his way to see a customer. He was not a professional security guard, but in the belt of his trousers he kept a revolver, which he had been authorised to carry because of the nature of his work. The street had been packed with people. An attack in broad daylight seemed unthinkable. But suddenly, the passenger on the motorcycle had reached out and snatched the salesman's bag. Taking out his weapon, the salesman had fired a few shots, one of which had hit the thief in the back; he was now in a critical state in hospital. A couple of police officers were stationed outside the operating theatre, hoping he would pull through so that they could question him. Another shot had grazed the leg of a young female student who had not even realised what was going on.

Yes, even in Florence, something like this could happen.

The police were searching for the motorcycle and its driver, but both seemed to have vanished into thin air. The wounded man, who had no identity papers, was not known to the police, which meant the two men were probably criminals from another city. There had been a whole series of robberies lately committed by people from out of town.

Ferrara was landed with the most difficult task: to assess the conduct of the victim, who was currently being questioned in the offices of the Robbery Squad. Would they have to charge him with voluntary homicide? Or would it be manslaughter while legitimately using his weapon? Could his reaction be considered commensurate with what had been done to him? It was a difficult judgement call. The statements by witnesses were confused and contradictory: as usual, there were those who had seen too much and those who had not seen enough. But the picture that was emerging was that the salesman had fired with his gun held high, which meant that he had intended to hit his target. The man himself, however, insisted that he had fired at the wheels of the motorcycle in an attempt to stop the criminals from getting away.

Ferrara was still thinking about all this when his secretary came into the room with a yellow envelope in his hand.

'This is for you, chief. A Carabiniere brought it in. It's from his commander.' He placed the envelope on the desk.

Ferrara opened it.

It was a dispatch classified top priority.

He read it.

Giovanna Innocenti, single, born Florence, 24 June 1968, daughter well-known family Innocenti, internationally renowned Florentine entrepreneurs, murdered in own apartment in Borgo San Frediano night of 24 to 25 June 2004. Victim found completely naked, her wrists secured to the head of the bed with a pair of handcuffs. Between her legs, a long-stemmed artificial black rose. Robbery currently

ruled out as motive. Prosecutor's Department informed.
Inquiries under way.

Marshal Edoardo Gori, Commander,
Criminal Investigation Division

Putting the sheet of paper down on the desk, Ferrara muttered to himself.

The secretary pricked up his ears. He knew that his chief was alone in the room, so he was surprised by that muttering. He wondered if the reason had something to do with the contents of that envelope. He was about to get up from his desk and go closer to the door, but he stayed where he was and continued working at the computer. Then he broke off, stood up, and stretched. He had just spent a long time recording his colleagues' overtime hours. It was almost the end of the month and the *Squadra Mobile* had exceeded the budget assigned to it by quite a margin – something that had been happening with increasing regularity of late. When would they receive payment for the extra hours from the ministry? Would it be months? Or even years? He took a step forward, then turned back and sat down again at his post. His natural shyness and indecisiveness gaining the upper hand again.

Giovanna Innocenti ... A long-stemmed black rose ... Innocenti, a very high-profile name in Florence ... Killed on her birthday and saint's day ... Handcuffed to the bed ... A rose between her legs ...

This was all very unusual.

Ferrara beat on the desk with his fist.

Setting aside his reflections on the robbery in the Via di Novoli, he re-read the dispatch from the Carabinieri, and started thinking.

The scar on the dead woman.

The threatening letter.

Now this horrifying murder.

Three incidents in the course of just three days.

Too many for Florence.

Strange . . . But strangest of all was that black rose.

29

A sudden memory.

Ferrara was certain that it was something important. He closed his eyes and tried to focus. His mind ran through images – some recent, some distant and fragmentary – of murders, kidnappings, photographs of crime scenes, reports, notes, letters . . .

Yes, that was it!

He reopened his eyes, leapt out of his chair and went straight to the cupboard where he kept his personal archive.

The files were arranged according to place and year. What he was interested in right now was his last time in Florence. Somewhere in these files, his unconscious was telling him, he would find what he was looking for. After leafing through document after document, he at last came across an ordinary white commercial envelope, addressed to him and postmarked *Florence, 15 April 2003*. There was no sender's name on it, but there was something unusual: the upper right-hand corner was partly burnt. He opened the envelope and took out a sheet of paper, folded in three. A few lines, printed off a computer, just like the address. He walked back to his desk, sat down, took a deep breath and began to read.

Dear Chief Superintendent Ferrara,

Soon the roses will bloom again and the hooded ones will take leave of their senses, not only in Florence, and you won't be able to do anything except smoke those stinking cigars of yours, whose name is the only good thing about them.

PS One word of advice. Try not to go boar hunting, because you might find yourself in the wrong place at the wrong time. You might even be mistaken for a boar . . .

No grammatical or syntactical mistakes. None of those errors that often characterised anonymous letters. The contents, while cryptic, were explicit.

He remembered what he had thought at the time: that this letter alluded to the dark, mysterious face of Florence. It was an aspect of the city that had been around since the medieval days of magicians, hermits, healers – or fake healers – and people who attended black masses and satanic ceremonies, old practices that still survived in odd ways, like that man he had seen with the tarot cards in the Via dei Calzaiuoli the day before.

He wondered if it had been a mistake to underestimate that letter, and if he might still be in time to remedy that mistake. In his mind, the phrases he had just been reading continued to echo.

Roses . . . The hooded ones . . . Roses . . . The hooded ones . . . And you won't be able to do anything else except smoke those stinking cigars . . .

He read once again the dispatch from the Carabinieri.

The black rose . . .

Enough!

He went to the window and looked out at the street. It was half empty. Rain had started falling again, pounding on the tarmac and forming dark puddles. Someone hurried past, hugging the walls. For a few moments he watched the big raindrops beating on the roofs of the cars. Time seemed to stand still. He was back in his childhood, when he would break off from his homework and spend a few minutes looking out at the rain falling on the roofs, the street, the passers-by. He could still hear the sound. So many dreams! He had been in a hurry to grow up, to face the world and discover its mysteries. In those days, he would have liked time to go faster, but all too often it had slowed down until sometimes it seemed to have stopped altogether.

He set aside his memories and came back to the present. He realised that, in the face of bitter reality, all his illusions had collapsed. It turned out the mysteries he had wanted to discover had nothing wonderful about them. Like a fly caught in a spider's web, he was struggling to free himself. But all his efforts were proving to be in vain. For a moment he had the illusion that once again the web was closing in on him. This job was one he had chosen: a job that forced him to share other people's lives ... How many times, though, had he told himself that he would have preferred to enjoy his life with Petra in peace?

A sudden thought struck him: could the two letters have come from the same printer?

He sat down again and re-read the 2003 letter.

One detail puzzled him: the reference to hunting. He had never been a hunter, except of criminals. The thought of hunting defenceless animals was so abhorrent to him, he was actually in favour of it being banned. Many years earlier, in Calabria, his colleagues had given him a setter puppy in an effort to persuade him to go hunting with them in his free time. He had accepted the dog, won over by those gentle eyes that seemed to demand nothing but love, but he had not changed his mind. Susi had become a pet, an unforgettable friend, whose memory, so many years after her death, still saddened both him and Petra.

He took his black leather cigar case from his jacket pocket and extracted a half-cigar. He moved it back and forth between the index finger and thumb of his right hand, then lifted it to his lips and rolled it several times to moisten it. Then he lit it, took a deep puff, and watched the white smoke rising to the ceiling.

He lifted the telephone receiver and dialled Marshal Gori's number.

30

The meeting had been fixed for an hour later in the Prosecutor's Department. He set off without the enthusiasm he had once felt.

There were various reasons for his reluctance. For some time now, he had been seeing the Prosecutor's Department with different eyes. It seemed to him increasingly like another world, filled with bureaucracy and red tape, so different from the atmosphere of Police Headquarters, especially the corridors and rooms of his own *Squadra Mobile*.

And that feeling of strangeness had grown since the killing of his dear friend, Deputy Prosecutor Anna Giulietti. Every time he entered the office that had been hers and was now occupied by Luigi Vinci, he was overwhelmed by a sense of sadness.

Vinci had been working in Florence for nearly ten years. In his late fifties, of medium height, with dark eyes, he did everything he could to keep in perfect physical shape. He played tennis twice a week in a private club in Poggio Imperiale, and on Sunday mornings often went jogging in the Parco delle Cascine. As far as his work was concerned, he was not exactly known for his initiative. In fact, he was so timorous that the officers who had worked with him had nicknamed him No Balls.

Today he was wearing a blue sports jacket and a pair of matching linen trousers.

'So, Marshal, what happened when you visited the Innocentis?' was his first question.

Gori said that he had met only the victim's father, who had come to the door of the villa but not let him in. The man had not asked any questions about what had happened to his daughter, as he might have been expected to, nor about how the investigation was proceeding.

'To be honest, Deputy Prosecutor, he didn't seem especially grief-stricken. I'd say he was more indifferent than anything else and in a hurry to put an end to the visit as soon as possible. His one concern seemed to be to avoid a scandal that could damage the good name of the family. It's my impression we shouldn't expect any kind of cooperation from him.'

'Strange,' commented Vinci.

Ferrara nodded several times.

'Deputy Prosecutor,' Gori went on, 'it might be an idea to tap his phones.' Of course, he knew the suggestion would never be accepted: Alvise Innocenti was far too influential a figure in the city.

'I'll talk to the prosecutor, Marshal, and let you know,' Vinci said, cutting him off. Then, turning to Ferrara, he asked what idea the chief superintendent had so far formed about the murder and above all if he had any theories to explain the significance of that rose placed on the victim's pubic area.

Ferrara, considering it still premature to speculate that there might be a connection between this murder and the scar on the face of the dead woman, merely replied, 'I don't yet know all the details, but my office is willing to cooperate with the Carabinieri.'

'You must!' Vinci said immediately, raising his voice.

'I'll put all the papers at the chief superintendent's disposal,' Gori said.

'Thank you,' Vinci said, apparently satisfied by this show of willingness. 'But tell me, Ferrara,' he insisted, 'what do you think about the rose?'

'It might be a message,' Ferrara ventured.

'A message? Who to?'

'That's something we'll have to find out.'

'Well, get going on this. And please, not a word about the rose to the press.'

PART TWO

SPECIAL FRIENDSHIPS

31

It was a bright summer's day.

There was a close-up of a road sign – Montespertoli, the 'home of wine' – followed by a pan of the hills, revealing a large burnt oak standing there like a huge ghost, and a converted hayloft, completely isolated and surrounded by a high stone wall. To one side, an arbour with a table and chairs. Inside, a fairly large bedroom. Then two voices, a man's and a woman's.

'Are you sure?'

'Yes. You know it's the great dream of my life. I can't wait.'

'You'll become an initiate. As you already know, the organisation is composed, in addition to the initiates, of a Priest, a Prince, a Master and a Grand Master. I'm the Priest who'll initiate you. And remember what I said before.'

'What?'

'That once you're in, there are only two ways you'll ever be able to leave: by killing yourself, or being killed by another initiate. There is no middle way. Also that you must maintain secrecy, whatever happens ...'

'Yes, I know the rules. And I'll never want to leave, I swear.'

'And you must never betray us.'

'Never, I swear.'

'Let's get undressed.'

Now the two were completely naked.

Apart from the double bed, the room contained a wardrobe and a chest of drawers with a few candles, a human skull and a small case on it.

The man emptied the case of its contents: a small bag filled with earth, another filled with some kind of mixture and a small knife. Then he drew a circle on the floor, placed some candles around it, lit them one by one, then lit others at various points around the room. Then he said, 'I took the earth from a grave in the nearby cemetery. Enter the circle and lie down. On your back.'

They entered. He bent over her body and with the knife cut off a few pubic hairs before placing the skull over her genital area. Then he cut off a few hairs from her head and burnt them. They both started to breathe in the smoke.

'Don't be afraid, I'm not going to hurt you.'

And with the knife he made a few small cuts on her chest. He collected the blood in a small bowl and drank it, uttering some words in Latin.

He now performed the same operation on his own body, and she in her turn drank his blood, accompanying the gesture with the same Latin words. He then passed the knife over her body. With his own blood he wrote the number 666 on the woman's forehead. Then they had sex.

'Now you will be able to have the tattoo done in a place that's not visible. It's the sign of your membership.'

'I will. I'm really happy and you can count on me for ever. Thank you. It was beautiful. When can I meet the others?'

'In due course. You'll meet the Prince first, then the Master. First, you'll have to watch the video. But remember, you must never ask inappropriate questions.'

The TV screen went black. The amateur video had come to an end.

The man pressed the stop button and took out the tape. He stood up and put it back in its usual place in the safe, where he kept it jealously, together with his other 'treasures'.

Now at last he felt recharged. That old video, which he knew by heart down to the smallest detail, had strengthened his resolve. He felt almost stoned, approaching the state of heightened excitement that he liked so much.

His friendship with that woman, who as a child had played in the garden with miniature coffins and dolls stuck with pins, had proved useful over time and he was sure that he could always count on her. Ever since she had become an initiate – although in fact still his only initiate – their relationship had grown in strength, without turning into a real love affair. They were linked by the kind of special friendship you found between people who had interests in common, interests they had to keep secret from the rest of the world – his secrets being even more unmentionable than hers.

32

'Chief, I have something for you about that letter you showed me.'

Ferrara had just got back from the Prosecutor's Department and was turning into the corridor when Inspector Venturi came towards him, holding a couple of A4 sheets in one hand and a plastic carrier bag in the other. He was smiling, and there was a gleam in his sky-blue eyes.

Ferrara knew him well enough to know that whatever he had to show him must be important.

'Let's go in my office,' he said, continuing along the corridor.

As soon as they were sitting facing each other across the desk, Venturi handed him the sheets of paper. 'This is private information from a friend of mine.' He emphasised the word *private*. 'I showed her a copy of the letter because she belongs to a family who are experts on the occult. She has some amazing books on the subject, some of them really old and rare. I've seen them.'

His curiosity aroused, Ferrara began to read.

Soon the roses will bloom again: roses are a symbol of blood. The blooming could refer to the carrying out of murders.

Roses also have a specific meaning in the language of Freemasonry. Whenever a brother is buried, three roses are thrown on his grave, known as the three roses of St John, symbolising light, love and life. In addition, on St John the Baptist's day, 24 June, the summer solstice, some lodges celebrate the feast of the roses.

The hooded ones will take leave of their senses: the hooded ones could refer to Masonic lodges that use cloaks with hoods in their rituals, or else the initiates of secret societies, who wear them to celebrate black masses. Either way, they are typical ceremonial garments, whose colour changes from one occult group to another.

At this point Ferrara paused. Not the Freemasons again! He shook his head and resumed reading in silence.

And you won't be able to do anything except smoke those stinking cigars of yours, whose name is the only good thing about them. Clearly he's teasing you.

The expert did not go into greater detail than that. Nor did she comment on the PS about boar hunting.

Having finished reading, Ferrara looked up. Venturi pushed across the desk an article from *La Nazione* that he had found during his search on the web.

'Chief, this might explain the reference to boar hunting,' he said, looking pleased with himself.

The headline was: *Hunter killed: A mystery story.* Ferrara read on.

According to the article, during a boar hunt in the countryside near Florence, a fifty-two-year-old man had been accidentally killed by a hunter who had heard noises coming from the undergrowth and fired, thinking he was shooting a boar.

He looked at the date: the accident had happened only a few days before he had received the anonymous letter.

If roses meant a number of murders, he wondered if the murder of Giovanna Innocenti was merely the first. He let out an exclamation. 'The bastards!'

'These are crazy people we're dealing with,' Venturi said, picking up the carrier bag he had been keeping beside him on the floor and placing it on the desk. 'Chief, my friend has sent you these books. She says you might find some useful information in them about the occult.'

Ferrara pulled the bag towards him and took out the books: they were very old volumes, age-worn, consulted God alone knew how many times. He looked through the titles. He noticed that they had all been printed in Florence. He would never have imagined that such a literary genre had ever flourished in Tuscany, and perhaps continued to do so. He looked at the covers again, then lingered over the one that had particularly struck him. It depicted a naked woman on a horse, holding her hands raised behind her head. Around her, some hooded men were brandishing long sticks and trying to strike her.

At the bottom of the bag he found a note.

Dear Chief Superintendent Ferrara,

I send you these books in the hope they might be of help to you. Don't hesitate to contact me for further information. It would give me great pleasure to know I'd been of use to you.

Yours sincerely

Silvia de Luca

Ferrara put the note down, wondering why Venturi had decided to reveal his confidante's identity. He had always respected the woman's anonymity, conscious that the relationship between her and the inspector was strictly personal.

'I'll read the books that Silvia de Luca has been kind enough to send me. In the meantime though, thank her, and suggest a meeting. I wouldn't mind having a little chat with her.'

'Yes, chief, I think the time has come. Silvia knows a lot about many things. And I guarantee you, she's very discreet. She's proved that countless times. And I know she'd be happy to help.'

Left alone in his office after Venturi had gone, Ferrara was looking through the book with the woman on horseback on the cover when the telephone rang.

It was Deputy Prosecutor Erminia Cosenza, phoning to say that she agreed with him that the jewellery salesman should be arrested. From what was known, there could be no doubt that his actions had been deliberate. Many witnesses had seen him taking careful aim at the passenger on the motorbike.

That'll teach him to go around armed! Ferrara said to himself, after hanging up.

He set off for the forensics lab, taking last year's anonymous letter with him. Although he was quite sceptical, he thought it might still be worth comparing it with the one he had received at home.

The comparison, though, might take a few days.

33

She was sitting in the waiting room, a small room lit entirely by the fluorescent light that was always on, day and night, in the adjacent corridor, the light from which came through a large pane of glass into the room. The marshal's old acquaintances, certain disreputable-looking characters who haunted the barracks, informers who had come to betray their associates, witnesses waiting to be questioned: these were the people you usually saw in this room. This woman, though, did not belong to any of these categories.

She was leafing distractedly through one of those house magazines you always found in the waiting rooms of Carabinieri barracks and which were often the only publications available to visitors.

Gori opened his door. 'Please come in and sit down, signora,' he said, indicating one of the two chairs in front of his desk.

'My name is Sara Genovese and I'm Giovanna Innocenti's best friend,' the woman said, sitting forward in the chair so that she barely touched the back of it.

The name did not ring any bells so far as Gori was concerned, but he registered the use of the present tense, as if the victim was still alive. He wasn't surprised: he knew how long grieving could take. He rose from his chair and shook the hand she held out to him. Her fingers were long and thin.

In the meantime she had taken off her dark glasses. Her large blue eyes were swollen and red from crying.

'Were you born in Florence, signora?' he asked gently.

'Yes, I'm a Florentine.' After giving her personal details, she lowered her voice and said, 'Giovanna and I were at school together. In fact, we were classmates for many years. We were always inseparable.'

This woman might well know something, the marshal thought, as he listened.

'Only last night we were together, celebrating her birthday and name day. We had dinner at one of our favourite restaurants, Alfredo's in the Viale Don Minzoni. Then we stayed in my apartment until about nine.' She had said all this almost in one breath. Then, no longer able to hold back her tears, she burst out crying. Her lips quivered and she bowed her head, embarrassed to show herself in such a state. Gori looked at her well-tended hands twisting the strap of her Louis Vuitton handbag. The situation was both pathetic and embarrassing. The marshal stood up, went around to the front of the desk and sat down in the other visitor chair.

'I understand your grief, signora, but please be brave,' he said, gently placing a hand on her shoulder.

She took a white embroidered handkerchief from her handbag and wiped her eyes. 'It was her birthday!' she said between sobs. 'Her name day! And she was killed! I know I must be brave, Marshal, that I have to get on with my life, but the truth is, Giovanna isn't here any more and she's left a void, a huge void.' She lifted a hand to her mouth to stifle the sobs.

A sudden silence descended. It lasted a few moments, enough for Gori to take a closer look at her.

Her dark blue linen suit and her white silk blouse accentuated a nice figure, and with her sensual lips, well-groomed shoulder-length red hair and tanned complexion, she looked like a film star. He wondered if by any chance she was in show business.

'What work do you do, signora?' he asked, to break the silence.

'I have an estate agency, in the Porta al Prato, very near here. Giovanna is my partner. We set up the company a few years after we graduated.'

'Are you married?'

'Me?'

'Yes, you.'

'No. Nor was Giovanna.' She bowed her head again, as if staring at a spot on the floor.

'What did you do last night? After nine o'clock, I mean?'

The woman slowly looked up. 'We went first to the Bar Curtatone, and had a glass of champagne . . .' Her hair had slipped down over her eyes and she raised her hand to brush it back behind her ears.

'And then?'

'We watched the firework display from the Ponte Vespucci. There were lots of people there. We said goodbye at about eleven thirty. I watched her cross the bridge until she reached the other bank of the river.'

At that moment the telephone rang. It was the colonel.

'I have to leave the room for a few minutes,' Gori said as soon as he had hung up.

'Should I wait here?'

'If you wouldn't mind.'

When he returned, she was still sitting in the same chair, her eyes staring into space.

'Sorry about that, signora.'

'It's my fault, Marshal, for coming here without an appointment and disturbing you.'

'You didn't disturb me, it's my job.'

She looked him in the face for a moment. She seemed different, as if there were suddenly many thoughts swirling around in her mind.

'Did you notice anyone suspicious during the evening? Someone following you, perhaps? Please try to remember, signora. Even some quite insignificant detail might turn out to be extremely useful.'

'No, I'm afraid I didn't notice anything suspicious. And anyway, who could have imagined . . . '

'Did your friend seem different to you in any way? Did she seem worried or nervous?'

'No.'

'And in the previous few days?'

'No.'

'Do you know if she'd quarrelled with anyone? If there was anyone with a grudge against her?'

'No.'

'Some personal matter that—'

'Nothing like that, I can assure you.'

'Then who could have had a reason to kill her?'

'Nobody wanted to kill her.'

'And yet somebody did. Please forgive my insistence, signora, but in my job it's sometimes only by insisting, unpleasant as that may be, that we manage to jolt people's memories about things they may have forgotten or underestimated . . . '

'I only know one thing: what happened is absurd, incomprehensible. I seem to be living through a nightmare. I feel as if I'm on the edge of a precipice. We didn't have any secrets from each other. If I had the slightest suspicion, I'd tell you.'

'Did your friend have a lover? A married man, perhaps.'

'That's out of the question. What are you talking about? She didn't have anyone. I'm absolutely certain of that.'

'Other friends, people she saw a lot?'

'Not many,' she replied, and listed the names of a few acquaintances, all from the Florentine upper classes.

'If you do happen to remember anything, please let me know,' the marshal said by way of conclusion. He took a business card from his desk drawer and handed it to her.

She dropped it in her handbag, then put her dark glasses back on and got to her feet. Gori walked her to the door, still wondering why exactly she had come.

'Thank you for coming.'

'Marshal, will you catch the killer?'

'It may take time, but we'll do all we can. I know that catching him may in some way help to alleviate the pain of those who loved her, like you. And the members of her family, of course.'

At these words the woman pursed her lips slightly, as if in a grimace. She turned and walked away down the wide corridor, looking straight ahead, ignoring the glances some of the Carabinieri threw her. When she went out, the smell of her scent lingered in the air.

Strange, that pursing of the lips. It might be necessary to question her again.

These were the marshal's first thoughts. In his experience, witnesses often tried to cover up aspects of a victim's life.

Why had she pursed her lips when he mentioned the family?

Had she been telling him only half-truths?

34

'Who was that woman, sir?'

Sergeant Surace, who had just got back from the morgue, had passed Sara Genovese in the corridor.

'A friend of the victim's.'

'Quite a looker. Did she have anything interesting to say?'

'No, nothing special. I'm not even sure why she came. So, what can you tell me about the post-mortem?'

Before answering that, Surace informed him that no prints had been found on the wrapper from the disposable camera, the light bulb or the handcuffs. Then, leafing through his notes, he gave the details of the post-mortem.

'Cause of death: asphyxiation. She was strangled. The hyoid bone was broken. That much is certain. No other signs of violence. She wasn't raped or sexually assaulted, and her internal organs were healthy.'

'So it's confirmed there was no sexual violence?'

'That's right, sir.'

Gori's face darkened. If traces of sperm had been found, that would have been useful. But there were none, just as there were no residues of skin, fibre or other material under the victim's nails or on any other part of her body.

It seemed certain, then, that this murder was not sexually motivated.

'Go on, Surace,' Gori said.

'At the moment of death, the digestive process had finished. But there were traces of champagne . . . '

So her friend was telling the truth, Gori thought.

'Cuts? Fractures? Bruises?'

'Bruises only on the wrists. Occurred while she was still alive, because the blood was still circulating – at least, that's what the doctor said.'

'Of course, the handcuffs. He immobilised her while she was still alive. Anything else? Did you follow up on the artificial rose?'

'Petrucci's looking into that, but there are a hell of a lot of florists in Florence, even supposing it was bought here.'

'Yes,' Gori replied, 'there are lots of florists. But I doubt that many of their customers are crazy about the colour black.'

Surace nodded.

'Anything more specific about the time of death?'

'Between one and three, based on the degree of rigor mortis. Tomorrow, though, we'll get the preliminary report with all the essential elements.'

'Thanks, Surace. We really need to get going on this case.'

'Of course, sir.'

As soon as the sergeant had gone out, Gori remembered what the colonel had said in that abrupt tone of his when he had been summoned to see him in the middle of his interview with Sara Genovese: 'Get a move on with this! I want results now!' He had not even been given a chance to tell him that he had a friend of Giovanna Innocenti's in his office at that very moment.

Shaking his head, he picked up the phone and called Ferrara. He told him the results of the post-mortem, but did not mention the conversation with Sara Genovese. Of course, the law was the law, and the deputy prosecutor's instructions had to be carried out, but, as a loyal Carabiniere, he would first have to discuss it with his chief. After all, the motto of the Carabinieri was *Faithful throughout the centuries*.

Deciding that the moment had come to take a look at the material found in the victim's apartment, he took out the box of photographs and began looking through them. Many of them showed Giovanna Innocenti in the company of Sara Genovese, whom he had no difficulty in recognising. She hadn't lied about this either: they had clearly been very good friends. He closed the box and put it back in the corner. Sara, he thought, could well turn out to be useful in identifying other friends and associates of Giovanna's.

A good reason to see her again.

35

The meeting was about to begin.

They had just taken their seats in the high-backed leather chairs arranged around a solid walnut table. The room was large and the heavy curtains had been drawn over the windows to keep the world out. The wall to the right was entirely covered in books, some bound in black leather, others in red. From the ceiling hung a large crystal chandelier.

A single painting on the wall showed a triangle inside a circle. Inside the triangle was a flower and above it a royal crown with a cross attached to a plume. The flower, in its turn enclosed in a square, had five petals and a long stem. In the lower part of the triangle, an assortment of symbolic signs. Around the outside of the circle were some words in Latin.

'Before getting to the subject of our meeting,' Enrico Costanza began, 'I'd like to express our sympathy with Alvise and his family. We will do everything in our power to protect the family name. Scandal must be avoided at all costs. We will all rally round.'

The others nodded.

'Thank you,' Alvise said in response. 'Scandal must indeed be avoided, by every means at our disposal.'

'We're lucky the Carabinieri are handling the case,'

Costanza went on. 'If it was in the hands of the police, especially that chief superintendent who's just come back to Florence, that Ferrari . . . Ferrar . . . What's the man's name?'

'Ferrara,' one of the initiates said. 'Michele Ferrara.'

'God knows what this Ferrara would come up with. He's a loose cannon. His own chiefs, even the people in Rome, still haven't managed to get rid of him. He thinks he's tough. Maybe he thinks he's still dealing with the Mafiosi he knew back in Calabria and Sicily. He hasn't understood a damn thing about Florence and the Florentines. He seems incapable of grasping who holds the power here.'

'We managed to get him out of our hair for a year,' someone said, 'and now he's back.'

'I know, but mark my words, it won't be for long this time. Him and his ridiculous ambitions! How deluded can you be?'

'Ferrara's a serious danger,' Alvise Innocenti said, confident that he was speaking for everyone present.

'I agree,' Costanza said, 'especially after the fuss he caused with the Monster investigation. What was he thinking? Where was he going with that? And to think that he was warned . . .'

He made a movement in the air with his right fist. As he did so, the gold ring on the index finger of his right hand glittered in the dim light. It had a ruby set in it and a stylised flower carved on the stone. All the brothers wore the same ring.

'But we'll keep an eye on him,' Costanza resumed. 'We have men in the right places. It must be done discreetly, though. Now isn't the time to risk exposing ourselves, especially after what happened to Alvise. And now, let's get down to business. Our brothers across the Channel are urging us to finalise the financial operation we've talked about. We can't put it off much longer. If you all agree, I'll conclude the deal on Monday morning, when the Milan stock exchange opens.'

The gathering approved the proposal unanimously.

'All right, then. I declare the meeting closed.'

As the brothers rose, the host approached Alvise Innocenti and whispered in his ear, 'Don't worry, we're not going to abandon you. You'll be avenged for what's been done to you. That black rose was an attack on all of us.'

Alvise Innocenti merely nodded.

'You'll be getting news soon, Alvise, very specific news.'

'Thank you,' Alvise Innocenti replied. 'I never doubted that for a moment. It's important, though, that I be kept out of it all.'

He immediately regretted these words, fearing he might have offended Costanza. But Costanza merely nodded.

Did he even know the reason for Innocenti's caution?

36

That evening, perhaps because it was the beginning of the first weekend of summer, the club was full to bursting. The main subject of conversation was the murder of Giovanna Innocenti. Everyone knew the family, and the victim. Some already knew some details of the murder, even of the preliminary autopsy results. Much of the discussion focused on the presence of the black rose between the victim's thighs. There were some who claimed to have a good idea where the killer might be found.

In the meantime, on the first floor, the usual private client was knocking at the usual door. Before leaving home, he had taken a few pills – he had an increasing need for then – and now he felt really good.

The woman opened the door to him, without a sound.

This time she was wearing a kimono. She was waiting for him, but not for the usual delivery. She invited him to follow her to the bedroom, which was illuminated by the diffused light of a small red lamp in a silk lampshade on a low antique table. The air was dense with a sweet scent of jasmine. A small hairless dog, its leather collar adorned with precious stones, sat with its paws crossed on a red armchair, staring at the man but not moving or barking.

The woman let the kimono slide to the floor, revealing a

breathtaking body, with a flat belly and voluptuous curves. She was wearing only a lace G-string, a bra and self-supporting stockings, all in black. With studied calm, she raised her arms behind her back and unhooked the bra, and her breasts came free. Resisting the impulse to throw himself on her, he took a few steps forward, savouring the excitement that was taking over his body. He had been waiting for this. He had desired her for a very long time. And now was the moment. She was indebted to him, but not because of the drugs. It was a question of life or death. He put his arms round her waist and, as she began to take off his jacket and unbutton his shirt, he lightly touched her neck with his lips.

'Slowly,' she whispered, slipping off his boxers. He took off her G-string. They walked to the double bed, still clasped together, while the puppy, which had not moved, watched them indifferently. Their skin grew hot, almost incandescent. They were bathed in sweat. Soon their kisses became even longer, a prelude to the intense pleasure that lay ahead.

About an hour later they were sitting at a small table in a corner of the room. She took two crystal glasses and filled them with champagne. They crossed glasses and sipped at the drinks.

'Are you still worried?' he asked her.

'Yes, quite a bit,' she replied, looking him straight in his grey eyes. 'I know it was a mistake. I don't know if they'll forgive me.'

'No. Don't think that. Nothing happened. You've been one of us for quite a while now, and you've proved your reliability. Trust me.'

There was still an anxious look in her eyes.

'You don't seem convinced.'

Silence.

'Come with me tomorrow night,' he said. 'Everything's just the way it was before, you'll see.'

'Where? I don't want to go back to Pontassieve . . .'

'No, it'll be somewhere completely different, though still not far from here.'

'Are you sure?'

'Yes, I promise. I'll pick you up at eleven o'clock tomorrow night. But I won't come here. I'll meet you in the Piazza Santa Trinita, by the Column of Justice.'

'Will he be there, too?'

'Who?'

'The man I saw . . . last time . . .'

'Don't worry about that now. All right?'

She nodded, and they toasted their next encounter.

He dressed and left.

She went to the bathroom. She had to get ready to go downstairs, where everyone was waiting for her.

37

She was alone, walking down a narrow alley in the driving rain.

She was wearing a wide calf-length skirt and a white blouse that was rather too big for her. With her right hand she held up the umbrella, in the other she had a large bag. On her feet, a pair of boots. She was on her way home, a three-room apartment that overlooked that pedestrian-only alley. It was one of the privileges of living in the centre, not being disturbed by the traffic noise. But this also forced her to go down that stretch of street with her eyes open, because as soon as it got dark, the possibility of an unpleasant encounter increased. There was not much light, and not many passers-by. Only a few cats. It was the ideal refuge for drug dealers, with little likelihood of a police swoop.

It had been a very tough day: the usual assistant was ill and she had had to face the customers alone. A raging headache drove her on: she couldn't wait to get out of this maze of streets and safe in the privacy of her own home.

A sudden noise behind her made her jump. Footsteps, coming closer. She was about to turn when she felt herself being violently grabbed by her left arm.

Her heart started pounding.

Instinctively, she tried to resist. She managed to fold the umbrella, but a second figure joined the attacker. They pushed her into the darkest corner of the entrance to her building. One held her motionless, stopping her from crying out, while the other lifted her skirt, tore off her panties and thrust himself into her. When he was finished, the second man took his place. As they adjusted their clothes, one of the two whispered in broken Italian, 'Careful, not be stupid. Must pay. Is last message from our boss.'

They ran off.

Aching all over, the girl dragged herself up the stairs to her apartment, leaning on the banister. Her skirt was torn, her blouse practically in shreds. Her eyes were red. With difficulty, she dialled a number on her mobile: 'Come, please, come now! They really hurt me.'

She just had time to hear 'I'll be right there' before she collapsed on the floor.

That night, big black clouds heavy with rain hung over Florence. Summer seemed to have receded again. A sudden roll of thunder startled Petra. Instinctively she got out of bed, with her heart in her mouth, went to the door and checked that it was locked. It was not the first time that she had done this in the past seventy-two hours. She opened the shutter in the living room and glanced out at the terrace, and at that moment a flash of lightning pierced the darkness. She closed the shutter again immediately, and took a deep breath. Then she went back to bed. She clung to Michele, who was fast asleep, overwhelmed by the accumulated fatigue of the past few days. But she herself lay there in the darkness, unable to get back to sleep, unable to get rid of this fear that was making it hard for her to breathe. Every night, when she was a child, her grandmother had made her say a prayer to St Anthony: *O kindly*

saint, turn to me your benign gaze, console my heart ... Assist me
in times of sorrow and bless me and all those dear to me. Amen.

Repeating the prayer in her head calmed her. She slipped gently into sleep.

38

Saturday, 26 June

In the first light of dawn, the rain stopped, and the sky cleared.

The last clouds had been swept away by the wind, promising a bright, beautiful day. But not for Chief Superintendent Ferrara.

The front pages of the national dailies were occupied by the day's shock news: the murder of Giovanna Innocenti. The banner headlines were almost identical: SAVAGE MURDER. As usual, a description of the crime scene, reconstructed on the basis of the little that had filtered through the wall of silence put up by the investigators, was fleshed out with completely imaginary details.

But when he turned to the local papers, he was surprised to find not a single line about the death of Giovanna Innocenti on the front pages. The news was confined to small items in the inside pages, with headlines like MURDER IN SAN FREDIANO.

Only the victim's initials were given, which was usually the case when the victim was a minor.

None of the papers mentioned the black rose or the

handcuffs, he noticed. The one exception was *Il Tirreno*. Their reporter must have had those details from a reliable source, and the editor had either not been placed under any pressure, or had had the strength to ignore it. In the concluding lines the hypothesis was put forward that the killer was some kind of pervert or psychopath. They even attempted a kind of profile: a man, between twenty and thirty, leading a double life . . .

Ferrara stood up, went to the window and opened it. He needed to breathe some fresh air. But it wasn't over. He had just started to leaf through the newspaper again when a headline sprang out at him.

DESECRATION: A WARNING?

. . . news in the last few hours about the substance found in the coffin where the desecrated body lay. Examination has shown that it was burnt cigar tobacco, a tiny fraction of an ounce with a very small percentage of nicotine. The forensics experts were able to identify it through the use of sophisticated apparatus . . . It is well known that Michele Ferrara, the head of the *Squadra Mobile*, is a cigar smoker. Could this have been a warning addressed to him? It may still be too early to state this with any certainty, but it seems a likely hypothesis . . .

He looked for the name of the journalist who had written the article, but it was anonymous.

He stood up again and cursed out loud: 'Forensics! It was them! It can only have been them! They even knew the weight! The bastards!'

He slammed his fist on the desk, scattering the papers. He was beside himself. He bent down to pick up the sheets and summoned his secretary.

'Fanti!'

'Yes, chief?'

The secretary, alerted by Ferrara's angry tone, rushed in.

'I want to know where this came from,' he said, handing him the newspaper. 'Do you know anything about it?' He had to rule out the possibility that the leak had come from his own office.

Fanti cast a fleeting glance at it, his face waxen and even more hollow than usual. 'Wh-what do you mean?' he stammered.

'I'm not suggesting it was you, Fanti. What did you think I meant?'

'You know I never talk. I'm as silent as the grave.'

'I know. But did you by any chance notice any of our colleagues talking to one of those journalists who are always hanging around here?'

The secretary seemed to relax. You could say a lot against him – that he wasn't a good street cop, that he didn't know how to prepare reports for the prosecutors – but you couldn't question his loyalty to the chief. You couldn't even make a joke about it. He had always been extremely discreet, sometimes even quarrelling with his colleagues if they asked him for information on Ferrara's movements, or denying the obvious rather than compromise himself.

'I didn't see anything, chief. You know I always concentrate on my work.'

'Okay, Fanti, you can go.'

The secretary went out, looking like a whipped dog. As he sat down again at his computer, he gazed at the faces of the two smiling women he had chosen as a screensaver: his wife and his twelve-year-old daughter.

Ferrara, in the meantime, was still puzzling over how that detail about the tobacco had become an open secret.

Why had someone tipped off the press? Were they trying to sabotage the investigation?

39

Sara Genovese opened the door.

For a moment, there was an embarrassed smile on her face.

Half an hour earlier, she had phoned the marshal to fix an appointment: she had suddenly remembered something that might be of help to the investigation. Gori, who was dying to ask her more questions, had leapt at the chance to go and see her. In her own home she would feel at ease and might be more prone to confide in him.

On the way there, he had wondered what kind of information she could possibly have for him. Was she about to share some revelation about Giovanna Innocenti? Something that would help them understand the killer's motive? The killer had covered his tracks well, even getting rid of the murder weapon. If they managed to track him down, it was possible he would have lined up a convincing alibi, but it might not be so easy for him to conceal the motive that had driven him to kill.

The apartment was in the Via Il Prato, near the estate agency. The marshal had often passed it, sometimes even stopping to glance at the properties advertised in the window. Almost all had the words *Under offer* attached to them. But he had always merely limited himself to squinting inside the agency, never bothering to ask himself who ran it.

Now the person who ran it was here in front of him.

He almost didn't recognise her.

She was not wearing make-up and her eyes were so swollen they were almost closed. Her lips were pale, and her red hair hung loose on her shoulders. Very little remained of the refined, well-groomed woman who had made such an impression on him the day before. And not just on him. Now she looked so sad, it was really painful to look at her.

The marshal's eyes rested on the short red silk dressing gown, crumpled in places. As if guessing his thoughts, she said, 'Giovanna gave me this on a special occasion.' Then she fell silent again. They shook hands and she led him down a long corridor until they reached the living room. Here, with a wave of her hand, she indicated a white leather armchair, inviting him to sit down and arranging a cushion behind his back. Gori took a quick look around. A few impressive items of cherrywood furniture and some equally impressive paintings indicated that this was the home of a woman of class. The room, however, was very untidy. There were books and magazines strewn over the floor, glasses and empty bottles on a low table, clothes thrown here and there on a couple of seats and on the sofas. And on the ground, some red roses next to a precious crystal vase.

'It's very good of you to come here, Marshal,' she said, in her usual soft, calm voice. 'I'm sorry about the mess. I've been too upset to do any tidying.'

'I quite understand, signora,' the marshal said. 'But tell me, what is it you've remembered?'

She looked at him as if about to confide a secret. 'As you can imagine, I didn't sleep a wink last night. I kept thinking and thinking all night, and suddenly I remembered something. I don't know if it's of any help to you, but I'd like to tell it to you all the same.'

'Something you didn't remember yesterday?'

'Yes.'

'Go on.'

'About a year ago, Giovanna and I were witnesses to something.'

'What kind of thing?'

'It happened in the Parco delle Cascine. It was a Tuesday, and we'd gone there, as we often did, to take a look at the market.'

She explained that, as they were walking in the pine grove, not far from the avenue, their attention had been drawn to a man, half hidden by a tree, holding a camera, apparently of a professional kind, and pointing it upwards.

'We thought that was strange, because there was nothing to photograph up there, except the tops of the trees. Look at that idiot, we said, and were about to laugh when ... '

'When what?' he asked, his curiosity aroused.

'We realised the man was a pervert.'

'In what way?'

'We noticed that he was photographing a little girl. She must have been about two years old, no more than that. Lovely fair hair, a real little angel. She was wearing a short white dress, her father kept lifting her in the air and she was laughing. Every time she went up, her dress lifted, revealing her pink knickers. That's what the pervert was photographing. We were shocked. We saw the camera fall on the ground. He was very aroused.'

'And what did you do?'

'We were both disgusted and angry, Giovanna even more than me. She was on the point of running to the man and confronting him. Then she realised that it was more sensible to call the police. She dialled 113 on her mobile. About five minutes later, two plain-clothes officers arrived, but in the meantime the couple with the child had walked away towards the swimming pool and the photographer had followed them. We told the officers.'

'And then?'

'The officers located them. They surprised the man with the camera behind a tree, with one hand inside his trousers . . . He was . . . '

'Masturbating?'

'Yes. They arrested him for committing an obscene act in a public place.'

'When did this happen?'

'Last year, about the beginning of September. I remember it was still hot and we were dressed in summer clothes.'

Gori, who until that moment had not taken his eyes off the woman, now took a notebook and pen from his jacket and quickly wrote down a summary of the story. Then he asked if they had attended the trial and if they had received threats.

Sara Genovese said that the trial had taken place in February, and that the man had been found guilty, but she could not remember the exact sentence. No, they had not received any threats.

Gori noted this down, too. When he looked up again, he realised that she seemed relieved, as if telling him about the incident had relieved her of a great burden.

'I have a few things I'd like to ask you,' he said.

'All right, but first would you like a coffee?'

'Thank you.'

Sara walked away into the kitchen.

While waiting, Gori studied the apartment more attentively. He realised that, just as in Giovanna Innocenti's apartment, there was a tasteful mixture of old and new.

Against the walls were a number of tall display cabinets in English style. In one was a collection of Baccarat crystal. In the corner, next to the window, a small Empire-style desk. His attention was drawn to a photograph in an antique silver frame. He stood up to look at it more closely. It was a photograph of two women, with a large red granite statue in the background. He recognised them immediately: Giovanna Innocenti and Sara Genovese. In the photograph they were both smiling broadly.

At that moment, Sara Genovese came back into the room, carrying a tray with two fine porcelain cups with steam rising from them, a small plate of biscuits and a silver sugar bowl. She approached. She had noticed Gori looking at the photograph.

'That was taken when we were in Egypt. In the square outside the railway station in Cairo, near the statue of Ramses II. That was our last holiday.'

'When was it? This year?'

'No. Last summer. A really lovely trip. We were hoping to go there again this July for two weeks.'

She sat down and put the tray on the little table. Gori noticed that her hands were shaking.

'Sugar?'

'No, thanks,' Gori replied. 'I always take my coffee bitter.'

She handed him the cup, then put a small spoonful of sugar in hers. They lifted their cups to their lips. Sara Genovese held hers with both hands, but that did not prevent a few drops from trickling down from the corners of her mouth. She wiped them off with a napkin. Gori drank slowly, eating a biscuit between one sip and the next.

'So, Marshal, tell me, what else would you like to know?'

'I still can't get a clear idea . . . '

'Of who? Of me?'

'No, signora. Your friend and her parents. When I went to see Giovanna's father, his behaviour could only be described as unnatural. Of course, I'd like this to remain just between ourselves.'

'If it's any consolation, I have to say that, after all these years, I haven't been able to form a clear idea of Giovanna's parents either. In fact, I've never even met them.'

'How come?'

'Whenever I showed any interest in meeting them, Giovanna would do everything she could to dissuade me. Can you understand that?'

'Not really.'

'Several times I asked her to take me to her house or to the family estate near Pontassieve, but she always invented some excuse. The thing is . . . '

'Go on, Signora Genovese.'

'She never mentioned her father by name, or her mother, to tell the truth. She always changed the subject when the conversation turned to them, as if it was taboo. Even just saying the word "father", she would turn her head away and get very nervous. I think she hated him. I should say this was just my impression, but I knew her well and I'm not usually wrong about that kind of thing.'

A long silence followed. The marshal would have liked to clarify a few points but he had to weigh up the pros and cons, well aware that at the beginning of an investigation it was necessary to proceed with caution. Especially considering what Sara Genovese had just told him.

'I'd like to ask you again a question I asked you yesterday. Who might have had a motive to kill her?'

'Nobody. Giovanna didn't have any enemies.'

'As far as you know, did she ever meet anybody who, in your opinion, could have been dangerous?'

'No.'

'Any love affairs that went wrong?'

'No. She was popular and attractive, men liked her, but she never got into any unusual situations.' She stopped to think for a moment then said, 'We were fine like that. Neither of us wanted to get married.'

The marshal nodded. He understood the meaning of those words. There must have been something much stronger between the two women than he had first thought.

At that moment, the telephone rang on a cabinet near the sofa.

'Do you mind, Marshal?'

'Not at all.'

He heard her say, 'Yes I know when the funeral is, I read it in the paper. Thank you, at least you bothered to let me know, it was kind of you to call me. Yes . . . Yes . . . I'm with somebody at the moment . . . Okay . . . I'll expect you.'

'I don't want to seem impertinent, signora,' Gori said in a gentle tone when she had put the phone down, 'but I need to ask you a personal question.'

Sara Genovese stiffened. 'I have nothing to add. You detectives dig and dig into a person's life until you find the dirt. What gives you the right? You don't realise how painful all this is. I've already told you everything I know, Marshal.'

She crossed her legs and folded her arms, a defensive position that did not escape Gori. There was no point in insisting. Before taking his leave, he asked, 'Did your friend smoke?'

'No, never.'

'And do you smoke?'

'No, I don't smoke either. Neither of us ever smoked, not even out of curiosity when we were girls and all our friends sneaked into the school toilets to do it.'

'I'm very grateful to you.'

Sara Genovese walked him to the door and held out her hand very formally.

Who, then, had left that cigarette ash?

The same person who had brought the black rose?

40

'Giovanna, Giovanna!'

Closing the door behind her, Sara Genovese collapsed heavily into one of the armchairs in the hall, beside an enormous gilded mirror. She cried her friend's name out loud and burst into great wracking sobs. Tears began to streak down her cheeks. She wiped them away, then covered her face with her hands, remaining in this position for a long time, as if completely drained of strength. Finally she lowered her hands, placed them on her lap and wrung her fingers until the knuckles turned white. She stared into empty space.

That question of the marshal's ... How dare he pry into Giovanna's private life? They had been friends and sisters for years, but had reached that level of intimacy only once, during their last holiday in Egypt. She heard again Giovanna's voice uttering her father's name for the first time, recalling her difficult relationship with him, that wound which had marked her deeply and which time could not erase. Giovanna had told the story and Sara had listened in silence.

It was harvest time. In the air, the strong, sweet odour of must straining into the vats. Alvise Innocenti was sitting on a sofa in the little room in the basement he used as an office.

'Sit down here, next to me,' he had said to his daughter,

who was eleven at the time. She had obeyed. 'Promise me you'll always keep quiet,' he had whispered to her. 'You mustn't tell anybody, even Mummy.' Then he had leaned over and kissed her on the lips.

Tears had welled up in her eyes. And when her father pulled his trousers down and started playing those games that transformed a parent into an animal, she had burst out crying. That occasion had been the first of many, continuing all through the time she grew into an adolescent. She had become his pupil, ever more compliant – apparently – with her father's desires.

Sara Genovese heard the breath die in her throat. She was shaking all over now, and finding it hard to hold back her sobs.

That confession had been Giovanna's way of justifying her refusal when, as they lay side by side on the bed, Sara had asked her to return her love. No, she would never be able to love anybody, Giovanna had said. And from that day on, she had shared her pain and her anger verging on hatred towards her father. At the end of the story, consoling Giovanna with tears in her own eyes, she had sworn over and over on their friendship that she would never, ever betray that secret. She had added that she would always love her. She had understood why there had never been a real love, a serious stable relationship, in Giovanna's life and why she always spoke so harshly of men. She vowed that this promise would never be broken, not even now that Giovanna was dead.

'No, I won't say a word!'

The only problem was that this terrible secret might be a clue to the identity of the killer. If she kept silent, her silence would turn to guilt. She had to do something for Giovanna.

Gradually her heartbeat returned to normal. She stood up from the armchair, her eyes burning. For a moment, she swayed and almost fell. Then she remembered that the funeral was taking place in a few hours, at three in the afternoon. She knew she had to get a grip on herself, to be strong.

Before getting ready to go out, she sat down at the desk in her study and started writing a letter. A short letter, just a few words written in capital letters in her sloping, vaguely childish hand.

An anonymous letter.

41

He was standing stiffly by the window, looking out, but turned as soon as he heard the knock at the door.

'Come in, Marshal, I was expecting you.'

The first thing people noticed about Colonel Arturo Parisi was his impeccable uniform, with all those medals and distinctions pinned to his chest. Like something straight out of an album of military heroes or the pages of a historical novel.

He was clearly not in a good mood. 'What's the latest from the Prosecutor's Department?' he demanded.

'The deputy prosecutor has ordered us to cooperate with the police.'

'I agree, Marshal, but on condition that the reports are kept separate. That's essential. You sign our report and the police sign theirs. Those are the orders from our high command.'

'Very good, sir.'

'And please, let's be as discreet as we can. The Innocenti family have a name here in Florence.' He walked to his desk. 'It's best if we sit down,' he said, his tone still curt. 'I hope that's not the only news. I did ask you to move quickly on this.'

'I've questioned a friend of Giovanna Innocenti and have learned something about her life, though nothing vital.'

He did not mention Sara Genovese's silences, her hurry to be rid of him, her somewhat equivocal attitude in the last part of the interview, that sense he had that she was not telling him the whole truth about the relationship between the victim and her parents, especially her father.

'There's a lot of pressure in this case, Marshal. It needs to be wrapped up as quickly as possible.'

Gori nodded, stood up, saluted the colonel, and went out.

By now, it was almost one. He still had a long and demanding day ahead of him. And, as if that was not enough, he felt one of his headaches coming on. He closed the office and went to have lunch in a nearby trattoria, accompanied by Sergeant Surace. This case was not only difficult, it was shaping up to be an almighty mess. And one on which unspecified pressures would be brought to bear.

They were sitting at a table from where they could see the customers come in and out. They had already ordered, but Surace, who wasn't a patient man, signalled to the waiter and said, 'Bring me a Tuscan antipasto while we're waiting.'

'For you too, Marshal?'

'A few crostini, but don't take too long about it. We have to get back to work.'

'I know what you mean,' the waiter replied. 'You must be very busy with this murder.'

The two men nodded.

'You know, we hear all sorts of things here. Most of our customers are local, and you know what Florentines are like when it comes to gossip.' He leaned over the table in a conspiratorial manner and lowered his voice. 'They say the woman had a special friendship, if you know what I mean, with the other one, her partner ...'

Then he walked away.

'Did you hear that, Surace? A special friendship. That's why she got upset today as soon as I tried to ask a personal question.'

Gori was more certain than ever that Sara Genovese knew more than she was saying.

42

The weather was fair, the sky a clear blue, the wind light.

The basilica of San Miniato al Monte had gradually filled. The Innocentis were sitting in the front row, along with a number of fairly well-known figures from the city's political and business circles. Sara Genovese occupied a place almost at the back of the central nave. She had her arms folded and was wearing sunglasses. She was clutching a balled-up handkerchief in her hand. In the left nave, the marshal was leaning against a column, looking around at those present, his gaze lingering over those he knew. There seemed to be a lot of people who had come out of curiosity. He did not, however, see anyone from the press. Only once did his eyes meet Sara Genovese's, and he nodded in greeting. Organ music resounded in the air.

The body had been brought to the church straight from the morgue at the Institute of Forensic Medicine, without lying on display in a mortuary chapel or in her parents' villa. The coffin had been placed on the inlaid floor in front of the lower altar.

Sergeant Surace and Corporal Petrucci had remained outside. Petrucci had a camera with him and had been photographing visitors as they arrived. Now he was helping the sergeant to take down the licence numbers of the parked cars.

After the sermon and communion, the priest approached the coffin with tears in his eyes. He had been the one who had baptised little Giovanna. He sprinkled the coffin with holy water, bringing the ceremony to an end. The smell of candles and flowers hung in the air. The priest went up to the Innocentis and formally expressed his condolences. The couple had maintained an impassive air throughout the service. They were both elegantly dressed, but not in what might be thought of as mourningwear, unlike Sara Genovese, who was wearing a black suit. She had not exchanged a single word with them.

The cortège got under way. The Innocentis walked immediately behind the coffin, which was carried by the undertaker's assistants. Signora Innocenti was clinging to her husband's arm and dragging her right leg. A small group of mourners followed in single file. They reached the cemetery in a few minutes, and came to a halt in front of the family chapel. The burial plot was next to it, and the hole had already been dug in the earth. At a distance, a few journalists were watching and taking notes, and a photographer was discreetly taking pictures. There were many wreaths. The coffin was lowered into the grave and Giovanna Innocenti was swallowed up by the ground. For ever.

Then, as if at the end of a theatrical performance, the gathering began to disperse. First to move were the Innocentis, who stepped away even before the workers had started throwing earth on the coffin. As Alvise Innocenti passed Marshal Gori, he glared at him. It was only a momentary look, but it did not escape Gori. The cars set off. At their head was the Innocentis' dark E-Class Mercedes.

The marshal was the last to leave the cemetery. Just outside the gates, he was approached by Sara Genovese, who seemed to have been waiting for him. Her face contorted with grief, she looked around anxiously.

'Marshal, will you catch him?' she asked. 'Will you catch the bastard who took Giovanna?' It was the second time she had asked him that.

Gori stiffened. 'We'll do all we can, signora,' he replied resolutely. 'The investigation is ongoing and it's too early to say anything.'

He looked closely at her. Perhaps it was only an impression, but it seemed to the marshal that for a moment Sara Genovese's expression had hardened.

'I'm sorry,' she replied. 'I wasn't asking you to give away any secrets.' Then she said goodbye and walked away, looking around as if lost.

Leaning on the low wall, from which you could take in the entire city, the marshal watched as she descended the long flight of stairs. A minute or two later, Sara Genovese reached the Viale Galileo and got into the passenger seat of a BMW Z3 that was parked there with its indicators blinking. Gori tried to see who the driver was, but the car was too far away. It was clear, though, that whoever it was had been waiting for her. For a few moments he stood there motionless and half closed his eyes, repeating the woman's words to himself, as if to imprint them on his memory: *Will you catch the bastard?*

Was that question born out of a desire for justice, or was she trying to steer the investigation away from herself?

Meanwhile the cemetery workers were finishing their task.

They did not notice the man watching them from behind a chapel. When they too had gone, the man emerged from his hiding place, looked anxiously around, and cautiously approached the newly turned earth. He bent slightly, quickly crossed himself, and threw on to the wreaths and bunches of fresh flowers the red rose he had been holding in his hand. Then, with his head bowed, he walked unhurriedly to a side gate and left the cemetery.

43

Once back in barracks, they divided the tasks.

The marshal would write a report on his conversation with Sara Genovese and fix the date and time for another interview. Then he would contact Ferrara to try and identify the man who had been taking photographs in the Parco delle Cascine. And finally, he would take a good look at the material from the victim's apartment.

Surace, for his part, would check up on the licence numbers of the cars parked in San Miniato and, once the owners had been identified, collect as much information on them as he could, especially the ones they didn't know.

Petrucci would deal with the photographs.

Meanwhile, the Innocentis had got back to their villa. During the ride, neither had spoken a word. They had merely exchanged a few fleeting glances.

Now they were sitting side by side in two armchairs in the large kitchen.

'Would you like a green tea, darling?' the wife asked.

'Yes, Laura. Tell Karin.'

'No, I'll make it. Karin is busy with the pistachio biscuits. She got the Bronte pistachios that you like.'

She stood up. It had been a difficult day, and she was limping more than usual.

Alvise lit a cigarette and puffed at it greedily. He remembered what Enrico Costanza had said the previous evening:

Don't worry, we're not going to abandon you. You'll be avenged for what's been done to you. That black rose was an attack on all of us.

Had Enrico been telling him the truth?

For some time now, he had been feeling that his old childhood friend had changed. Perhaps it was due to the cancer eating away at him. But what if there was another reason? Something that had its roots deep in the past? Was a rift opening up between them? Had Giovanna's terrible death been an act of revenge by someone who hated them both and wanted to set them against each other?

He had to be careful. He couldn't trust anybody.

'Alvise, the tea is ready.'

Laura poured it into the cups and handed him his. He extinguished his cigarette in the ashtray and slowly began drinking. From time to time he passed a finger over the edge of the cup, trying to relax.

'Why did they kill my lovely Giovanna?' she said. 'Who could have done such a thing?'

'Drink your tea, Laura.'

'Please make space for her in the chapel, Alvise. I know she's nearby, but I don't like her being alone. People might talk. You know how things are here in Florence.'

'I will. I've already given instructions. There are a few technical problems to solve, but she'll be there.'

'That girl Sara had the nerve to come to the funeral,' his wife went on. 'It's a good thing she didn't come near us. If she'd tried, I would have sent her packing. She's given rise to so much gossip, damn her! Florence is full of it. God knows how many things she knows. It wouldn't surprise me if she had something to do with this horrible business.' She looked her husband straight in the eyes, as if expecting him to tell her something important.

'Who knows?'

'I wouldn't be surprised either if the bitch tried to implicate us.'

'What are you talking about, Laura? Just ignore her.' His tone had become sharper, and the cup shook in his hands, spilling a few drops on the tiled floor.

'Calm down, Alvise. We have no lack of contacts. We have to discover the truth, because . . . '

She left the sentence hanging and finished her tea. Then she put the cup down on the table and walked away.

He had always hated those shuffling steps of hers, but this time he barely heard them. Enrico's words were still echoing in his mind.

Don't worry, we're not going to abandon you . . .

He told himself once again that nobody could be trusted. He stood up and went out into the garden. He needed to be alone, breathing the fresh air of the hills.

She had been the one great love of his life.

He had met her at Enrico's stag party. He was not yet forty and was already married to Laura, in what was little more than a marriage of convenience.

The girl had immediately struck him by her beauty: her thin face, her perfect features, her sinuous body, her grey eyes, her skin as clear as porcelain. Her name was Elena. It was only later he learned that, even though she was only nineteen, she had led a somewhat dubious life, but that didn't stop him from falling madly in love. She was always ready to satisfy his sexual needs, however perverse.

It was not long after Giovanna was born that he found out Elena was also expecting a child. He had been overjoyed at the news. The baby would be the fruit of his true love. But Elena's unexpected death in childbirth had thrown him into a pit of despair. He had started to hate the person he held responsible for that death: his newborn son. He had removed him from his life, entrusting him to the woman who had been his own nursemaid when he was a child. And, on the rare occasions when he was able to see the boy, he had been incapable of embracing him, or even touching him. He had simply looked him up and down with a sneer on his lips.

Since Elena, he had never managed to love another woman. All that he looked for from women was pleasure as an end in itself. And only with very young women, women as innocent as he himself had once been. He had no desire to remember, only to get relief at all costs. Now, as he walked in silence back to the house, he moved his hand over his forehead, once, twice, three times, almost as if trying to wipe out the past.

That past which, however remote, was always there.

44

The marshal had already written the letter summoning Sara Genovese to appear, and had had it delivered to her. She was requested to come and see him at ten o'clock the next day, 27 June, even though it was a Sunday. He knew it wouldn't be easy to get her to talk, but he hoped that he could somehow persuade her to tell him all she knew, all she had been hiding.

Now he sat at his desk, supporting his chin with his right hand, thinking about what he had gathered so far. And his first thoughts were of the killer. He imagined him celebrating his success, laughing behind the backs of those who were struggling to get at the truth, and neglecting their own families and lives in the process.

He went over his notes – those he had taken at the crime scene and those from the interview with Sara Genovese – as well as the post-mortem results, trying to catch some clue between the lines, but in vain. Then he summoned Sergeant Surace, who was still busy at the computer.

'Found anything interesting?' he asked him as soon as he appeared.

'I'm still checking the names. There are a lot of them. Some very big names, too . . . '

'I want to know about all of them, and I mean all. Find out what there is on the Internet, see if any of them have records.'

Surace nodded. 'That's exactly what I'm doing, sir.'

'Good, good.'

'Have you summoned Sara Genovese, sir?'

'Yes, for tomorrow.'

'I think she's hiding something, maybe out of fear.'

'Do you suppose she could be involved in some way?'

'I wouldn't rule it out, though the MO suggests a man.'

'She might have had an accomplice. After the funeral today, I saw her get in a car driven by a man. It was the BMW I told you about so that you could cross-check it against the list of cars.'

'There was no BMW Z3 parked near the cemetery.'

'What do you mean?'

'I saw the Genovese woman arrive. She came from the direction of the steps and seemed a bit out of breath. She looked quite pale and I didn't recognise her at first.'

'That means the driver probably dropped her in the Viale Galileo and waited for her there.'

Just then, the marshal remembered the words he had over-heard her say during that brief telephone conversation: *I'll expect you.*

'Someone gave her a lift. Someone who didn't want to be noticed. Why? Who was it?'

Surace suggested that it might be useful to check the names of the clients of the estate agency.

'Good idea. When I question her tomorrow, I'll ask her to let me have the names and details of all sales and negotiations, beginning with the most recent.'

'What if she asks for a warrant?'

'Then we'll get one.'

This might turn out to be the chink of light they needed.

That evening Ferrara received the preliminary report from forensics comparing the anonymous letters.

There were similarities between the two. They both used the same font – Times New Roman – and size – 14, all of which was quite standard. And both had been printed using an inkjet printer, but of a very common brand: HP. In other words, there was no way of determining whether they had or had not been sent by the same person.

The letters would now be sent to the central forensics service in Rome for further technical tests.

Ferrara decided to return home earlier than usual. He was looking forward to having a quiet dinner with his wife Petra, watching a little TV, chatting about the summer holidays, which were coming up soon. Maybe he would read one of those novels from the book club his wife subscribed to in the hope that he would eventually find time for them.

And finally get a good night's sleep.

He could not have imagined that, less than six hours later, his sleep would be interrupted and his plans for tomorrow would have to be put on hold.

45

Sunk in the usual armchair, he was reading *The Da Vinci Code* and finding it really fascinating.

Reading was his way of relaxing.

On the floor, a half-full bottle of Scotch. From time to time he would pour a little into his glass and add a few small cubes of ice from the crystal bucket on the table. Just a little, because he had to stay sober for the appointment he had planned.

Every now and again he would place the bookmark in the page he had opened and stand up. From the window he would glance out on to the Piazza Santa Croce, which was packed with tourists as well as the usual vagrants and foreign drug dealers who had made it their base. He hated them, more than ever now. And soon he would have to do something about it.

At eight o'clock he finally closed the book. He had finished reading about the rose, which, in the symbolism of the Priory, was a synonym for the Grail. The rose which, at the time of the Romans, had been a symbol of secrecy, commonly placed in front of a closed door as a guarantee of privacy.

How interesting.

He got down on the Persian rug and did a hundred press-ups, to get his muscles working. It was something he did every day. Then he went into the bathroom, took off his perspiration-soaked sweatshirt, and stepped into the hydro-massage shower. He closed his eyes, lifted his hands to his temples and pressed them hard. He took a deep breath. He stayed there for more than a quarter of an hour, letting the hot water lash his body, then got out, dried himself and put on the white dressing gown with his own initials sewn on the left-hand pocket.

He went into the bedroom. It was 21.26 by the clock on the bedside table.

He still had more than an hour and a half to go.

He lit a lamp and stood for a long time in front of the wardrobe mirror. He let the dressing gown slide to the floor and looked at himself for a few moments. He was pleased, really pleased, especially with the long thick sideburns he had allowed to grow. He was six feet tall and weighed just over twelve stone. He had long arms, broad shoulders and narrow hips. It was a perfect body, and he liked to keep it in good shape. His big grey eyes looked back at him from the mirror, eyes some people found strikingly cold.

Then he lay down on the bed. He knew he would not sleep, although he hoped for a little rest. But the ghosts of the past, surging up from the deepest recesses of his heart, began to torment him. He saw once again an out-of-focus image, which often recurred in his dreams and had lately been appearing with greater and greater frequency. A tall, solidly built man was staring at him without the slightest emotion, or rather, with scorn. He himself was only a child. He made a gesture in the air with his hand, as if to wipe that vision from his mind once and for all.

Soon he would be doing it for real.

The hour was approaching.

46

Night of Saturday, 26 to Sunday, 27 June

Her complexion was coffee-coloured. Her hair was black, and so shiny as to appear unnatural. Her angelic face was turned to the floor, emphasising her long, thin neck. Her arms were raised behind her head, and her feet placed one in front of the other. Her eyes were half closed.

She was a very beautiful woman, even more attractive naked than dressed.

Behind her, the altar with its twelve neatly aligned black candles, their flickering providing the only light.

She was not alone.

A number of hooded figures wrapped in black cloaks stood watching her, almost contemptuously. All at once, one of them separated from the group, went behind the altar and stopped in front of a crucifix fixed to the wall. The figure of Christ, upside down, seemed to sway in the candlelight. As all of those present formed a circle, holding hands, the celebrant murmured a few incomprehensible words and came up behind the woman, who was still as motionless as a marble statue or a model posing for a sculptor. He lifted her left arm, and the thin sharp blade glittered for a moment. With a decisive gesture, he moved it across her throat from right to left, severing her carotid artery, her jugular and the other veins and arteries of the neck, as neatly as if he were slitting the throat of a young goat. The woman emitted a moan, fell first to her knees, then face down. She was dead even before she touched the tiled floor. Saliva and blood spilled from her mouth. And then only blood, gushing out over her chest and on to the floor.

Two of the figures turned her on her back, stretched her arms by the side of her head, then parted her legs, while another retreated towards the door. The woman's eyes were wide open, as if about to come out of their sockets.

The celebrant bent down and, with a scalpel, cut her from the sternum to the pubis, making an incision so deep that her guts spurted out. He took parts of her organs and placed them in a thermal bag. Another man, who had been holding a can, poured liquid from it, first over the body and then all around. The crackle of a long match echoed unnaturally. Then the match was thrown, producing a flash of light in the air.

The hooded men went out into the grey night. Once outside, they separated.

A slight fog had fallen, shrouding the woods.

Meanwhile, flames had started rising very quickly inside the little church. Dense black smoke started to pour out through the open door.

Soon the fire would engulf the building.

She had received the severest of their punishments for having seen the face of someone who should have remained anonymous.

It had been chance, a piece of bad luck, but an unforgivable error all the same.

47

The ringing of the telephone echoed insistently in the silence of the room.

Petra stifled a cry of fear. She was used to the phone ringing at night, but she was particularly sensitive at the moment.

Ferrara reached out his arm to the bedside table and picked up the receiver. It was only a brief call, and as soon as it was over he leapt out of bed, his hair tousled and his eyes swollen with sleep.

Waking up on Sunday morning usually had a different feel from the rest of the week. Knowing he didn't have to hurry because the driver wasn't waiting for him outside, he would stay in bed and laze about until late, even when he had slept all night, and listen to Petra, who always got up at the usual time, moving about the apartment, busy with her household chores.

But today was not going to be a Sunday like any other.

Less than an hour later he was at the scene.

The area had already been marked off with red-and-white tape.

It was a surreal spectacle: fire engines, police cars, powerful floodlights illuminating the small church and the surrounding area as if it was daytime.

He looked in through the door. What he saw was horrible.

The firefighters were still at work. He looked up and instead of a ceiling saw a huge cloud in a leaden sky. On the floor, a body. The arms and legs were bent: the fire had shrunk the tendons. He hoped that whatever had escaped the flames had not been blotted out by the hoses. He took a few steps back, lit a cigar, and waited for the operations to be completed.

In the distance he could see the lights of the houses of Sesto Fiorentino, a large municipality bordering Florence, its hills covered with villas built over the course of the years by aristocratic families.

Suddenly he heard someone call his name.

It was the young officer from the operations room, who was there in a coordinating capacity. He was bathed in sweat and looked quite nauseous. Clearly he was not used to horrors like this.

'Chief Superintendent,' he said as he approached, 'as soon as we got here, we were struck by the smell of petrol and burning flesh. The body was still smoking. Then, just outside the perimeter we discovered, by the light of the searchlights and the torches, a gallon plastic jerrycan with traces of petrol. Lying on its side, without a top. There are still some shoe prints on the ground, and some seem to have been left by boots.'

'So the fire was started deliberately,' Ferrara commented.

'We're still searching the area for clues, though making sure we keep everything intact until forensics arrive.'

'Good work. Carry on like that. But hurry up, I can hear thunder in the distance, it's going to rain soon. And rain will help whoever did this. Any prints might be wiped out, completely or partly.'

'Right, chief,' the young officer said, and walked off.

Ferrara threw the rest of his cigar on the ground and put it out with the sole of his shoe. The image of the charred body was now imprinted in his mind, and would remain there for ever. It was one of the cruellest deaths he had ever seen.

The fact was, you never became entirely desensitised to the sight of murder victims, and this particular corpse was truly horrifying.

48

There were two of them, one walking just in front of the other. Ferrara watched them as they approached.

'I'm Umberto Bartolotti,' the one in front said, holding out his hand as they came level. 'I own this land and all the buildings here. To be more precise, I'm in partnership with other people, including my brother Dante, who lives abroad.'

He was a tall, thin, very distinguished-looking man in his late thirties. He was wearing a Burberry coat over black trousers and a pair of calf-length boots.

'Chief Superintendent Ferrara. Pleased to meet you.'

'I've heard of you. My caretaker here' – he indicated the short, rather squat man behind him – 'told me about the fire. He lives with his family down there, in one of our houses. Can you tell me what happened, Chief Superintendent?'

'I'm afraid it's too soon to say. Perhaps you could answer a few questions first.'

'Of course.'

'Have you noticed anything strange in the last few days or months? Anything that drew the attention of your employees?'

'Not as far as I know, but let's ask the caretaker. Pietro, come here.'

The man stepped forward, and Bartolotti repeated Ferrara's question.

'No. Nothing strange. The last incident was two years ago.'

'What incident?'

'Another fire. The police in Sesto Fiorentino know all about it. They were the ones who came that night.'

'Are you sure you didn't notice anything suspicious? Please try to remember. Maybe something you thought was unimportant at the time.'

He would have to talk to his colleague in Sesto, Ferrara was thinking.

'I've sometimes found the perimeter fence broken, or the gate to the church forced.'

'Had anything been stolen from the church?'

'There was nothing to steal, Chief Superintendent.'

'What could it have been, then?'

'Kids daring each other, maybe. But more likely the junkies who hang out in the Etruscan tombs down there.' He pointed towards the area to his left.

'Did any of these break-ins strike you as especially serious?'

'No.' It was a curt, confident no.

'When was the last time you noticed something like that?'

'A few weeks ago.'

'About what time?'

'Just as it was starting to get dark, as usual.'

'Did you report the damage?'

The man exchanged a glance with Bartolotti, then said, 'No, because nothing was stolen.'

Ferrara did not insist. He took two business cards from his wallet and said, 'Here's my mobile number. Phone me if any of the other employees think of something.'

'Of course, Chief Superintendent,' Bartolotti replied. 'After all, it's in my own interest, too.'

Ferrara said goodbye to them and went back inside the church. The pathologist and a couple of forensic technicians had arrived almost simultaneously a few minutes earlier and were already hard at work.

He stood there watching in silence.

'The body is a woman's.'

Franceschini, the pathologist, had approached Ferrara and begun to give him his first impressions, but was forced to pause several times to clear his throat because of the smoke.

'Let's go outside, I need air.'

They went out, passing under the red-and-white tape.

'Cause of death?' Ferrara asked.

The question might have seemed superfluous, the answer being an obvious one, but the doctor guessed why it had been asked. He shook his head. 'I know what you're referring to, but we'll have to wait for the post-mortem to determine the primary cause of death. It might not be down to smoke inhalation.'

'Why?'

'Because the woman may have been killed before the fire. There are a couple of things that lead me to believe that ... ' He stopped and heaved a deep sigh.

'Like what?' Ferrara asked, unable to restrain his curiosity.

'For instance, as far as I can see, there are no traces of burnt material. So in all probability, the woman was naked.'

'What else?'

'There are traces of viscera on the abdomen ... ' He stopped for a moment to cough. 'But I'm not going to say anything until I've carried out a post-mortem, Chief Superintendent, in case I jump to erroneous conclusions. Besides, we have to remember that the crime scene has been contaminated by the work of the firefighters. The water used to put out the fire might have wiped out important traces.'

'Did you find anything that could help us to identify the victim?'

'In the case of victims who have been burnt, we can usually guess their approximate age by examining the internal organs, but for a more reliable identification, we need more than that.'

'I know.'

'The teeth might tell us something, provided we have the X-rays with which to make a comparison. There's something else . . .'

'What?'

'I have the impression that, by the time it was set on fire, the body was no longer intact, but let me complete my work and then I'll be able to be more precise.'

'I'm relying on you.'

'Frankly, I think you're going to have a hard time finding prints. Everything's been destroyed.'

'When will I be able to have your preliminary report?'

'I should know something by this afternoon. I'll call you then.'

'Thanks.'

'But for now, Chief Superintendent,' Franceschini said as he walked away, 'I think you should take a look inside. You might see something interesting.'

Ferrara went back into the church and let his eyes wander over the scene. They came to rest on the wall to his right, which was blackened by smoke. What he saw made him start. He went closer to the wall and saw, only just distinguishable, a written number: 666. Above it, a five-pointed star, two of the points turned upwards. There was also some kind of indecipherable drawing. He ordered one of the forensics team to photograph the wall, in long shot and close-up, after cleaning it as best he could. Moving behind the altar, he noticed an iron crucifix, hanging upside down.

Soon afterwards he was joined by the head of the firefighters, a fat man with a large nose, his face dirty with soot, his eyes half closed. He looked tired and had several days' growth of beard. He had taken off his helmet and was wiping his forehead and bald cranium with a handkerchief.

'What can you tell me?' Ferrara asked.

'The fire was definitely started deliberately, in several places. The church has already been made safe.'

'Thanks. Please send me a copy of your report.' As he said goodbye to him, he noticed an old burn on the man's hand.

Once alone, he walked to where the body lay.

The face was burnt off, the features erased. The head was completely black, apart from the white teeth, and looked smaller than you could ever imagine a head to be. There was no longer anything human about what had once been a human being.

He stood there as if nailed to the ground. He imagined the woman gradually enveloped by the flames, begging for mercy. In years to come, even many years, he would be able to indicate with absolute certainty the exact point where these charred remains were. He would be able to reconstruct the scene in every detail and smell the smell the little church had that night.

He left the church.

It was nearly dawn.

He saw Teresa Micalizi coming towards him. She had just arrived, together with a patrol from the *Squadra Mobile*. She was wearing designer jeans, a cotton pullover and a pair of trainers. Her eyes were slightly red from lack of sleep, but she still managed to look radiant. He asked her to follow him. She was too young in his opinion to go in and face that terrible scene.

In the meantime, the sky was becoming clearer and the first light had reached the treetops.

They set off towards the Etruscan area indicated by the caretaker.

At that moment, outside a renovated farmhouse, Umberto Bartolotti was talking to his caretaker.

'You didn't have to mention that incident two years ago, Pietro.'

'I'm sorry, signore, but I only spoke about it so that policeman wouldn't get suspicious. He always knows everything, so I took it for granted he knew about it.'

'You're really one of a kind. I've known you since you were little and yet you always manage to surprise me. I'll have to tell my brother what happened last night. And the other partners, too.'

'Yes, I think you should. We don't want the police to contact them first. You know what Signor Dante's like.'

Umberto Bartolotti nodded.

Ever since he was a child, he had admired his elder brother for his strength, his self-confidence, his ability to inspire respect and to get all the care and attention of both their parents. As he grew up, he had tried to emulate him, not always successfully: he had not always made the right business decisions and had got into financial difficulty. Through it all, Dante had always remained his point of reference.

'If you do find out anything, Pietro, tell me first, and I'll tell the police. Understood?'

'Of course. You know you can count on me. I can keep a secret.'

'I know. You're as loyal as your father was. You'd go through fire for me, I know.'

'No, don't talk about fire today,' Pietro said with a smile.

But Bartolotti did not return that smile. That was not like

him: he had always let himself be led by Pietro's contagious smile, even when the man spouted nonsense.

This confirmed to Pietro what he had thought when he had seen Bartolotti the day before: the man was suffering, and couldn't hide his sadness. He seemed to have aged suddenly. That other business was probably causing him a lot of headaches. All those kids . . .

'I don't think the police will let go of this too soon,' he resumed. 'It's not just the local lot this time.'

'True, Pietro, but don't forget they're all cut from the same cloth. Anyway, keep in contact with your policeman friend. I have to go now.'

They said goodbye.

Bartolotti got in his Porsche and set off. The roar of the engine even reached Ferrara's ears.

49

The air was cool, with a lingering smell of wild grass and damp leaves. The woods were silent except for the shuffle of their steps on the broken branches.

They soon came to a clearing and looked around. On one side was a farmhouse, surrounded by a stone wall with an iron gate in it. Beside the gate, a niche containing an image of the Madonna and Child.

Presumably the caretaker's house, Ferrara thought.

On the other side, a smaller clearing than the first one. They walked in that direction. After a few more yards, emerging from the ground in places they saw outcrops of rock and stone in various sizes, some piled one on top of the other.

'What's this?' Teresa said. She leaned forward, pointing to an object on a stone just in front of her. Beside it lay a hypodermic syringe.

'It's a skull!' Ferrara replied.

At that moment, the peace of the place was broken by a terrible moan that echoed through the air.

Teresa, who was not used to these nocturnal sounds, froze. 'What was that?'

'An owl, Teresa.'

'That skull's so small. Could it be a child's?'

'No, Teresa. It's an animal. A dog, or more likely a cat, given its size.'

He motioned for her to continue. With a nod of the head, he indicated the track, overgrown with weeds, that cut through the wood.

'Let's go this way.'

The track was about three feet wide. After a while, they came to the remains of the Etruscan graves. Just then, Ferrara heard his mobile phone ringing. He looked at the display. It was the Commissioner.

'Ferrara?' the voice at the other end yelled.

'Yes?'

'Yet another murder! They're getting very worried in Rome. The Head of the State Police is beside himself. He wants results, now. Did you hear that, Chief Superintendent? Now!'

'Of course. We're working as fast as we can. I'm at the scene now. Don't worry, we won't waste any time.'

'Keep me informed of developments. If you discover anything important, let me know immediately, so I can bring the chief up to speed. He wants to be called directly, this time.'

'Unfortunately, we don't know anything yet. All we know for sure is that the charred body was a woman's.'

'I already knew that. And she was naked. The head of pathology, Lassotti, called me just a while ago. Do you realise what it means, finding the charred body of a naked woman in a deconsecrated church? And we don't even know who she is. An addict? A prostitute? A respectable woman?'

'I'll keep you informed,' Ferrara replied, ignoring the questions. It wasn't the first time he had had to investigate a murder case where the victim's identity was unknown. Always in the past they had turned out to be foreign prostitutes, women nobody had reported missing. Would it be the same now?

They said goodbye and hung up simultaneously.

Maybe this time, Ferrara told himself, his superiors would finally believe him. In the past, whenever he had suggested that certain crimes might have an occult motive, it had been dismissed as pure conjecture.

'What is it, chief?' Teresa asked, seeing him looking around with his hand tight on the grip of his gun.

'Nothing. Let's go back. We have a long day ahead of us. You'll have to get used to it.'

She smiled. But he didn't notice.

50

Forensics were nearly finished.

The firefighters had already put the body in the coffin, to be transferred to the Institute of Forensic Medicine, and now they were listening to Deputy Prosecutor Vinci's instructions.

Ferrara and Teresa Micalizi watched from a distance as two members of the forensics team, a youngish man and woman, prepared a mixture of chalk and water, using the same technique dentists used. They poured the chalk into the water slowly, mixed it in until it was completely absorbed, then poured the mixture carefully over the prints found near the church. Then they lifted off the moulds. Vinci, who had come closer, was also following the operation. He was in a tracksuit with a hood. You certainly would not have guessed his profession from his appearance.

'I won't be able to go running in the Cascine today,' he said to Ferrara. 'I hope at least I don't miss my tennis match this afternoon . . . ' He gave an ironic smile. 'Since you got back, Chief Superintendent, I haven't had a moment's peace.'

'I was supposed to be heading out of the city for lunch, but it's all part of the job,' Ferrara replied, remembering that he ought to phone his friend Massimo to cancel the appointment. He and Petra could go to Forte dei Marmi another Sunday.

'I was joking, Chief Superintendent.'

Vinci and Ferrara took another look at the signs on the walls, especially the unmistakable 666.

'We need to find out if there are satanist groups operating in this area,' Vinci suggested.

Ferrara nodded. 'I agree. These signs, the fire, the burnt victim, the fact that it happened in a deconsecrated church . . . Everything seems to point to some kind of secret society.'

'This time, Chief Superintendent, I'm inclined to think the facts are proving you right. At last, you might say.'

They talked some more about what needed to be done next.

Meanwhile, the firefighters, with the police looking on, barred the entrance to the little church, placing sturdy wooden planks against the iron gate in the outside wall. On the central plank they placed a board, signed by the officer from the operations room, with the words: CLOSED BY ORDER OF THE AUTHORITIES. It was a few minutes to seven.

The discovery of the charred body made the seven o'clock news on all the radio networks. This was in every way an attention-grabbing piece of news: there would be no prizes for guessing what would make the front pages of the newspapers next day. Obviously, the news bulletins didn't give any information about the identity of the victim, merely suggesting it might be someone who had disappeared in the last few days or hours. As yet, nobody was attacking the conduct of the police. But that was sure to come.

51

Sunday, 27 June, Yorkshire, England

The men were drinking tea.

They were in an old castle, its courtyard surrounded by stone turrets, its magnificent grounds filled with centuries-old trees. A fairy-tale building, a place of enchantment and mystery, not far from Fountains Abbey.

The men, who were all smartly dressed, were sitting in comfortable green leather armchairs in the private study of the castle's owner. They had been discussing the news from Florence, and not just the official version as broadcast on the radio.

Sunlight filtered through half-closed shutters, and the interplay of light and shade was reflected on the impassive faces of those present.

Sir George Holley, tall, white-haired, well groomed, put down his cup of tea and resumed speaking. Everyone's eyes were on him.

'We'll be buying the shares in Piazza Affari tomorrow, it's been confirmed, but as for the future, I say we'd best wait. The market isn't stable . . . '

The others nodded.

There was another pause. Sir George lifted his cup to his lips and took a sip. The others did the same.

'As for the other things,' he went on, 'our people in Italy are doing what they can and are quite optimistic. They've confirmed to me that they have the channels they need. I'm being constantly updated, and can confidently state that the situation is under control.'

'George, I fully share your view. We have every confidence in them, but perhaps they could do more ... We can't afford even the slightest mistake, I get the feeling some errors have already been made ... '

The person speaking was the youngest of the guests, a tall, handsome, aristocratic-looking man. He was there as a wealthy, highly respected investor with unlimited capital, involved in financial operations that were completely legitimate, at least in appearance. But, in other circles, a long way away, he was known as the biggest drug trafficker to have appeared in the world of organised crime over the past few decades. A crime boss who needed the collaboration of people who were not only competent but also, most importantly, above suspicion to help him manage – and launder – his illegal profits.

The others agreed.

They drained their cups.

'Now let's arrange our next meeting,' Sir George finally proposed.

Just then, there was a light knock at the door and a liveried butler entered the room.

'Sir George, everything is ready outside,' he said.

It was 8.22 by the grandfather clock against the wall. Time to go.

They stood up.

The fox hunt was about to start. For them, this was a necessity, like living and breathing.

They put on their black hunt caps, an indispensable component of the uniform, and left the room in silence.

Outside, the rays of the sun illumined their red jackets.

The dogs, almost all beagles, were getting restless. The centuries-old ritual could begin. A ritual that would be repeated for ever, unless those Members of Parliament who considered it cruel succeeded in getting it abolished. Sir George Holley, though, was optimistic: he was sure the vote would go in their favour.

52

The steep, winding road that led down to Sesto Fiorentino was not well maintained. But his mind was elsewhere and he had not even noticed.

Ferrara's thoughts kept returning to the horrors of the last few days. The scar on the dead woman. Giovanna Innocenti crucified in her bed. The black rose. And now that woman burnt to a cinder. The smell of charred flesh was still in his nostrils and his mind was full of images of the emblem of the devil, the great beast of the Apocalypse, the upturned crucifix, the pentagram with the two points turned upwards. The threatening words of those two anonymous letters echoed in his ears.

The roses, the hooded ones . . . We're getting closer.

He wondered if it was just coincidence.

No, that wasn't possible.

He decided that the time had come to meet Venturi's friend, the expert on the occult.

They were waiting for him.

Marshal Gori was sitting in an armchair in the waiting room, speaking to Venturi. As soon as he saw him he called out, 'Good morning, Chief Superintendent.'

'Marshal, please go in.' Ferrara opened the door to his office. 'One moment and I'll be with you.'

He led Venturi into the secretary's room. Now that they were out of earshot, the two could talk.

'Venturi, I want to meet that friend of yours, this morning if possible, sometime today at any rate.'

'Shall I get her to come here, chief?'

'If she can. Or else we can go to her house, or anywhere she feels comfortable. She can choose.'

'All right. I'll let her know straight away.'

'Thanks.'

At last he walked into his office.

'Nasty business,' the marshal began, holding his briefcase on his lap.

Ferrara nodded several times. 'We need to join forces,' he said.

'That's why I'm here, Chief Superintendent. It's what both the prosecutor and my colonel want.'

'Thanks.'

They exchanged their respective news. Ferrara was struck by one detail he had previously been unaware of: the camera wrapper discovered at the scene of Giovanna Innocenti's murder.

'Curious,' he said.

Gori gave him an inquiring glance. 'Why?'

'Because a cleaner at the chapels of rest remembers finding a similar wrapper the morning the scar on the dead woman's face was discovered.'

'Did you get hold of it?'

'It was already gone.'

'What a pity. What make was it?'

'Unfortunately the witness didn't notice.'

Maybe they had underestimated the importance of that detail, Gori told himself.

The situation in Florence was getting more and more complicated by the hour. Ferrara and Gori agreed to keep in constant contact. At least once a day they would meet personally, either here at Police Headquarters or at the Borgo Ognissanti barracks.

Before leaving, Gori left on Ferrara's desk a copy of the papers dealing with Giovanna Innocenti's murder, and said that he would be questioning the victim's friend, Sara Genovese, later that day.

It could be a crucial interview. At least, he hoped so.

53

There was nobody about at this hour.

Kneeling, she arranged a bunch of tuberoses, Giovanna's favourite flower, in a vase. Then she put her hands together, raised her eyes to heaven, and began to pray.

Sara Genovese had spent a sleepless night, then at last had got up and gone to her study, switched the lamp on, opened the photograph albums and leafed through them. There, before her eyes, were all the lovely moments she had spent with her friend. She lingered over a photograph that Giovanna had given her years before, at her insistence. It showed her friend as a teenager standing in front of some big wine barrels. She looked pretty in her short flowered skirt, with her shoulder-length hair. But there was a touch of sadness in her eyes. When she had first seen the photo, Sara had been struck by that expression, although back then she did not know how hellish Giovanna's life must have been at that age. Now, she lifted it to her lips, as large tears slid down her cheeks.

'May God strike you down!' she repeated several times. 'May you rot in hell, Alvise Innocenti, you pervert!' Closing the album angrily she had left home, unusually early in the morning for her.

Now, in the little cemetery, all that could be heard was the murmur of her prayers. Her face bent towards the grave, she uttered in a thin voice, 'Giovanna, I'll see you avenged, I promise. It will be the one aim of my life.'

When she heard a police helicopter flying over San Miniato al Monte towards the hills, she crossed herself and walked away.

In her heart, there was only one thought, now more insistent than ever.

54

In the meantime, Ferrara had already made a few telephone calls.

First, to Massimo to cancel their appointment. He had told his loyal friend about the incident in the church and received an unexpected offer of help. 'I know a priest who's a real expert on these things. He's been coming to my bookshop for years and I have a very good relationship with him. Just let me know and I'll arrange dinner.'

Then to the Commissioner, to bring him up to date.

To the police station at Sesto Fiorentino, to find out about the fire in the little church two years earlier. On that occasion, he was told, two gamekeepers had seen a man running away just after the fire had broken out, but they had not managed to stop him. The fire had been classified as an accident, most likely a by-product of an attempted robbery. The investigation, however, had not been conclusive. The fact that no objects of value had gone missing, other than some papers, the contents of which the caretaker had been unable or unwilling to divulge, had meant that they couldn't rule out the possibility that the fire had been caused deliberately. Ferrara learned that the property belonged to a company that also owned a large dairy farm in the Emilian Appennines, and was given the names of all the shareholders.

At last he was able to call Petra and explain why he had had to leave so suddenly in the middle of the night. She seemed reassured and told him that she had spoken to her friend Monika, who had promised to come and see her in August.

Then he put on his glasses and began looking through the newspaper articles Venturi had brought him a few days earlier. He lingered over one of them.

CHAPELS, CEMETERIES, DECONSECRATED CHURCHES: THESE ARE THE HAUNTS OF SATAN

Black masses and satanic rites in cemeteries and abandoned buildings in the Florentine countryside. Black Sabbaths, nocturnal meetings, thefts of sacred objects and relics from chapels, fetishes, animals with their throats cut, jinxes, candles: this is the other face of Florence, a city that has inherited the grim legacy of Satan . . .

Yes, this was Tuscany, he thought. And Florence with its two faces.

The white and the black.

The sunny and the shadowy.

The sunny side, with its great heritage of art and history, made it an object of envy throughout the world, which was why so many Americans, English and Germans chose it as a second home. The shadowy side, the secret side, lurked behind the scenes and only came to light when freakish crimes such as these were committed.

The article continued with a series of interviews with witnesses describing incidents that had taken place over the past few years: a young man who recalled finding the headless skeleton of a dog, a man who had seen the head of a goat stuck in the gate of a cemetery, an old married couple who, returning home after dark, had seen several cars parked outside a deconsecrated church.

Ferrara summoned Teresa.

'What is it, chief?' she asked, coming in with a plastic coffee cup in her hand. Watching her as she sat down, Ferrara noticed that she looked tired. She put the cup down on the desk and glanced at the newspaper page he handed her.

'What do you think?' he asked.

'Well, there are two things linking a number of these incidents. One is that they took place around the summer solstice. The other is that they occurred in or near deconsecrated churches in the hills above Florence.'

'Well spotted. You're quite right.'

'The only thing that puzzles me, chief, is that none of the people interviewed are named. Not even their initials are given. Why? And the article is unsigned.'

'Do you think it's an invention?'

'We can't rule it out.'

'What would you say to checking directly with the newspaper?'

'Do you want me to do it now?'

'That's why I called you.'

Teresa leapt to her feet and went out.

55

It was 10.02 by the clock on the wall when there was a resolute knock at the door.

'Come in.'

Sara Genovese appeared in the doorway.

'Please sit down, signora,' the marshal said, indicating the chair to his right in front of the desk.

But she stood there, seeming to stare at the photograph of the President hanging on the wall behind the marshal.

'Why have you summoned me?' she asked, at last turning her gaze to Gori. 'And why was it necessary to send a Carabiniere to my apartment? Couldn't you just have phoned?' From her tone, it was clear she was annoyed.

'Calm down, signora. It's the normal procedure for an official summons. Please sit down.'

She hesitated for a few moments more, continuing to look at him as if trying to discern his real intentions. At last she sat down.

'All right, Marshal, go on,' she said, looking at her wristwatch.

'Are you in a hurry, signora?'

'It's Sunday, I have things to do.'

'In that case I'll get straight to the point. Was there more than just friendship between you and Giovanna? We've heard rumours—'

'Marshal, let's not beat about the bush. I was in love with Giovanna.'

'And Giovanna ...?'

'No, she wasn't like me. I told her how I felt last year, during that trip to Egypt. We'd drunk a little more than usual. We were very happy and ...' She paused for a moment, and when she spoke again it was in a calm tone, with not a trace of the nervous tension she had displayed when she came in. '... and we spent the night together, in the same bed ...' She paused again, and her eyes lit up: it was as if a great weight had lifted off her. ' ... Just that one night. But we didn't become lovers, as I'd hoped, as ...'

She fell silent yet again, and Gori, like an indecisive boxer, was not sure whether the time had come to strike the decisive blow. In the end, he asked the one question that mattered to him.

'Signora, what do you really know about your friend's relationship with her father?'

Sara Genovese began to shift uneasily in her chair, to intertwine her fingers. Her face turned as white as marble and she stared into the distance.

No, she told herself, she couldn't betray her. Not now.

'I don't know what to say,' she replied. 'I've already told you, I have no way of knowing. Giovanna never talked to me about her parents.'

'So she never confided any secrets to you?'

She shook her head.

'Are you sure?'

'Yes ... My throat's a bit dry, Marshal. Could I have a glass of water, please?'

Gori reached out his arm to the little cabinet behind him,

opened it and took out a bottle of water. He filled a plastic cup and handed it to her.

Sara drank the water, then took a deep breath and looked Gori straight in the eyes. 'I knew her well, she confided in me, but I repeat: she never told me any family secrets. I gathered she'd had an unhappy adolescence, but that's all I know.'

'Unhappy in what way?'

She frowned as if she had remembered something but had immediately repressed it. 'I really can't say. Please don't ask me any more questions.' She looked again at her watch. 'I really have to go.'

'I'd like to know more about your friend's difficult adolescence,' insisted Gori, even more grim-faced.

Silence.

'I remember once when the subject of babies came up, she told me she didn't want children. I think that had something to do with her past. But please don't ask me any more. It was just women's talk, nothing explicit. It's all just speculation on my part, you understand.'

Sara Genovese wasn't telling the truth. That was clear from her reaction, but Gori realised he needed to change the subject. He would ask the deputy prosecutor for authorisation to investigate her, perhaps tap her phones. If she was hiding something, they would find out.

'Does a black rose mean anything to you?' he asked.

Sara Genovese frowned. 'A black rose?'

'Yes.'

'There's no such thing.'

'There are artificial ones.'

'Ah. But why do you ask?'

'Did your friend ever talk to you about black roses?'

'No, never. I don't understand your question, Marshal.'

'Did you ever see artificial flowers in Giovanna's apartment?'

'No. Her favourite flowers were white tuberoses. She liked roses, too, but red ones.'

Gori did not insist. It would have been pointless. And besides, he did not want to reveal details of the investigation that had not yet been released to the public. Why was Sara Genovese still so reluctant to talk? He had been watching her closely throughout, noting her gestures, her posture, the various signs of stress. He would have liked to use different tactics to force her to tell the truth, but he knew there would be other opportunities.

'All right, signora, we've finished,' he said. 'But I'd like a Carabiniere to accompany you. Perhaps you would let him have a list of clients of your agency, starting with the most recent.'

Sara Genovese pursed her lips slightly. 'Provided it only takes a few minutes.'

More doubts were crowding into Gori's mind.

56

The satanism angle was starting to seem the likeliest avenue to explore, and Ferrara decided he had to confront the subject directly.

The discovery of the charred body in the deconsecrated church was a strong pointer that he was on the right track, especially when he remembered another case a few months earlier in a different part of Italy, in the province of Varese, involving a group in their early twenties, fans of heavy metal music, who had called themselves the Beasts of Satan. A number of young people had been killed, others had been reported missing by their families. Others still had committed suicide in very suspicious circumstances. One girl had been eliminated because in the eyes of the group she represented the Madonna and had to die.

The banality of evil . . .

The moment had come to get a better idea of the worshippers of Satan in Florence.

He was just thinking about his coming encounters with two experts on the occult when there was a knock at the door.

'Come in,' he said.

It was his deputy, Francesco Rizzo.

'What are you doing here?' Ferrara said, rising to his feet

and going to him. 'Shouldn't you be in Rome, at the management course?' They embraced affectionately, like two old friends meeting after a long time.

The burly but introverted Rizzo, sometimes touchy but uncommonly loyal and generous, was someone he'd always felt he could trust implicitly. Over time, Rizzo had shown himself to be a true friend, one who believed in the sanctity of friendship, as well as a highly perceptive investigator whose opinions on cases were always welcome.

'I've missed you,' Ferrara said.

This was a rare admission. Aside from his wife, there weren't many people with whom Ferrara felt able to show his feelings.

'We're dealing with some very nasty cases here, Francesco. Murders with a lot of unusual elements.'

His chief's use of the word 'nasty' alerted Rizzo to the likelihood that these cases would not conform to the rule that said murders needed to be solved within hours or at most days. He immediately had a sense that it would take them weeks, if not months, to solve them. That's if they ever did manage to solve them.

'Chief,' he replied, 'I only came for the weekend, but I'd like to stay if I can be of use. I'm prepared to ask for leave from the course if necessary.' By now they had moved into the sitting area.

At that moment Fanti came in, holding a cardboard tray with two glasses. He put it down on the little table and immediately went out again.

'Nothing escapes good old Fanti,' Rizzo said with a smile. 'He never changes.'

'I don't know how he does it,' Ferrara replied, also smiling for a moment. 'But sometimes I think he must have four ears and four eyes.'

'No, chief, the fact is, he knows you really well. He's like a well-programmed robot.'

Both men laughed.

They sipped their coffee in silence.

'Francesco, I admire your willingness to help, but let's not talk about leave. Just say you're staying in Florence on unexpected police business that can't be put off. I really need you. And not only me, the boys too. Everyone. I'll talk to the Commissioner.'

'Things certainly don't seem to be going well at the moment, chief.'

'You're right,' Ferrara replied. 'This is the worst it's been since I came to Florence, and that's going back nearly ten years.' He brought Rizzo up to date on all the cases. 'The Carabinieri are handling the Innocenti murder, but we're cooperating. Just this morning Marshal Gori left me copies of all their papers.'

'So we're working together?'

'That's right. Each investigating our own cases, but coordinating our activities.'

'That's a first,' Rizzo said, taking the Carabinieri file that Ferrara held out to him. 'I'll read it right away, chief. I'd really like to help the boys.'

'Good. Let me know what you think. We didn't find any clues at the crime scenes, and so far we have no suspects. The first thing you can do is attend the post-mortem this afternoon.'

'I'll be there.'

He got up to leave, and Ferrara followed him out.

In the corridor they ran into Venturi, Sergi, and a few other colleagues, anxious to say hello to Rizzo. Venturi shook Rizzo's hand, then turned to Ferrara and told him that his friend was ready for the meeting.

'How about we head over there in an hour's time?' Ferrara said.

57

Little more than an hour later, they were already in Galluzzo, the hamlet near Florence famous for its monastery.

For the last mile or so, they had been stuck behind a bus. Forced to go slowly, they had not noticed the man in the jeep a few cars behind them. At that time, Ferrara and Venturi were busy discussing the Beasts of Satan killings, as well as a case in Chiavenna in 2000, in which three girls had brutally stabbed a nun after luring her to an isolated part of the village. They had sacrificed her to the devil and then gone off to an amusement park to have some fun.

Silvia de Luca lived in a small three-storey apartment block that looked out on the central square. Her apartment was on the ground floor. They rang the lowest bell, next to her name, and a female voice immediately replied. A few moments later, the door swung open. The woman was wearing a pair of black trousers and a long-sleeved cotton sweatshirt, also black. She stood aside to let them in and they followed her along a narrow corridor. Through a half-open door, Ferrara caught a glimpse of two young children, a girl and a boy, engrossed with their PlayStation. There were posters of famous singers and members of the Fiorentina team on the wall behind them, and the floor was strewn with toys.

'Nice children,' Ferrara said, addressing the woman.

'They're my whole life. Since I lost my husband last year I've lived for them and my daughter. The boy's six and the girl's almost eight.'

'Do they live with you, signora?'

'No, but I have them here most of the day. I look after them when my daughter's at work. On Sundays, though, we eat all together.'

At the end of the corridor was the door to the living room. Against a wall was a very old trunk, covered with a crochet tablecloth. In a small cabinet, which functioned as a bookcase, were a number of volumes with crumpled spines. In the middle of the room stood a round table and four wooden chairs. There was also a three-seater sofa with flowered uphol-stery. No paintings on the walls. A modest but neat home.

Silvia de Luca invited them to sit down on the sofa.

Ferrara began by explaining the reason for their meeting. He went through the strangest details of the crimes, lingering over those connected with the scene in the deconsecrated church.

The woman answered them in a low voice so as not to be heard by her grandchildren. She had learned about the crime from the TV news, she said. She explained that she had been interested in satanism and black magic for almost twenty years, and that her husband had shared her passion.

'Yes, I know you're an expert. Venturi told me, and that's the reason I'm here. I'm sorry to have to bother you with my ques-tions, but you could be of great help in our investigations.'

'It's no bother, Chief Superintendent. In my opinion, what happened in that church was a genuine satanic ritual, a human sacrifice. Everything points to it: the six-six-six, the upturned crucifix, the pentacle, the fire ... There's absolutely no doubt in my mind.'

'But what do they all mean?'

'Six-six-six is the number of the beast, Satan, the Antichrist. It's used by satanists of every tendency . . .'

'That much I knew.'

'The upturned crucifix symbolises the opposition to Christ's cross. Some satanists wear necklaces with an upside-down cross. It's even appeared on some album covers . . .'

'Record albums?'

'That's right, usually associated with heavy metal music. There's a certain fad among some groups of young people.'

Ferrara nodded, thinking of the Beasts of Satan. 'What about the pentacle?'

'When a single point is at the top it refers to the divine, but when there are two points on top, as in this case, it represents Satan and is used to invoke evil spirits. Often it's drawn inside a circle, which limits its power.'

'So the murder of that woman could be interpreted as a sacrifice?'

'Precisely. And the victim must be completely naked because, according to their beliefs, that symbolises their altar.'

'Yes, she was.'

An expression of satisfaction appeared on the woman's face. The fact that the victim was naked had not been made public, nor had it been reported by the media.

Silvia de Luca continued, giving them more detailed information, some of it historical in nature, on black magic, and on the satanic parody of the central ritual of Christianity. The sacrifice of a human being, she explained, was held to be the best way to invoke Satan. In this connection, she cited Aleister Crowley – not a satanist but one of the most celebrated occultists in history. He had called himself the Great Beast and considered it normal for a death to occur during the celebration of a ritual with a sexual orientation.

'In Florence there are devoted followers who worship Satan with black masses and magic rituals. And that happens on fixed dates, like the changes of the season, or when there's a new moon or a full moon. On these occasions, the participants have sex among themselves and make sacrifices, not necessarily human ones, convinced that by doing so they will increase their strength and become supermen and superwomen.'

'That's ridiculous!' Ferrara commented.

Just then, they heard a loud metallic clang, followed by a voice crying, 'It's nothing, Mother, a pot fell down.'

'That's my daughter,' the woman explained. 'She's cooking. Unfortunately, I've become used to these noises. She suffers from rheumatism in both hands.'

'I'd like to ask you something, Signora de Luca. Was there anything that didn't seem right in the details I just gave you?'

'Yes, there was one thing that struck me.'

'What was that?'

'Usually, satanist groups don't expose themselves so openly. They observe absolute secrecy, and keep their rituals strictly to themselves.'

'Can you tell me something about the groups operating in Florence?'

'There are several.' And she listed some: the Kremmerzians, the Crowleyans, others dedicated to the worship of Lilith or Isis. 'In the Talmudic tradition, Lilith was the first wife of Adam, with whom she gave birth to demons. People invoke her when they want to obtain magical powers. They're the most evil and dangerous of all. You have to remember though, Chief Superintendent, that analysing the various ideologies and their practices isn't at all easy, because many of their writings are kept secret. Obviously there are things that can't be revealed. But I'll tell you what I can.'

She went on to explain that the Kremmerzians took their name from Giuliano Kremmerz, also known as Ciro Formisano, a Neapolitan alchemist. Within the sect were various sub-groups. One of the most important was the Order of the Mantos, composed of a few rich people, highly placed in Florentine society.

The Crowleyans revived traditional satanic writings and rituals.

'What kind of rituals do they practise?' Ferrara asked.

'Rituals that involve the ingestion of their own semen, the use of blood and the breath exhaled in the act of violent death, the use of anatomical parts taken from the victims, including sexual organs, to make seals . . . By seals, I mean objects on which to concentrate to receive strength.'

'So, summing up, would you say that a satanist group was responsible for what occurred in that church?'

'In my opinion, yes, even though they didn't observe the usual secrecy.'

'What about the other cases? The scar on the dead woman, the murder of Giovanna Innocenti . . . What do you make of those?'

'The one thing that comes to mind is the temporal element.'

'What do you mean?'

'The twenty-fourth of June is the third night of Tregenda, a night when the witches gather. It's an important date for satanists, one on which they celebrate special rituals.'

At this point, the woman stood up. The two officers did the same.

'We're very grateful to you, Signora de Luca.'

'It's been a pleasure, Chief Superintendent. I hope I've been of some use. Don't hesitate to contact me again if there's anything else I can help you with.'

They heard yelling. 'Grandma, Grandma!'

'I'm coming, children.'

Silvia de Luca walked her visitors to the door.

'What a nice woman,' Ferrara said to Venturi when they were outside. 'A pity there are so few people willing to help.'

'Yes, chief,' Venturi said with a smile. 'She's a very special woman.'

Yes, Ferrara thought, this friendship between Inspector Venturi and Silvia de Luca was yet another kind of special friendship.

58

He had been standing beside the kiosk in the square, turning his head from time to time to look at the main door of the apartment block. He had followed the two policemen there in his jeep, which he had then parked in a side street, out of the way of prying eyes. As soon as he saw them come out, he checked his watch again. He calculated that they had been inside for just over an hour. He waited until they had driven away in their Alfa 156, then walked towards the block. He memorised the names on the three bells.

It wouldn't be too difficult to find out who they had been visiting.

It was his intention to keep an eye on the building, at least for a couple of days. Apart from the jeep, he would also use the Mercedes SLK so as not to arouse suspicion. While waiting for new instructions, he would clarify his ideas. In the end, though, his instinct would prevail.

As it always did.

PART THREE

THE WORSHIPPERS
OF SATAN

59

An imposing iron gate barred their way, the pillars on either side surmounted by marble lion's heads.

Beyond the gate was a long drive, lined by cypresses so high that the sun barely filtered through. At the end of it, the Innocentis' villa. The whole impression was one of great affluence.

'Ring the bell, Surace,' Marshal Gordi ordered, pointing to the video entryphone to their left.

Surace lowered the window and pressed the white button.

The gate immediately opened wide. The blue car with the word CARABINIERI on the side had been seen on the monitor at the main entrance.

They drove through the gate and proceeded along the smooth white gravel drive until they came to an open space in front of the villa, where a number of large, expensive-looking cars were parked.

At the front door they were met by a young woman in a black satin dress and a white apron bordered in lace. The collar and cuffs were white. On her head was an elegant bonnet, also white. She looked at them with a degree of curiosity before letting them in.

Alvise Innocenti came towards them along the corridor. He

had not shaved, and he looked tired. He was as fat as the marshal was thin. He was wearing a white linen suit, and there was a mixture of annoyance and suspicion in his eyes. It was obvious he regarded them as intruders, undesirables. Reluctantly he shook hands with them and said curtly, 'To what do I owe this latest visit, Marshal? Wasn't the last one enough? I don't have much time.'

He looked at them closely, as if trying to see right through them.

'We need to ask you some more questions,' Gori replied. 'I realise you're a busy man, and that now might not seem the appropriate moment, but the more time passes, the more difficult it will be to identify your daughter's killer. It'll only take a few minutes.'

'Not a moment more. Follow me!' His tone was as sharp and brusque as before.

He led them down long corridors, which criss-crossed at various points. It was a labyrinth, but one filled with old paintings, expensive porcelain, marble and bronze statues, and heavy velvet curtains. The two Carabinieri looked at each other several times. For them it was an unreal world.

They entered a large room with a coffered wooden ceiling, book-lined walls and a large English-style desk. In one corner was a lounge suite in dark chocolate-coloured leather. The room was full of light, thanks to the wide French windows that extended from the floor to the ceiling. Through them, a limpid blue sky was suspended over a harmonious landscape of magnificent green hills with similarly luxurious villas scattered over them. Outside, rotating sprinklers watered the lawn, watched over by a gardener.

Alvise Innocenti sat down in the large armchair behind the desk, filling it with his fifteen-plus stone. He motioned the two Carabinieri to sit down in the visitors' armchairs. Just above his head hung a pair of crossed antique swords. The rest of the wall was covered with a multi-coloured tapestry depicting a hunting scene. The general atmosphere was one of great refinement.

'If you've come here for information, you've had a wasted journey,' Innocenti said immediately, throwing them a hostile glance and playing with a packet of cigarettes in his pudgy hand. 'I hadn't seen my daughter for nearly two months. The last time she was here was on the thirtieth of April, my wife's birthday. A fleeting visit, as usual.' There was an expression of contempt in his eyes, the contempt of a powerful, self-confident man. 'But let's be done with these preliminaries. Why don't you come straight to the point?'

'What we'd like from you is to know if there's anybody you suspect.'

'No, absolutely not. After she graduated, she went to live on her own. She had her life. She started her business, but I think you already know that. Am I right?' There was a slight sneer on his lips. He took a cigarette from the packet, lit it, puffed at it, and blew smoke towards his guests.

'Yes, we know about the estate agency,' Gori replied, waving the smoke away with a nervous gesture of the hand.

'Precisely! With that friend of hers, Sara ... I can't remember her surname, or perhaps I never knew it.' He had raised his voice slightly.

'Genovese.'

'Yes, that might have been it. Anyway, she's a woman about whom there are a lot of rumours, which may not be mere gossip.'

'What kind of rumours?'

'They say she's a lesbian.'

'We're not interested in that,' the marshal cut in. 'We're only interested in crimes, and being a lesbian is not a crime.'

'I know, but a close relationship like that . . . What more can I say to make myself clearer?'

'You've said quite enough.'

'I see you understand.'

'Did your daughter have any enemies? Did she move in dubious circles?'

'What are you talking about? She was brought up in a respectable household.' His tone had become even colder.

'Signor Innocenti, the only reason I insist is because I want to find out the truth.'

'Yes, of course, that's your job.'

'Can you remember any particularly difficult time in your daughter's life? During her teenage years, for example?'

'What do you mean, Marshal? What are you trying to insinuate? As I said, she was brought up in a respectable household. I have the impression you're simply wasting time and I won't allow her memory to be tarnished.' He fixed them with a hostile glare.

'So you haven't formed any opinion about your daughter's murder?'

'None whatsoever.'

Gori could feel a cold wind of hatred in the air. It was only a momentary sensation, but enough to convince him that he had not been mistaken.

'And what's your opinion, Marshal?'

'I haven't yet formed one,' Gori said. 'But I'd like to ask you one final question.' His eyes were hard now, inquisitorial.

Innocenti studied him with a mixture of curiosity and menace, but the marshal remained composed.

'Are there any objects belonging to your daughter in the house? Old ones, maybe, from when she still lived with you . . . Letters? Diaries? Gifts? If there are, I would be grateful if you could allow me to see them.'

'Marshal, I don't understand what you're getting at. Have you by any chance come to search the house? If you have a warrant, then show me.' The muscles around his mouth seemed to contract. He was starting to lose patience with this informal interrogation.

'No, I don't have a warrant, and we have no intention of carrying out a search. It's a simple request, made in a spirit of cooperation. That's all we're asking for: your cooperation. For you to hand over to us, of your own free will, any objects belonging to your daughter, so that we can examine them. That's all.'

'There's nothing. As soon as she graduated she went to live in San Frediano and took everything with her.'

The marshal had rarely questioned an individual so unforthcoming. He could have lost his temper, but he held it in check. It was clear that the man was putting up a defensive barrier around himself.

To protect the family name? Or for some other reason?

Perhaps, like Sara Genovese, he was afraid of being involved in the investigation. These were people whose lips were sealed.

The penetrating stare, the tension in his voice, the way he held the marshal's gaze while maintaining that air of superiority mingled with defiance and ill-concealed sufferance, were all details which, taken singly, could be interpreted as symptoms of the stress he must be feeling at this time of mourning. Considered as a whole, though, they expressed nervousness, fear and anger, as well as contempt.

Gori had met quite a few murderers, some of them highly unlikely suspects. He was well able to spot those details that were invisible to an untrained eye.

'We'd like to speak to your wife, if she's at home.'

Alvise Innocenti had stubbed out his cigarette in the ashtray and was about to stand up when he froze. 'Why?'

'She might know something. Daughters often confide more in their mothers.'

'I think that's extremely unlikely. Besides, my wife can't be disturbed right now. Let me remind you that we are in mourning and we have visitors. If you insist, I'll have to phone my friend, Chief Prosecutor Fiore.'

These last words did not surprise the marshal at all: he had assumed that Innocenti would mention the prosecutor sooner or later.

'I understand that now may not be the best moment,' Gori replied, drily and formally. 'But we shall have to meet again.'

He stood up, and Surace did the same.

As Innocenti led them back to the front door, Gori sneaked a glance inside the drawing room. He saw several people standing there, among them Signora Innocenti. Rich as she was, she gave the impression of a woman who had given up on her own femininity. Her body was thin and sluggish, with a stooped back, and her complexion was grey and dull. He had just enough time to observe that she walked with a limp. He had not noticed it at the funeral.

'Good day to you, Signor Gori,' Alvise Innocenti said when they reached the front door, lowering his voice at the word 'Signor'.

Was it a concealed threat, implying that he would not have the rank of marshal for much longer?

As they walked away, he thought he heard the man murmur, 'Fools!'

'He won the first round,' Surace said as they got in their car. 'What an arrogant bastard ... What the hell did he mean by that "Signor"? Was he trying to intimidate us?'

'His manner doesn't fool me,' Gori replied. 'Did you notice he never called his daughter by her name?'

'And did you notice that he's a smoker?'

Gori nodded. Several times. In the meantime, Surace had turned the key in the ignition. The marshal had time to cast a last fleeting glance at the villa. At one of the windows on the ground floor he glimpsed Alvise Innocenti, watching them. But then the face disappeared, so quickly as to leave him in doubt as to whether he had really seen it.

They hadn't really made any progress, but the visit had served to make them aware that they couldn't expect any help whatsoever from the victim's father.

They had also, perhaps, had a confirmation of Sara Genovese's words: Giovanna must have suffered a serious trauma in her adolescence. And it was quite likely that her father had had something to do with it.

60

Teresa had come back from *La Nazione*. And she was not sure how to face her chief.

The visit to the paper had not been a success, as far as she was concerned. For any of the others, it would have been all in a day's work.

Afraid he would think she'd bungled it, she felt the need to confide in a colleague, even though she barely knew any of them. She was walking towards the main entrance of Headquarters when she heard a horn tooting. She turned and saw Sergi, just parking a large car and signalling with his hand for her to wait. She stopped, thinking as she did so that it looked quite a luxurious car for a police officer on a salary of just over 1,700 euros a month.

'Someone from Rome has been trying to get hold of you, Superintendent Micalizi,' he said as soon as he caught up with her.

'Who?'

'Maurizio. He said he was a friend of yours and asked me to tell you to call him back as soon as possible.'

'Thanks, Inspector.'

'Are you tired or not feeling very well? You look so pale!'

'No. I'm fine. It's just that I may have a problem.'

'Personal or work, if you don't mind my asking? If it's the latter, I might be able to help you.'

'Just work.'

'Then hop in and we'll go and grab a coffee.'

During the ride, Teresa confided her problem in him. At *La Nazione*, she had learned nothing about the article the chief superintendent had sent her to inquire about. She ought to have insisted, not let herself be put off by the editor's excuse of professional confidentiality.

'Do you think I screwed up, Inspector?' she asked in a shaky voice.

'Don't get so upset about it. The newspaper world can be a hard one to crack. What happened to you could have happened to any of us, even after years of service. Don't worry about the chief. He knows these people better than anyone.'

His words seemed to encourage her. 'Thank you, Inspector. Let me buy you a pizza some time.'

'Surace, I'll leave you this . . .'

It was the report on their meeting with Alvise Innocenti.

'Read it and then countersign it. We'll send it to the deputy prosecutor. I think it's good to have it down in black and white as a record of how the man behaved. Then it'll be up to the Prosecutor's Department to decide what to do about him.'

'Right away, sir,' Surace replied, picking up his pen to sign.

'What have you been up to?'

'Finishing going through the photographs.'

The licence plates of all the cars present at the funeral had been checked and for each owner they had compiled a file with the essential information: name, place of residence, profession, any previous convictions, any court cases pending, and so on. Each file had a photograph attached.

'Good. Remember to send a copy to Chief Superintendent Ferrara, along with your report.'

'I'll send both over today by courier, sir. Or we could take them ourselves when we go to the meeting later.'

'Good idea. Let's take them.'

'As soon as I'm finished with this, I thought I'd take a look at the list of clients from the estate agency.'

'Excellent. Good work, Surace.'

61

The stream of visitors offering their condolences had stopped for a while, leaving Alvise Innocenti and his wife free to talk at last.

'Who was that busybody staring at me?' Laura Innocenti asked. 'As he went by in the corridor, he glanced in and gave me a nasty look.'

'One of the two plain-clothes Carabinieri who came here.'

'What did they want?'

'Nothing. They still haven't grasped who they're dealing with. Questions, questions, questions. If we had anything here belonging to our daughter, if I suspected anyone . . . They're fishing for information, don't you see?'

'Why? Are we supposed to do their job for them?'

'They want us to cooperate.'

'But we don't know anything. How can we cooperate? They're the ones who ought to be giving us information.'

'Laura, just leave them to their business. They're idiots, amateurs. As I said, they don't realise who they're dealing with. Let's think about us. On the first of July I'm going to England.'

She set off for the kitchen to give orders to the maid, dragging her left leg on the floor.

He couldn't stand that leg any more, he thought, watching her walk away. His wife's limp was no longer just a fact of everyday life. He was actually starting to hate it.

62

Visiting hours had been over for a while. Nobody had come to see her that Sunday.

From the bed next to the window, with her back propped on the pillows, she had spent all afternoon looking out at the waters of Starnberg Lake. The weather was gorgeous, and a number of regattas had been in progress. As the snow-white sails glided over the calm waters of the lake, she'd imagined the competitors on the boats: their tension, their efforts, their joy. As always, she had been a silent fan, watching from a distance. Over time, she had found a way of killing the endless hours. Even watching the ferries crossing the lake, or the motorboats with their roaring engines, was a pleasant pastime. Small pleasures, perhaps, but as she had been bedridden for years, such things meant a lot to her. Her favourite scent, Chanel No 5, hovered in the room.

She was dozing off when the telephone on her bedside table started ringing. She passed a hand through her thin white hair, gathered in a bun on the back of her neck, and answered.

'Oh, it's you! Where are you calling from? Oh, from Florence . . . Why are you phoning? Has something happened? Nothing? Well, let's hope so. Don't worry me, you know I can't move from here . . . What am I doing? Nothing, looking at the lake, there have been regattas today ... Me? Yes, I've been fine. So are you coming next week? I'll be expecting you. Don't forget the chocolates!'

She sent a kiss down the line and put the phone down. Her eyes, a little misty now, moved back to the waters of the lake.

The sun would soon be setting.

63

It was seven in the evening and they were in the big room on the second floor of Headquarters.

Rizzo, just back from the Institute of Forensic Medicine, entered with his briefcase still in his hand. He greeted all those present and took his seat in the one free chair, between Teresa Micalizi and Sergi. Deputy Prosecutor Vinci and his chief Luca Fiore were also at the rectangular table. Fiore had the reputation of being a very practical man who never wasted time on trivialities and, when he wanted, usually got results.

Vinci was the first to speak.

'I'm pleased to see that the *Squadra Mobile* has been reinforced,' he said, turning towards Teresa with a smile. 'At last, a member of the fair sex in this office. Welcome! I hope you get on well here.' From the expression on his face, it was easy to see what he was thinking: What a pretty girl – I wouldn't mind taking her running with me in the Cascine.

Teresa turned crimson.

Vinci invited those present to take stock of the investigation. 'Then we'll trade ideas.'

This was the usual procedure.

In a complex case, a deputy prosecutor always asked the opinion of his colleagues, but in the end he was the one who decided how the investigation would be conducted. Long gone were the days – like the first decade of Ferrara's career – when the police had more autonomy and the prosecutor only intervened in rare cases; for example, if the culprit confessed. Then, in 1998, a new penal code had revolutionised relations between the police and the prosecutor, relegating the former to an ever more subordinate role. Now the prosecutor was the true chief and, as such, entitled to direct all aspects of the investigation from beginning to end. Ferrara had found it hard to adapt to the new system: he was a detective of the old school, and there weren't many like him left. The vast majority thought only of their careers, wanting to advance as quickly as possible, and so they supported the prosecutors in everything and meekly awaited instructions before making a move.

Inspector Venturi began to summarise what he had discovered so far from his researches on the Internet.

On a number of English-language sites, he had found the case of the Chicago Rippers, which went back to the beginning of the 1980s. In Chicago from June 1981 to September/October 1982, a number of women – definitely six, perhaps seven, or even more – had been kidnapped, mutilated and killed. None, however, had been burnt. The last victim, dumped on a riverbank, had been able before she died to provide the police with a few details, especially about the van she had been forced to climb into when she was kidnapped. Four men had been identified as the killers; all were satanists. In the apartment where they usually celebrated their rituals, the officers had found traces of human sacrifice.

'You say the victims were mutilated,' Vinci said. 'In what way?'

'Their left breasts were removed.'

'Curious. Just like some of the Monster of Florence murders.'

'Precisely.'

'Did you know about the Chicago case?' Vinci asked Ferrara.

'No,' Ferrara replied. 'This is the first I've heard of it.'

The others, including Gori, also claimed ignorance.

'Of course it's only mentioned on the English-language websites,' Venturi said.

'I suggest we contact the Chicago police or the FBI for information.'

The others nodded.

Venturi continued his report, moving on to the information he had gathered on the Bartolotti brothers. 'I want to know everything about those two, and I mean everything,' Ferrara had told him when he had phoned that morning from the little church.

Dante Bartolotti, Venturi reported, was an important figure in the financial world. Single, fifty-five years old, he lived in New York, on the Upper East Side, where he was a majority shareholder in a number of companies, mostly in the oil and construction industries. He had interests in various parts of the world, from North America to Asia and the Middle East. He was definitely an influential man.

His brother Umberto was an engineer, though he worked only intermittently, mostly on jobs for friends and friends of friends. He was well known in the city, and moved in aristocratic circles. Almost forty-five years old, he too was single; it was rumoured that he was gay, but this might be nothing more than gossip based on his never having been in a serious relationship. What was not gossip was the fact that, as a result of some ill-advised investments, he had found himself in financial difficulty – something he had apparently not told his brother about. It was also said that he had a great passion for cars and that every year he followed Formula One races around the world. When he was eighteen, he had even taken part as a driver in the last year of the Sicilian races at the Madonie Targa Florio circuit. That was in 1977, when one of the competing cars had come off the road after Buonfornello and crashed into the spectators' stands, killing two people and seriously injuring three. Since then it had been suspended and turned into a rally.

'I'm waiting for further information, which I hope to get some time today. One of my informers is digging up a bit of dirt about their company, which owns not only the property where the church is located but also, together with others, a dairy farm in the Apennines, which is apparently the subject of much talk.'

'What kind of talk?'

'Apparently there's a home on the property for children who've been taken into care. People are saying the children have been abused.'

'The usual malicious gossip!' Prosecutor Fiore cut in, angrily. 'I think we should concentrate on what we know for sure.'

Venturi simply nodded.

Then it was the turn of Inspector Sergi, who had been scouring the Etruscan tombs and the surrounding area, trying to get information on the people who hung around there. So far, without much success, apart from vague mentions of a group of drifters who had established some kind of base near the woods.

'Keep trying. We must be able to get their names.'

'Okay.'

Then Marshal Gori spoke up, with information about the owners of the cars. He had the list with him and gave it to the prosecutor and Ferrara, together with photographs.

'Some of the names are unfamiliar, and we're still looking at them. I should have more to tell you quite soon.'

He then gave an account of his interview with Sara Genovese, and handed over a copy of the statement.

'What can you tell me about the photographer in the Cascine?' Vinci asked.

'We identified him, thanks to the chief superintendent, who found the case in police records.'

'What do we know about him?'

'Not a lot, apart from that incident in the park.'

'Is he free?'

'Yes. He was sentenced, but he appealed, and is currently awaiting a decision on that appeal.'

At this point, Ferrara proposed a short break: they still had a lot to get through, and a pause would certainly do them all good. When the meeting resumed, Vinci reported the results of the post-mortem.

The victim was indeed female, aged between thirty and forty. She had been killed with a knife and set on fire when she was already dead. The collarbone had been broken with a cut from right to left.

'Franceschini is certain that some of her organs were removed, perhaps the liver or part of it. As soon as possible, we'll be getting the results of the histological and toxicological tests, which will tell us if she'd taken any drugs.'

He explained that the teeth had remained intact, which would make it possible to identify her if they found her X-rays.

Prosecutor Fiore's next contribution to the meeting was to declare, in an authoritative tone, 'My colleague Deputy Prosecutor Vinci will now give you your instructions, and I advise you to keep to them scrupulously. Please don't embark on any personal initiative that hasn't been cleared with my office first.' In uttering these last words, he looked pointedly at Marshal Gori.

Had he already received a complaint from Alvise Innocenti?

The police would put taps on the phones of Umberto Bartolotti and the caretaker, in the hope that something useful might emerge from their conversations. They would also continue their inquiries in the vicinity of the little church in the hope of locating witnesses. All employees on the property were to be formally questioned.

It was at this point that Ferrara intervened and asked for authorisation to acquire the records of all mobile phones from which calls had been made in the area of the crime – for the moment, during the twenty-four hours preceding the fire.

Vinci glanced at his chief, then declared himself in agreement.

The Carabinieri, meanwhile, would tap Sara Genovese's phone and continue their investigations into the photographer in the Cascine, as requested by Gori. The marshal made another proposal: to formally question the Innocentis.

This time Vinci's glance at Fiore was a longer one, and it was the chief prosecutor himself who spoke.

'Marshal, send us a preliminary report on all you've gathered thus far, along with an official request, and Deputy Prosecutor Vinci and I will consider it.'

'Of course, Prosecutor,' Gori said.

With these words, the meeting could be considered concluded.

64

Enrico Costanza was waiting.

He was looking out of the window at the reddening sun. This evening, though, he could not savour the enchantment of its colours, the red and orange hues of the sunset. There was a veil of melancholy over his eyes. What bothered him most was that time was going by too quickly. He still had many things to do, all of them important. And he was anxious to know if his old friendships still held fast after all that had happened. He would soon be able to verify that personally.

When the telephone rang, he took a deep breath.

At last!

He walked to the desk and lifted the receiver.

'Yes?' he said in a firm tone.

'It's me,' said the voice at the other end. 'Any news?'

'No.'

'We have to follow this through. You know what I'm talking about ... The people here need to be sure ... '

'Yes.'

'We need to know their moves. Do you understand me?'

'Of course. We've already made arrangements. We're being very careful.'

'Good.'

They were careful not to speak more explicitly, even though they were sure their phones were not being tapped.

'Thank you.'

'Will I see you on my birthday?' asked the voice at the other end.

'Of course. I'll be with you tomorrow night.'

When the call was over, he returned to the window and again looked outside. But the red ball of the sun had already sunk below the horizon. The colours of nature had disappeared and the mantle of darkness was gradually descending on the hills.

Costanza closed the shutters. He went back to the desk, lifted the receiver, and dialled a number.

It was a brief phone call, as cryptic as ever.

65

Ferrara also received a call before leaving the office.

It was Gianni Fuschi, phoning to tell him what they had gleaned so far from the shoe prints. Two were distinct: the soles must have been quite new. They were from a man's hunting boots, size 43–44. A third print belonged to the worn sole of a Nike tennis shoe, size 36.

'A woman's?' Ferrara asked.

'Quite likely. The length and depth of the print suggest it was someone light and thin. I'll let you have the detailed report tomorrow.'

'Thanks.'

When he got home, he found his wife in bed. She was still awake and the TV was on.

He bent over her and gave her a kiss.

'Your hair stinks of smoke,' Petra said to him. 'You must have smoked more than usual.'

'It's not only cigar smoke. If you only knew what else it was . . .'

'Don't say another word. You know I don't want to know any details.'

'I know, I know. I'm going to take a shower.' He gave her another kiss and headed for the bathroom.

'I'll make you something to eat, Michele,' she called, getting out of bed.

As he stood beneath the jet of hot water, Ferrara thought again about the victim. He tried to imagine her in her last hours, with her family, maybe with her husband or her lover. What if she had been a prostitute? Who had she been with before she was reduced to that state? He tried to imagine her: she may have been beautiful, alluring. And above all unaware that, in the dead of night, someone was going to kill her and set her on fire.

When had she realised she was about to be killed? Had she known about the ritual, or was she completely ignorant? Was she herself an initiate?

'Is everything all right?' Petra asked, putting her head in at the door of the bathroom.

'Yes, fine.'

'I've already laid the table.'

'I'll be right out.'

The salad bowl was filled with lettuce and tomato. He had a steak and Petra a sole *alla mugnaia*. The dinner was washed down with a good glass of Chianti and finished off with a fruit salad.

At last he could collapse in his black leather armchair. It was just after midnight. As usual, he put his feet up on the stool, ready to tackle the work he had brought home with him. He wanted to draw up a chart with the essential features of the crimes, an indispensable tool for a detective, to be updated as new facts emerged. It was work that required patience, and would keep him busy for quite some time.

He could not imagine, even remotely, what was about to happen.

Right there, just outside his own home.

66

Night of Sunday, 27 to Monday, 28 June

He ran out on to the terrace.

A number of gunshots had rung out suddenly. Two, three, four, maybe even five.

He saw people running on the Ponte Vecchio. It was like a stampede. Something, perhaps a person, lay on the ground in front of the bust of Benvenuto Cellini.

'Petra, I'm going out!' he called.

'Michele—' she said, but the door slammed immediately.

Ferrara ran down into the street dressed just as he was, in a sweatshirt and jeans. Once outside, he heard the wailing of police sirens in the distance. Gradually they came closer. He turned to his left and saw a flashing light on the roof of a patrol car. He ran the last fifty yards, panting, and found himself faced with yet another terrible scene. A thin young dark-skinned man lay on his back on the pavement. Blood was gushing from his chest and head, and he was shaking convulsively. Ferrara knelt by him. The man's chest heaved a few times, then stopped moving. In the meantime, the pool of blood continued to spread.

He touched him. No pulse. Not even a weak one. The man

had died, right there in front of his eyes. He had a closer look and realised that the man could not have been more than twenty-five. He stood up and looked around. A small group of onlookers were leaning over the side of the bridge. A policeman went up to them and told them to move away. In the meantime, Ferrara had been joined by the officers from the patrol car. He ordered them to get in touch with the operations room at Headquarters: the pathologist would have to be sent for, and whichever deputy prosecutor was on duty would need to be informed.

Another murder within twenty-four hours; this one right in the heart of Florence!

As he waited, he lit a cigar and began walking slowly along the bridge. Beneath it, the waters were as flat as a plank. Rings of smoke rose slowly into the air after him, to be dispelled immediately by the wind. He could not recall a similar crime, in the very heart of the city, and at this hour, with the tourists enjoying the view of Florence by night from one of its most beautiful spots, and the lights of the buildings reflected in the river.

Suddenly he heard someone calling him.

'Chief Superintendent!'

It was a police officer, informing him that the pathologist and the deputy prosecutor had arrived. Stubbing out the remains of his cigar with his foot, Ferrara went to meet them. It was Vinci and Franceschini. The two of them were back on duty again.

'Who is he?' Vinci asked immediately.

'A foreigner, I think. No idea of his identity yet.'

'Did you see anything, Chief Superintendent?'

'I heard the shots from my apartment and came running. He died before my eyes.'

In the meantime, Franceschini had bent over the body, taking care not to step into the spreading pool of blood.

'He was hit in the chest and head,' he said.

'Any cartridge cases?' asked Vinci.

'No,' Ferrara replied. 'The killer must have used a revolver.'

'Quite likely.'

Some thirty yards away, over towards the Piazza della Repubblica, the first crime reporters began to appear, along with some photographers. A cameraman from a local TV channel was filming the scene.

When would all this horror end?

67

'*La Nazione* here,' a woman's voice replied, after a few rings.

The man at the other end held a small recorder to the receiver. The microcassette had already been inserted. He pressed play.

'I'm speaking on behalf of the FAF,' a metallic voice said. 'We killed him with marked bullets. Tell the police that if they won't make an effort to keep the city safe, we'll do it for them.'

There was a click, and the line went dead. The man had hung up. The switchboard operator looked at the display, but didn't see any indication of the caller's number.

In the meantime, the man was walking away from the phone booth in the direction of the Parterre car park, where he had left his car.

He had done what he had to do. He had righted a wrong.

No papers had been found on the victim's body, nor had any match been found in the fingerprint database. Was he an illegal immigrant? There was no way of knowing. Perhaps he had only been in the city for a few days, or even a few hours.

From an external examination of the body, it emerged that he had been shot three times, and that the shots had been fired from a revolver. The diameter of the bullet holes suggested the use of small calibre cartridges.

An apparently inexplicable homicide, although Deputy Prosecutor Vinci was in little doubt about the motive – a settling of scores, perhaps between organised groups of street vendors or drug pushers, a theory supported by a number of previous incidents, although none as serious as this.

68

Monday, 28 June

At eight in the morning, images of Florence appeared on the screen.

It was the TV news on Channel 5.

First, a view over the city. Then the Ponte Vecchio. On the tarmac, the white marks left by forensics of the outline of the body were still quite visible.

A voiceover said, 'Murder in the heart of Florence.'

Ferrara sat up in bed and increased the volume. The item lasted just over two minutes. A lot, for a national news broadcast. The piece concluded with a brief statement by the Commissioner, filmed in his office, standing next to the Italian and EU flags. He invited possible witnesses to come forward, guaranteeing them anonymity.

As a coda, the reporter mentioned, in very general terms, that another murder had been committed, this one in a deconsecrated church in the countryside near Florence.

Ferrara switched off the television and got out of bed.

During the night, his men had not been idle.

Some had questioned people living in the vicinity of the

Ponte Vecchio; some had carried out raids in the places where foreigners usually hung out, some had contacted their informants in the hope of finding a lead. They were all exhausted, with bags under their eyes and mouths foul with too much coffee. Some had not been home for more than twenty-four hours.

The activities had been coordinated by Superintendent Luigi Ciuffi, head of Narcotics, who had even used some of his undercover officers for the task. Ciuffi was someone Ferrara greatly admired. He was always thorough and meticulous, giving one hundred per cent. He possessed a quality that was growing ever rarer in younger officers of his rank: he was always ready to be called on, day and night, including public holidays.

And so that morning, in the corridors and offices of the *Squadra Mobile*, there was a constant coming and going. The telephones could be heard ringing, the printers humming continually.

The night's 'haul' had been substantial: prostitutes, pimps, pushers, unauthorised street vendors and illegal immigrants. All people with something to hide: the only way to extract information from them was to threaten to stick your nose in their business. The famous 'cage' had been put to use: far from the parts of Headquarters frequented by the law-abiding public, this large room on the ground floor was where suspects were held before being transferred to prison or a reception centre. Some of last night's intake had had to sleep on the floor, which had done nothing to improve their mood.

Two police vans were parked outside the building, ready to take those illegals who were to be deported to the ports of Ancona and Bari, or Leonardo da Vinci airport in Rome. And there was a knot of photographers waiting on the pavements opposite, ready to photograph them as they were led out in single file and loaded in the vehicles.

It was the kind of low-life trawl that might have given the citizens a greater sense of security if carried out regularly. Instead, such measures were only undertaken when something alarming had happened, like the previous night's incident. It was difficult to get enough men together from the other sections, and even more difficult to make sure they would be paid the requisite overtime because of all the budget cuts. Every other morning, the Commissioner himself delivered a lecture to his section chiefs on the need to limit overtime and any trips outside the city. They were becoming more and more like accountants.

Now it was almost nine, and Ciuffi and his men, helped by their colleagues in the Immigration Office, were finishing their questioning of the people who had been brought in. They were hoping that somebody would at least give them an inkling as to the identity of the killer or the victim. Of the latter, nothing was yet known. Nobody had showed up to identify him. It was as if the young man was of no interest to anyone.

Teresa Micalizi, too, was still busy in her office.

At the beginning of the operation she had said to Ciuffi, 'I'm sure one of the girls will speak more freely to me as a woman.' Now, after many hours and many interviews, she had to admit that she had heard a lot of unlikely stories and gruesome details that seemed straight out of the pages of some old novel. They were all too scared to speak the truth, she had told herself, to overcome her discouragement.

Ferrara arrived at nine thirty that morning.

As he passed the door of Teresa's office, which was ajar, he peered in. He saw Teresa on the little couch, talking calmly to a slim blonde girl with a very light complexion sitting beside her. The girl was wearing a skimpy top that left her midriff bare, a very short black skirt and high-heeled shiny black leather knee-boots. She was so young, Ferrara thought she might be a minor. He did not go in, closed the door noiselessly and continued along the corridor, looking in at the other offices.

69

Florence would be different from now on.

There was no escaping the fact, not with news of the satanic ritual in all the papers, not to mention the murder on the Ponte Vecchio.

Now Florentines were liable to become alarmed at the slightest thing. And naturally they would be asking, What's going to happen next?

It was a nightmare.

There were events that changed the life of an individual and events that changed the life of a city. The days when you could live a normal life in Florence would soon be nothing more than a pleasant memory.

Sitting at his desk, Ferrara leafed through the newspapers as he slowly sipped his coffee. The local ones, unlike the news on Channel 5, had given ample space to the incident in Sesto Fiorentino. The headlines were almost all along the same lines: *Murder during satanic rite! Satanists in Florence!*

The victim, whose identity was still unknown, was variously described as being between thirty and forty, and the middle pages of *La Nazione* carried a photograph of the church with the police cordon around it.

In *Il Tirreno* there was an interview, accompanied by

photographs, with a famous expert on religion in Italy. This expert gave an overview of the satanist groups operating in Tuscany, but without going into much detail.

Of the killing of the foreigner, only *La Nazione* carried a brief item under 'Breaking news'.

It was 10.16 when Commissioner Adinolfi put in an appearance at the *Squadra Mobile*.

Even redder in the face than usual, he was clutching an envelope in his right hand as he hurried nervously along the corridors, glancing in at the offices that had their doors open. A few officers, startled by his presence, came and stood in their doorways to watch him. Something very serious must have happened.

The Commissioner entered Ferrara's office.

'Chief Superintendent Ferrara, we have to talk,' he began, waving the envelope in the air.

Ferrara stood up, came around to the front of the desk and made his way to the armchair next to the one where Adinolfi had seated himself. He waited, thinking that, whatever was in that envelope, it must be really serious if, instead of summoning him to his own office, the Commissioner had come to see him personally.

It was the first time that had ever happened.

'Read this!' Adinolfi said, handing him the envelope. There was an indefinable expression on his face. Dismay? Anxiety? Fear? God alone knew. Perhaps it was just the torment of someone who would have to deal with the political repercussions of everything that was happening.

Ferrara opened the envelope and took out a sheet of paper headed *La Nazione*. He unfolded it and read the contents.

It was the transcript of an anonymous telephone call that had come in to the newspaper's switchboard.

I'm speaking on behalf of the FAF. We killed him with marked bullets. Tell the police that if they won't make an effort to keep the city safe, we'll do it for them.

'The editor himself brought it to me a few minutes ago,' the Commissioner said. 'In order not to compromise the investigation, they haven't published it today, but they will before long. Well? Is it true that the bullets were marked?'

'There hasn't been a post-mortem yet. It's being done this afternoon. We should be able to confirm that then.'

'Why haven't the bullets been recovered?'

This was proof that Adinolfi had never conducted an investigation in his career. Ferrara explained to him that the bullets were still in the body and that no others had been found at the crime scene.

'It's possible some ended up in the Arno!' the Commissioner remarked sarcastically. 'Inform me as soon as you have the post-mortem results. I have to keep the Head of the State Police in Rome updated. If this is confirmed, we'll have to get Special Ops involved. There may be a political motive to the shooting, perhaps of a racial nature – although they say they've never come across the initials FAF.'

He had clearly already been making inquiries.

'I'd be happy to have Special Ops on board,' was all that Ferrara said.

'Do the initials mean anything to *you*?'

Ferrara thought about it, then said no.

'It could be a new group, something like Florentines Against Foreigners,' Adinolfi ventured.

Ferrara said nothing.

'Do you have a lead yet?' the Commissioner asked. 'I assume so, with the number of men you've got on duty,' he added, his tone still sarcastic.

'Nothing concrete as yet, but everyone's working flat out, as always.'

'You don't sound very optimistic!'

'How can I be optimistic in a case like this? We still don't know anything about the victim and there's a shortage of witnesses, even though there were plenty of people in the vicinity of the bridge at that hour.'

'Insist! Bend over backwards. Someone has to come forward sooner or later. I've already made an appeal on TV, I don't know if you saw it . . . '

Ferrara nodded. 'Yes, I did.'

'And hasn't anyone phoned yet? A relative?'

'We did have a few calls, which we're in the process of checking, but I don't think any of them were serious.'

'But how is it possible that nobody saw or heard anything? Here we are in the cradle of art and culture, the centre of the Renaissance . . . People can't just stay silent.'

'When you're dealing with a murder like this, all cities are the same. People are scared, they prefer to mind their own business. Even in Florence.'

'Anything from the informants?'

'Not yet, but the squad are working on it. One of them may come up with a lead.'

Adinolfi stood up. 'I'll leave you the transcript. I've asked the editor to keep as quiet as he can about it. Good luck!'

He walked slowly out of the room, even more stooped than usual.

70

Meanwhile, Teresa Micalizi was knocking at Ciuffi's door.

'I may have something,' she said in an excited voice.

'Come in, tell me what you've got.'

Teresa sat down. 'I've just been questioning a Russian girl who was promised work in the fashion business here in Italy. She certainly has the looks to be a model. She's still in my office, in a pitiful state.'

Ciuffi nodded. This was nothing new to him. A constant stream of young people, some still minors, had passed through his office over the years. He could still hear their tearful voices as they told him their stories, their shattered dreams. These were the victims of the trafficking in human beings that was going on right here in Florence in the third millennium. Many would never see their families again.

'I persuaded her to help us,' Teresa went on, 'although she's afraid for her life and the lives of her relatives in Moscow.'

'What exactly did she tell you?'

'She knows one of the guys who organises the unauthorised street vendors on the Ponte Vecchio. He's also a drug dealer. She reckons he's been having some problems lately.'

'How does she know him?'

'She's slept with him several times, at his place. He paid her in money and the odd twist of heroin. The last time, a few days ago, he was very nervous. She heard him talking on his mobile.'

'What about?'

'He said something like: "If he did that, he deserves a lesson, but I'll deal with it, and you deal with the debt ..." That's all she managed to hear.'

'What language was he speaking?'

'Italian.'

'How did she first meet this guy?'

'Through her pimp. She's too terrified to tell us anything more about him, but I get the impression he's a big drug dealer who operates all over Tuscany.'

'Is she at least willing to tell us where he lives?'

'Yes. It wasn't easy to persuade her, but in the end I think I gained her trust.'

'Good. Go back to her and don't leave her alone. I'll talk to Ferrara.'

If they could identify this person, Ciuffi thought, and check the records of his mobile phone, they might be able to get somewhere.

Teresa went back to her office, feeling pleased. But she found the young woman with red, swollen eyes. She had obviously been crying throughout Teresa's absence, and when Teresa entered, she looked up, her eyes filled with terror.

Was she already having second thoughts?

71

Once alone, Ferrara had taken another look at the transcript of the call to *La Nazione*.

The claim didn't seem at all credible to him. There was something old-fashioned in the tone: it reminded him too much of those communiqués from terrorist groups in the sixties and seventies.

He thought about how to proceed, then summoned Venturi and showed him the transcript.

The inspector reminded him of an episode a few years earlier, when a group of youths had set fire to a tramp sleeping on a bench in the Parco delle Cascine. On that occasion, too, the act had been thought to be racially motivated, then that was ruled out when it had emerged from the investigations that the culprits were just local yobs.

'Venturi, go to *La Nazione* and question the switchboard operator. The name isn't given on the transcript, but you can ask the editor. We have to find out more. Maybe the operator remembers the voice of the anonymous caller. Check if by any chance it was recorded.'

At that moment Ciuffi entered the room.

'Anything new?' Ferrara asked.

'Maybe, yes, chief.'

'Go on.'

Ciuffi told him what he had heard from Teresa, commenting at the end, 'It may be a lead.'

Ferrara nodded. 'Worth following up, I'd say. Organise a raid for tonight. Anything else?'

'Nothing, chief, except that Florence is changing. Nobody's talking. Nobody's come forward – not a relative, not a friend of the victim. Which means either he was completely alone here, or that the people who knew him are scared because he was an illegal. We don't yet know his exact nationality. From the look of him, I'd say he might be a Moroccan.'

'Florence has already changed!' Ferrara replied. 'Have they all taken a vow of silence, like in Sicily? Well, from this evening, I want officers on uninterrupted duty on the Ponte Vecchio and the adjoining areas. I don't want anyone selling so much as a match until one of them decides to talk.'

'Right, chief,' Ciuffi replied with a smile. 'We'll make it a no-go area. You can count on it.'

He and Venturi were just about to leave the room when Fanti came in with the coffees. He placed them on the table and went out in silence, tall and thin as a nail.

They drank the coffee straight down and left.

'What about the bullets?'

'Just three, Chief Superintendent,' Franceschini replied. He looked tired and drawn, as if he had not slept for several nights. 'Twenty-two calibre lead bullets. They're on the trolley.'

He was wearing a white coat that looked rather big on him, rubber gloves and a mask. He had started the post-mortem early, because the director, Lassotti, had called a meeting of all the doctors for 3.30 and he dared not miss it. In the air, a strong smell of disinfectant.

'Just three bullets?' Ferrara asked, glancing at the corpse. He saw that the standard Y-shaped incision from the chest to the pubic region had already been made, and the internal organs removed. The cranium, too, had been opened.

'Three,' the doctor repeated, with a touch of irritation.

The others must have gone astray, Ferrara thought. Fallen in the river, as the Commissioner had said, although he had meant it as a joke. 'What can you tell me?' he asked.

Franceschini explained that death had been caused by an internal haemorrhage as a result of gunshots, probably fired in rapid succession. Two bullets had reached the thorax and punctured the aorta, while the other had penetrated the occipital region. Although the first two had ravaged vital organs, like the lung and heart, the third seemed to have been the decisive one. In addition, the trajectories of the first two bullets went from the front to the back along an almost perfectly horizontal line, which meant, at least hypothetically, that the victim and his killer must have been standing facing each other. The third bullet, on the other hand, had been fired from above, when the victim was already on the ground.

Ferrara thought this reconstruction sounded correct, but said nothing.

'Death took only a matter of minutes,' Franceschini added.

Ferrara knew that the small calibre was deceptive. Contrary to what those who knew little about guns and ammunition might think, the .22 could cause the same if not worse damage as bigger bullets like the 7.65 or even the .38. And for a very simple reason: usually a .22 wasn't powerful enough to exit the body and so it bounced about inside, wreaking havoc on the organs it came into contact with. In addition, a pistol of that calibre, even a revolver, was easy to conceal about the person, which made it a favourite with hitmen.

'I'd like to take the bullets,' he said.

'No problem, Chief Superintendent.'

Franceschini went to the trolley, picked them up, put them in a small plastic bag and handed it to him.

'Here they are. Do with them what you will. My work is done here. I'll let you and the deputy prosecutor have my report as soon as possible.'

There was a kind of sarcastic sneer on his face. Ferrara ignored it, said goodbye and left.

Next stop: forensics.

'You know, Michele,' Gianni Fuschi said, after examining the bullets carefully, 'although they're twisted out of shape, I can see they have traces of red paint.'

Marked! Just as the anonymous caller had said.

They were in a large room with windows that looked out on the Piazza Indipendenza. It was packed with equipment and apparatus: computers, test tubes, chemicals, optical and electronic microscopes and so on.

'You mean they're not in their original state?'

'The killer, in my opinion, painted them before loading them in the magazine, though I can't think why. In all my years, this is the first time I've seen someone do something like that to bullets. The pathologist may have thought it was blood, but it isn't, it's indelible paint.'

'That's a new one on me, too.'

'And you've seen a lot of homicides, Michele.'

Ferrara nodded. 'Gianni, please let me have your report as soon as possible.'

'I just need to write it up. You'll have it by this evening.'

They said goodbye.

It was becoming clear that Special Operations would need to be involved in this case.

72

Meanwhile, Sergi and a few men, among them his sidekick Ricci, had been going through the woods on the hills of Sesto Fiorentino.

Without neglecting the investigation into the desecration at the New Chapels, Ferrara had given Sergi the job of continuing the search for possible witnesses who might be able to identify the satanists who frequented the area around the little church.

That morning, crouching on a hill, they had finally noticed something interesting. They could not take their eyes from their binoculars.

'I've counted four of them so far,' Ricci said.

'Me, too, Pino.'

'That house must be their base, Inspector.'

It was about half a mile from the ruined church and well camouflaged by trees. Perhaps it was an old hayloft, long disused and abandoned.

'Do you think we should search it, Inspector?'

'Don't be too hasty. We have to find out a bit more before we go in and take a look.'

'Whatever you say, chief.'

They fell silent and continued looking through their binoculars.

73

No, she had not had second thoughts.

The Russian girl had overcome her entirely understandable reluctance and confirmed to Teresa that she wanted to co-operate. She had given her the address of the dealer she had talked about.

Now it was almost six in the evening and she was getting ready to leave Headquarters to be transferred, together with some of her compatriots, to Fiumicino airport in Rome, where she would be put on a direct flight to Moscow.

'Remember, Karina,' Teresa said, while they were still alone in the office, 'if you have any problems, call me right away.' She slipped into the girl's hand a slip of paper with the telephone number of Headquarters and her own mobile number.

For the first time, a slight smile appeared on the girl's face. She put the paper in a plastic supermarket bag that contained her meagre belongings. Then, moved, she hugged Teresa, murmuring in her foreign accent, made even stronger by the emotion, 'Thank you.'

A policewoman took her out. From the window, Teresa watched her get in the bus and continued watching until the vehicle disappeared.

When the last of the illegals had left the building, Ferrara drew up a balance sheet of the operation with Ciuffi. In all, seventy-eight people had been repatriated, most of them suspected of dealing drugs or selling counterfeit goods. Soon they would call a press conference to announce the details to the media.

They were grabbing a bite to eat before the operation planned for that night.

Sergi went in first and held the door open for her. They were in the local trattoria in the Via San Gallo, near Headquarters. They sat down at a corner table, facing each other. As soon as they arrived, the owner recognised the inspector and led them to a corner table, the furthest from the entrance and also the quietest. They sat down facing each other.

Teresa Micalizi was radiant. She was going to work that night, too, but she didn't mind at all.

Sergi, on the other hand, had just got back from Sesto Fiorentino and seemed pensive.

'Have you telephoned your friend?' he asked.

'Friend? He's only a colleague. No, I haven't called him. To tell the truth, with all the work we've had, it went right out of my mind.'

The waiter came and they ordered a big steak for two with a side order of baked potatoes. To drink, the house red.

'I can't wait to get going,' Teresa said. 'Ciuffi has organised a whole series of raids and house searches.'

'It's going to take all night. But I'm sure it'll be very interesting for you. You'll get a chance to learn in the field. Florence is going to be an excellent training ground for you.'

'I can't wait,' she repeated, her eyes shining with a mixture of admiration and envy for her older colleague.

The waiter approached with the wine and poured it.

'To a brilliant career,' Sergi said. They raised their glasses.

After drinking, Sergi removed some traces of wine from his beard with a paper napkin.

'I'm well aware of the sacrifices I'll have to make,' Teresa said. 'My father was in the force. He had the old police rank of marshal.'

'Really? Where did he serve?'

'Various cities. Our family was constantly on the move. The last few years, in Milan, where . . . ' She hesitated.

'Where?' Sergi prompted.

'Nothing.' Her face had grown sad.

'Did something happen?'

'He was killed in a shoot-out with robbers.'

'I'm sorry. I've been in a situation like that myself. I carry a reminder of it under this beard. A scar that'll never go away.'

He turned pensive again. He was about to tell her that he, too, came from a family of police officers, but at that point the waiter arrived with their steak, already sliced, and they attacked it with gusto.

When the bill was presented, Teresa insisted on paying. 'Don't forget, Inspector, I owe you one.'

'Yes, but that was a pizza! That can be next time. Let's go Dutch.'

As Teresa took the money out of her purse, Sergi glimpsed a photograph of a mature man with a large moustache, wearing a marshal's uniform.

Her father.

Simultaneously, she noticed that her colleague's wallet was quite bulky.

He must have another source of income, she thought. His family, maybe?

74

Before going home, Ferrara summoned Venturi and Sergi.

'What did you find out at *La Nazione*?' he asked Venturi.

'Nothing more than was in the transcript, except for something about the voice. It sounded metallic, that's what the switchboard operator said.'

'Did they record it?'

'No. I was told they get so many calls from cranks and maniacs, they don't bother to record them. But I was assured they will from today in case the same person calls again.'

'And the initials? Were those the correct ones?'

'Yes. She was sure about that, she says she heard it clearly and wrote everything down on a piece of paper. That's why she's sure of the text.'

'Good. Write a detailed report and send a copy to Special Ops.'

'Special Ops?' Venturi asked, exchanging a rapid glance with Sergi.

'Yes. They're involved too.'

'Don't tell me the bullets really were marked.'

'Yes, they were.'

Venturi did not reply.

'Chief,' Sergi said, handing Ferrara a small file, 'I've

brought you the list of employees of the chapels, plus those staff from the Careggi Hospital who might have had access.'

It was a long list of names, all unfamiliar, except for Gustavo Lassotti, the director of the Institute of Forensic Medicine, and his colleagues.

'Good,' Ferrara said. 'I want to know if there's anything in our records on any of these people, even the ones we already know.'

'I'll get on to it right away.'

'There's something else I've been thinking about for a few days.'

'Go on, chief.'

'Could there possibly be an underground passage connecting the chapels to the nearby hospital, or coming out into open country? That would explain why nobody saw anything.'

'I'll check,' Sergi replied, looking somewhat sceptical.

'Seeing that there was no sign of a break-in, we also have to consider the possibility that whoever got in had a key.'

'What about the couple who were already inside?'

'There's nothing to indicate they had anything to do with it. Besides, they would have needed a key to get out through the side door. That might explain why the security guard didn't notice anything.' Then, changing the subject, Ferrara asked, 'How are things going at Sesto?'

Sergi told him about the little house they had spotted. He was in no doubt that this was the satanists' refuge. His men would continue the stakeout throughout the night.

'Good. Go to the Prosecutor's Department tomorrow morning and get a search warrant. We mustn't waste any time.'

'All right, chief.'

As soon as they'd left the room and were out of earshot, the two inspectors discussed the involvement of Special Ops. Neither man expected anything good to come of it. They knew how their colleagues worked, and both could remember occasions when Special Ops had proved reluctant to share their findings with anyone else.

This was only going to complicate the investigation into the latest murder.

75

Yorkshire, England

That evening, the grounds of the castle were more brightly lit than usual.

The air was saturated with the scent of flowers, and the pleasantly cool temperature made the place even more enchanting.

Plain-clothes policemen ensured the safety of the guests, who included politicians, businessmen, bankers, and the presidents of European and non-European multinationals, as they strolled about the grounds.

It was Sir George Holley's seventy-fifth birthday, although he looked at least ten years younger. There were no lines around his eyes or at the corners of his lips, and his hands were long, delicate and unblemished. He seemed ageless, as if time moved at a different rhythm for him.

He had decided to celebrate his birthday with his friends. Though in reality most of the guests were, at best, close acquaintances.

'Happy birthday, my dear George!'

These affectionate words came from Enrico Costanza, who had just got out of a large black chauffeur-driven Jaguar. He was wearing an elegant dark blue suit and an eye-catching bow tie instead of his usual tie. The two men were the same age, but the advance of his illness made Costanza look a lot older.

'Enrico! What a pleasure to see you. I never doubted for a moment that you would come.'

They embraced. Enrico was definitely someone he regarded as an old friend.

They had known each other for more than forty years and both belonged to the same Masonic lodge, within which there was a subsection for a chosen few.

'The pleasure is all mine, George. It's a real honour and privilege for me to be here at your party. I brought this little gift for you from Tuscany.' He handed him a neatly wrapped package with a note pinned to it. 'I do hope you like it.'

Sir George slowly opened the package and took out a gold Rolex, its face adorned with precious stones. It had been personalised: his initials and date of birth were engraved on the case.

'It's wonderful,' he said, turning his lively blue eyes to Enrico. 'Thank you. Thank you so much.'

'I also brought you something else,' his guest continued, and handed him a thin envelope. 'You know what it's about. Everything's been sorted, just as it had to be.'

'Thank you. I'll open it later, when everyone's gone. But please: I don't want a repeat of this, and let's hope nobody finds out about it.'

'I know I've been careless, very careless, but I didn't think it would happen at that particular moment. Anyway, everything's been sorted and there are no more risks. Trust me.'

'Let's hope you're right. What about your stepson?' He looked Enrico straight in the eyes, as if studying his reaction.

'He's still very loyal. He's all I care about since Elda died.'

'Are you sure?'

'I can vouch for it. But why do you ask?'

At that moment, a uniformed waiter appeared with a tray of cocktails and they had to interrupt their conversation. They took two glasses and raised them.

'Many happy returns!' Enrico said.

'Thank you, my friend.'

The waiter put the empty glasses back on the tray and continued moving among the guests.

'Thank you again. Now, Enrico, let's mingle.'

They passed from one small group to another, joining in each conversation long enough to exchange a few jokes.

By the time he was fifty, Sir George Holley had already reached the pinnacle of his success. He had everything that could be desired from life: a splendid family, health, luck in business. And not only that. He was also a powerful man, one of those who could decide the fate of nations. His children, one son and one daughter, had each given him a couple of grandchildren, who adored him and who would one day inherit his huge fortune.

They moved towards a group of five men, who were chatting among themselves in a corner of the grounds: a group who, when people they did not know well passed close to them, changed the subject and started discussing the wars in Iraq and Afghanistan, George Bush's blunders, world terrorism . . .

But their reaction was quite different when they saw their host and their Tuscan brother approaching. They all knew Enrico Costanza well: they, too, had been waiting for him. One after another they embraced him.

'What a good idea to meet here,' one of them said.

'Yes,' Sir George agreed. 'We won't attract any attention, not even from all these policemen. They're doing their duty, protecting us!'

The group burst out laughing, then Sir George asked Enrico to report the latest news from Italy.

He gave them a detailed account, concluding with the words he had previously used to Sir George: 'Everything's been sorted.'

'What about the investigation?'

'They're groping in the dark. They suspect Umberto Bartolotti, the son of that old man who ruined so many innocent lives. And so we've killed two birds with one stone. That family will have to disappear for ever. Which is only fitting, considering the harm it's done, even to some of us, am I right?'

The others nodded.

The handsome, aristocratic-looking young man seemed particularly pleased, as if at last the moment had come to settle an old score. But then his face clouded over. 'What about that chief superintendent who's come back?' he said. 'What if he starts prying?'

'Leave him be,' Enrico cut in. 'We have an important advantage. We're in a position to know all his moves. We know what he's going to do before he does it, which gives us time to change our plans.'

'Do you think they might suspect our informant?' Sir George asked.

'No,' Enrico replied, without a shadow of uncertainty. 'My contact is above suspicion. Talking of which, when this business is over, we'll have to do something for him. He's going to be increasingly useful to us. Thanks to him, I have something else to report . . . '

Everyone's eyes were on him.

'A couple of bugs have been placed in the chief superintendent's office. We'll know everything, including the information he usually keeps to himself. And we'll be able to hear everything he says on the phone.'

'Excellent!' said Sir George, who had already been informed of this initiative. 'With that in mind, I say we wait and follow developments. As far as our contact is concerned, he'll get his reward when the time comes. We never forget people who help us.'

They all nodded.

They knew very well that with money they could buy anything and anybody, and they could help those who helped them with promotions and raises, in England as in Italy and the United States. Most of these men had inherited the power they possessed from their fathers and they intended to pass it on to their own heirs. It went well beyond financial power; what they had was stronger than any government or state organisation.

76

After dinner, Ferrara resumed the task he had interrupted the previous evening.

And so, while Petra idled, he sat down in front of the computer to look again through the cases. He went through all the files, studied them, and from time to time tapped at the keyboard, compiling a chart that listed the most important details. Just before two in the morning, he printed the sheets and stared at them for a while.

Then he switched off the program and the computer.

When he got up from his desk, he glanced at the grandfather clock against the opposite wall and realised that he had been sitting there for nearly two hours. His eyes were smarting and he felt sore. He switched off the lights and immediately slipped into bed, taking care not to disturb Petra, who seemed at last to be sleeping well again.

77

Yorkshire, England

It was almost midnight, and by now all the guests had gone.

Sir George, however, had still not gone to bed. His curiosity was too great, and he had to satisfy it.

He went up the stone steps to his favourite room. He loved the leather sofa and armchairs there, and the 42-inch plasma television. He locked the door, took the DVD from the envelope Enrico had given him, inserted it into the player, and flopped into one of the two armchairs. He pressed play on the remote control.

'Let the show begin!'

The first shot showed a few figures approaching the church. Then a completely naked woman appeared. The camera focused on her for quite some time. A close-up lingered over a tattoo close to her groin: a black rose. The woman was standing in front of an altar with twelve candles. Six on each side. Behind her, an upturned crucifix. She was standing with one foot in front of the other. She had her arms raised behind her head and her face turned towards the floor.

A man came up behind the woman. He was hooded and wore a long cloak. He raised his left hand and struck her in the neck with a small knife. The woman collapsed on the floor. The image was static for a while, then the camera moved to frame other hooded men. Then the flames, getting ever higher.

Sir George watched the film a second time. Finally, he pressed stop and took the DVD out. He returned it to the envelope, stood up and went to a large mirror on one wall. He reached out his right hand and pressed a button hidden behind it. Then he put a corresponding pressure on the upper part and the mirror opened outwards, revealing a space of about six square feet. On one side was a collection of videocassettes and DVDs, lined up side by side. He added the latest one and closed the mirror.

Excellent work, he thought. Always so careful and meticulous.

He switched off the light and closed the door.

Now at last he could go to sleep.

Only one doubt remained, and it was a major one. Could they be sure the woman hadn't talked?

78

Night of Monday, 28 to Tuesday, 29 June

They had to decide how best to proceed.

They could lie in wait until somebody came home, or the owner came out, and then go in. At night, however, lying in wait could arouse suspicions. Or else, they could go in now, without knowing exactly what they would find inside. This was the simplest choice, but also the most dangerous, because the people inside the house would have time to react, maybe to start shooting.

After discussing it with his men, Ciuffi opted to go in, counting on the element of surprise. First they would surround the building, which was on the Via Pistoiese, far from the centre, in an area inhabited mainly by Chinese. They knew that it was a four-room building. The bolt on the gate had been replaced by a piece of barbed wire, twisted to form a loop knot.

Ciuffi rang the bell, yelling, 'Police! Open up!' Hearing no sound of footsteps approaching the door, he ordered his men to knock it down. A few minutes later they were inside.

Under their jackets, to minimise the risks, they were wearing bullet-proof vests. Teresa was among the first to enter. Like the others, she had a duty pistol, a Beretta 92/S.

Everyone was asleep. Even the owner of the house, curled up in a corner of the double bed.

He was a strong-looking, dark-skinned man of about forty, with a shaven head and a bull-like neck. He must have weighed at least fifteen stone.

Next to him in the bed was a young girl, little more than a child, with clear skin and blonde hair. She was naked and tried to cover her small breasts with the sheet. She seemed confused and terrified.

'Don't be afraid, we're police,' Ciuffi said.

Teresa went to her and gently placed a hand on her shoulder. 'Don't be afraid,' she too said.

The man suddenly leapt out of bed, stark naked. He threw a threatening glance at the girl, as if to intimidate her and stop her speaking. He got dressed while the police officers watched. From the other rooms came yelling in an incomprehensible language. There were seven men, all Moroccans. They had been made to get out of their bunk beds and stand with their faces turned towards the wall.

This place was more like a refuge than an ordinary apartment: everywhere there were cigarette butts, pages from newspapers, squashed beer and Coke cans, plastic bags, discarded paper tissues in the corners. The walls were filthy. Here and there the paint had peeled off. Only one window had a creased curtain, unhooked in several places. In one of the rooms they found piles of goods: all fakes, although good ones that could have fooled an untrained eye. They were still in their boxes, with nothing on the outside to indicate either the person they were intended for or who had sent them.

'Search all the rooms thoroughly,' Ciuffi ordered, after making sure the situation was under control. 'You, come with me,' he said to the owner of the house, who perfectly matched the description the Russian girl had given them.

He led the man into the kitchen. There was a small electric oven, a couple of pots encrusted with sauce and grease, a refrigerator and a table with four chairs.

Teresa stayed in the bedroom with a couple of officers and began searching it. It was her first search and she ignored the dirt. She remembered what she had learned at the academy: First, have a general look round, then make sure that those present are isolated and kept within sight, then check every object, piece of furniture, garment and so on, calmly and methodically. Then make a note of the place where each of the things to be taken away was originally found and the name of the officer who found each item. All these details would be needed in order to write up an accurate report.

The girl, who had put on a T-shirt and sat down on a chair, was now following the actions of the police officers with great curiosity. She seemed bewildered and even younger than before. When Teresa brought her the T-shirt, the young woman had murmured, 'I'm sixteen and he makes me work. If I don't, he beats me up.'

'To what do I owe this visit?' the owner of the house said calmly, even before Ciuffi had asked him any questions. 'My papers are in order. This is the first time in seven years you've checked up on me.'

'What about that girl?' Rizzo asked.

'She's young, but in her country, the Czech Republic, she was already walking the streets. Did you know that?'

'All I know is that I've found her in your bed, which means you've been having sexual relations with a girl who might be no older than fourteen or fifteen.'

'That's not her age and I'm helping her.'

At that moment a young officer appeared in the doorway,

followed by Teresa, who was holding a small transparent plastic bag in her hand.

'Sir, we found this in the toilet cistern,' the police officer said with a triumphant expression. Traffickers of this kind must be devoid of imagination to have used such a common hiding place. 'It's heroin,' the officer added.

'Good work,' Ciuffi said, with a smile.

Teresa looked pleased.

Karina had been telling the truth. And Teresa was seeing the fruits of her own labour. Relying on her own human gifts rather than on her role as a policewoman, she had managed to gain the trust of the Russian girl.

'When you've finished,' Ciuffi said, 'take all this back to Headquarters.' He grabbed the house owner by the arm. 'You're under arrest.'

The man did not seem at all intimidated. 'I don't know anything about those drugs,' he said. 'Someone else must have been hiding them.'

Ciuffi nodded without replying.

79

Little more than two hours later, everyone they had rounded up was in Headquarters. They were led out of two cars and a van and taken to different offices of the *Squadra Mobile*. Teresa had brought the girl in her car.

The corridors were still as they had left them: as bright as daylight.

Now they had to wait for the men's identities to be determined and for tests to confirm the nature and quantity of the drugs. They would have to establish whether they should charge only the owner of the house with possession or all those who lived there. Would any of them claim ownership, maybe in an attempt to clear the others? The police would grill them, but would they get any answers?

And all this would have to be done as quickly as possible. According to the code of criminal procedure, they could not detain these people for more than twenty-four hours, after which the case fell within the jurisdiction of the Prosecutor's Department, which would have to decide whether or not the arrests and the confiscation of the drugs was valid.

The owner of the house, identified as Nabil Boulam, had not been lying when he had declared that his residence permit was in order. He had come to Italy nearly seven years earlier and had formalised his position thanks to the Act of Indemnity 2002. At that time he had been working for a doctor – at least, that was what his papers said – as a domestic help.

In the meantime, Ciuffi had done a lot of thinking on what needed to be done, focusing on two factors above all.

One was the telephone call overheard by Karina: 'If he did that, he deserves a lesson, but I'll deal with it, and you deal with the debt . . . '

What did he mean by "lesson"? Murder? And what about the reference to debt? A missed payment for drugs? Or for fake merchandise?

The person Nabil Boulam had spoken to could not have been Moroccan. Otherwise, in order to avoid being understood by the Russian girl, Boulam wouldn't have spoken in Italian but his own language.

But there was nothing to make Ciuffi doubt that Karina had been telling the truth, especially after the discovery of the drugs.

The second factor was the likelihood that the man killed near the Ponte Vecchio had been trying to do some business of his own on Nabil Boulam's territory.

But was that enough to pin the murder on Boulam?

Ciuffi found that hard to believe.

It seemed to him unlikely that the man would commit a murder on his own territory, unless it had been unpremeditated. But if that had been the case, he certainly would not have stayed put in his own home, and he certainly would not have been keeping that quantity of drugs on the premises. And no weapons had been found on him during the search – although he could have hidden the murder weapon somewhere, or thrown it in the river.

Now Boulam was sitting in front of the desk for his first interview, while Teresa was talking to the girl in her office.

The game had begun.

'Quite a bit of heroin, more than half a kilo!' Ciuffi began, looking him in the eyes for a moment to catch some reaction. Then he looked at Boulam's hands and noticed the nicotine-yellowed fingers. He looked like the kind of person who smoked his cigarettes down to the last remaining scrap of tobacco.

'It's mine, Superintendent. It isn't true that I didn't know anything about it. The others have nothing to do with it.'

'Are you sure?'

'Yes.'

'How did you get hold of it?'

'You can't interrogate me without my lawyer. The law says I have a right to one.'

'I see. You don't want to be helped.'

'No, I made a mistake and it's right for me to pay.' His tone was sharp and resolute, his face like stone, his eyes cold, his back straight. He folded his arms. It was obvious that he had no intention of communicating further.

Ciuffi called an officer and had him taken to forensics for a gunshot-residue test, just to cover all the bases. Then, while waiting for him to be transferred to prison and the documents to be drawn up, they would keep him in the holding cells.

They were getting nowhere fast, Ciuffi told himself.

And yet, just over an hour later, Nabil Boulam was again sitting opposite Ciuffi.

The superintendent wondered if the man had changed his mind. After the forensics tests, he had asked on his own initiative to see Ciuffi once again.

Was he going to spill the beans in return for favours?

'All right, go on.'

The man heaved a big sigh and began speaking. He explained the deal he was proposing.

A deal that might prove useful to both parties.

80

Tuesday, 29 June

'How did it go last night?'

Ciuffi shook his head like a pendulum, a hint of a smile on his face. He exchanged glances with Teresa, then said, 'A profitable night, chief.' He went over the details of the operation, while Ferrara looked from him to Teresa and back again.

'So the Russian girl was telling the truth?'

'Yes, she was,' Teresa replied, with a hint of self-satisfaction in her voice.

'And this Nabil Boulam didn't want to go to Sollicciano prison. Did he tell you why?'

'He said he has a lot of enemies in there and he didn't think he'd get out alive, but that was as far as he'd go.'

'What exactly did he give you in return?'

Ciuffi explained that they needed to check on a rape that had happened a few days earlier. It had been committed by the Moroccan killed on the Ponte Vecchio, and was probably the reason why he had been eliminated.

'Did he tell you the name of the rape victim?'

'He said he didn't know it.'

'Or the name of the Moroccan who was killed?'

'He wouldn't tell me that either, though I'm sure he knows it.'

'Yes, he knows it all right.'

The two men nodded.

'Chief, I got the feeling he wanted to say more but didn't dare. So he supplied us with a motive, but didn't compromise himself more than he had to. My guess is, he didn't want to lose credibility in the circles he moves in.'

'In other words, he wants us to get there by ourselves. Unless, of course, he's involved in some way. So, do we know of any rapes in the last few days?'

'Only one, an American student who attends the Institute in the Via Brunelleschi.'

'We have to get in touch with her.'

'A patrol has already gone to fetch her.'

'Good, keep me informed. Did you confiscate his mobile phone?'

'We didn't find it. In fact, we didn't find a single mobile in the whole house. He told me he doesn't own one.'

'And yet the girl heard him talking on a mobile.'

'He may have it hidden somewhere.'

'Send a team to search the apartment again. There may be hiding places we missed.'

'I'll send them right away.'

'What prison is Nabil Boulam in?'

'Pisa. I talked to the deputy prosecutor on duty and he authorised it.'

'I think we'd better pay him a visit.'

'So do I, chief. He's going to have to tell us a bit more.'

Ciuffi left the room, leaving a copy of his report charging the Moroccans with being accessories in the illegal possession of drugs as well as being members of a criminal association dealing in narcotics. Nabil Boulam was additionally charged with aiding and abetting illegal immigration and sexual violence on a minor.

Teresa was about to follow him out, but was called back by Ferrara.

'Teresa, wait a moment.'

She turned abruptly. 'What is it, chief?' she asked in surprise.

'You've done a really good job.'

He did not yet know her well, but he was getting the idea that she knew what she was doing. Teresa's face lit up. All traces of her initial surprise had gone. This was real praise, the first she had had since she had joined. Her thoughts went immediately to her father.

'Thank you,' she said, 'but I only did my duty. Right now, I'm dealing with the girl. For the moment I'll try to get her sent to a home for minors.'

'Thanks, Teresa. Keep up the good work.'

81

Rizzo, who was just back from forensics, came into Ferrara's office.

'Anything new?'

'We may have something.'

'Let's hear it.'

'There are still only three decent shoe prints, as Gianni Fuschi told you on Sunday evening, but it's possible there might be more. The others don't seem to belong to the shoes already identified. Plus, the technicians have been trying to reconstruct the various directions they went in.'

Rizzo set down the sheet of paper he was holding in his hand. Ferrara leaned over to take a close look at it, placing his elbows on the desk. What he had in front of him was a genuine map drawn up by a good draughtsman.

'At a certain point they diverge,' Rizzo said, indicating a point on the map. 'As if the people have separated. Some seem to have gone into the mountains, over towards Monte Morello, others down towards the village, but after a while there are no more prints because they hit first a gravel path, then a paved road.'

Ferrara nodded. 'That confirms the hypothesis that it was a group following a pre-arranged plan, maybe even one that had been announced in advance . . .'

'Announced in advance?'

'Precisely, Francesco.'

He opened the top drawer of his desk and took out the photocopy of the anonymous letter from 2003.

'Read that, Francesco,' he said, handing it to him. 'An expert on the occult I spoke to gave a plausible explanation for the hooded ones and the roses . . . '

He waited until Rizzo had finished reading, then continued: 'I think it's worth paying Bartolotti a visit. I get the feeling he knows something. We already have his phone tapped, a visit from the police might be a way of stimulating him to make a few calls. What do you think'

Rizzo nodded. 'It seems like a very good idea, and if you don't mind, chief, I'd like to be the one to go.'

'Excellent.'

'How about tomorrow morning?'

'Perfect! That'll give us more time to listen to his conversations. And I'd like Teresa to go with you.'

'I'll tell her right away,' Rizzo replied, leaving the room.

In the Borgo Ognissanti barracks, the Carabinieri, too, were debating what to do next.

Among the day's mail, which had been placed on the marshal's desk, was a letter addressed to him personally, with no indication of the sender. An anonymous letter.

It was a single sheet of squared notepaper, the words on it written in capital letters:

MARSHAL GORI,
INVESTIGATE ALVISE INNOCENTI. HE'S A PERVERT.
HE SEXUALLY ABUSED HIS DAUGHTER WHEN SHE
WAS A TEENAGER. HE MUST PAY FOR HIS SINS.
A FLORENTINE

Gori and Surace passed it back and forth to each other several times, studying it carefully.

'What do you think?' the marshal asked.

'Makes sense,' Surace replied. 'Sexual abuse would explain the bad relationship between father and daughter, the fact that she left home as soon as she came of age, even his behaviour since her death.'

Gori nodded. 'And who do you think this "Florentine" could be?'

Surace smiled. 'Sara Genovese,' he replied without hesitation.

'Very likely,' Gori replied. 'Anyway, take this letter to forensics and let them have a look at it. We may find a few prints.'

'I'll do that right away, sir.'

It was time to confront Alvise Innocenti, and maybe Sara Genovese again also. The marshal was not afraid of Innocenti. He knew certain kinds of character well. He wasn't impressed by luxurious houses, butlers, cars, wealth displayed with ill-concealed pride. Of the two of them, it was Alvise Innocenti who ought to be feeling uncomfortable, who ought to be feeling fear, real fear, just like the lowliest criminal when the law catches up with him. In that splendid villa, buried in greenery, in perfect harmony with the lines of the Tuscan hills, there was probably a skeleton in the cupboard, a hidden story involving father and daughter. It must be uncovered, whether it was connected with the murder or not.

Without wasting any time, the marshal, having been given free rein by the Prosecutor's Department, to whom he had sent a preliminary report as requested by Prosecutor Fiore, drew up a formal summons and entrusted it to a patrol to deliver to Alvise Innocenti. He was to present himself at the barracks the next morning, Wednesday, at ten o'clock, to be interviewed as a third party with knowledge of the facts. The moment had come to clarify his relationship with his daughter and, if necessary, Gori would ask him straight out where he had been and what he had been doing on the evening and night of 24 June.

Innocenti would have to supply equally direct answers, supported by alibis.

Perhaps the marshal had found a way to untangle this whole intricate web.

82

In the meantime, Special Ops had obtained from the phone company the records for the switchboard of *La Nazione*.

The call had been made from a public phone booth in the Piazza Libertà with a prepaid five-euro phone card. The only call made on that card so far, but the company would monitor the card day by day for further use.

Ferrara was about to be updated by Ciuffi about the American student when the telephone rang.

He immediately recognised the voice. It was Giuseppe Barba, the head of Special Ops, a tall, burly officer with sleepy eyes and an unmistakable voice, almost as delicate as a little girl's.

'Thanks, Beppe, let's hope they inform us of other contacts,' Ferrara said, before hanging up.

'Well?' he asked Ciuffi.

'This isn't our case,' Ciuffi said. The American student, it turned out, was a young woman of seventeen who had accused the customer of a club in the Via Guelfa. She had drunk a lot and the man had tried to take advantage of her. She had managed to break free, had landed him a kick and taken refuge in the toilet, where she had asked other girls for help. The man was a young Florentine with no previous convictions, out of his head on a mix of alcohol and drugs.

'You're right, Luigi, this can't be our case. And I think it's urgent that we talk to Boulam again. Ask the deputy prosecutor for authorisation for an interview in prison.'

'I'll get right on to it, chief.'

'Did you get the results of the gunshot-residue test?'

'The lab just sent them to me. No traces. The expert was categorical. Nothing from the new search of the house either, chief. No weapons. No hiding places.'

'All right. All the more reason for him to tell us more, especially the truth.'

Ciuffi nodded. 'I'll grill him. We need to know about that call Karina overheard.'

The situation was critical, to say the least.

It was brought home to Ferrara as never before that his squad was not well prepared to deal with a case that had a satanic element to it. What was lacking was a ground map of the groups operating in the area and also of the deconsecrated churches spread around the Florentine countryside. His 120 men, who certainly weren't idling, were insufficient. They had other cases to solve, apart from all the routine duties that hadn't gone away: robberies, drug dealing, money laundering ...

What he had to do, then, was strengthen the team, hire more staff to cover the area and prevent further crimes. But how? He certainly couldn't take his men off cases in progress, so, after setting aside the idea of asking Rome for reinforcements, he decided to call on officers of the police mobile unit, whose main remit was public order. Based in a barracks in Poggio Imperiale, near the Piazzale Michelangelo, the mobile unit was made up of good officers, who knew how to move about and were dying to play their part.

He decided to raise it with the Commissioner, who liked the idea.

By that afternoon, four teams had been formed. Inspector Sergi was put in overall command. The territory was subdivided into quadrants. A team with specific tasks was assigned to each. It would identify suspects and keep watch on the isolated areas where the deconsecrated churches were located, if necessary using night-vision goggles.

Ferrara had employed a similar strategy in the 1980s, when he had worked in the Aspromonte, in Calabria, arresting kidnappers and releasing hostages. It was work that required patience, but it had paid off: the detailed map that had been drawn up, showing every sheepfold and cave and ravine, had turned out to be an essential tool in his success.

He would use the same tactic now, but with very different targets.

This time they would be hunting down the worshippers of Satan.

83

By now it was afternoon.

And at last Venturi brought in to Ferrara's office the long-awaited records of the mobile phone calls made from the area around the deconsecrated church, specifically from the Via Sanminiatelli, the street that climbed the hill from Sesto Fiorentino.

'There weren't many calls in the evening and night time during the twenty-four hours leading up to the murder. Twelve, to be exact. And I'd say that only one is suspicious, the one at eleven minutes past two in the morning. The mobile in question is registered to a woman named Beatrice Filangeri.'

Venturi passed him the records, on which he had highlighted that call in yellow.

Ferrara examined them.

The name Beatrice Filangeri didn't ring any bells for him.

'There are two phones here registered to the same person.'

'Precisely, chief. The phone that was called also turns out to be registered to Beatrice Filangeri.'

'A very short call, only a few seconds. We have to find out more.'

'I'll get on to it. But perhaps, chief, we need to go back more than twenty-four hours. At least to a week before the murder, to see if any of the twelve phone numbers on these records recur,' Venturi suggested.

'Excellent idea! And while we're about it, let's also examine the whole of Sunday and Monday. You never know.' Something told Ferrara they were on the right track.

'I'll put in a request with the Prosecutor's Department straight away,' the inspector replied with a smile on his lips, as he went out.

Was it really a lead? Instinct told Ferrara it was. But by itself, it wasn't enough.

That evening, Ferrara had an invitation to dinner.

Massimo Verga had organised it in order for his friend to meet Father Giulio Torre, that customer of his who was an expert on the occult.

The priest was young, with an honest, open face. The first impression was of a person of great charm, very different from the traditional priests Ferrara had known when he attended the local parish church in his native Catania.

They chose Il Latini in the Via dei Palchetti, one of the oldest restaurants in the city, where it was still possible to sample genuine Tuscan cuisine. They were familiar with Ferrara there, and the owner knew that, if he came there with someone else, it was best to be discreet. That was why, when he telephoned to make the reservation, they offered him a place either in the least crowded corner of the main room or on the first floor, which was even more secluded.

'Have you been here before?' Ferrara asked as they examined the menu, sitting in the almost deserted room on the upper floor. From the ceiling hung haunches of uncooked Tuscan ham, and the good smell of home cooking hovered in the air.

'Several times, Chief Superintendent,' the priest replied, a smile breaking over his chubby face. 'It's one of my favourite restaurants.'

'Then you don't need me to advise you on what to choose.'
Father Torre shook his head.

'He knows very well what to eat here,' Massimo interjected.

They ordered directly from the owner, the original Latini's son, who was still sprightly despite his advanced age and went out early every morning to personally stock up with fresh produce from the surrounding countryside. A gentleman of the old school, who treated his customers with great courtesy, an almost paternal familiarity.

While waiting for the food to arrive, Ferrara took up the subject that was foremost on his mind.

'Coincidences do exist in life, of course,' he said, 'but perhaps out of professional scepticism I'm always reluctant to accept them. And in this case there are too many of them. As I mentioned to you, in the last few days there have been three incidents that appear to have something connecting them. Only the fourth, the killing of the foreigner, seems so far to be a case apart, possibly having a racial motive.'

Urged on by his guest, he presented the facts in greater detail.

The desecration at the chapels.

The murder of Giovanna Innocenti.

The charred woman, apparently killed and set on fire during the celebration of a ritual.

'This last incident definitely has satanic elements. At least, that's what I've been led to believe by a reliable source.'

Father Torre had followed the account attentively, occasionally nodding approval. 'I agree with you, Chief Superintendent. This last incident does indeed have features typical of satanism. Unfortunately, there are people around who worship evil, even in its most extreme forms. I graduated in theology, specialising in demonology, so I've had a chance to study the phenomenon, and have even written a few books about it.'

'Ah, that's interesting.'

'If you like, I can let you have some of my publications; a couple are about satanism and the practices of certain secret societies in our country. I'll also send you a study on the same subject produced by the Ministry of the Interior. It dates from the early nineties. It's the only one of its kind and is still valid today. They must have it at Special Ops. I know that because, at the time, I helped to compile it.'

'I'd be very grateful, Father,' Ferrara replied, while reflecting inwardly on the absurd lack of communication between the different sections of Headquarters. Why had his colleague Barba, whom he met almost every morning during meetings with the Commissioner, never mentioned this study? It was all news to him.

In the meantime, a waiter had arrived with trays of uncooked ham, salami, fried courgettes, and potato rissoles, also fried.

Massimo filled the glasses with Nobile di Montepulciano. Father Torre held his up to the light: it was a fine garnet red colour. After the toast, he drank it all down in one go. 'Full and round,' he commented. 'One of the best Tuscan reds.'

'Definitely,' Ferrara confirmed, deciding not to mention the fact that in his native Sicily some younger entrepreneurs had started to produce excellent wines that would soon be widely admired.

'Chief Superintendent, the scar on the corpse and the murder in the church might be connected, but to be certain I'd need to read the documents. Maybe not all of them, but at least the most important, like the crime-scene reports. I'd also need to see the photographs. Images sometimes tell us more than words and reveal details that may seem insignificant to you police officers but are actually clues. I hope I'm not being indiscreet . . .'

'Not at all. I have no doubts regarding your ability to form a judgement.'

In the meantime, Massimo had refilled the glasses. The priest immediately lifted his to his lips.

'I need to form the broadest possible vision of the events,' he said. 'But I can already tell you that the scar on the corpse has a very specific esoteric significance.'

'What is it?'

'In satanism, and in the occult generally, there's a strong need to push beyond the limits. Anyone committing an act like that does so as a kind of challenge. The certainty of being discovered makes him feel particularly powerful.'

'If it's a challenge, who are they challenging?'

'That's for you to discover.' A smile crossed the priest's increasingly red face.

'What kind of personality could have committed such an act?'

'Not your classic psychopath. No, someone influenced by the esoteric culture, by popular magic, someone who – it can't be ruled out – wanted to challenge even himself, his own abilities.'

They drank again, and then the waiter approached with a large tray.

'Here we are,' he said, placing it on the table. 'Top-quality meat from Signor Latini's estate. True Florentine beefsteak. I recommend that you don't leave anything over.' His mouth opened in a wide smile, displaying his nicotine-blackened teeth.

'Truly delicious,' Father Torre said, after tasting the steak. 'As always. The kind of thing you can only enjoy in certain Tuscan restaurants.'

They fell silent and set about eating. And by the time they had finished there was indeed nothing left on the tray.

'What can you tell me about the charred woman?' Ferrara asked, taking another sip of wine.

Father Torre shrugged. 'From the details you've given me, I deduce that a genuine ritual was performed in that church. The woman was killed as a sacrifice to Satan.'

'What do you make of the fact that parts of her organs appear to have been removed?'

'That confirms that this was a human sacrifice. Organs are used by the initiates in their meetings.'

'Father, you've been very helpful. Would you be willing to examine all the documents and write a report?'

'Yes, of course.'

'Then I'll ask the deputy prosecutor to appoint you as our consultant.'

'That would make me very proud.'

They changed the subject. A few minutes later, the waiter arrived with the coffee and a bottle of grappa from San Gimignano.

The bill was paid by Massimo. Outside the restaurant, they said goodbye and went off in different directions.

Massimo and the priest set off together towards the Piazza della Repubblica, while Ferrara headed along the river to get home.

One thought was uppermost in his mind: the scar on the dead woman had been a challenge.

But who were they challenging?

Him?

84

Wednesday, 30 June

Teresa and Rizzo were surprised to be received by a thin young man in black trousers and a white shirt, his face stippled with acne. He looked no more than sixteen, maybe seventeen. Certainly a minor.

'I'm Dario,' he said simply, as he let them in.

He explained that Signor Bartolotti had yet to come back from his usual morning rounds of the farm, which supplied a number of shops in Tuscany and Emilia-Romagna with typical Tuscan produce. He admitted them to the living room.

'Please sit down,' he said, indicating two armchairs. 'Would you like a coffee while you're waiting?'

Both declined the coffee. They sat down and began to look around the large room with great curiosity.

The young man took up position by the window, like a guard dog, and stood there, sometimes looking outside, sometimes at the two visitors.

The room was filled with period furniture. On the walls, paintings that appeared genuine works of art. On the floor, large Persian rugs with floral patterns.

Suddenly both police officers' eyes were drawn, as if by a

magnet, to a perfect copy of Leonardo da Vinci's *St John the Baptist*: the saint with his finger raised, turning a languid, ambiguous gaze and a soft smile to the spectator. One of the Tuscan master's most mysterious works. They were so absorbed by it, they did not notice the arrival of their host.

'Good morning, officers,' a voice said behind them.

They turned.

'Good morning,' they both replied.

As they stood up and shook hands with Bartolotti, Dario crept out of the room.

For a moment, Bartolotti's eyes came to rest on Teresa's face.

That morning, Teresa Micalizi had dressed with great care. She was wearing a grey suit and a pair of high-heeled sandals. There was no trace of tiredness on her face. She looked impeccable.

She returned his gaze. What a charming man, she thought.

'I see you were admiring my St John,' he said with a smile. 'Were you struck by his boyish face framed by all those curls? His smile? Or was it the lifted finger? Do tell me!'

'All three,' Teresa replied, remembering her frequent conversations with her mother, who was a great art lover, 'but especially the darkness around the saint.'

'I see you know what you're talking about. Are you really a policewoman? I have my doubts.'

'Would you like to see my badge?'

'No, I believe you. Probably, like me, you'd rather contemplate the works of Leonardo than do your job. I'd love to continue talking about art, but I imagine you're here for another reason. Let's go into my study.'

Teresa and Rizzo followed him into a room furnished soberly with antique English furniture. On the walls were various oil paintings and a collection of nineteenth-century sabres. Behind the desk, on which sat a fine yellow leather blotter and a pair of period silver ink pots with small glass bottles, was a painting depicting the Madonna and Child. Below it, a little fireplace with a shelf in Carrara marble, on which stood two vases of fine porcelain.

Bartolotti invited them to sit down. He himself took his seat in a very old walnut armchair with carved uprights and helical crosspieces and supports.

At that moment, there was a light knock at the door, and Dario came in.

'Your coffee, Signor Bartolotti,' he said, putting the tray down on a little table.

'What about the officers?'

'They didn't want anything.'

'Well now, what can I do for you?' Bartolotti said, after sipping his coffee and smoothing his hair.

'We're here to see if you can help us,' Rizzo began, glancing at his colleague, who nodded. Then they both looked at Bartolotti, hoping to catch anything on his face that might betray what he was thinking.

'I really don't know how. I read all that talk in the newspapers about satanic rites, marks on the wall, and so on. Frankly, I find it all rather ridiculous. I can't believe there are people who go in for that kind of thing.'

'Unfortunately there are.'

'The world is getting sicker every day.'

'How long has the church been deconsecrated?'

'Ever since the fire that largely destroyed it. It used to be the family chapel. My brother and I were both baptised there.' He did not move a muscle as he said this.

'Do you have any idea who the victim might have been?' Teresa asked.

'No, I ... I have no idea,' he said, stammering slightly. 'Haven't you identified the woman yet?'

'No.'

Again the two officers exchanged glances.

'Have your employees come up with anything?' Rizzo asked.

'No.'

'Can they be trusted?'

'Absolutely. I've known them for many years. Pietro, the caretaker, has always worked for us. He took the place of his father, who was a real jack of all trades.'

'Would you be able to provide us with a list of your staff? It'll help us with our inquiries. Purely routine, of course.'

'No problem. I'll tell my secretary.' He picked up the phone and gave the order. 'It'll be ready in a few minutes.'

'Thank you.'

'But surely you don't suspect any of them?'

'No, but we have to explore every avenue, especially at the beginning of an investigation.'

'I understand. But if you'll excuse me, I really have to go now.' Bartolotti rose from his armchair.

Teresa and Rizzo followed him towards the exit, where they waited a few minutes.

Dario came running from a small building opposite, which presumably housed the offices.

'The secretary asked me to give you this,' he said, handing an envelope to Bartolotti, who immediately gave it to Rizzo without checking the contents.

The two officers thanked their host, said goodbye and left.

As soon as they got in the car, they looked at each other and both said, simultaneously, '"Haven't you identified the woman yet?"'

'Francesco, how did he know that? The papers only mentioned a charred body.'

'I knew that hadn't escaped you. I think we're going to have to take a closer look at this one. Either he's involved in some way, or he must have someone feeding him information, maybe in forensics.'

'I agree.'

'Let's pass the list to Sergi so that he can question these people, if he hasn't already done it.'

They set off. As they drove away, they saw a group of young people tending to some animals inside an enclosure.

'Kids, sent here because they don't have a family,' Rizzo commented. 'Or at least, no real family.' He had read about the home set up here, as well as some of the rumours.

'Sad, isn't it?' Teresa said.

In the meantime, Bartolotti had summoned Pietro. There were a few details he needed to know.

85

It was 10.20 and Alvise Innocenti had still not appeared. Waiting for him in his office, Marshal Gori was becoming increasingly impatient.

On the desk, there were no photographs showing him in his private life. Even the walls were bare. On the wall opposite were some shelves containing volumes on criminology and the history of the Carabinieri, and – the only evidence of his personal taste – a few books on Roman history. He loved the Imperial age and particularly admired Augustus.

As he waited, he ran through the list of clients of the estate agency, which Surace had left for him on his desk. None of the names rang a bell. He was reflecting on this when the sergeant arrived with a cup of steaming coffee in one hand and a sheet of paper in the other. Gori drank only a sip, then unfolded the paper and read.

'Sit down, Surace,' he said. 'The Innocentis' family doctor has certified that Alvise Innocenti has a serious heart problem and needs absolute rest and treatment for at least twenty days, unless there are complications, in which case it'll be longer. We'll proceed as per regulations and send the certificate to the deputy prosecutor, but in the meantime let's go there ourselves. If nothing else, we may finally be able to speak to his wife.'

Both men thought this illness was an excuse.

It was Laura Innocenti who opened the door to them. She did not seem at all surprised. She led them down a long corridor to the wing opposite the kitchen, where a greenhouse had been built on to the back of the villa.

'Please make yourselves comfortable. My husband needs absolute rest and can't see you. Perhaps you didn't receive the certificate?'

'Yes, we did receive it.'

'Well, I'm at your disposal. I brought you in here because this is where I spend most of my time. My daughter, too, when we lived together. We can talk freely here.'

They all sat down on wicker chairs around a table. They were surrounded by a large variety of plants, most of them evergreens.

After a glance around, the two Carabinieri took a good look at Laura Innocenti. It was the first time they had seen her properly. She was dressed in black. She had wavy, medium-length iron-grey hair and very blue eyes. There were lines on her face. Around her neck hung a mother-of-pearl rosary.

She lifted a hand to her lips, then asked, 'Tell me, is there any hope you'll find my daughter's killer?'

'We're doing everything we can, signora, but we'd be grateful if you could clarify certain points for us. We know very little about Giovanna's life. Can you tell us if there was anyone in whom she confided? Or if anything happened in her past that left a mark on her?'

'My daughter was very independent. When she came of age, she went right out of our lives. Young people want to be independent very early. As far as her past is concerned, all I can tell you is that she was a happy child and a happy teenager. She grew up in a loving environment. Ours is a very respectable family, I don't think I have to prove that to you.'

As she said these last words, she raised her voice slightly.

After a brief pause, she resumed, 'You might be able to find out more from Sara Genovese, her friend – and I emphasise *friend*. A sweet girl, whom I never had the pleasure to meet personally because my daughter never gave us the opportunity. But I know she was like a sister to her.'

'What kind of life did your daughter lead before she left home? Was she always with the two of you?'

'Generally, yes, but she also spent time in the countryside around Pontassieve, where we have another house and our vineyard. I assume you already know that, too.'

'Perhaps she met someone in Pontassieve who caused her problems?'

'Not as far as I'm aware. What I do know is that she used to have parties there with her friends.'

'Who were her friends?'

'Schoolmates, children of friends of the family, a few neighbours . . . All respectable people, of course. We never allowed her to associate with anyone dubious. I don't know if I've made myself clear . . . '

'Yes, signora, you've made yourself very clear. But please allow me one last question.'

'Go ahead, Marshal.'

'Do you remember where your husband was on the night of June the twenty-fourth?'

'Why do you ask me that?' Her face turned red. She seemed on the verge of losing her temper, but held back.

'It's just routine.'

'Well, it's easy enough to remember. He was at home with me.'

'Are you sure?'

'Yes. We're a very close couple. He was here.' She had raised her voice again.

Then, with the help of a stick, she stood up. 'Please excuse me. I have to take flowers to the cemetery.'

'We're very grateful to you for seeing us.'

Gori and Surace stood up and followed her.

As they walked down the same corridor as before, they noticed that a door was now ajar.

86

Ferrara opened the file and began reading.

This was the dossier compiled by Inspector Venturi on the person the two phones were registered to.

BEATRICE FILANGERI
Collation of Official Documents and Report

BEATRICE FILANGERI, née Guido, born Florence 10/02/1968, resident there, in Vicolo de' Greci, no number.

Identity Card AC7698325, issued Town Hall Florence 05/05/2000

Passport AA1765423, issued Police Headquarters Florence 12/07/2002 [see Appendix A]

Driving licence ABFI0754310

Weapons licence: none

Weapons possession: yes [see Appendix B]

Various: see Appendix C

Report:

The subject, divorced, comes from a family of retailers. An only child, she attended a school of performing arts.

She runs a chocolate shop in the Via Giuseppe Verdi.
She has never been stopped during police operations.
Not known to Vice or Narcotics. One charge of theft
when she was a minor, but the file does not seem to be
available. Perhaps, given the time passed, it has been
pulped or placed in the underground storerooms.

Report compiled in accordance with your instructions.

Signed: Inspector Riccardo Venturi

Florence, 29/06/2004

Ferrara lingered over the photograph attached to the passport
application contained in Appendix A. The face meant nothing to him. The woman had short dark hair.

Appendix B consisted of an application for authorisation to
purchase a pistol, a 6.35 calibre Beretta, to keep in her home.

Appendix C showed the report of the theft of her Nissan
Micra, a year earlier, as well as the fine she had had to pay for
contravening the hygiene rules in her chocolate shop.

The inspector had spent a couple of hours shut up in
records, on the top floor of Headquarters, which housed files
on all those who had had dealings of any kind with the
police – not only people who had committed offences but also
those who had applied for licences or reported crimes. He had
pulled out all documents that mentioned the woman's name,
read them carefully, taken notes and made a few photocopies.
By the end, his eyes had been smarting from the dust and his
nose itching.

'Can you pop in for a moment, Venturi?'

Ferrara still had the inspector's report in front of him and
the telephone receiver in his hand when Fanti came in, looking very agitated. Ferrara realised that something serious must
have happened.

'S-sorry, chief,' Fanti stammered.

'Calm down and tell me what's happened.'

'There are two women through there. They have information . . . '

'Calm down! Who are they?'

'Two Brazilian women. They work in some kind of private
club . . . '

'And?'

'They've come here because they think the person burnt in
that church might be their boss.'

'Send them in.'

They were both very beautiful.

Ferrara introduced himself and Inspector Venturi, who
had now arrived, and asked them to explain why they had
come.

'Our boss, Signora Madalena,' one of the two replied, 'has
been missing since Saturday night. And today is Wednesday.'

'I'm her niece,' the other woman said, apparently the more
upset of the two. 'My name is Ana Paula and I'm Brazilian.'

'Is your aunt Brazilian, too?'

'Yes, but she's been living in Florence for nearly twenty
years and . . . '

'Go on.'

'I'm afraid she might be the person burnt in that church,
the one the newspapers have been talking about for two days
now.'

'What makes you think that?'

The two women exchanged a long look. Then the niece
spoke again.

'My aunt had been using drugs for some time. And she was
often depressed, especially lately.'

Ferrara nodded.

'The person who supplied the drugs was the man she had an appointment with on Saturday night.'

'Where?'

'I don't know, but definitely outside the club. I saw her go out just after eleven and she never came back. But she had told me she was going to see a friend and would be back late.'

Silence descended.

The two women looked at each other again.

'Do you know the name of this friend?' Ferrara asked after a couple of minutes, during which a great many thoughts had come rushing into his head.

'No,' they both replied, almost in unison.

'Have you ever seen him?'

'Sometimes,' the niece replied, while the other nodded.

'Where?'

'At the club.'

'What's the name of the club?'

'The Madalena. It's a private club.'

'Could you describe this person?'

'Tall, regular build, quite good-looking . . .'

'How old?'

'About forty, perhaps a bit younger.'

'Is he a member?'

'No. He came from time to time to see my aunt in her apartment, and then went away again immediately.'

'Was he her boyfriend?'

'No, not as far as I know.'

'What was he, then?'

'I gathered he was the one who gave her heroin.'

'How did he get in? Was he known at the door?'

'That's possible, but you'd have to ask the doormen.'

'Why are you so convinced it's your aunt?'

The two women looked at each other once again. The niece

joined her hands on her knees. She was in obvious difficulty. She had assumed the typical attitude of someone who is undecided whether or not to tell the truth.

'Yes, signora?'

'When I read that some kind of magic ritual was being performed in that church, I thought of my aunt . . . '

'Why?'

'She's always been interested in the occult, ever since she lived in Brazil, in São Paulo. She loved to read tarot cards. She often read them for me. One day she implied she was interested in deconsecrated churches and I gathered she had gone to visit some near Pontassieve. The last time, she came back at dawn and she was very upset.'

'Did she tell you why?'

'No. She didn't tell me and I didn't understand, but she must have seen something disturbing . . . I can't even begin to imagine what.'

'I need to talk to the door staff at the club,' Ferrara said.

'I can give you their names. There are always two of them and they alternate. One starts work this evening at nine.'

'Good. Now follow Inspector Venturi here and you can lodge a formal missing persons report.'

A lover of the occult, tarot cards and deconsecrated churches – maybe it really was her . . .

87

There was news for the Carabinieri, too.

The lawyer Girolamo Rizzuto, with an office in the Via Strozzi, had been in touch with Sara Genovese to tell her that she had been named by Giovanna Innocenti as her sole heir and to summon her for four that afternoon.

Gori had found out from the tap on her phone and had immediately arranged for Sara to be followed. In order not to arouse suspicion, he would wait before questioning her again.

He was going through the details with Surace when Corporal Petrucci knocked at the door, came in and handed over an envelope.

Something else new.

Sara Genovese was punctual.

At exactly four o'clock that afternoon, after showing a client around an apartment, she rang the doorbell of the lawyer's office. A plain-clothes Carabiniere, standing among a crowd of tourists queuing outside Palazzo Strozzi to visit an exhibition, saw her go in through the solid front door.

Rizzuto told Sara Genovese that Giovanna Innocenti had drawn up her will six months earlier, making her the sole beneficiary. No mention of her parents.

She was astonished.

'Did Signora Innocenti talk to you about it?' the young lawyer asked.

'Not at all! It's a complete surprise ...'

When she came out, the Carabinierie followed her discreetly along the Via della Vigna Nuova, across the Piazza Goldoni and down the Via Borgognissanti, all the way back to her apartment.

So Giovanna had made her will months ago. But why? Had she had a premonition?

88

The two club doormen, summoned for five in the afternoon, presented themselves punctually at Headquarters.

They were both young men with good physiques, who looked as though they spent a lot of time at the gym. They were questioned separately.

Neither of them had a police record. They had never been arrested, never been reported to the police. Two years earlier, one of them had submitted an application for permission to carry a weapon on the grounds that he often carried money and valuables for the Madalena; this had been corroborated by the club's owner in a written declaration in which she assumed full responsibility.

He was the one Venturi decided to start with. Perhaps because, if the man proved reluctant, he could always be threatened with having his licence revoked.

His name was Biagio Puliti and he was twenty-seven years old. His Lycra T-shirt emphasised his solid chest. Tall, with fair hair swept back from his forehead and kept in place with a liberal application of gel, he looked like one of those fairly good-looking young men whose one ambition was to be on a TV talk show and pull lots of girls as a result.

He was visibly ill at ease, perhaps afraid to say the wrong

thing. He hesitated, weighing his words, even when giving the simplest answers. When Venturi decided that the time had come to question him about more delicate matters, Biagio Puliti wavered.

'Did you ever let anyone into the club who didn't have a membership card?' the inspector asked.

'No. Only members are allowed in.'

'Are you sure of that?'

'Of course.'

'Signor Puliti, we have reason to believe that an individual was sometimes admitted who wasn't a member. Someone who may have said a pre-arranged word or phrase and was allowed in to see the boss. Tell us the truth.'

The man's jaws contracted. He shifted on his chair. The reply was a long time coming.

'Signor Puliti, perhaps I didn't make myself sufficiently clear. If you don't tell us the truth, we'll be forced to revoke your weapons licence. We issued it to you, and we can take it away whenever we choose. Have I made myself clear now?'

The witness shook his head. 'If you take away my licence, I won't be able to work again. For me it's essential.'

'Then tell me the truth. I asked about this individual because I already have some idea of the answer. Come on, you haven't taken a vow of silence.'

Venturi had raised his voice. It was the crucial moment of the interrogation.

The man felt the inspector's eyes on him. At last he spoke up. 'Yes, there was someone I sometimes let in who wasn't a member. Always the same person.'

'You see, it wasn't so difficult after all. Carry on.'

'Signora Madalena told me to let him in.'

'And what was the man supposed to say?'

'He never said anything to me. He always showed one of

the club's business cards, signed on the back by the signora. That was his pass. That's the truth, but I beg you, don't ruin me. I have a son who's only two.'

'We don't ruin people, Signor Puliti, but we don't like being given the run-around either. Are you aware that your boss may have been murdered?'

'Murdered?'

'That's what her niece thinks.'

'Oh, no! She's such a good woman!'

'How many times did you see this man?'

'A few times.'

'How many? Two, three, how many times?'

The man was silent for another moment or two. Then he said, 'Twice, three times at the most.'

'Think hard. Are you sure it was only two or three times?'

'I think so.'

'Was he alone?'

'Yes.'

'Did you ever see him with anyone inside the club?'

'No. I swear I didn't. I never saw him in company. I would have known if he'd gone anywhere near our girls. Whenever he came, he went upstairs and then left.'

'When was the last time you saw him?'

'I think it was last Friday. Let me have a look at my diary.' He took from the inside pocket of his jacket a little diary and went through it quickly, then said, 'Yes, that's right. It was last Friday. I was on duty. And I remember he was up there longer than the other times.'

'Can you describe him physically?'

'About six feet tall, a bit taller than me, I'm five-eight. Longish hair. Quite fair, I think. No beard or moustache. A round kind of face and . . .'

He broke off for a moment.

'And?'

'. . . I remember he had these longish arms. It struck me when he showed me the business card. He was also a bit buttoned up, I don't know how to put it . . . I mean, he was quite standoffish, didn't want to talk to anyone. Looked very bright, though. I don't know if I'm explaining myself well.'

'You're doing fine. Can you remember anything else about him? Some unusual mannerism, a twitch?'

Puliti seemed to be thinking hard, but said nothing.

'Okay,' Venturi said. 'I'm going to call someone from forensics so that we can put together an identikit. In the meantime, try to remember.'

While Puliti was talking to the expert in another room, Venturi questioned the other doorman. After a few moments' hesitation, he admitted that he had seen the guest on several occasions. Maybe six or seven times during his shifts, always late in the evening.

Then the inspector went to see Ferrara to bring him up to date and receive new instructions. He would have to go with a team to the club to check Madalena's apartment.

'If we're lucky,' Ferrara said, 'we'll track down the dental X-rays we need for a comparison. I'm sure the niece, Ana Paula, will be willing to help. If not, let me know and we'll get a search warrant.'

89

There were prints on the anonymous letter.

Corporal Petrucci's envelope contained the report of the fingerprint expert. Some of the prints had fourteen or fifteen characteristic marks, others sixteen, seventeen or more, which meant they were perfectly usable. There was only one possibility in tens of millions that even a fragment of a print with seventeen marks could have been left by an individual other than the one to whom it had been attributed.

And the prime suspect could only be Sara Genovese.

After a murder, the police and Carabinieri often received anonymous letters, some written by fantasists, others by people working out a grudge against a relative, an old friend, or a neighbour. In among them, though, there were letters that actually told the truth and helped to bring murderers to justice.

This letter might well fall into the latter category.

Gori and Surace were weighing up the best way to proceed. It was not an easy decision.

'Sir,' Surace suggested, after they had discussed it for some time without coming to a conclusion, 'we could summon her on the pretext that we want to take a statement about the incident in the Parco delle Cascine, and take advantage of her being here to get her prints, maybe from the paper she touches when she signs, or else from a glass. We could offer her a drink of water or something. What do you say?'

'That's certainly possible,' Gori replied. 'The incident in the park was mentioned as part of an informal conversation, and we never took a statement. I don't see why Sara Genovese should suspect anything.'

'And then, once we have a positive match, we can question her about the anonymous letter.'

'And the inheritance.'

'When should we summon her?'

'Tomorrow morning at eleven.'

'Good. I'll issue the summons right away.'

90

There were no problems. Ana Paula was perfectly willing.

She let the police officers into the first-floor apartment above the club, holding in her arms, like a baby, her aunt's puppy. It looked sad, perhaps because it was missing its mistress.

'I've been looking for the X-rays, Inspector, they must be around. I'll keep searching while you look in the bedroom. Almost all my aunt's things are in there.'

Putting the puppy down on a chair, she walked into the adjacent room, used as a storeroom.

When, after about half an hour, she came back with a box in her hand, the officers were still searching. Some objects had been placed on the bedside table. She gave a quick glance, then asked, 'Anything useful?'

It was Venturi who replied.

'We found drugs, perhaps heroin,' he said, indicating a small jewel box. 'It was in the top drawer of the bedside table, along with some hypodermic syringes.'

She was not at all surprised. 'It was that man who brought her the drugs. And these?'

'Diaries, address books. We'd like to examine them back at Headquarters. Do you have any objection to our taking them away?'

No, she replied after a moment's reflection, she didn't have any objection, provided everything was brought back eventually. Those books and papers belonged to her aunt and she would like to keep them.

'Don't worry, you'll get everything back.'

Venturi lifted the lid of the box that Ana Paula had brought in.

'These are all the X-rays my aunt had taken in the last few years, Inspector.'

'X-rays of her teeth?'

'Among other things. She suffered from a bad case of paradentosis and was in treatment for several years. As she also suffered from arthrosis, I think there must also be X-rays of her spinal column.'

'Thank you. We'll examine all this at Headquarters, if you don't mind.'

'You can take them away, but please give them back.'

'Of course. I promise.'

'Thanks.'

The officers finished their search. Ana Paula watched them leave, the puppy once again in her arms.

The orphaned puppy – if indeed its mistress was dead.

Any remaining doubts were to be swept away within a few hours.

Ferrara was at home when he got the telephone call from Franceschini. The dental X-rays handed over by the niece matched the teeth on the charred corpse.

Ferrara immediately telephoned the deputy prosecutor, who had already been informed by the pathologist.

So it was Madalena who had been the victim of the satanic ritual.

But why?

PART FOUR

SURPRISES

91

Night of Wednesday, 30 June to Thursday, 1 July

He parked the jeep in the same side street, a long way from the main square.

Then he set off with the resolute stride of someone with a very specific destination. The moonless sky was pitch-black, the only light coming from the street lamps around the square and the intermittent glow of the traffic lights at the junction.

The little building, too, was completely dark, but by now he knew everything he needed. The layout of the apartments, the people who lived there, their habits. He opened the front door with a copy of the key. He had had it made for him by an acquaintance, a criminal from Prato who was an expert in that kind of work, after taking a cast two nights earlier. Then, using a second key, obtained by the same method, he opened the door to Silvia de Luca's apartment.

Once he was inside, he took the black hood from the inner pocket of his winter jacket and put it over his head.

He had studied the apartment with great care. He knew that it consisted of five rooms, and that only one person slept here at night: this supposed expert on the occult and black magic, who was helping the police. He quickly walked along the corridor to the bedroom and stood outside the door, listening. The only sound he heard was the woman's faint snore. He opened the door, turning the handle slowly, and closed it behind him without making the slightest noise. His eyes were accustomed to the darkness. He was a true professional.

Silvia de Luca was curled up on the left-hand side of the double bed. She was wearing a white linen nightdress. He had been watching her continuously from early that afternoon and, soon after eleven at night, he had seen her come to the windows to close the shutters. From the street she had seemed to him a very attractive woman, still capable of a sex life, but he was not there to rape her. He had to kill her. And then do something else.

The silk scarf filled her mouth in an instant.

Still half asleep, she was unable to cry out, and took a few moments to understand what was happening. Instinctively, she tensed every muscle of her body. Her attacker held her down on the bed while she thrashed about. It was a real struggle. The woman was turning out to be stronger than he had imagined. She was fighting for her survival, trying to push away the hands that were throttling her. Desperately, she reached out a hand, took hold of his hood, tore it from his head, and with her other hand grabbed him by the hair.

But he did not panic. Tightening his grip on her neck, he beat her head against the iron bedhead, repeatedly, until he felt her grip weaken. One last time, harder than ever, and it seemed to him that her cranium had split into a thousand pieces. He turned her over and, holding her face down with one arm, looked for the hood with his free hand. It was in her right fist. He wrenched it free and put it back on his head. Then, with both arms, he lifted the body from the bed and threw it down on the floor.

He turned her on to her back and looked in her eyes. They

were lifeless. Blood was gushing from her smashed head, staining her nightdress. He lifted the garment right up to her neck then tore it away from her head and threw it irritably on the bed. He laid the body out again, now almost naked, on the floor. He took off the knickers, pulled a knife from his jacket and made a few precise incisions in the skin. Then he arranged her with her arms and legs outspread.

But he had not finished.

He turned on the lamp on the bedside table, and with the blade of the knife extracted from under the nails of the woman's hand the pieces of fibre taken from the hood. He put them in his pocket together with the weapon. Then he took out a necklace and put it round her neck. He checked her pulse. Nothing.

Silvia de Luca was dead.

He picked up the nightdress and the knickers and put them in a small plastic bag. He replaced them with other garments that he had brought with him. With one last glance at the corpse, he left the room and walked back down the corridor to the apartment door.

He was about to open it when he heard a noise.

Someone had just entered the building. It must be the nurse upstairs who always came back late, he told himself.

He stood there motionless, his ear against the door. In his right hand, the knife, ready to be used. The steps continued up the stairs. He heard the sound of a door closing. He had not been mistaken. He put the knife back in his pocket and stood there for a few more minutes, then took off his hood, left the apartment and then the building, and headed back to the jeep.

As he walked away, he glanced back at the building. It was completely quiet. In the square and on the pavements there wasn't a soul about. He imagined the woman's body in the position in which he had left it and her daughter's face when she came in at about eight in the morning to drop off the children on the way to work. He checked his watch. It was just before five o'clock. As he reached the first houses of the city, he passed a police car and the blood in his temples began throbbing. But the officers took no notice of the jeep and drove past.

He put his foot on the accelerator. Fortune had smiled on him yet again!

92

Thursday, 1 July

The marshal was in the colonel's office, bringing him up to date on the progress of the investigation, especially with regard to the anonymous letter and the victim's inheritance, when the telephone rang. It was the Carabinieri commander at the Galluzzo barracks.

The call was a brief one.

'Shit!' the colonel yelled at the top of his voice, after he had hung up. 'That's all we needed. What the fuck is going on in this city?' Then he fell silent.

Gori continued to look at him, not daring to open his mouth. He had never before heard the colonel express himself in such terms. He assumed that whatever had made this man, usually so polite and measured when talking to his officers, lose control like that must be something terrible.

When Parisi at last spoke, it was to tell him about the murder of Silvia de Luca.

'I want you on the scene now,' he ordered.

'Absolutely, sir,' Gori replied, moving swiftly to the door.

After he had gone, Parisi sat there motionless, staring into the distance. When would they get back to normal? It was as if Florence was under attack by hordes of murderers.

Or was it only one?

The same news soon reached the operations room at Police Headquarters, and surprised Ferrara as he was busy with his morning meeting with his colleagues, where they were discussing the latest developments, and especially the identification of Madalena as the victim of the satanic ritual.

Ferrara was just suggesting that they release to the press the identikit produced with the help of the two doormen when the call came.

His face clouded over as he listened, then he slammed down the receiver.

'Bad news, chief?' Rizzo asked.

'Silvia de Luca has been killed,' he replied, looking straight at Venturi, whose face immediately darkened. 'I'm going to the scene. Venturi, come with me. The rest of you, continue the meeting. Francesco, I'll leave you to organise a press conference for the release of the identikit. We can't waste any more time.'

Rizzo nodded, wondering who this person was and why the news had so disturbed his chief. He would have liked to go with him, but he knew that his presence at Headquarters was indispensable right now.

'If I'm not back in time, Francesco,' Ferrara went on, 'you hold the conference. And have enough copies of the identikit made to distribute to every patrol in the area.'

'Of course, chief,' Rizzo replied.

But Ferrara was already in the corridor. Tormented by the thought that he had made a mistake.

In the days that followed, he was often to wonder whether

Silvia de Luca would have been killed if he had not gone to see her at her home.

Yes, he had made a mistake.

An unforgivable one.

93

There were a number of people outside the building. And several Carabinieri cars, some double parked.

The driver stopped the Alfa 156 with a screech of tyres, and Ferrara and Venturi jumped out.

The neighbours were looking out of their windows, horror-struck. In the square, locals were gathering in small groups, talking heatedly, their eyes fixed on the building where Silvia de Luca had lived. She had not been the most forthcoming of women, and many of them had found it difficult to connect with her. She had also, occasionally, been the subject of gossip.

The first journalists had already switched on their microphones for the interviews. Others would soon arrive, and of course there would be photographers, too.

Ferrara and Venturi found Marshal Gori in the bedroom.

Together with the other Carabinieri, Gori was staring in silence at the woman's body. She lay in a pool of dark blood, now congealed. The floor around her head was completely saturated with blood. The sight made Ferrara's stomach lurch. He exchanged glances with Venturi and recoiled slightly.

The marshal came up to him. 'Wounds on the hands, feet and chest, as well as the head,' he said. 'Her head was definitely beaten against the bedhead.'

The corpse was completely naked and the killer had left on the soles of the feet and in the palms of both hands marks that recalled the nails on the body of Christ. He had also placed the body in the same position as that of Giovanna Innocenti.

Was it a signature?

Ferrara hoped that the woman had not been raped, that at least she had been spared that.

'We know from her daughter,' Gori went on, 'who's in another room with my sergeant, that a nightdress is missing. Her mother never slept without one, not even in the middle of summer. The one that's missing is a white linen nightdress that she herself gave her mother for her birthday.'

'Maybe the killer took it away with him.'

'Precisely. This is looking more and more like the work of the same man who killed the Innocenti girl. We didn't find her underwear either, or any sign of a break-in at the apartment.'

Ferrara nodded. By now he had studied the Innocenti case and knew everything there was to know about it.

'The killer must have been someone she knew,' he said.

'That's what we thought about the Innocenti girl too,' Gori replied.

Could they both have been killed by someone they knew? Ferrara wondered. But what connection could there possibly be between the two women?

'The daughter told us something else,' Gori went on. 'She said her mother met you and a policeman friend of hers on Sunday.'

'That's true, Marshal,' Ferrara replied immediately. 'I would have told you. She gave us some suggestions about the incident in Sesto Fiorentino. She was an expert on the occult. The policeman friend was Inspector Venturi here. We were together.'

Venturi nodded. 'She was a dear friend, very special.'

'And she lived alone,' Gori said. 'Her husband died last year.'

'I knew she was a widow,' Ferrara replied. 'She told me on Sunday.'

The pathologist arrived. Once again, it was Piero Franceschini. Immediately afterwards Deputy Prosecutor Luigi Vinci arrived. He was not on duty that day, but when the news had reached the Prosecutor's Department, the chief prosecutor had entrusted him with the case because of its possible connection with the previous ones, in accordance with the rule that allowed the same prosecutor to deal with two different crimes simultaneously provided they were thought to be linked.

Ferrara thought it best to inform Vinci of the conversation he had had with the victim on Sunday.

'When we've finished here,' Vinci replied, 'and this includes you, Marshal, we should all meet in my office and discuss the matter in more detail.' He looked at Ferrara for a moment, as if thinking he might be hiding something. 'I need to know absolutely everything about that conversation, Chief Superintendent. Oh, and by the way, before I came here, Prosecutor Fiore asked me about you. He wants to talk to you, though I don't know what about.'

What could he possibly want? Ferrara wondered. He smelt a rat: he wasn't often personally summoned by the chief prosecutor. Usually his relations with the Prosecutor's Department were limited to direct contact with the various deputies who were in charge of cases. He couldn't imagine what Luca Fiore wanted with him.

In the meantime, Franceschini had been examining the body. 'The skull is fractured,' he said, his fingers in the dead woman's hair. 'She was struck violently on the head several times. There are signs of a struggle on her forearms and hands. One nail of her right hand is broken. She may have scratched her attacker.'

At that moment, Corporal Petrucci approached the little group, holding a small plastic bag in his gloved hand.

'They aren't the victim's,' he said, addressing the marshal. 'The daughter denies that categorically. The mother didn't wear a G-string, and besides, the bra is much too small.'

'What is it?' Vinci asked.

'We found a red G-string and bra on the bed,' Gori said. 'We thought they were the victim's.'

'Let me see,' Vinci said.

Petrucci took the garments from the bag and carefully laid them on the bedside table. He turned them over several times, then, after everyone had looked at them carefully, put them back in the bag.

'Thank you,' Vinci said. 'Let's allow the pathologist to get on with his work.'

Franceschini's external examination of the corpse was meticulous.

There were visible haematomas on the victim's body, especially on the arms, confirming that she had tried to defend herself. Franceschini also noted that the wounds to the feet, hands and chest had been made when she was already dead. A quick test with his portable kit suggested that the woman had not been subjected to sexual violence. From the measurement of both the rectal temperature and the room temperature, as well as from the presence of hypostatic stains, death could be assumed to have occurred the previous night, between two and four in the morning.

When he had finished, Franceschini took off the victim's necklace and handed it to the marshal, who in the meantime had put on a pair of gloves. It was a gold necklace. Gori stared at the small medallion. He turned it over and was startled to see on the back of it the words: TO GIOVANNA FROM SARA.

And a date: 24 JUNE 2000.

It was Giovanna Innocenti's necklace.

There was no end to the surprises in this case, he thought bitterly.

The first thing he wondered was why Sara Genovese had not told him about the necklace. It was quite likely that the G-string and bra had belonged to Giovanna, too.

The two cases were linked. There could no longer be any doubt about it. But what was the thread that connected them?

During the search of the apartment, which took several hours, the technicians from the Carabinieri forensics team found a couple of long hairs, complete with their roots, which suggested they had been pulled out. They were on the floor, next to the bed. Their structure and light colour suggested that they had not belonged to Silvia de Luca. They were packaged up to be sent to the lab for DNA testing, where they would be compared with samples taken from suspects. Assuming there were any.

No sooner did Ferrara step out of the front door than the photographers began snapping him. He walked quickly towards his duty car. The reporters from the tabloids ran after him, bombarding him with questions.

'What do you think of all these murders, Chief Superintendent?'

'Talk to the Prosecutor's Department. Ask Deputy Prosecutor Vinci.'

'Tell us something, Chief Superintendent,' someone cried. 'Anything!'

Ferrara did not reply.

'Does this murder also have something to do with

satanists?' one journalist insisted. 'People around here are saying some odd things about the victim.'

'No comment,' Ferrara replied, getting into the Alfa 156.

He did not realise it, but perhaps he was making another mistake by antagonising the press. On other occasions, he had been shrewd enough to make them feel they were getting inside information, when in reality he was only feeding them unimportant titbits.

'Where shall I take you, chief?' the driver asked.

'To the Prosecutor's Department.'

The car set off, screeching on the tarmac.

Now to see what the hell Luca Fiore wanted . . .

94

The door opened.

And Ferrara caught the words of the prosecutor to the person who was just leaving:

'It's always a pleasure to see you.'

Ferrara looked vaguely at the smartly dressed old man who came out. Something about him looked familiar.

Then, from behind the door, which was still ajar, he heard the words: 'Come in, come in.'

Clearly he was expected. The secretary must have told Fiore he was here over the intercom.

Ferrara went in, still wondering why that old man's face had struck him as familiar.

Luca Fiore was sitting at his desk. Behind him was a painting depicting a knight in armour, fixed lopsidedly to the wall. The few times he had been in this office, he had always found it in the same position, as if neither Fiore nor the cleaning lady took any notice of it. Maybe the prosecutor liked it that way.

'Come in, come in, Chief Superintendent!'

Ferrara walked up to the desk. He was expecting to be invited to sit down, but no such invitation came.

'Tell me, Chief Superintendent, what were you thinking of?'

'Me?'

Fiore did not have the reputation of being an unpleasant man, but his manner and above all the tone in which he had just addressed Ferrara revealed a side to his personality the chief superintendent had previously been unaware of. The hostility was tangible. With some difficulty, he suppressed the instinct to simply turn and walk out and forced himself to maintain his natural composure.

'Yes, you. What were you thinking of?' The tone was openly aggressive now, as if he could barely contain his anger.

'I don't know what you're referring to,' Ferrara replied, still with no idea where Fiore was going with this. 'I'm simply doing my duty.'

'Your duty! Your duty! Did I or did I not tell you that any personal initiative had first to be agreed with this office?'

'Yes, you did. And that's what we're doing. We're carrying out your deputy's instructions.'

'And what authority did you have from my deputy to search the Madalena Club and seize the membership list?'

'My men didn't search the club, and didn't seize anything.'

'I heard differently.'

'Then you must have heard wrong. The owner's niece allowed us access to her apartment and willingly handed over some material, which we'll give back after we've examined it.'

'It comes to the same thing, Chief Superintendent. You didn't inform us of this activity. My colleague Vinci told me you phoned him last night, but didn't tell him anything about the material you took away.'

'I would have told him about it this morning. Last night it was late and I just told Deputy Prosecutor Vinci about the X-rays, informing him that they had been handed over by the niece of her own free will.'

'Well, I don't want it to happen again, Chief Superintendent.

I caution you against taking initiatives. I'm going to write a formal letter to your Commissioner today. Now tell me, have you been investigating the owner of this club?'

Ferrara was in no hurry to answer. There were too many thoughts that were crowding into his mind.

'I assume you haven't had time . . . '

Ferrara nodded.

'In that case I order you to inform me as soon as possible about anything that emerges. Investigate the woman herself, nothing else. Do you understand?'

All Ferrara could do was nod again.

The telephone rang.

'Hello? Yes, send him in.'

He put the phone down and said to Ferrara, 'You can go and see Deputy Prosecutor Vinci now. Don't forget: each man must respect his own role. I don't want any abuse of power.'

Ferrara walked towards the door, muttering under his breath words to the effect that Fiore was an idiot. So intense was this thought that for a moment he was afraid he had actually said it out loud.

Clearly, among the material collected from Madalena's apartment, there was a membership list, a list that must be worrying some people. That made him all the more eager to investigate Madalena. And the list would be the first thing he would look at.

95

After waiting almost an hour in the corridor for the others to arrive, Ferrara finally made it into the deputy prosecutor's office. By this time he was seething with anger and resentment.

'At this point,' Vinci started by saying, 'it seems the likeliest hypothesis is that we're dealing with a serial killer.'

That meant they'd now be calling in the usual experts, Ferrara thought, who would give the usual advice: Look for a solitary type, from a dysfunctional family, perhaps with an obsessive and domineering mother. A man who finds it hard to connect with people, especially women. In fact, he hates women so much that he kills them. He may be impotent, unmarried, or else married and divorced . . . et cetera.

'What do you think?' Vinci asked. 'Organised or disorganised?'

Vinci was referring to the classification proposed in 1988 by former FBI agent Robert K. Ressler, who had become director of the organisation's Behavioral Sciences Unit at Quantico in Virginia. According to Ressler, the organised killer chose his victims on the basis of common elements such as age, race, appearance, lifestyle and so on. With the disorganised killer, on the other hand, the victims were chosen purely at random.

'Definitely organised,' Marshal Gori replied.

He had attended a course at Quantico in the late 1980s, when both the police and the Carabinieri had sent some of their officers for training with the FBI to learn more about serial killers, a little-known phenomenon in Italy at the time.

'It's proved by the choice of victims,' Gori continued. 'Giovanna Innocenti and Silvia de Luca. This second murder confirms it. The objects found, the underwear, especially the Innocenti girl's necklace. We still have to establish what they have in common.'

Vinci nodded, but Ferrara seemed to be listening with only half an ear.

'Carry on, Marshal.'

'We have to assume that we're dealing with an individual who's apparently quite normal, although probably with an above-average IQ. He won't be easy to track down ... '

'We're all conscious of these difficulties,' Vinci intervened. 'But he may have made a mistake last night.'

'Yes, that's true,' the marshal said. 'The hair ... I've already given instructions to our experts in the forensics department to run tests.'

'All right,' Vinci said, dubiously. 'But then whose hair do we compare it with?'

There followed a long silence.

'And what might be the motives that have driven him to kill?' Vinci asked. 'Since you've had training in this, Marshal, why don't you go through it for us?'

Gori listed the five types of serial killer: the visionary, the missionary, the thrill killer, the control freak and the lust killer.

'And which category do you think our man belongs to?' Vinci asked.

'That's a problem. Considering the crimes, I'd say either a visionary or a thrill killer.'

'Meaning what?'

'The visionary kills because he's received orders given by imaginary voices. In this case, if there's a connection with the incident in the church, that might have been Satan.'

'So the cases might be linked? What makes you think that?'

The marshal thought for a moment, then replied, 'At the moment there's nothing to link them, apart from the fact that it was in connection with his investigation of the murder in the church that Chief Superintendent Ferrara went to see Silvia de Luca. But I don't think we should rule out the possibility that it's all part of the same criminal project.'

'So Satan could be the voice giving orders to the killer?'

'That's right.'

'And the thrill killer?'

'He's someone who gets a particular pleasure from killing. Murder provides him with a real thrill, a kind of emotional orgasm.'

'The kind a gambler feels when he wins a bet?'

'Precisely! The murders seem to have a sexual connotation, but the killer didn't rape his victims: his pleasure came from killing them as brutally as possible.'

'I understand. Well, I think, Marshal, that you've given us some very valuable pointers. But several people seem to have been involved in what took place at the church. That hardly seems to fit with the idea of a lone killer.'

'That's the one element that doesn't seem to fit,' Gori admitted.

'Perhaps now we can hear what the chief superintendent thinks,' Vinci said.

Ferrara had continued to listen distractedly to this little lecture. For him it was nothing new. In his mind he kept replaying the image of Silvia de Luca as they had found her, naked and crucified on the floor, and in his ears he heard the words of Luca Fiore. He had thought over and over about the man he had passed on his way into the prosecutor's office. He could not swear to it, but he had the feeling the man was a well-known political figure, someone who had been prominent a few years earlier but had since faded from the scene.

Was it possible that the politicians were getting involved?

He was just asking himself that question when Vinci addressed him.

He pulled himself together. 'If it wasn't for what happened in that church,' he began, 'the idea of a serial killer might be feasible. But I find it difficult to believe that a lone killer could have killed the woman in the church, at least in that way. Several people must have been involved, the shoe prints prove that. And only in this last case are there elements pointing to satanism, which leads me to think we're dealing with a group of criminals who are satanists.'

'We certainly can't ignore those elements,' Vinci said. 'But tell me, Chief Superintendent, what idea have you formed about that other case?'

Ferrara found himself in a difficult position. If he gave his version, he would have to reveal the contents of the anonymous letter from 2003, the one that mentioned the roses and the hooded men. How would Vinci react when he discovered that he had kept the letter in a folder for more than a year? No, he couldn't mention it. Just as he couldn't talk about the letter he had received at home. He would come across as someone who saw plots and personal enemies everywhere.

'Come on, Chief Superintendent,' Vinci urged him.

'Assuming that the same person killed Giovanna Innocenti and Silvia de Luca, I wouldn't rule out the possibility that he was also involved in the other crimes . . . '

'You mean the disfigurement of the dead woman and the woman who was murdered and then set alight in the church?'

'Precisely.'

'So the killer might be part of a group?'

Ferrara nodded. 'Not that that gets us any closer to finding him.'

'Then what do you suggest?'

'I think we have to start with what we know for certain.' He went over the latest developments in the case of the murder in the church, including the identikit of the man Madalena had met on Saturday night and the search of her apartment in the presence of her niece. In doing so, he realised that Vinci was unaware that his own chief had been complaining about this very search.

'Have the material examined and then send me a report. Unless your men find something interesting, everything should be returned to the niece.'

This confirmed that Luca Fiore had said nothing to him.

'We'll release the identikit to the press today,' Ferrara said. 'It may prompt someone to come forward. If we can identify the man, it may lead us to his possible accomplices.'

'What do you think, Marshal?' Vinci asked.

'I agree with Ferrara, although I have a *but* . . .'

'What is it?'

Gori told them about the anonymous letter accusing Alvise Innocenti. In his opinion, it was imperative to find out if Innocenti had been involved in any way in his daughter's murder.

Vinci looked aghast. 'Alvise Innocenti? Do you realise what you're saying, Marshal? Not just a father killing his daughter, but Alvise Innocenti . . .'

'If whoever wrote that letter turns out to be telling the truth, then we really are dealing with a monster. And a monster is capable of anything. Alvise Innocenti's behaviour continues to be extremely strange.'

'But if he were involved, there'd be a connection between Alvise Innocenti and the man in the identikit. Don't you think so?' Vinci looked from Gori to Ferrara and back again.

The two men nodded.

'And why kill Silvia de Luca?' Vinci asked, staring at Ferrara. 'Did they know she was helping you? And if so, how did they find out?'

'That's a mystery,' Gori replied.

Ferrara said nothing, merely shook his head several times. He looked more worried than ever.

'Let's think about the concrete facts,' Vinci said, cutting short a debate he was convinced would go nowhere. 'The identikit, the hair found at the scene of the crime, the shoe prints, the phone taps ... You'll have to question Alvise Innocenti as soon as he's recovered. Let's take a coffee break before I issue more instructions.'

'Deputy Prosecutor,' Ferrara said, 'I think I should tell you something about my conversation with—'

'Let's have coffee first, Chief Superintendent,' Vinci interrupted him, getting to his feet.

Once he'd brought the coffee, Vinci turned to Ferrara. 'Well now, Chief Superintendent, what exactly did Silvia de Luca tell you? Would the woman have been able to play an important role in identifying the people in the church?'

Ferrara gave him a detailed account of the conversation.

'From what you tell me, the woman was potentially a useful source of information,' Vinci said. 'Which means her death could well be linked to the one in the church.'

Ferrara nodded.

'In that case, Chief Superintendent, they must have known about your visit. Not only that, they must have known she was talking to you as some kind of informant. Who knew you were going to see her?'

'Only myself and Inspector Venturi.'

'Do you trust Venturi?'

'Absolutely.'

'Then it's a mystery. But, if we accept that there is a connection with what happened in the church, this whole satanist angle looks increasingly solid. There has to be a group behind all this.'

'I'd like to add one thing. It's only an intuition at the moment, so just take it for what it is.'

'Go on. I know how accurate your intuitions can be. My poor colleague Anna Giulietti often told me that.'

There was a few seconds' silence.

The memory of Anna Giulietti made Ferrara's stomach lurch. That terrible attack had deprived him of not only an irreplaceable colleague, but also a great friend.

Her death had been the work of the Mafia. And the fact that a great deal was known about the Mafia and their associates meant that they could be effectively countered.

But when it came to this serial killer or these Satan-worshipping murderers, nothing was known: the territory they covered, the names of the members, what they looked like . . . These sick individuals were able to go about their business undisturbed. They might well be above suspicion. Which was why, in all probability, no informer, however alert or reliable, could provide any useful information.

'The lone killer might be playing a double game,' Ferrara said at last, breaking the silence.

'What do you mean by that?'

'Some of the murders seem to have had more than one objective.'

'Are you saying that he's been pursuing his own interests while at the same time following the instructions of a group?'

Ferrara nodded. 'Precisely. But, again, it's only an intuition.'

He would have liked to add Father Torre's hypothesis that the scar on the corpse in the chapels might be a challenge, but he held back. It would have been premature to bring that up. They simply didn't know enough yet.

'I'll give it some thought,' Vinci concluded.

The meeting continued for another half an hour.

The prosecutor divided various tasks between the police and the Carabinieri. They were all in the same boat now. Which meant they would sink or swim together.

'Let's keep the matter of the underwear to ourselves for the moment,' he said just before they left. 'It's the kind of detail that might bring the loonies out of the woodwork. We'd only end up with lots of false confessions.'

Ferrara hoped that this would not turn into another open secret.

96

By the time Ferrara got back to his office, the press conference was already over. All the journalists present had agreed to publish the identikit, Rizzo told him.

Then Ferrara brought his colleague up to date on the meeting in the Prosecutor's Department, but without mentioning Luca Fiore's complaints.

'I'm not convinced by the idea of a lone serial killer either, chief,' Rizzo said when he had finished. 'It's an obvious deduction, after finding one victim's necklace on the other's body. But it's too obvious. In my experience, seizing on a theory like that can easily lead you up the wrong path entirely. You know as well as I do that, in our work, once you've pursued the obvious to a dead end and realised how wrong you were, it may be too late to get things back on track. No, I agree with you. First we have to trace the man who Madalena was meeting on Saturday night, and then we'll know how to proceed.'

'Good, Francesco. You always see things in concrete terms. Long may you continue like that. Scientists and scholars are all very well. We have to take their theories into account, but not let them dictate our every move. Day-to-day detective work, as we know, is another matter entirely.'

'That's what you always told me,' Rizzo said. 'And it's what I try to live up to in my work.'

'But there's one thing I don't understand, Francesco.'

'Go on.'

'And it's something that's really bothering me.'

Rizzo looked at him with a mixture of curiosity and anxiety. 'I'm listening.'

'I can't figure out how they discovered Silvia de Luca was helping us. Do you see what I'm getting at?'

'Of course. Who knew about it?'

'Venturi and me. I would have told you, but I didn't get the chance.'

'Did the victim's family know?'

'Her daughter certainly did. She was in the kitchen when we visited.'

'Maybe the daughter told someone about it without thinking.'

'It's possible.'

'Maybe we should talk to her.'

'Yes, I think we should. Now let's go and get a coffee.'

A sudden thought had crossed Ferrara's mind.

A terrible thought.

'Francesco, I think I'm being watched.'

These were the first words that Ferrara uttered when they were outside Headquarters.

'Watched?' Rizzo echoed, incredulously, as if he wanted to be sure he had heard correctly.

'That's right. Someone's keeping an eye on me.'

'Who could it be?'

Ferrara did not reply. Rizzo was about to step off the pavement, but Ferrara stopped him. 'No, Francesco, let's not go to the café opposite. Let's try one a bit further away.'

Once they had turned the corner, they walked under the

arcades, passing a long queue of foreigners waiting their turn to be admitted to the Immigration Office through a side door. As usual, most were Chinese.

'Someone must be following me,' Ferrara said. 'Someone who knows my habits, knows where I live. And I haven't even noticed.'

'It isn't possible, chief. Someone as careful as you would certainly have noticed. It just isn't possible!'

'Unless it's someone from the office. A mole. It wouldn't be the first time something like that has happened in the police.'

It was a thought that horrified him more than corrupt or lying politicians or even ruthless killers. Discovering that he had a corrupt colleague who had aligned himself with criminal elements would be a terrible blow. Like being betrayed by someone you loved.

Rizzo was silent, lost in thought. From the look in his eyes it was obvious that he was sceptical.

'Have you noticed anything out of the ordinary, Francesco?'

'No, I don't think so.'

They continued walking.

'Has anybody been asking you any unusual questions? Or behaving suspiciously?'

Rizzo hesitated. 'No, chief, not in the office, and not outside. And anyway, only two people knew about the meeting with the victim. You and Venturi. And I don't think there can be any doubt about Venturi's loyalty.'

'No, of course not. I'd trust him with my life.'

'Well, then?'

'There's one other possibility, and only one.'

'What's that?'

'My office itself is under surveillance. Someone's investigating me, using illegal methods. It could be the work of spooks.'

'The secret services?'

'Maybe not officially. Rogue agents, that's what I'm thinking.'

Rizzo nodded. 'That wouldn't surprise me,' he replied. 'If the Freemasons are involved, which seems likely from the anonymous letter you showed me, anything's possible. They have brothers everywhere: in the telephone company, in the secret services, and in our own administration. Remember the P2 scandal.'

'Let's not discuss the case in my office any more,' Ferrara said. 'Or rather, let's not discuss anything serious there. And we have to think carefully about how we behave.'

Rizzo nodded again. 'You're right. They may have planted a bug.'

'Maybe more than one. There's no alternative, Francesco. But we have to play it cool and not make it obvious that we know something. When the time comes, we'll have the room swept for bugs. And not only mine.'

'I agree absolutely.'

They had reached the café.

A good coffee was just what they needed.

97

Ferrara found Ciuffi waiting for him in his office when he got back.

'How did the prison interview go?' he asked immediately.

'Not too well, unfortunately.' Nabil Boulam had confirmed everything he had already said without adding anything new, except about the phone call heard by Karina. 'He was quite upset at first, when he realised she was the one who gave us his name. When I insisted, he gave me his version.'

'Which is what?'

'That he was talking to one of his customers.'

'Whose phone was it?'

'Karina's.'

'Ah-ha! And what was the customer's name?'

'He doesn't know. Doesn't know where he lives, can't even remember the reason for the call. It might have been to make an appointment, he says.'

'In other words, he didn't want to tell you. This Nabil fellow knows more than he's saying.'

'Definitely. We could get hold of Karina's mobile number.'

Ferrara thought about this. 'How?' he asked. 'God knows who the telephone was registered to. We'll have to contact her.

I'll tell Teresa. Or rather, no, I'll deal with it myself. I have a contact in Moscow, he works in the Italian embassy.'

'Excellent idea. At least it would prove that Boulam's lying.'

'In the meantime, prepare a report for the deputy prosecutor. He's the one who should question Boulam at this point. Then, if he continues lying, he'll risk an additional charge of making false statements to a prosecutor. That might force him to tell the truth.'

'I'll get right on it.'

Ferrara joined Venturi in his office.

He found him poring over the Brazilian woman's papers, putting them in order and making notes. There was quite an assortment: bank documents, bills, passports, a pack of letters, some of them yellowing.

'Have you examined the whole lot already?' Ferrara asked immediately, thinking of his conversation with Prosecutor Fiore.

'I haven't finished yet,' the inspector replied. 'They're all mixed up and so far I've only found this . . . '

He pointed to a 2004 diary open at Sunday, 20 June.

Ferrara put on his glasses and read:

Mistake last night but not mine. It was him! Will something happen? I'm af— I'm sad.

Afraid? What was she afraid of?

Then his gaze came to rest on the bottom of the page. A flower had been drawn in black pencil.

A black rose?

'Did you notice this?' he asked the inspector, pointing to the flower.

'Of course,' Venturi replied. 'And so far I haven't found the same drawing on any other page.'

'Anything else?'

'Yes. Another entry for Friday the twenty-fifth of June.'

Ferrara turned the pages until he reached that day:

At last! Now I've been reassured. I feel confident again.

'Anything else?'

'No, so far nothing interesting. There are verses on some pages. They sound like the ramblings of an addict to me.'

'She was afraid because of a mistake that wasn't hers ... What mistake? And then she says "It was him!" Who? But after a few days she feels reassured. Who by? And about what? We have to look into her past. And I think it might be a good idea to question her niece again, but in depth this time. She needs to explain to us what her aunt was afraid of. We can't rule out the possibility that she was part of a secret society, and became its victim. It certainly wouldn't be the first time a secret society had killed one of its own.'

'I'll do that, chief.'

'But tell me, did you also get the club's membership list?'

'No. Why? Should I get it?'

'Not yet. I'll tell you when.'

'Okay, chief.'

Ferrara was pensive for the rest of the day.

Shut up in his office, and in a very bad mood, he imagined the killer safe and sound somewhere, savouring his successes and waiting to strike again. And that could happen at any moment, this very day, right now. A killer who had not made any mistakes, had not left any traces. Except for the hairs at the last crime scene. How many people were still to die? How long would it take to catch him? And if he really belonged to a secret society, would they ever manage to get him?

He thought again of Prosecutor Fiore's concern about the membership list, the diary entry written only a few days earlier, that flower drawn in black. Why had Madalena been afraid? What mistake had she made? And who had reassured her about it?

But what made him especially anxious was the suspicion that he was being watched. Who by? And how? Was his office bugged? How many bugs were there? Was somebody trailing him? If they were, it must be a professional, because he hadn't noticed a thing.

And finally, the most painful question: was the mole one of his own men? But who among them could have gone over to the other side?

The possibility that Silvia de Luca had been killed because of the information she had freely given him and Venturi weighed on him like a stone. When he got home, he found it hard to hide from Petra the anguish tormenting him, and it kept him awake for a long time that night. He felt that something precious had been stolen from him: his absolute faith in his colleagues.

Without a real team, what was the point of his job?

98

Friday, 2 July

It was like a madhouse.

It was as if, in some act of historical revenge, the building had gone back to being Bonifazio's Hospital, rather than Headquarters.

The sound of footsteps in the corridors. Raised voices in the offices, especially those of the inspectors. Telephones ringing constantly. Doors opening and immediately being slammed shut.

But this turmoil was not the kind usually to be found in detectives' offices on the eve of an important police operation. Quite the contrary. It was the newspapers that had unleashed this.

The news had been dominated by the identikit of the presumed killer, along with the details released at the press conference.

And there was something else.

Especially in *La Nazione*.

After a summary of the latest crimes, much space was devoted to the incident in the church and the identification of the victim: Madalena Miranda Da Silva, thirty-eight years old. The newspaper published a photograph, quite an old one, in which she appeared in all her beauty. An in-depth article by their chief correspondent, an apparently insignificant little man, lambasted the police, especially the *Squadra Mobile* and its chief, for their shortcomings. Among other things he wrote:

> Florence is at the mercy of criminals: the new Mafiosi from Eastern Europe, serial killers, and now satanists, who celebrate their rituals with impunity in our beautiful hills, which are once again dripping with innocent blood . . .

The piece concluded with a series of questions:

> Who will defend our honest citizens? Should we be thinking of arming ourselves? What are the police doing?

The murder of Silvia de Luca was reported on another page of the newspaper. According to its author, unconfirmed rumours suggested that she had been an expert on the occult and black magic who might have been killed in connection with the investigations into the ritual in the church.

The report ended with a question: *Could she have been helping the police?*

There was also an article by a famous Roman criminologist, who maintained that detectives these days relied too much on computers, technology, all the latest scientific gadgetry. Perhaps, he wrote, the time had come for the detective who used his brains and intuition – a figure who had become little more than a nostalgic memory – to make a comeback and reinstate the traditional methods.

One thing this expert especially regretted was the fact that modern detectives were unable to conduct an interrogation.

Have you ever wondered why we no longer get people confessing to a murder?

For me, the answer is simple: we lack detectives capable of obtaining a confession through effective interrogation techniques. Interrogation is a true art, an art that has been forgotten.

Ferrara read this article with an open mind and was forced to admit that, by and large, he agreed with the criminologist's views. It was only a pity that, reading between the lines, it could be seen as yet another attack on his own abilities.

In the *Corriere della Sera*, a summary of the latest events in Florence was followed by an article with the banner headline:

THE SECRET LIFE OF FLORENCE'S VIPS

Most of the text purported to be an account provided by a contact of the journalist, a contact not even referred to by his initials in an effort to safeguard his privacy. Assuming, that is, that he even existed.

This person had apparently once moved in exalted circles in the city. In an attempt to overcome boredom, he claimed, it was fashionable for upper-class Florentines to take part in black masses:

> In discotheques and private clubs, there is always someone, once darkness has fallen, who suggests a black mass. You just have to know the right person to contact, a devotee of the occult, and within a short time this person arrives with cloaks, hoods, candles and willing young women. At the end of the ceremony, an orgy is guaranteed . . .

He recounted a personal experience:

Some years ago, an old friend of mine persuaded me to join his secret society, which had about twenty members, all in their thirties and forties, and all from the upper middle-class. The society was structured in a hierarchical way and met in the Poggio Imperiale area at monthly intervals to celebrate a black mass at which an animal was sacrificed . . .

Ferrara was furious, to say the least.

All that was missing from the news coverage was the fact that Giovanna Innocenti's underwear and necklace had been found at the scene of the latest murder. But he wouldn't be at all surprised if these details were to feature in future articles.

He knew that there was a generation of young journalists who were indifferent to the principles that had guided their mentors. They were ready to do anything for the scoop of their lives, even if it might prejudice the outcome of a police investigation. They were so blinded by their own ambition, the disastrous consequences of their actions probably never occurred to them.

99

The Commissioner was beside himself.

It was obvious from his face, which was even redder than usual. He looked as if he might explode at any moment. The press room on the first floor, next to the chief of staff's office, was besieged by journalists. The public relations officer, faced with a bombardment of questions which he could not answer, was having difficulty containing them.

With Headquarters reeling from this onslaught, Ferrara, convinced that the investigation needed to crack on at an even faster pace, summoned his men.

He gathered them in Teresa Micalizi's office. Being the newest arrival, she was the least well known outside the department. At least in theory.

The tempo of an investigation could suddenly speed up as a result of an anonymous tip-off or the discovery of an apparently banal detail that turned out to be important, if not actually crucial. It was clear, after the last murder, and especially after what had appeared in the press, that they desperately needed to move up a gear. As if the detectives had to abandon their ministry-approved cars, all those Fiats, Alfa Romeos and Hyundais, of which there were fewer these days anyway, and get behind the wheel of a powerful Ferrari or

Lamborghini. Yes, that was the frame of mind that Ferrara wanted to instil in his men.

When the squad were all present, Ferrara told his secretary that he absolutely did not want to be disturbed and closed the door. Fanti remained on the lookout in the corridor.

'We need results,' Ferrara began, in a voice that sounded different to them. 'And we need them soon. As I'm sure you've all read, the newspapers are attacking us, some quite directly. *La Nazione,* to be more precise. We need to put all our resources into these cases. Twenty-four-seven. Starting now.'

They all nodded.

'What about the other cases in progress?' Ciuffi asked.

'The urgent ones must continue, but these latest events are our top priority. Especially the murder in the church and the murder of Silvia de Luca, which are almost certainly connected.'

Ciuffi was tempted to point out that every case was urgent, and that they had instructions from the deputy prosecutors that must be carried out, but he realised now was not the moment. He had never seen his chief looking so determined.

'Okay,' was all he said by way of reply.

'Good. The identikit has appeared. That's the one positive thing in today's newspapers. Let's hope someone comes forward. But while we're waiting for that to happen, we need to go through the various hypotheses and work out a plan.'

His men nodded once again.

100

'Good morning, Marshal.'

It was 11.05 when Sara Genovese entered Marshal Gori's office, where the marshal and Sergeant Surace were waiting for her.

The meeting, fixed for eleven o'clock on Thursday morning, had been postponed for twenty-four hours after the murder of Silvia de Luca.

'My colleague will be present at the interview,' Gori began, nodding towards the sergeant.

'Another interview?' Sara said in surprise.

'We need to take a formal statement about the incident with the photographer in the Parco delle Cascine, that's all.'

'You know I'm always pleased to help,' Sara replied. From her tone it was obvious she was reassured.

'All right. If you could just repeat what you told us before, my colleague will draw up the statement.'

Sara Genovese went through the incident again, right up to the sentence passed on the paedophile.

Gori had to fight the temptation to interrupt and ask her about the anonymous letter, Alvise Innocenti and the inheritance. But he couldn't afford to make any false moves.

When he had finished writing, Surace pushed the statement,

which amounted to three pages, across the desk towards the woman.

'Could you please sign every page?'

Sara Genovese read through the statement with great concentration, holding the pages with both hands. Then she put them down on the desk and signed them. Gori and Surace did not move.

'Can I offer you a coffee in return for the one you gave me the other day?'

'Thank you very much, Marshal. That'd be nice.'

Surace left the room and came back soon afterwards with three glass cups, without handles, full of steaming coffee. They drank in silence, then Sara Genovese said that she had to go.

'Thank you for your help, signora,' Gori said, rising from his chair and shaking her hand.

A few minutes after she had left, Surace set off at top speed for the forensics lab.

Ferrara was so absorbed in his reading, he did not even notice that Fanti had entered his office. Not that his secretary made any particular noise during his appearances, but Ferrara, even when he was busy with files, always felt his presence. Not this time, though.

'Chief, your coffee.'

'Thanks, Fanti,' Ferrara said, without looking away from the sheet he had in front of him. 'Put the cup down on the table.'

The secretary did so and immediately went noiselessly back to his room.

Ferrara continued reading.

Half an hour earlier, he had received an envelope by priority mail. It came from Florence. The sender: Giulio Torre. He had opened it with a curious expression on his face. Inside were a couple of books, some typewritten notes and a hand-written letter, which he read first.

Dear Chief Superintendent Ferrara,

As promised, I am sending you some of my publications on the subject we discussed, hoping they may be of help to you. I also took the liberty of writing in the attached note some of my reflections on the basis of the information you were so kind as to provide me with. I thank you once again for giving me your trust.

Please do not hesitate to contact me if you need further information. Good luck in your work.

Yours sincerely

Father Giulio Torre

He concentrated on reading the note.

The thing that really grabbed his attention was the significance of the cloak in the language of black magic. It was a ceremonial garment, whose colour varied from one occult group to another and according to the kind of ritual that was being celebrated. At gatherings in the countryside, it was black in order to merge with the surrounding darkness.

When he had finished, Ferrara remembered that he had decided to have the priest named as a consultant. He lifted the receiver and telephoned Vinci to propose the appointment.

101

Lunchtime.

He sat down at one of the tables in the Caffè Gilli. Today was Friday. Cod *alla livornese* was always on the menu on Fridays, and he felt a great craving to eat it before he left. He ordered it from the waiter, then, while waiting, opened *La Nazione*.

And this time his eyes were drawn straight to an item on the front page.

A piece of news he had not expected to read.

At least not in such detail.

He put his dark glasses back on again.

Meanwhile, a short distance away, Teresa Micalizi was sipping an aperitif.

She was standing at the counter of the Caffè Rivoire in the Piazza della Signoria, just opposite City Hall. The historic venue was popular with tourists and Florentines who wanted to enjoy a good coffee, a drink or an excellent chocolate in a delightful setting.

From time to time she took an appetiser from a crystal bowl and lifted it to her mouth.

She was early. She had an appointment with Sergi in front

of City Hall and every now and again she turned and glanced outside. She needed to apply for residence, as laid down by police regulations, which officially required an officer to reside in the place where they worked. Having yet to find an apartment to rent, thanks to the exorbitant prices, she intended to give the address of the police barracks where she was staying. Just like the vast majority of unmarried police officers.

A man, sitting with a woman at a table, stopped talking as soon as he saw her and stood up.

'Excuse me a moment,' he said to the woman, who immediately took a fashion magazine from a bag and began to leaf through it distractedly.

The man, meanwhile, had started walking towards Teresa, who was gazing in wonder at the window display with its tempting array of chocolates and sweets. On her first free weekend, she thought, she would take a box to her mother in Milan.

'I didn't know you came here, too,' the man said, coming up behind her.

Teresa had just speared an olive with a toothpick and was lifting it to her mouth. She turned with her hand suspended in mid-air. An expression of surprise spread across her face.

It was Umberto Bartolotti, looking very elegant.

He shook her hand warmly. He seemed happy to see her again.

'It's the first time I've come here,' Teresa replied. 'I've only been in Florence for a few days.'

'Then you have lot of things to see,' he said with a smile. 'Provided your work gives you enough time.'

'You're right. I'd really like to be a tourist, but I'm here to work.'

'There's always time. Listen, I read that you identified the woman. Is that right?'

'Yes.'

'Madalena?'

'Yes. Did you know her?'

'Not personally, but I think someone told me about her.'

'About her or about her club?'

'About her.' He changed the subject. 'Can I buy you an aperitif?'

'That's very kind, but I've already paid.'

'Another time, then. Goodbye, and good luck with your work.'

'Thank you again.'

Teresa watched him as he walked back to his table and took a good look at the woman with him. She was young, tall and slim, with smooth shoulder-length red hair.

He certainly wasn't gay! The information they were given wasn't always correct, she thought, remembering what she had read about Bartolotti not being known to have any steady relationship in his life.

Teresa hurried out towards City Hall. Her heart was beating faster, and not only because of the speed at which she was walking. The encounter with Bartolotti, whom she continued to find fascinating, had been a pleasant surprise.

But what about the woman? Once she had got over her surprise that Bartolotti had a female companion, she realised that the woman's face was not entirely unknown to her. But she couldn't place her.

Was she an actress, perhaps?

102

Yorkshire, England

Sir George Holley put the receiver down.

For a few moments, he looked out of the window of his study. The countryside, illumined by a lukewarm sun, was resplendent in green.

His guests were waiting anxiously for him to say something.

'Things are going well,' he said. 'They're still groping in the dark. Everything, and I mean everything, is under control. Steps have been taken to have that madman transferred.'

The brothers seemed relieved by the news. Some of them smiled.

It was the news they had been hoping for: the transfer of that chief superintendent. Once that was taken care of, they would see about settling accounts within their own ranks. Because mistakes had to be paid for. Everyone had to pay. Even those who considered themselves untouchable. Even Enrico Costanza. And perhaps not only him.

After all, it was for the sake of their secret association: the Black Rose.

*

He felt good.

Really good.

For a couple of reasons.

Firstly, because his plan was coming to a conclusion and everything was going smoothly.

Secondly, because he was still under the influence of the strong emotions he had experienced in the last few hours.

What more could he want?

They were sitting next to one another on the sofa, talking. The living room was, as always, perfectly neat and tidy, almost fanatically so.

In the background, the seductive voice of Amy Winehouse, his favourite singer of the moment.

We only said goodbye with words
I died a hundred times

'I won't be away for very long,' he said to his companion. 'Two, three days. I need the usual box of chocolates for tomorrow morning, but remember this time to make them just the way I said. You have to add the things I told you. Do you understand?'

'Yes, I understand,' she assured him, then asked him how old his stepmother was.

'Seventy-nine. She'll be eighty in October.'

'And with all the illnesses she has, she still won't die?'

'She has lots of problems, but they look after her very well. It's not like it is here.'

A kind of grimace appeared on the woman's face. 'Are you going by plane as usual?'

'I'm not sure yet. I may take the train.'

'Please be careful.'

'Don't worry.'

'You know I couldn't manage without you,' she said in a low, sweet voice.

'I know, I know,' he replied.

He moved closer to her, put his arms around her shoulders and began kissing her. First on her neck, then close to her left ear, then on the lips, while she unbuttoned his shirt. They slipped slowly on to the floor.

Getting dressed again, she said to him, 'I have to go now. Tomorrow morning, before opening the shop, I'll bring the box of chocolates, made just as you want them.'

'Wrapped in plain coloured paper, please.'

'Right. See you tomorrow.'

Once he was alone, he picked up the newspaper, and this time read all the items on the front page. Then he stared once again at the identikit with a degree of curiosity. Perhaps not only curiosity. He recognised his features, especially that eye-catching moustache.

He chuckled to himself. He was becoming famous!

For a few minutes he pondered the situation. Someone must have talked about him, must have described him to the police. It was a problem.

What could he do?

A solution came into his mind and he felt good again.

He leapt to his feet and ran into the bathroom.

He took the electric razor, switched it on and, looking at himself in the mirror, trimmed his moustache until it was a normal size. That would stop it being an important detail for those who were looking for him. Then he changed the colour of his hair to jet black. And with a pair of contact lenses he changed the colour of his eyes from grey to brown. He looked at himself for a long time in the mirror. And saw a different man.

Anyway, he had to go tomorrow, come what may, he said to

himself. He went back into the living room, where the soft voice of Amy Winehouse filled the empty space.

He walked to the stereo and raised the volume, dismissing his pleasant fantasies. He couldn't wait until it was time to go into action again.

The final objective was still to come. His true revenge.

The hour had come to settle his accounts with that bastard who had ruined his life before he even came into the world. The hour had come to savour the sweet taste of revenge, watching him die, reading in his eyes the terror of the moment when he was about to strike. It was something that would be talked about in this city for a long time to come. You could bet on that.

It was the last piece of the mosaic, the final stage of his plan, and it would work. He was certain of it.

103

In the evening Ferrara received the preliminary post-mortem report.

It was fairly comprehensive.

Time of death. Presence of signs of struggle on the arms. Removal and first analysis of the internal organs. Taking of samples of various bodily fluids and sending them to the toxicology lab for tests.

Diagnosis on the cause of death: epidural haematoma, following repeated blows to the cranium.

Silvia de Luca had died as a result of the killer violently striking her head against the iron bedhead.

He was reading the report a second time when the Commissioner summoned him to his office.

'Chief Superintendent, the Ministry wants to transfer you to the Bundeskriminalamt in Wiesbaden for a certain period of time. Consider it a promotion.'

The cold words struck Ferrara like a bullet in the chest. Caught off guard, he stared back at Adinolfi with a look of bewilderment on his face. 'Wiesbaden?'

'Yes. As Italian liaison officer. It's a very prestigious position. Your wife is German, isn't she? I'm sure she'll be happy to spend some time back in her own country. What do you think?'

Ferrara's first instinct was to reject this offer outright. It was not his custom to keep a low profile, to be diplomatic. Didn't they consider him a loose cannon at the Ministry? On this occasion, though, he did everything he could to curb his rebellious instinct.

'I know this is a promotion, Commissioner, and a prestigious post, one that many of my colleagues would like, but I prefer to stay in Florence, at least for a while.'

'Ferrara, my dear Ferrara, you can't stay in Florence for ever. That's the way it is in this job: transfers, promotions, new experiences ... And you can't keep endlessly clashing with our superiors. It's counter-productive. You'll condemn yourself to staying a chief superintendent for the rest of your life. You'll never become a commissioner. You know there's an age limit for every rank and that, after a certain point, if you haven't been promoted, you'll be obliged to retire.'

It occurred to him that this was the second time in a matter of days that Adinolfi had called him 'my dear Ferrara'.

It also occurred to him that Petra might indeed be pleased.

'Commissioner,' he said, 'if the Head of the State Police thinks this transfer is a solution, I'll consider it.'

'Think of it as a temporary solution, anyway. For a year, possibly extendable for another year. And don't forget, officers posted abroad enjoy special benefits, including financial ones. That's not to be sneezed at these days. What do you think?'

'I'll let you know.'

'Think it over, although I'm pretty sure the Head of the State Police has already made his mind up. I'd be surprised if the papers aren't already waiting to be signed by the Minister of the Interior. A few more days so it can be registered with the Court of Auditors, and then you'll be notified.'

Ferrara did not reply. It would have been pointless. It was

the same old tune. He knew it well. A 'proposal' was made, but the decision had already been taken without his knowledge. He'd been through it all before. He knew he would have to accept.

The Head of the State Police had more than one reason to get him out of Florence: the threatening letter, the letter about the roses and the hooded men, which he had not shown the Prosecutor's Department but had handed over to forensics and the Commissioner, as well as all the crimes committed over the past few days that remained as yet unsolved. He certainly could not boast a great success rate lately. Not to mention whatever the chief prosecutor had written in his letter of complaint, the contents of which had not been made known to him. Had Luca Fiore expressly demanded his transfer? If that was the case, his hopes of remaining in Florence were slim indeed.

He took his leave of the Commissioner and went back to his office, thinking all the while what a strange profession it was, being a police officer.

As soon as he was back at his desk, he summoned Rizzo, Venturi and Sergi.

'We have to get a move on!' he began once he had gathered them in Teresa Micalizi's office.

Teresa, sitting in a corner, seemed to be busy examining some papers.

'We can't afford to waste any more time,' he went on, and he revealed what he had just been told by Adinolfi.

The faces of the officers, including Teresa, changed. They all felt as though knives had been plunged into their stomachs and twisted, without their being able to defend themselves.

'But, chief ...' Rizzo ventured.

'No, Francesco, don't say anything. Let's just think of what we can do in the little time remaining to me. I don't want to leave you with this mess unsorted.'

'We're ready.'

'Good. Then here's my plan . . . '

Sergi and his team would swoop on the house near the Etruscan tombs. The deputy prosecutor had already issued a warrant.

Rizzo and Teresa Micalizi would deal with Beatrice Filangeri, the registered owner of those two telephones. They would summon her to Headquarters and question her. And once they had learned the name of the user of the second phone, they would do the same with him or her.

Venturi had obtained additional records from the phone company. He had studied them and had concluded that the call he had originally pointed out, the one made at 02.11, was still the only suspicious one, the only one that required clarification. The others had all been repeated calls between the same phones, whose owners lived in the area. There was no reason to suspect them.

'Even the late-night calls?' Ferrara had asked.

'Couples, chief, especially engaged people and lovers, talk for a long time at night,' Venturi said.

'We'll get moving on this tomorrow,' Ferrara concluded.

They all expressed their agreement.

Was this the right lead to pursue? Given the circumstances, they had to try.

Before bringing the meeting to a close, Ferrara communicated the latest information that had arrived from Moscow. The official at the Italian embassy had managed to trace Karina, who denied ever having owned a mobile phone in Italy.

So Nabil Boulam had lied. And now it was up to the deputy prosecutor to convince him that, if he wanted to avoid another trial, he had better tell the truth.

Ferrara was already at the door, about to leave the office, when Teresa Micalizi took a sheaf of photographs from a file.

'Chief, look here!' she said, opening it and placing it on the desk.

Ferrara put on his glasses, glanced at the photograph Teresa was showing him, and gave her a questioning look.

'This woman was with Umberto Bartolotti this morning,' she said.

'Where?'

'At the Caffè Rivoire. I saw them together, sitting at the same table.'

'Ah!'

'These are the photographs the Carabinieri gave us of those present at Giovanna Innocenti's funeral.'

Ferrara looked at the photograph again and read the caption: *Sara Genovese, friend of the victim.*

'We'll have to tell Gori and liaise with him on how best to proceed. In the meantime, let's carry on listening to the girl's phone calls.' He turned to Venturi. 'Anything new on that front?'

'Nothing interesting, for the moment.'

That evening, a smile spread across Petra's face when she heard the news.

Perhaps St Anthony had heard her prayers.

He was taking her back to her country, away from all these dangers.

The next day, in the nearby church, she would light a candle in front of the image of the saint.

PART FIVE

THE LAST PIECE

104

Night of Friday, 2 to Saturday, 3 July

Alvise Innocenti and his wife drove through the iron gate in their Mercedes, proceeded along the tree-lined drive, and pulled up outside the main entrance to the villa. They got out and walked towards the massive wooden door. Neither of them noticed the silent figure sitting cross-legged on the damp grass in the shadow of the trees, dimly lit by the moon glinting through the branches. He had gone over everything an infinite number of times. Now he was convinced that the moment had come to keep the promise he had made himself. He had calculated every tiny detail: his dreams were finally going to come true and he would not make the slightest mistake. His plan was perfect.

He had checked the windows one by one. They were dark, no movement from inside. The villa appeared deserted. And now, hidden amid the trees, he had seen them arrive.

He waited just over half an hour, and then, slipping out of his hiding place, moved cautiously but rapidly towards the back of the villa. He approached the kitchen window and looked in. There they were, the woman with her back to the window, standing at the refrigerator and taking out the dinner prepared by the maid, and the man sitting in a time-worn yellow leather armchair by the fireplace, reading a newspaper. He looked distracted. Was he thinking about the summons from the Carabinieri? He had managed to put it off, but for how much longer? Surely not for very long, unless his friend Fiore intervened.

The man standing outside let his gaze wander about the room: he was not surprised to discover that it was just as he had imagined it. It was very large and furnished with immaculate taste. It must be comfortable and intimate. One wall was covered with copper pots and an impressive assortment of spices.

He took a wooden ladder he had brought with him and hidden in the garden. He walked to a point beyond the kitchen window and climbed silently to the first floor. The adrenalin was growing with each step he took: by the time he reached the top of the ladder, he could feel it coursing through his veins. He felt focused and alert, ready to confront anything unexpected that might happen. He knew their habits, knew that they did not usually set the burglar alarm until just before they went to bed. He cautiously opened the window without making any noise, climbed over and finally was inside the bedroom. From there he moved cautiously, imagining the faces of the couple when they saw him. The house was quiet. When he was close to the kitchen door he held his breath.

He was consumed by hate.

Hidden behind the half-open door, he watched them for a few more minutes.

Now.

He cleared his throat.

'What a wonderful surprise!' he announced, flinging the door wide open. 'You really are a beautiful couple!'

He was a few steps from them and his voice hit them from the back. They turned, startled.

The woman let out a scream, then put both hands on the refrigerator in order not to lose balance. 'I beg you, Lord, save us.' Her eyes were wide open and she was trembling. Her husband was on the point of rising from the armchair, before realising how pointless that would be, with the barrel of a gun aimed directly at him. He looked at the finger on the trigger. It was in position. He sat down again. He tried to remain calm.

The intruder had a hood over his head. He was leaning against the doorpost. With his left arm held out, he took aim, pointing it first at one then the other. As if still undecided which one to shoot first.

'What on earth do you want?' Alvise Innocenti demanded in a firm voice, his face as red as fire. 'Who the hell are you? Is this a robbery?'

'What do I want?' the hooded man echoed, now aiming his gun directly at Alvise's face. 'What do I want? Don't you know what I want?' There was a sarcastic throb in his voice. Through the gaps in the hood his eyes glinted, dark and ghostly.

'That's precisely what I'm wondering,' Alvise replied. 'What are you planning to do?'

'I'm planning to take you away with me. Just you. You and I will go for a nice ride. And I can assure you, it'll be worth it.'

'Is this a kidnap? Tell me how much you want, I'll give you the money right now. We can come to an arrangement.'

'No, it isn't a kidnap!' the man replied, his gun still pointed at Innocenti. 'And there isn't enough money to pay me. Is there?'

Alvise Innocenti fell silent. A sudden realisation struck him: he wouldn't get out of this alive. Nor perhaps would his wife.

'Get up and follow me!' the intruder ordered, quickly moving to the woman and placing his gun against her head.

'Move or I shoot her. Make up your mind. I don't give a fuck about this crippled whore. But I know it's different for you. Whores have always been your thing, and some of them even left you their souvenirs. Isn't that so? Or have you forgotten?'

The woman could hardly breathe, she was trembling so much. 'I beg you,' she said. 'We'll give you whatever you want.'

Silence.

Alvise Innocenti had understood. He knew now who this intruder was. A fire flared up in his stomach, and for a moment he put his forearms on the armrests of the chair.

'Where are you taking me?'

'Oh, I don't want to spoil the surprise. Come with me and you'll see. I can tell you this, though. It'll be a one-way trip. No return journey planned.'

Innocenti at last stood up.

'I'll follow you,' he said. 'But leave my wife alone. She has nothing to do with this. Don't do her any harm.'

'I know she has nothing to do with this,' the hooded man replied. 'So just to please you, I'll do as you say.' He struck the woman's head with the butt of his gun. She let out a groan and collapsed on the floor.

'You're mad,' Alvise Innocenti cried, taking a step forward. 'What the hell are you doing?' He would have liked to jump on the man and disarm him. If only he had a gun, too . . .

'Stop!' the other man said. 'Stop if you don't want me to kill you both right here and now. And now don't talk any more. I don't have any time to waste, especially with you.'

Alvise Innocenti stopped in his tracks. He stood there with his hands raised, as if to defend himself.

He was starting to panic. He's going to kill us, he thought, unless I can somehow . . .

The hooded man crouched and placed over the woman's

mouth a handkerchief soaked in a liquid he had taken out of his jacket. She would be out for several hours.

'Bastard!' Alvise Innocenti cried. 'You'll pay for this.'

'Yes, you're right. I'm a bastard. A bastard who's come to settle an account that's been pending for thirty-six years. And now I really don't think you should be in any more doubt. I could take my hood off, but I don't want to give you that satisfaction. You don't deserve it. And as for making me pay, I think you should know that your friends have also become my friends, and nobody will avenge you. You're no use to them any more.'

He went to Innocenti and put a pair of handcuffs on his wrists. It's you who brought me to this point, he thought, closing the handcuffs so tight that Alvise Innocenti grimaced with pain. You loved screwing every whore within reach, while you had a wife expecting her first and only daughter!

'What on earth are you going to do? I don't want to die! Listen to me—'

'Be quiet!'

They left the room. Innocenti could feel the barrel of the gun in his back, pushed in so hard that it hurt. A few steps and they were in the garden.

In the dark.

105

They came to a large outbuilding used as a tool shed, with a cellar. Inside, there was a strong smell of wine in barrels. On one side were stainless steel wine presses and fermentation vats, which had been active in the days before the work was shifted entirely to the estate at Pontassieve. Against the opposite wall, crates of bottles were piled, ready to be shipped.

Alvise Innocenti was shoved against a barrel.

'What are you planning to do to me?' he murmured in terror.

'Turn round!'

Now they were facing each other.

'Can you still not imagine what I'm going to do to you? Do you still think I want your money? I don't need money, that's not what I came for. I want to kill you, you son of a bitch. You ruined my life. And not only mine . . . Was it here you came and put your hands under your daughter's skirt?'

'Who told you that?'

'What does it matter, pig? And anyway, what the hell interest is it of yours? It's taken me years, but I know everything about you. Your daughter was twice a victim because of you: you raped her and I killed her out of revenge. In the few moments remaining to you, try to imagine how much she suffered. Her end, when it comes down to it, was a liberation.

But now you also have to pay for what you did to her. I will show no mercy.'

The hooded man moved the gun to his right hand and with his left took a small knife from his jacket.

'Noooo ...'

He sank it into the man's belly, up to the hilt. Then he slowly pulled it out.

'That's only the beginning,' he hissed, staring into Alvise's horrified eyes.

Alvise Innocenti bent forward, teeth clenched. He let out a series of weak gasps, but was immediately stabbed again with the knife, savagely, repeatedly.

He closed his eyes. His thoughts were a storm of terror and memories. Soon they would abandon him. For ever.

Simultaneously, the hooded man was seeing in his mind, like old out-of-focus snapshots, the sexual violence undergone by his half-sister. When Alvise Innocenti collapsed on the ground, mortally wounded, his attacker barely heard his last, almost incomprehensible words. His last sighs. He got to his knees and took his pulse. He could feel nothing.

Innocenti was dead, his eyes wide with terror.

The killer took the scalpel from his pocket. He opened the man's trousers and skilfully cut off his genitals. The smell of blood filled his nostrils. He took a black hood from another pocket and put it over Innocenti's head. A gesture that might cost him dear, but that no longer bothered him. Now he had accomplished the sole objective of his life, the one he had experienced for so long in his imagination. And that chief superintendent, so hated by the others, had in a way become a figure of sympathy to him. Perhaps, if he was really intelligent, he might be able to save his own life.

Before leaving, he took a few photographs. Then he went back to the kitchen.

Laura Innocenti was still unconscious on the floor. He went to her, placed the gun against her head, cocked the trigger, and squeezed it.

Now his mission was finally over. Or almost. Soon he would begin to live, really live. He slipped out of the villa. He would go and rest for a few hours before he left.

His departure could no longer be delayed.

106

Saturday, 3 July

By just after eight in the morning, the Innocentis' villa was swarming with police officers, Carabinieri, magistrates and technicians. Some twenty people, all visibly tense. The atmosphere was unreal. Ferrara and Gori, who had arrived almost at the same moment, had looked at each other anxiously.

The chief prosecutor and his deputy, Vinci, were following the operations closely.

What surprised them all, though, was the arrival of Gustavo Lassotti, director of the Institute of Forensic Medicine. He looked even more troubled than the others.

It had been some years since Lassotti had last been seen at a crime scene. He taught at the university and, when he was not giving lectures, was off at some conference or other, or in his office among his papers.

He put on latex gloves and knelt to examine the body of Alvise Innocenti, which lay in a pool of blood. The first thing he did was to remove the hood from the head. He was about to put it in a plastic bag when he noticed there was something inside it. As soon as he had it in his hands, an expression of disgust appeared on his face. It was a photograph of Giovanna

Innocenti lying dead on her bed. Lassotti handed it to the chief prosecutor.

In the meantime, in a corner, a young Carabiniere had found the wrapper from a disposable camera. A Kodak. He approached Vinci to show him his find, but as he did so he caught a glimpse of the body and immediately fell to the ground like an apple from a tree. He had fainted. Two of his colleagues lifted him and took him inside the villa.

There were many bizarre elements.

The hood.

That the victim was a Freemason was well known. But what did it mean that he was lying dead with a hood over his head? What was the killer trying to tell them? Had he wanted to indicate that Innocenti had belonged to a secret lodge?

Then the photograph.

It was a signature. Father, mother and daughter killed by the same hand.

The handcuffs and the Kodak wrapper proved that the killer was following some kind of ritualistic pattern.

The cutting of the genitals.

The confirmation that Alvise Innocenti had been an abusive father, as indicated in the anonymous letter.

This latest murder finally put paid to any remaining notion that this was a serial killer choosing his victims at random. But why the Innocentis? What harm had they done, to be murdered so brutally? The killer could only be a professional.

Or a group of professionals?

When he had finished, Lassotti went on to perform an external examination of the woman's body. She had been found on the floor of the kitchen, lying on her back, with her arms and legs spread. This immediately struck both Ferrara and Gori. It was exactly the same position as the other victims. On her forehead Lassotti noticed a small bullet hole, but there was no cartridge case on the floor. There was a dark ring around the hole. That meant she had been shot from very close range, almost point blank. It had been an execution.

Had a .22 calibre revolver been used again?

Just as in the murder of the unknown foreigner?

Was that merely a coincidence? After all, the murder of the foreigner didn't seem to fit the pattern.

Or was there a connection between the two crimes?

If that was the case, what could the Innocentis and the murdered foreigner have in common?

What was the thread that linked them?

Had it been another challenge?

Or the same challenge?

Too many questions. And no certain answer.

Gori and Ferrara left the house and walked to a secluded part of the garden to compare impressions. Ferrara immediately informed Gori of Teresa's discovery that Sara Genovese knew Umberto Bartolotti.

'What a mess, eh?' the marshal said. 'What does your instinct tell you, Chief Superintendent?'

The answer was not long in coming. 'Nothing, for the moment. You have any ideas?'

'Maybe, especially after what you've just told me about Sara Genovese. The morning your colleague saw her, she'd been to see me.'

He explained what he had learned, and put forward his own hypothesis.

In the meantime the forensics team continued to do their work, while Prosecutor Fiore looked on.

No journalists had yet put in an appearance, but Ferrara was sure that once the double murder of the Innocentis became known, the media would be full of it. Florence would once again be in the spotlight, just as it had been in the days of the Monster. The foreign press would send their own correspondents. And there would soon be all kinds of complications, as always happened when high-profile names were involved.

What about the Head of the State Police? It wasn't difficult to imagine how he would react to such an escalation of horror.

But as far as Ferrara was concerned, his professional future had already been decided.

107

It was almost eleven.

Teresa Micalizi preceded the woman into the room.

She was just over five feet tall, and thin – more than thin, bony. She could not have weighed much more than six stone. She was wearing a brown leather jacket, a white T-shirt, jeans and trainers. There was no make-up on her waxy face. Her identity card said she was thirty-six but, perhaps because of her girlish build, she looked much younger.

Teresa Micalizi had tracked her down to the chocolate shop in the Via Verdi, which usually opened at ten in the morning, even on Sundays and holidays, much to the delight of tourists heading for Santa Croce.

'Sit down,' Teresa said, indicating one of the two chairs for visitors. She took her seat on the other. Rizzo was already sitting behind the desk.

'What's your name?' he asked.

'Beatrice Filangeri,' she replied. 'Can I have a glass of water? I'm not used to this.'

'Of course.'

Rizzo picked up the phone and made the request to Fanti. After a couple of minutes, the secretary entered with a bottle and some plastic cups.

Beatrice Filangeri drank in silence, while Rizzo looked at her surreptitiously. Now that he had a better view of her, he noticed the lines around her lips and eyes, which seemed to indicate a life of excess. Then he looked back at the computer screen, which displayed the results from the files and Venturi's report. Only two authorisations from the police: one for the issue of a passport, the other for the ownership of a semi-automatic pistol. And only one charge reported to the authorities, quite a long time ago. Venturi had managed to dig out the file from the basement of Headquarters.

Rizzo began with some simple, rather vague questions, to judge her reactions, and listened carefully to her answers. He knew that observation and listening were two important principles of interrogation. Both were key to understanding the personality of the person you were questioning.

'Do you have a criminal record?' he asked in a reassuring tone, just to test her honesty.

'No.'

'Are you quite sure, signora?'

The woman frowned.

Rizzo glanced again at the computer. 'I should tell you straight away that we believe you were once charged with theft,' he said, his tone slightly severe now. He thought he noticed a touch of tension in her face.

Her eyes narrowed. 'Oh ... But that was a very long time ago. I was a young girl. Let's just say it was a dare among schoolfriends. Don't tell me you're dragging that old misdemeanour up again?'

'A dare? Is that what you call stealing a candlestick from the chapel in a cemetery?'

'It was a joke. My friends persuaded me. I was young. The prosecutor shelved the case, and it never went to trial. Isn't that in your records?'

'Yes, it is.'

'Please, tell me the truth. Why did you bring me here? This young lady was very polite, but I've never before received a visit from the police. Do I need a lawyer?'

'No, not for the moment,' Rizzo said. 'Whether you'll need one in the future depends on what you tell us. I'm interviewing you as what we call a third party with knowledge of the facts.'

'Knowledge of the facts? What facts? Don't tell me it's about that candlestick.'

'No, no. That's water under the bridge. I need to ask you some questions about certain circumstances that we believe you need to explain to us.'

'Need to explain? Explain what?'

'We just need certain things clarified.'

'And I don't understand what you're talking about!'

Rizzo began typing on the computer.

Name, profession, educational qualifications, criminal record. The usual preliminary questions and answers.

Then the interview really got under way.

'Could you tell us what you were doing on the night of Saturday to Sunday last in the Via Sanminiatelli in Sesto Fiorentino?'

'Where? I don't know any Via Sanminiatelli.'

'I think you do.'

'You're wrong. I don't know what you're talking about, I don't know what you're accusing me of. Why are you asking me these questions?'

'Because we need to know certain things.'

They went on like this for almost half an hour, with the woman obstinately denying everything. Every now and again she would shrug her shoulders. She seemed to have placed a barrier between herself and the truth. Her repeated protestations of 'You're wrong' were interspersed with ever more prolonged silences. Rizzo, for his part, had the feeling that he was getting nowhere.

He changed tactics.

'What's the number of your mobile phone?' he asked.

She gave it to him from memory, without any hesitation.

'Do you have a contract, or is it pay-as-you-go?'

'Pay-as-you-go.'

'Is that your only number?'

'What do you mean?'

'Do you have any other phones? Are you on any other networks?'

Silence.

'Please answer my question.'

She thought for a moment, then said, 'I don't think so. In the past, years ago, I had others, but I stopped using them and I don't even remember the numbers.'

At this point Rizzo took the phone company records from his desk drawer.

'Well, signora, here we have the number of your mobile phone, the same number you gave us just now.' He pointed to the call at 02.11 on Sunday 27 June. 'Do you see it?'

She leaned forward until she was almost touching the sheet of paper. Her expression did not change. 'The number is mine, but I don't know what it's got to do with your investigations.'

'The fact is, signora, that the number called turns out to be yours, too. You can see it with your own eyes.'

The woman leaned forward again.

'So, what can you tell me?'

Silence again, an even longer one.

Then she looked straight at Rizzo, with a mixture of anger and disgust in her eyes, and said, 'I was on my way home.'

'Who did you call?'

'I don't remember.'

'But it was only a few days ago. How can you not remember?'

'If I tell you I don't remember, I don't remember. And anyway, it was a personal matter. You can't invade my privacy.'

'Signora, if you carry on like this, you run the risk of being charged as an accessory.'

'An accessory?'

'That's right.'

'To what?'

'There was a murder that night, and you were in the vicinity at about the time it was committed. Do you understand now?'

'I don't know what you're talking about, Superintendent. I have nothing to say and my private life is my own affair.'

'Signora, we summoned you to clarify your position. If you aren't able to do so, we can only assume you must have a reason.'

'I don't know anything about any murder. What do you want from me? Leave me alone.'

'You're not doing yourself any favours with your attitude, signora.'

'I'm not saying anything more without my lawyer,' was her curt reply. She straightened in her chair and folded her arms.

Rizzo stamped the statement and handed it to her.

The woman did not even look at it. 'I won't sign it.'

'That doesn't matter. We'll sign it and note that you refused.'

The woman said nothing.

108

'So much violence, so much brutality.'

It was Prosecutor Fiore who was speaking, addressing Vinci in the kitchen of the Innocentis' villa.

Ferrara and Gori approached.

At that moment, Ferrara's mobile phone began ringing. It was Rizzo, calling to bring him up to date on the interrogation of Beatrice Filangeri.

'I'll call you back in five minutes, Francesco,' Ferrara said. He immediately informed the two prosecutors.

Vinci exchanged a knowing look with his chief and said, 'Search the woman's apartment. Consider the warrant already issued. Tell your deputy, given the urgency, and the fact that I can't write it out here, to inform the lady that I issued the order orally and that I'll write to her confirming it later today.'

Ferrara phoned Rizzo back and passed on the instructions.

The apartment was in a rundown old block with a colourless facade.

The police officers entered together with Beatrice Filangeri, with Teresa Micalizi beside her.

There was a strange atmosphere in the apartment. It was extremely untidy, especially in the bedroom and kitchen. The sheets were heaped on one side of the bed, and there were what looked like semen stains on the mattress. Empty whisky bottles and dirty glasses lay everywhere, on the floor and even on the television set. The floor was covered in dust. The place was a pigsty. In the bathtub and wash basin in the bathroom, they found hair of a length and colour different from Beatrice Filangeri's. The hairs were about two inches long, and seemed to belong to someone middle-aged.

But the first real surprise was hidden under the cushion of a leather sofa.

It was in a small room that seemed to be used for domestic chores. There was an open ironing board and a heap of linen in a basket on the floor. On a chest stood a small TV set and a stereo.

An officer, his hands protected by gloves, picked up a transparent envelope. Inside it was a small knife.

With a satisfied expression, he showed it to Rizzo.

On the jagged blade were dried reddish stains.

Perhaps blood.

Suddenly, like the sky when a strong wind sweeps away the clouds, Rizzo's expression changed. A gleam of joy appeared in his eyes. This search was starting to appear in a new light. A clearer light. He looked at Beatrice Filangeri. She turned white, like someone caught red-handed, but said nothing.

Was this knife the murder weapon?

If it was, they had her.

Until a few hours earlier, or even just a few minutes earlier, the investigators had been groping in the dark, speculating blindly about the terrible events of the past few days. But that might be about to change.

'What can you tell me about this knife, signora?' Rizzo asked.

The woman sighed and said nothing.

'Do you do underwater fishing?'

'No.'

'It's quite dirty. Is this blood?'

She made an effort to control herself, then looked around her anxiously and began to say, 'I think it's better ... ' but immediately broke off and shifted her gaze to an indeterminate point in the room.

'It's better what?'

Silence.

'You were saying: "I think it's better ..."' Rizzo insisted.

She smiled. 'I've forgotten what I was going to say.'

'What can you tell me about this knife?'

'Me?'

'Yes, you. You were just about to tell me something.'

'I can't remember.' She turned her head away.

Rizzo decided not to insist. There would be time back at Headquarters to broach the subject again. He was convinced that the woman had been about to confess, like the culprit who, knowing he's been discovered, prefers prison to the anguish of uncertainty. He gave orders to turn the apartment inside out.

The police officers began their search with a new spirit of optimism.

There were more surprises in store for them.

109

There were some very unusual volumes in the bookcase.

Volumes about magic, the occult and satanism.

On a small table was a pack of tarot cards. And in a cubbyhole they found a box with an old leather-bound photograph album. Some of the photographs showed a little girl playing in the garden of a villa. In others, the same little girl was shown standing with a veil over her head beside three miniature white coffins.

Another large box contained a number of disquieting objects, including some sinister, if not downright evil-looking, rag dolls, all with pins stuck in their heads, and some clumsily made little wooden coffins.

Souvenirs of Beatrice Filangeri's troubled childhood.

While the other officers continued inspecting the premises, Rizzo was examining the computer in a small room used as a study. In the files he found mostly documents relating to the woman's commercial activities. The same was true of her e-mail folder, apart from some messages exchanged with the same small number of correspondents. He wrote the addresses in his notebook, then ordered the computer to be taken back to Headquarters, where it could be examined more carefully.

In their search, the officers disembowelled the mattress and pillows on the bed and the cushions on the sofa and armchairs, leaving heaps of foam and down on the floor. They took everything away: the box, the books on satanism, the photographs, videocassettes, CDs, DVDs, as well as the Beretta 6.35 mentioned in the files. Then they placed seals on the door of the apartment.

As soon as he got in the duty car, Rizzo called Ferrara.

'Congratulations!' was the response at the other end of the line.

It was almost four in the afternoon, and Ferrara and Vinci had just arrived back at Headquarters.

She entered Teresa Micalizi's office, looking quite calm and innocent.

She was accompanied by a court-appointed lawyer who seemed to be under the impression that, for perhaps the first time in his career, he had been assigned a case that would make him famous. He looked about thirty. He sat down next to his client and exchanged a few words with her, while Teresa watched. Then he glanced at his watch and started drumming on the desk with the fingers of his right hand, as if to indicate that he was wasting valuable time. Soon Ferrara and Vinci appeared, and took their seats side by side behind the desk.

The lawyer took the penal code and the code of criminal procedure from his bag. Wherever lawyers went, these volumes went with them.

His name was Luciano Vitale and, according to the business card he handed Vinci, he could be reached via the offices of a famous lawyer.

'I've advised my client not to answer,' he began in a severe tone that Ferrara thought somewhat forced. 'We want to know first of all exactly what she's accused of and what evidence the Prosecutor's Department has in its possession, if any.'

Vinci went through the contents of the statement and Rizzo's report: the telephone call at night from the Via Sanminiatelli, the implausibility of the reason put forward – 'I was on my way home' – the refusal to name the person called, denying that she had any memory of events, personal facts, her allegation of violation of privacy . . .

After which he said, 'Signora, do you confirm these statements that you didn't want to sign?'

The woman exchanged a quick glance with her lawyer, who limited himself to making a kind of grimace with his lips. Then she replied, 'Yes, I do.'

'Signora, you must tell us the truth. We need to know what you were doing there that night, who you were with, and who you called on your mobile phone. If you tell us the truth, we might be able to help you. There may well be extenuating circumstances. Your lawyer will be able to explain that to you.'

'Deputy Prosecutor,' the lawyer intervened, 'my client has made her position very clear. She confirms her previous statement, but it has no value as evidence. Signora Filangeri was not summoned in the usual way, as laid down in the code, but taken almost by force from her own commercial premises, which she was obliged to close, with subsequent loss of income. I fail to understand the charge.'

Vinci and Ferrara looked at each other.

Either this young man had had very good teachers at university, or he was the son of some criminal lawyer. Maybe both.

'Therefore,' he continued with a sneer, 'the questions asked of my client must be more specific. Her presence in that area, assuming she was there, isn't sufficient reason for her to be committed for trial, and she understands that. Isn't that so?'

'All right then, signora,' Vinci said, going straight to the most damning piece of evidence they had, 'tell us about the knife the police found in your apartment. And remember, you're being investigated, at present, for the offence of aiding and abetting.'

'What knife?' the lawyer asked.

'The one the police found while searching your client's apartment. It was hidden under a sofa cushion and there are dried stains on the blade that we will submit to tests.'

'It's obviously animal blood. My client must have eaten some steak and forgotten to wash the knife. But you think . . . I want an expert of our choice to be present at the test you intend carrying out. If my client is accused of aiding and abetting, the test must be carried out in agreement with both parties, in accordance with article 360 of the code of criminal procedure.'

'Signor Vitale, we know the law. Rest assured, you will receive due notification when the time comes. In the meantime, I admonish you not to answer for your client. I remind you that you can be present at the interview and make observations, but the law does not give you the right to replace the accused.'

'I'm sorry, Deputy Prosecutor.'

'All right, I'll let it go this time, but please don't let it happen again. If it does, I'll have to notify the Bar Council.'

'Don't answer,' the lawyer said to the woman, then, looking Vinci straight in the eyes, 'The interview ends here. We will consider resuming it when you have specific questions rather than vague ones, and only after the laboratory tests have been carried out. In the meantime, I should like to have a private conversation with my client.'

'That's your prerogative, Signor Vitale,' Vinci replied in a somewhat irritable tone, exchanging a knowing look with Ferrara. 'The law allows you that, and I'll authorise it as soon as you've provided me with a written request. In the meantime, your client is in custody, and she will be taken from here to prison. You can have your conversation there.'

The woman stood up and left the room together with Teresa Micalizi.

There was fear in her eyes.

110

It was already dark by the time Venturi got back to Headquarters.

With the help of the Carabinieri, he arranged around his office the boxes with the material taken from the Innocentis' villa.

Vinci, Ferrara and Gori had in the meantime gathered in Teresa's office.

Gianni Fuschi knocked to announce the result of the test on the knife found in Beatrice Filangeri's apartment. He had a broad smile on his face.

'I get the impression you're bringing good news, Doctor,' Vinci said.

'Yes, I think I am,' Fuschi replied, glancing at Ferrara. 'My technicians have only just finished.'

'Go on,' Vinci urged.

'The stains on the knife are human blood. And, if authorised, we'll proceed with a test to determine the type.'

'And then?'

'And then the DNA, too, though that will take longer.'

'Good. However, we'll have to do the tests in the presence of the accused's lawyer and an expert of his choice.'

'No problem. The test is repeatable, because I've used only a very small sample.'

'For now, don't touch anything else. Tomorrow, we'll notify the lawyer and fix a time and place.' Vinci paused. 'There's one thing I don't understand.'

They all looked at him.

'Why didn't they get rid of the knife? Why did they keep it, if it still had blood on it?'

'I can think of an explanation,' Ferrara said.

'Go on.'

'We have to remember that a ritual murder was carried out with that knife, which gives it a particular significance for the initiates of a secret society. They have to guard it in order to use it again. For them, it has an almost sacred value.'

Vinci then turned back to Fuschi. 'What about the hairs?' he asked.

'We're getting there, Deputy Prosecutor. From the tests we can determine blood group and DNA and compare them with those found at the scene of Signora de Luca's murder, which the Carabinieri currently have.'

'But those tests aren't repeatable, are they?' Vinci asked.

'Precisely! That's why we need your authorisation.'

'You have it, but we'll have to inform the accused and her lawyer about those tests, too.'

'Of course.'

'Tell me, Dr Fuschi, did you find any prints on the handle of the knife?'

'A few, but unfortunately they're not the accused's. We compared them with those taken when she was brought in and they don't correspond at all.'

'Thank you for the good news, anyway,' Vinci concluded, and immediately turned to Gori. 'Marshal, I'd like you to make the hairs taken by your men available to Dr Fuschi.'

'Of course.'

It was now Gori's turn, and he announced that he had again

summoned Sara Genovese. 'I'm expecting her tomorrow, and she'll have to explain her relationship with Umberto Bartolotti. Just as she'll have to explain the contents of the letter accusing Innocenti. She's definitely the author of that anonymous message. We compared the fingerprints and there's no doubt.'

'Perfect!'

Ferrara raised his hand. He had had an idea, an intuition, or perhaps he just wanted to cover every base.

'Gianni, when the bullet is removed from the body of Signora Innocenti, if, as seems likely from the bullet hole, it turns out to be a .22 calibre, I'd like it to be compared with those taken from the body of the foreigner killed near the Ponte Vecchio.'

Vinci looked at him in surprise. 'What's that got to do with anything?'

'You never know,' Ferrara replied.

'Do it,' Vinci said to Fuschi.

At last they were dealing with concrete data. And they would soon have the first test results, which, they hoped, would confirm their theories.

That was the true value of science: to confirm or refute, but never to replace traditional investigative methods, which were the daily bread of every good detective.

111

The surprises were not long in coming.

In the now silent rooms of the *Squadra Mobile*, the staff, directed by Rizzo, were combing through the objects and documents taken from both Beatrice Filangeri's apartment and the Innocentis' villa.

Fanti, who had been asked to check Filangeri's computer, had come upon an exchange of e-mails with the same person, whose address was Leober@free.it. The last messages bore the date Saturday 26 June. One bore the time stamp 21.03: *Let's meet at the usual place and agreed time. Please be punctual. Love.*

The reply had been immediate: *Okay.*

Then Fanti and Rizzo took a look at Beatrice Filangeri's collection of videos and DVDs. Most were love stories and thrillers. They divided them up, and viewed the contents by playing each one in the computer or VCR for a few minutes.

Rizzo had got to his seventh film, *An Officer and a Gentleman.* The title was written on the case in a black marker.

But it wasn't *An Officer and a Gentleman.*

There was no sign of Richard Gere.

Or Debra Winger.

There were quite different images. Cruel, violent images,

beyond anyone's wildest imagination. Captured without pity, emotion, or the slightest humanity.

Images of the murder of Madalena Miranda Da Silva. There she was, filmed in close-up, completely naked as the flames began enveloping her.

Rizzo clicked stop.

'Bingo!' he said to himself.

He picked up the phone and called Ferrara at home.

'We're there, chief,' he announced triumphantly as soon as he heard Ferrara's voice.

There could be no doubt about it now. Beatrice Filangeri had been involved in the ritual held inside the church.

112

It was after eleven o'clock at night.

Even though the day had been particularly heavy, Ferrara was not resting. Quite the contrary. After dinner he had sat down in front of the computer to update his outline. It was a way of putting some order into his thoughts, and there were a lot of important new elements to be added.

But first he telephoned Deputy Prosecutor Vinci at home.

What a strange city, he said to himself as he put the phone down after the call.

Then he resumed typing.

Case: Chapels of Rest
Date: Night 21–22 June
Perpetrator: Unknown, at least two people
Suspects: Couple noticed by son of dead woman; staff with
    free access
Investigations: Woman perhaps anorexic – Filangeri?
    Man: Doctor?
    Burnt tobacco leaves
    Wrapper disposable camera (make?)
    List employees chapels and hospital
    Secret passage?

Case: Threatening letter
Date: 22 June
Perpetrator: Anonymous
Suspects: None
Investigations: No prints
    Used HP inkjet printer
    Perhaps linked to anonymous letter 2003 (roses, hooded ones ...)
    Masonic references?

Case: Murder of Giovanna Innocenti
Date: Night 24–25 June
Perpetrator: Unknown. A man. Perhaps accomplices
Suspects: Man who knew victim well, same who killed father and mother
    Sara Genovese: Accessory or accomplice? Had most motives: jealousy, inheritance
Investigations: Murder weapon not found
    Artificial black rose
    Cigarette ash, handcuffs
    Wrapper disposable camera Kodak (no prints)
    Inheritance to Sara Genovese
    Anonymous letter on father of victim: sexual abuse
    Phone tap Genovese

Case: Murder of Madalena Miranda Da Silva
Date: Night 26–27 June
Perpetrator: Unknown
Suspects: Satanists
    Visitors to spot
    Metalheads?
    Beatrice Filangeri and other user with phone registered in her name

Investigations: Prints of shoe soles (3). One a woman's
   (size 36)
   Satanic symbols
   Listen telephone Bartolotti and caretaker Pietro
   Bartolotti knows Sara Genovese
   Phone records
   Contact Filangeri
   Search Filangeri: knife with traces blood, occult books,
   DVD with film of murder
   Diary victim: was afraid, drawing of flower
   Identikit man appointment, her drug dealer

Case: Murder of Moroccan
Date: Night 27 June
Perpetrator: Unknown
Suspects: None
Investigations: Phone call to *La Nazione*: initials FAF –
   5-euro phone card
   Collaboration of Special Ops
   Phone booth Piazza Libertà
   3 bullets calibre 22 painted red
   Illegal street sellers, drug dealers
   Search Nabil Boulam: arrested for drugs etc.
   Reticent on phone call – comparison with bullets
   Innocenti

Case: Murder of Silvia de Luca
Date: Night 30 June–1 July
Perpetrator: Unknown
Suspects: Same person who killed Innocenti
Investigations: Used knife
   Underwear?
   Hair (one with root attached)

> Found necklace Giovanna Innocenti, G-string and bra
> perhaps Innocenti?

> Case: Murders of Alvise and Laura Innocenti
> Date: Night 2–3 July
> Perpetrator: Unknown
> Suspects: Same person who killed daughter and Silvia de
>   Luca
> Investigations: Used knife and gun
>   Small bullet calibre 22
>   Knife found at Filangeri's?
>   Genitals severed
>   Handcuffs (like Giovanna Innocenti)
>   Photo murdered daughter
>   Black hood
>   Wrapper disposable camera Kodak (prints?)

When he re-read the notes before switching off the computer, he asked himself why the killer had left a disposable camera wrapper at the scene of two of the murders and, perhaps, also at the chapels of rest. Had it been a way of putting his signature to the crimes? Or was he making fun of the investigators? Or telling them that these killings were ordered by someone who required photographic evidence?

It was usually serial killers who left clues and issued challenges.

He thought specifically about the murders of Giovanna Innocenti and Silvia de Luca. Neither of the two had been robbed of valuables: jewellery, watches. Both appeared to be serial killings with a sexual element; it seemed the killer had wanted to be close to the victims, to feel them struggle and succumb. He had invaded their privacy, strangling the first one, striking the head of the other violently against the bedhead.

Both methods must have given him a thrill, which the use of a firearm probably would not have done. But Laura Innocenti had been killed with a gun and her husband had had his genitals cut off.

Something wasn't right.

What was he missing?

What was the common denominator? The connection? For the Innocenti couple, simply the fact that they were Giovanna's parents?

No, it wasn't enough.

And besides, he might not be dealing with a serial killer, a pervert, a psychopath – or at least, not only that. There had to be another motive, and it had something to do with whatever terrible secret it was that the Innocenti family had harboured.

113

Meanwhile, the man, with his now jet-black hair and dark eyes, was travelling.

He had not taken the plane but the train. He could not afford to make any mistakes, especially now. He had left just before ten in the evening, after spending the whole day in his farmhouse near Montespertoli. He felt sure of himself. For the journey, he had chosen a classic light grey suit and a striped tie. He looked like a young executive. He doubted that anyone would be able to recognise him. In his first-class compartment, there was only one other passenger, an eye-catchingly pretty blonde, who was returning home from a holiday in Florence. In other circumstances, he would have flirted with her, but he had no wish to draw attention to himself, so he kept his eyes down and concentrated on the last chapters of *The Da Vinci Code*.

From time to time he would think about Ingrid. She inspired very mixed feelings in him. On the one hand he still loved her, but on the other he knew that her death was essential. She was the last source of danger. The only person who might realise who had killed the Innocentis. To assuage his misgivings, he told himself that she only had a few more days to live anyway, maybe weeks, a few months at most. Those chocolates, so well prepared by Beatrice, would solve the problem. For ever.

He would get to Munich at about 6.30 the next morning and go straight to his favourite hotel, the Bayerischer Hof on Promenadeplatz, bang in the middle of the city, a symbol of its elegance and wealth.

With its gym, its shopping gallery, its restaurants, the Bayerischer Hof was one of the finest hotels in Munich. It was a hotel he had often chosen for his monthly visits. He was particularly fond of a restaurant on the lower ground floor, where he could eat his favourite würstel with sauerkraut, accompanied by tankards of Weissbier.

That evening Sir George Holley had a long phone call.

And the news he received was not at all reassuring. Quite the contrary.

The call had covered a number of topics: the killing of the Innocentis, the interminable search of their villa, the arrest of a woman, the latest news about the investigations . . .

Some of the details were particularly worrying: the hood over Alvise's head, the photograph, the bugs that had not recorded anything from Ferrara's office all day.

That hood terrified him.

Had it been left on purpose? Like that artificial black rose between Giovanna Innocenti's thighs?

Why?

And then the photograph inside the hood . . . what did that mean?

He had started to suspect that Enrico's godson was not to be trusted. He had acted on his own account, putting their organisation at risk.

If that was true, it was another mistake on Enrico's part.

How would he justify himself to the others?

This time, Sir George really couldn't help him.

114

Sunday, 4 July

ALVISE AND LAURA INNOCENTI
EXECUTED IN THEIR OWN VILLA

That, or something like it, was the banner headline on the front page of almost all the papers. They all published a photograph of the villa. Some also ran Alvise's photograph, with captions like: *The world's best-known producer of Florentine wines.*

There were few details on the method of the double murder, but in every item there was speculation on a connection with the murder of the couple's daughter. Now, even *La Nazione* gave her full name, not just her initials, when mentioning her death. The leading article concluded with the words: *Who hated the Innocentis so much? Another riddle for the police!*

Sollicciano prison, 9.00 a.m.

'My client wishes to avail herself of the right to silence.'

They were in the interview room. Deputy Prosecutor Vinci

had just sat down behind the iron desk. Sitting across the desk from him were the accused and the young lawyer, who, after the conversation he had just had, had been chosen by the woman as her attorney.

'What do you mean? Perhaps I didn't make myself clear yesterday. I told you your client must answer. This is the second and final time I'll remind you of your role and your rights.'

'I don't intend to answer,' said the prisoner with an innocent air.

'Deputy Prosecutor,' the lawyer intervened, 'my client's statements were made under extreme emotional duress after she was taken from her shop. Such methods, as I've already had occasion to explain, do not fall within the procedures prescribed by law for the summoning of witnesses. Article—'

'Spare me the article,' Vinci cut in, irritated by the man's self-important tone.

'Not only that, but the police violated my client's privacy. By what right did they obtain the telephone records?'

'You'll be able to read that in the custodial order I'll be issuing in the next few hours. And there was no violation of privacy.'

'I'll apply to the appeal tribunal to have her released.'

'Do as you see fit,' concluded Vinci. Turning to the woman, he asked, 'So, signora, you intend to avail yourself of the right to silence?'

'Yes,' was the curt response.

Vinci drew up a brief statement, closed his briefcase and left the room. The prison officer who had remained behind the door led the woman back to her cell.

She would be staying there for a long time.

Vinci knew that for sure, having been informed of the latest developments the previous evening, including the fact that Beatrice Filangeri had in her possession a film of the ritual murder of Madalena.

With that DVD, they would nail her once and for all. No appeal court would agree to release her.

It might only be the beginning. The woman might be just one piece in the puzzle they would have to complete. But clearly she was an important piece. There was no doubt about that.

As soon as he left the prison, Vinci called Ferrara and brought him up to date.

'How about you?' he asked. 'Any news?'

'Some.'

'Go on.'

'We've identified the recipient of her e-mail. A team has gone to the man's house, in Piazza Santa Croce, to bring him into Headquarters.'

'Good. Hold him there and question him. Keep me informed. In the meantime I'll prepare the warrants for the technical tests. They need to be carried out as soon as possible.'

'Right.'

Having hung up, it struck Ferrara that he might have made a mistake. It might have been better not to arrest the woman but to bug her phone and tail her a while before bringing her in. A couple of undercover officers keeping surveillance might have been able to gather more details about her accomplice or accomplices. But then he told himself that the pressure of events had dictated that things needed to be done in a hurry. Not to mention the attacks from the media, pressure from the higher echelons of the police, and the fact that he did not have much time left in Florence.

But if it had been a mistake, was it still possible to remedy it?

He would give it all he had.

In the last few hours, luck seemed to have smiled on him.

115

Meanwhile, Teresa Micalizi was talking to an elderly man who, despite the heat, was wearing a smoking jacket and a pair of woollen trousers.

It was Leonardo Berghoff's neighbour.

Previously, she had knocked repeatedly and for a long time at the door of Berghoff's apartment without getting any response.

The shutters over the windows that looked out on the square were closed. Either the man had shut himself up at home, having heard what had happened to his friend Beatrice, or he wasn't in.

Certainly, no sound came from inside.

And so, before deciding to knock the door down, she had rung the bell of the one other apartment on the same floor.

'Signor Leonardo isn't in,' the old man said, adjusting his jacket, 'so there's no point insisting and making all that racket.'

'Are you sure he isn't in?'

'I saw him leave yesterday, carrying his case. He goes away for a few days every month.'

'Do you know where he's gone?'

'I think to visit that poor woman who brought him up.'

'His mother?'

'She has the same surname, but people round here say . . . '

'Yes?'

The man smiled. 'They say he isn't her son and that this apartment was bought for her by a lover.'

'Who was this lover?'

'I don't know. As I said, it's just neighbourhood rumour. Many years ago, we used to see a lot of different men coming to the apartment. That was when the rumours started.'

'What else do people say?'

The man gave a wicked smile. 'They say she came to Italy to be a maid, or rather, a kind of governess, and that she was kept by one lover after another. With each one, she rose in the world. She was a beautiful woman, you know, always wearing expensive clothes, covered in jewellery. A real head-turner.'

'And where does she live now?'

'That, I don't know. Abroad, I think. She's German, you know.'

'You don't have the address?'

'No. We were never particularly close. Just good morning and good evening.'

'I see. And what work does this Leonardo do?'

'Why are you asking all these questions? Has he done something?'

'Oh, no,' Teresa lied, hoping her tone was convincing. 'We found something valuable that we think belongs to him, and we want to give it back.'

'Well, I don't know how I can help you. Come back in a few days. If I happen to see him first, I'll tell him to get in touch with the police.'

'But what work does he do?' she insisted.

'I don't know. If you want my opinion, I don't think he does anything.'

'How does he live?'

'I have no idea.' He gave a sarcastic smile. 'That's for you lot to find out. There are so many people these days, even in this square, who do nothing from morning to night and live in the lap of luxury. Not like in my day —'

'I see,' she cut him short. 'Thank you very much. If you happen to see him first, phone me without telling him.' She handed him a business card.

The man nodded and smiled. 'Got it!' he replied.

The officers left the building and returned to Headquarters.

All except one, who took up position in the square, with his back towards the church, in order to keep watch on the building.

116

Meanwhile a drama was being played out at the Corsi di Borgo Ognissanti barracks.

After some hard questioning, Sara Genovese had been forced to admit that it was she who had written the anonymous letter accusing Alvise Innocenti. It was something she had hesitated over for a long time, she had confessed in tears, something she had done only out of love for her friend. She had sworn over and over that Giovanna had never told her she intended to leave her the inheritance. The news had come out of the blue, she insisted.

Now, her eyes red and swollen, she was drinking coffee, watched by Gori and Surace, who had exchanged knowing looks several times during her confession, both convinced that the time had come to break her down.

'Signora,' Gori said, after she had put the cup down on the desk, 'do you know a man named Umberto Bartolotti?'

'Umberto who?' she asked, staring ahead of her.

'Umberto Bartolotti, the engineer.'

Silence.

Sara Genovese seemed to be in a trance, as if she could not focus on her thoughts. This interview had been too much for her. She felt drained, without strength.

'Look,' Gori said, and showed her Umberto Bartolotti's passport photograph. 'Do you recognise him?'

She looked at it so closely she almost touched it, as if her vision was blurred. Then she moved her head in an almost imperceptible nod.

'Is that a yes?' the marshal asked.

'Yes,' she breathed.

'Could you please tell me how you met him and what your relationship with him is?'

'I have to go to the toilet. May I?'

Surace took her there and came back with her after almost ten minutes. Quite a long absence, during which she had tried to refresh her face, wiping away the last traces of make-up in the process.

'Yes, I know him,' she began when she sat down again, even more white in the face.

'Go on.'

With a trembling voice, Sara Genovese explained that he was an old acquaintance. When she was little more than a child, because of the bad relations between her parents, who neglected her, she had been entrusted by the court to the children's home on the estate belonging to Umberto Bartolotti's father.

At this point, she burst into sobs again.

There followed a long pause. Several times, Gori was on the point of urging her to go on, but held back. He did have a heart after all.

She resumed speaking without prompting.

'Almost all of us were abused,' she said in a thin voice, looking around as if to make sure that only the two Carabinieri were listening to her.

'By Umberto?' the marshal asked.

'No. He was a victim, too. There were men and women.

The women taught us some little "games" – that was what they called them – to please the men, some of them elderly, who came at night.'

'Who were they?'

'I never found out. They wouldn't let us see their faces.'

Silence again. A heart-rending silence. The past was still with her, and still very painful.

Sara Genovese sipped at her water.

'And what's your relationship with Umberto now?' Gori asked after a few minutes.

'We're friends. Just friends. He became a client of mine at the agency. I'm handling some business for him. Right now, he isn't doing very well and he needs to sell some of his property. Including the estate where those poor young people grew up. They were such fragile kids, with uncertain futures. I don't know how I would have ended up if I hadn't met Giovanna. That was another reason I loved her so much.'

Gori and Surace looked at each other, and decided to bring the interview to a close.

It was an interview they would not easily forget.

117

'I just got back from City Hall, chief.'

'How come? Didn't you already go there to ask for your residence permit?'

'Yes, I did, but this time I went to see what I could find out about this supposed mother and her son.' She smiled. 'They all know me at the registry office by now and they've become extremely helpful.' She handed him a photocopy of the family record.

'They're German.'

'Yes, chief, from Munich. It turns out the woman was taken off the register nearly ten years ago, but he still has his residence here. I also had them give me the photograph from his last identity card. It was issued at the end of 1999.'

'Let me see.'

She handed him the photograph.

'Never seen him before,' he said after examining it attentively. 'I see his mother, if that's who she is, went back to Munich.'

'Yes.'

Then she told him what she had learned from the neighbour.

'Excellent work!' Ferrara exclaimed. He liked Teresa more and more. She was bright, motivated, intelligent.

'It looks as though our man has escaped,' he said. 'But at least we have their details. If the woman's living in Munich, that might be where he's gone.'

Teresa nodded.

'I'll contact the liaison officer at the Bundeskriminalamt in Wiesbaden,' Ferrara said.

It was one of the channels of procedure in such cases. For most inquiries abroad they had to turn to Interpol, which was bureaucratic and therefore not always quick in its responses. But in the case of Germany, they could contact the Italian liaison office, which was based in Wiesbaden, at the headquarters of the German criminal police. He opted for this latter solution, convinced he would save time.

It was where he would be working himself very soon. Fate seemed to be playing a game with him.

He looked for the number, and with the little German he had learned over the years from Petra, managed to make himself understood by the switchboard operator, who put him through to the right department.

His conversation with the liaison officer was a long one and concluded with Ferrara agreeing to immediately send the photograph of the man they were looking for.

The bureaucratic machine was under way.

Late in the morning, two important pieces of news reached Ferrara, within a few minutes of each other.

The first was the result of the ballistics report on the bullets extracted from Signora Innocenti's cranium. They were .22 calibre, and the grooves shared the same characteristics as those found on the bullets that had killed the Moroccan. They had all been fired from the same weapon. There was no doubt about it.

The second piece of news concerned the weapon used to

kill Alvise Innocenti. The murderer had not used just any old knife, but a dagger with a long jagged blade. The kind used for underwater fishing. Exactly the same kind as the one found in Beatrice Filangeri's apartment.

No prints, though, had been found on the wrapper of the disposable camera, or on the photograph.

Why had the killer taken photographs of the crime scene? Several crime scenes, in fact. Definitely in the murders of the Innocentis, husband, wife and daughter. Perhaps also at the chapels. What connection could there be?

The first thing that came to Ferrara's mind was that the killer must derive some kind of erotic fulfilment in the act of killing, and that looking at photographs of it afterwards aroused him. Alternatively, he was working for someone else and had taken those photographs to show them his handiwork. Or he wanted to challenge the intelligence of whoever was pursuing him. But what if all three of these reasons were valid?

At any rate, it confirmed that all these acts had been committed by the same person.

Of course, it was rare for criminals to flaunt their crimes in this way, especially when they committed them in the same geographical area. But this was a highly unusual case.

The unrepeatable forensic tests must be carried out as a matter of urgency if they were to catch this killer.

Ferrara picked up the phone and called the deputy prosecutor to remind him to issue the warrants.

'I'll send them in the morning,' Vinci replied before hanging up.

Ferrara was now convinced that the murders were not the work of a madman, a sex maniac or a sadist, as might have been supposed in considering the murders of Giovanna Innocenti and Silvia de Luca individually. Nor were they the work of a racist group, as whoever made that phone call to *La Nazione* wanted them to believe. That must have been an attempt to derail the investigation.

No, these murders had their own logic. Which in all probability had something to do with the Innocentis.

What was still lacking was the motive.

Financial?

Revenge?

Or both?

118

Munich

It was a warm, summery day.

The tables on the café terraces in the Marienplatz were full. It was almost midday and tourists were starting to gather around the column in the centre of the square, which had a gilded statue of the Virgin Mary on top. They were all staring at the clock tower of the New Town Hall, waiting to see the mechanical figures which, when the chimes sounded, would start to move, re-enacting two events in Munich's history: the dance of the coopers to ward off the plague in 1517 and a famous marriage celebrated in the square in 1568. It was a spectacle that delighted not only children but also their parents.

To get a better view, Leonardo Berghoff went into the Hugendubel, the multi-storey bookshop opposite, and took the glass elevator to the top floor. From there, you were so close to those little figures, you felt as though you could touch them with your hand. As soon as they began to move, he took a series of photographs. He remembered the times Ingrid had brought him here when he was a child.

First the figures in the top row moved: two men on horse-back, going in opposite directions, fighting each other with their lances. Then the ones in the lower row started dancing, turning round and round, while a figure in the middle raised his arm to conduct the dance.

Since the weather was so fine, he then walked to the Englischer Garten.

For a few minutes he lingered on the bridge and looked down at the surfers defying the raging waters of the Eisbach, the small but very rapid tributary of the Isar, at the point where it formed a waterfall just over three feet high.

Tomorrow he would pay a visit to the woman who for many years he had thought was his mother.

His last ever visit.

1 p.m.

On the screen of the little TV set, tuned to ZDF, the news began.

The first images were of the war in Afghanistan, showing the aftermath of the latest Taleban attack. A huge crater in the tarmac. Wrecked cars. Mangled corpses. Gutted buildings. Kabul was not getting any safer. God alone knew where it would all end.

Then the item gave way to other news. Terrible news from Italy.

And the woman, lying in bed, suddenly became more attentive.

She knew those places. They were familiar to her.

The images were of Florence, its lovely hills. There was a shot of a luxurious villa where a double murder had apparently been committed. She recognised it immediately, even though she had not seen it for many years.

Her heart began to pound.

Then, when she heard the names of the victims, she felt a chill go through her body.

She knew them, too.

Especially him, Alvise Innocenti.

And she realised that what she had so often feared had finally come to pass. Deep down she had always hoped she would be mistaken. But she wasn't.

When the item finished, she closed her eyes. How many times had she sat down in one of those yellow leather arm-chairs near the fireplace in the kitchen, with little Alvise on her knees! Alvise who, when he was only fourteen, had been such a tall, strong young man. After his parents had died, she had been like a mother to him.

She felt a pang in her heart. It became ever more intense, and she suddenly found she could not breathe. She reached out her arm and pressed the button next to the head of her bed.

Within a few moments a tall, sturdy nurse entered the room.

119

Monday, 5 July

'Chief, there have been more calls, all from the same number!'

Venturi had entered Ferrara's room with a sheet of paper in his hand. He seemed very excited.

'Go on.'

Ferrara had been discussing with Rizzo what to do next. Things were moving to a climax, and they couldn't afford to waste precious time. Rizzo had offered to go to Munich. Maybe if there was an Italian superintendent with them, the local police would move more quickly and efficiently.

'I just got this from the phone company. Someone has been trying to contact Beatrice Filangeri in the last few hours.'

'Let me see.'

Venturi handed him the sheet of paper.

Ferrara examined it. 'Several calls in quick succession,' he said, 'first to her mobile and then to the landline in the chocolate shop. Whoever it is obviously doesn't know she's been arrested.'

Venturi nodded. 'That's for sure. And the last number corresponds to the Hotel Bayerischer Hof in Munich.'

'Bingo!' exclaimed Rizzo. 'Now at last we know where to find him.'

'We have to contact our German colleagues and leave immediately for Munich,' Ferrara said.

'I'm ready to go straight away, chief,' Rizzo said.

'We'll go together, Francesco,' Ferrara replied. 'I'll ask the Commissioner to authorise the mission. In the meantime, inform the liaison officer in Wiesbaden.'

He got up from his chair.

As Ferrara left the room, Rizzo hoped the Commissioner wouldn't kick up a fuss about the mission. Ferrara, meanwhile, was hoping the Commissioner wouldn't bring up the budget cuts as an excuse. What had they been reduced to? It would end up with them having to pay their own expenses and being reimbursed in a year, if they were lucky.

But Adinolfi didn't kick up a fuss.

On the contrary, he greeted the suggestion with something approaching enthusiasm. 'Perfect, Chief Superintendent, that way you'll start getting to know your German colleagues. This mission may help you to feel more confident in your new environment. Quite a stroke of luck, I'd say.'

'We'll leave today, on the first available plane,' Ferrara said.

'*We?* What do you mean, "we"?'

'Superintendent Rizzo is coming with me.'

'Why? Can't you handle it on your own?'

'Rizzo offered to go even before this latest development. And I'd like him to see this investigation through to the end. He's been working flat out for days. He should get some personal satisfaction from it.'

'Chief Superintendent Ferrara, what matters is the result, not personal satisfaction. But we'll see.'

Typical! Ferrara thought. Never having been directly involved in an investigation himself, Adinolfi had no concept of the sacrifices his men had to make, or how their personal lives suffered. What did he know of the pleasure they felt when they got a result?

'Commissioner, I insist that Rizzo comes with me,' he said aloud. 'He knows the case thoroughly and his presence may be vital.'

'The ministry is bound to question the need to send two officers. I can foresee all kinds of problems. Do you realise the straits we're in at the moment, with all these cuts?'

'If there's a problem, tell the ministry I'll pay Rizzo's expenses out of my own pocket.'

'You'd be prepared to do that?'

'Yes, I would.'

'Then I don't think there'll be any problem. You can get ready. I'll start the process of authorisation.'

Ferrara left the room, almost slamming the door.

It had been yet another confirmation, if he still needed one, that it was becoming ever more difficult for the police to do their job to the best of their abilities. The force he had known in the eighties and nineties, he thought sadly, was nothing but a distant memory.

120

Munich

Meanwhile, Leonardo Berghoff was crossing the foyer of the Hotel Bayerischer Hof.

He looked around casually, as if searching for someone, then handed in his keys at reception, paid in cash, and went out through the revolving doors.

Once outside, he looked up at the sky.

It did not look promising. Dark clouds were chasing one another in the distance. The climate of Munich was unpredictable. It could change several times in the course of the same day, especially at this time of year, and you never knew whether to put on light or heavy clothing in the morning. You needed a raincoat, or at least an umbrella, maybe a small one you could keep in a bag or in a briefcase, ready for every eventuality.

He walked to one of the taxis parked outside, and got in. A doorman in an impeccable uniform and black bowler held the door open for him. He slipped a ten-euro note into the man's free hand.

'*Vielen Dank,*' the doorman said, smiling.

He knew this guest: he was Italian, he had seen him on previous occasions.

'*Bitte.*'

Then, turning to the driver, he gave the address.

As the car set off, he glanced to his left, towards the big statue of Maximilian Emanuel of Bavaria, the prince who had lived at the end of the seventeenth century and the beginning of the eighteenth and had become famous for defeating the Turks. Next to it, some children were chasing each other while their mothers or babysitters looked on.

He looked at them with a touch of envy.

121

'You can't see Frau Berghoff today.'

The receptionist spoke quite good Italian. Like so many Germans in Munich. It was sometimes said that Munich was the northernmost city in Italy. Many of the locals spent their holidays in Lake Garda or Lake Iseo.

'Why?'

'She's had a heart attack.'

'A heart attack?'

'*Ja!*'

'Where is she?'

'Klinikum Starnberg.'

He left the nursing home with the box of chocolates in his hand. He called a taxi and gave his next destination.

But he could not see her there either.

She was in a serious condition.

After a heart attack at her age, nearly eighty, there was little chance she would survive.

He took a room in a hotel by the lake, not far from the railway station.

He was tempted to phone Beatrice again, but that might be risky. In fact he had already made a mistake by calling her a few hours earlier, from the hotel in Munich. But why was her telephone off? What had happened to her? He had tried again at the chocolate shop at 10.25, and even that attempt had failed.

Now, shut up in that room by the lake, he felt his anxiety growing.

Rizzo had updated the Italian liaison officer in Wiesbaden on the latest developments.

'Let's hope he's still there,' the officer had replied. 'And let's hope he registered under his own name.'

He explained that in Germany, unlike in Italy, guests registering at hotels did not have to show any identity documents, they just had to fill in a form with their name, date of birth and place of residence; sometimes only the name. Anyone who had something to hide could easily give false information. And this man certainly had every reason to cover his tracks.

'I'll call the Polizeipräsidium in Munich right away,' the liaison officer had said. 'And I'll send them the photograph you sent me.'

122

London

'He must know!'

They were sitting on comfortable red leather armchairs in a beautiful nineteenth-century private reception room in the Hotel Russell, a Victorian building with an imposing facade in the heart of Bloomsbury. The windows looked out on the gardens in Russell Square, where squirrels were jumping in the trees. From the centre of the ceiling hung a splendid crystal chandelier with twenty candle-shaped bulbs.

Sir George was unable to hide his own anxiety at the latest news.

'He doesn't seem to be using his office any more,' he went on. 'He must have discovered the bugs. And now he's holding meetings in the office of a woman police officer, the latest arrival, or in his deputy's office – that plump fellow who seems to worship him as if he was a god.'

'What about our source?' one of the brothers asked.

'Nothing. He hasn't been able to go in. He's too busy outside.'

'All the time?'

'When he got back to Headquarters, the deputy prosecutor

was in the room. They'd made an arrest and were in the middle of an interview.'

'An arrest?'

'Yes.'

'Who?'

'The daughter of old Filangeri, the baker. That redhead who turned the bakery into a chocolate shop.'

'I don't recall the name.'

'She isn't one of ours.'

'Why did they arrest her?'

'That son of a bitch who betrayed us made a mistake.'

'Who do you mean?'

'Enrico's godson. He was taking his revenge on Alvise, and put a black hood on his head to direct the investigation towards us. And that's not all . . .'

Sir George went over Enrico's mistakes in detail. The initiates listened attentively.

'Now his godson is in Munich, as usual,' he continued.

'If you authorise me, I'll deal with it,' the aristocratic-looking young man said.

The others exchanged glances, followed by knowing nods.

'All right,' Sir George replied. 'Go ahead and deal with it. Your moment has come. Betrayal must be paid with blood. Then we'll deal with Enrico. We've waited too long for that.'

A smile appeared on the young man's face. 'I have some excellent contacts in Germany, men I trust absolutely. I'll leave for Munich today on the first available flight. Consider him a dead man.'

They all stood up and moved into another room for breakfast.

Hunted.

Yes, that was how he felt. A hunted lion.

It wasn't only the police who were searching for him now. The brothers who had accepted him into their ranks would be on his trail too. They would have known from the hood over Alvise Innocenti's face, from the photograph, and perhaps also from the fact that his godfather's face had been seen by Madalena. Madalena's death should have been enough to put an end to the matter, but he had then gone further, he had acted in his own interests, putting the organisation at risk.

In addition, Beatrice seemed to have vanished into thin air. Had she been arrested?

Damn, he thought, he had been wrong to phone her from the Bayerischer Hof. He'd be all right, though. Even if the police went there, they wouldn't find him. But what about the taxi drivers? Damn!

He took his suitcase, paid in cash and left the hotel in Starnberg.

He gave the taxi driver his new destination: 'Schwangau.'

'Schwangau?'

'*Ja, bitte!*'

Within an hour, he would be in the heart of the Bavarian Alps, at the beginning of the so-called Romantische Strasse, which winds for 220 miles through natural beauty and historic towns all the way to Würzburg.

For him, though, that border territory, with its medieval castles, was the last destination, the end of the line.

123

Tuesday, 6 July

By 7.30 in the morning Ferrara and Rizzo were on a direct flight from Bologna to Munich. They arrived at 8.10, and were met by a police officer in a BMW, who drove them straight to Police Headquarters, close to Frauenplatz in the centre of the city.

The Polizeipräsidium is a large building with a green facade and red roofs, similar in appearance to a large barracks. Above the secondary entrance on Augustinerstrasse are two figures on either side of an oval window. On one side, a man in a suit of armour, his hands clutching the hilt of a sword, on the other a woman with long golden hair and a cloak, carrying in her arms a heap of ears of corn. Symbols of justice and fertility. The main entrance is on Ettstrasse, through a large iron gate with stone columns on either side, surmounted by two reclining lions that seem to be looking at each other.

It was through this entrance that Ferrara and Rizzo entered that morning. Waiting for them in the little square they found their colleague from Wiesbaden, a thin man of about thirty-five. His name was Rodolfo Ferro and he had been the liaison officer for just over a year. After briefly paying their respects to the Commissioner, a tall thin man with a refined manner, they were led into the office of Markus Glock, the Director of the Criminal Investigation Department.

Glock was tall, sturdy and fair-haired. He was about the same age as Ferrara, but had a much lighter complexion. He knew a little Italian, enough to make himself understood and to understand without Ferro having to act as an interpreter. As a student, he had attended a language course in Milan.

First, he updated his guests on the latest developments.

The receptionists and doormen at the Bayerischer Hof remembered Leonardo Berghoff well. He had often stayed there, although they had found him changed compared with previous visits. But they did not know him as Leonardo Berghoff. In the computer he had been registered under the name Filippo Presta, an Italian living at 100 Via Cavour, Parma.

'That was to be expected,' Ferrara commented, nodding his head.

Glock went on to tell them that his men had questioned all the taxi drivers who had been on duty in the rank outside the hotel from the moment the guest had arrived. They had been shown the photograph and one of them, after a few moments' hesitation, had recognised him. He said he had driven him on Sunday morning to Starnberg, first to an old people's home and then to a hotel by the lake.

'Where is that?' Ferrara asked.

'About fifteen miles from here. But he's not there any more.'

'You mean he's already left?'

'Yes, after a few hours, in another taxi.'

'Where to?'

'Schwangau.'

'How far is that?'

'It's in the Bavarian Alps, south-east of Munich,' Rodolfo

Ferro said, before Glock could even open his mouth. 'It's a skiing resort and also a weather station.'

'We have to go there,' Ferrara said. 'As soon as possible.'

'There are several hotels there,' Glock said, 'but if he hasn't run away again it shouldn't be too difficult to locate him. I'll put two patrols on it, as well as the one that's already on its way there from Starnberg.'

'Thanks,' Ferrara replied.

124

Leonardo Berghoff was sitting in the Restaurant am Park in Schwangauer Strasse, about four miles from Füssen.

He had taken a room in a hotel near the terminal where tourists caught buses to visit the castles. There, too, he had not given his real name, or that of Filippo Presta from Parma. No, now he was called Giulio Adorno with an address in Bologna.

He had become even more cautious, his suspicion verging on paranoia. He couldn't fail in this, the last game he would play. The last challenge. This time it was a challenge to himself: not to get caught and, if possible, not to kill anyone else.

He was eating pig's knuckle with sauerkraut, drinking his favourite beer, Weissbier – he was already on his second tankard – and reflecting on some aspects of his life. He didn't feel the slightest guilt for the crimes he had committed, or any pity for the victims. Except one: Giovanna, his half-sister, on whose grave he had placed a flower on the day of her funeral. He had not hated her, but she had been part of his revenge on Alvise Innocenti.

From where he was sitting, he could see the castle of Neuschwanstein with its crenellated towers. It stood out in all its beauty and majesty on a rocky spur, as if the rocks themselves, and not the hand of man, had given birth to it. Below it, a centuries-old forest. In the distance, the waters of a lake. A fairy-tale location, but also one filled with melancholy, perhaps because the ghost of Ludwig II still hovered over it.

Leonardo Berghoff had liked that strange king, considered by some to be mad, ever since his adolescence, when Ingrid had told him about his life. She had even taken him to visit the various castles and over the years he had often come back alone to Neuschwanstein, the king's favourite refuge.

The sense of sadness and mystery this place somehow conveyed to him had led him, in his desperate flight, all the way here. For the last time. He wanted to go up once again on to the bridge across the stream, the Marienbrücke, where Ludwig loved to stroll in the evening or in the middle of the night and admire the castle, illuminated by the lights of hundreds of candles.

Yes, it was from there that Leonardo Berghoff wanted to look at the world for the last time.

Between one sip of beer and the next, he planned out the rest of the day. He had not tried to phone Beatrice again. He was convinced now that something serious must have happened to her, and he did not want to do anything to compromise her further. She was his own personal initiate, never having become a full member of the lodge of hooded ones.

Several times he had told himself, perhaps only to preserve the illusion, that as soon as she discovered he had been trying to phone her, she would call him back.

Now, though, he had other things to think about.

Above all, he had a letter to write, the contents of which were gradually taking shape in his mind.

125

The search wasn't easy.

The three patrols divided up the tasks. One would concentrate on Schwangau. Another, with Glock, Ferrara and Rizzo, would reconnoitre Füssen. The third would focus on the adjacent areas.

Each officer had a photograph of the fugitive. None of them, however, had seen him.

And none of the hoteliers who had so far been shown the photograph had recognised him as a guest. No, that face meant absolutely nothing.

It had already grown dark by the time the patrol car with the Italian officers drew up outside the Park Hotel, which was situated on the road leading to the castles of Neuschwanstein and Hohenschwangau.

Glock and Ferrara got out of the Opel Vectra and walked to the hotel. They were greeted by the doorman, a tall fat man. As soon as he saw the photograph, he said without hesitation, 'He just left.'

Glock and Ferrara exchanged rapid glances.

The man indicated the direction the guest had taken on foot: the bus terminal from which you caught the bus to the castle of Neuschwanstein. But at this hour, the buses had stopped running. The two officers rushed out, while the door-man looked on in astonishment. They drove more than a hundred yards and, just as they reached the bus terminal, they saw a figure leaving the main road and setting off along the path leading through the woods and up the mountain to the castle of Neuschwanstein.

At the sound of a vehicle braking hard, Leonardo Berghoff turned and saw the police car in the distance.

He immediately started running up the path as if chased by the devil.

Glock and Ferrara set off after him. Rizzo and his German colleague, who had parked the car close by, followed them.

They ran for a while in single file, then stopped for a few moments to catch their breath. The man seemed to have vanished into thin air, swallowed by the darkness.

They still couldn't see anything but trees.

They continued along the path as it climbed through the forest. All at once, Ferrara thought he saw a crouching figure on his right, in amongst the tall thin trees. He approached slowly, followed by Rizzo, regretting that he was not armed. Their two German colleagues, however, were, and they were just a few yards behind.

'You there!' Ferrara cried.

Silence.

They cautiously inspected the area.

Nothing.

A false alarm.

Perhaps it had been an animal.

They continued along the main path, the silence broken only by the sound of their steps.

126

After a good half hour, the pursuers had left the castle of Neuschwanstein behind them on their left, and had arrived at a fork in the road. One branch led to the Marienbrücke, the other to Bleckenau. For Ferrara and Rizzo, these were unknown places. But not for Markus Glock. He and Ferrara turned left towards the Marienbrücke, while Rizzo and the other officer continued to the right. Glock and Ferrara followed a narrow, curving tarmac road, as it ascended the slope. After a few minutes, they came in sight of the bridge, with its floor of long wooden planks and its iron side rails. They could clearly hear the noise of the waterfall, which formed a little lake at that point before continuing its course downstream.

It was then that they saw a figure. It was him, Leonardo Berghoff. Tired, but with a self-satisfied smile on his face.

'Wait here,' Ferrara murmured. 'I'll move in closer.'

Glock would have liked to remind him that they were in Germany, on his territory, and that it was up to him to direct the operation. But he made no objection. Better to indulge his Italian colleague. He stopped and crouched on the ground. Ferrara was already walking towards the middle of the bridge.

'Stop, Chief Superintendent!' Leonardo Berghoff cried. They were no more than ten feet apart and he had recognised him.

'Give yourself up,' Ferrara replied. 'The whole area is sur-rounded, you can't escape. I have a lot of questions to ask you.' He took another step forward.

'Don't come any closer, or you'll force me to kill again,' Berghoff said, pointing a gun at him with his left hand. The barrel shone for a moment in the darkness. 'You're a real bloodhound, Chief Superintendent, but you haven't under-stood my game, my challenge. And yet I sent you some very clear messages! I wanted you to open your third eye.'

'You were only a pawn in a game bigger than you. I need to know who's behind all this.'

A brief silence.

'It's not as simple as you may think,' Berghoff said. 'I was carrying out a plan of my own. It was my revenge and I used the Black Rose to—'

Just then, there was a distant flash in the darkness, followed by a whistle coming fast through the air and a muffled scream.

Leonardo Berghoff swayed and fell. As he did so, he instinctively pressed the trigger of the gun, which was still pointed at Ferrara.

Another flash.

A shot broke the surrounding silence.

In a matter of seconds, Ferrara found himself crying out with pain and fear. His left arm seemed to have been cut clean off, he could no longer feel it. His right hand went to his shoulder and he felt a warm, viscous liquid. Blood. His hand was covered with it. Then he crouched, waiting for another shot, the one that would kill him. On the ground, unarmed, he was now an easy target.

Glock emptied the magazine of his gun. Leonardo Berghoff rolled over on the ground and lay still. His wide-open eyes seemed to stare at the castle.

In the meantime, from the other side of the bridge, a man

in black overalls began to dismantle his precision rifle with its silencer and infrared sight. Then he put the pieces back in his rucksack and set off along a path that climbed the mountain. There had been no need to fire any other shots. His mission had been accomplished. The aristocratic-looking young man would reward him well for it.

Confused images.

A screaming siren.

In his field of vision, Ferrara thought he saw a man in a white coat. He stared at him. He realised that he was on a stretcher. He put his right hand on his left arm and felt a thick bandage. After a while, there were no more jolts, just excited footsteps close by him. They were wheeling him into a hospital. Here he exchanged a few words in Italian, or at least he had that impression. Then his mind went blank.

127

Wednesday, 7 July

A bad dream?

Or was it all true?

The room was quite large and completely white. There was another bed apart from his, but it was empty. There were two windows, through which the mountains could be seen. Silence. He tried to move, but without succeeding.

He had only just recovered consciousness that morning.

He wanted to look at his watch, but realised he did not have it. In its place was an eye-catching bandage that covered his whole arm. On his right he saw a tube leading down to his arm. Above it, a white, transparent container, full of liquid. He looked around. There was nobody here. He was alone. He felt a sense of confusion, but his mind gradually started to clear, to go back in time, replaying the images of the last hours and that flash in the thick darkness of the forest. The pain in his arm and shoulder. The blood. The black rose. The stretcher. He remembered everything, or almost everything. His brain was working again.

He was still thinking about those last hours when a tall blonde nurse came in. She looked at him almost fearfully.

Then she smiled. But he felt exhausted. All he wanted to do was close his eyes and sleep.

'Please, tell me where I am,' he said, returning her smile. The woman did not reply. She had not understood.

'*Wo bin ich?*' he insisted in his poor German.

'Klinik Füssen,' she replied.

'The hospital at Füssen? *Danke.*'

The nurse put a thermometer on his tongue to take his temperature: 37.8. At that moment a pink-faced, relaxed-looking young man entered.

'I'm Dr Torrisi, the surgeon who operated on you.'

Ferrara smiled.

'How are you feeling?'

'Very well, thank you.'

The doctor checked the contents of the drip, then carefully took off the bandage and replaced the needle. Ferrara grimaced, but the pain disappeared immediately.

'Is it serious?' he asked.

'No,' the doctor replied, as he put a new bandage on, 'but you will have to stay here for two weeks. I took a .22 calibre bullet from your arm.'

When he had finished, he whispered something in the nurse's ear and went out to continue his rounds. Other patients were waiting for him.

Ferrara thought of his wife. He would have liked to have her there. She could spend the night in the other bed. She would give a personal touch to this room, recreating their own home in microcosm.

And as he imagined Petra's presence, he felt the urge to smoke a cigar. He made an effort to suppress it. By now, he thought, they must already have informed her. How worried she must be!

She must hear my voice, and soon, he said to himself.

But he was alone again.

128

When Glock and Rizzo came to see him, he was awake, but lost in thought.

His mind was still occupied by the events of the night and above all by the thought of Petra. He smiled at them and breathed, 'Thank you.'

Then: 'Did you catch the man who did it?'

Looking at Rizzo, he thought, At last! I can use his mobile phone to talk to Petra.

'Unfortunately not,' Rizzo replied, adjusting his pillow for him, then sitting down on the edge of the bed. 'He managed to get away. We only found the position from which he fired the rifle shot. Beyond the bridge, on a little rise. They searched the whole area last night. They even used helicopters, but there was no sign of the sniper. He disappeared.'

'What about Leonardo Berghoff?'

'He's dead.'

Ferrara's face darkened.

'We found this in his trouser pocket,' Rizzo said, taking out a photocopy of a letter. 'Can you hold it with your right hand, chief?'

'I'll try.'

He took it, making sure that the drip was not dislodged as he did so. Rizzo helped him to put on his glasses.

He started reading.

The letter was addressed to him.

Chief Superintendent Ferrara

If you're reading this letter, that means you've won, and I'll try to expiate my sins by – perhaps – saving your life.

He stopped for a moment and let out a deep breath. Glock and Rizzo watched him with concern.

He resumed reading.

My whole life has been marked by evil, ever since I was born. Then came the day when I understood who I really was. Not that lively, good-looking child loved to distraction by his mother. No, that woman was not my mother. I discovered at the age of sixteen that I had been brought into this world by a high-class prostitute and that my natural father was that bastard Alvise Innocenti, who raped his own daughter. It was then that I, too, began to fall into the abyss of evil. Real evil. The evil that has given me the strength to survive and take my revenge, but which at the same time has turned me into a true monster.

Another pause, during which Ferrara looked from Rizzo to Glock several times.

Back to the letter.

I'm certain that by now you'll have understood, so it's pointless for me to continue with my personal story. You have sufficient intelligence and intuition to reconstruct the latest events in Florence, including the murder of the illegal immigrant. Yes, even that one. Men who rape women have no right to exist, or even to be put on trial.

And now for the plan I put into action: I carried out my revenge while at the same time following the instructions of people you would do well to leave in peace if you care about your own safety. It's a fringe group within a powerful Masonic lodge, with members in every field of society, including politics and state institutions, both in Italy and the outside world. A group which has been hindering your every move from behind the scenes, and which could take drastic action against you if its secrecy were to be endangered. I don't know the leaders, but I know for certain that they represent the blackest evil.

But I will give you two names connected to them, though in different ways. One is that officer of yours they call Serpico. The other is former senator Enrico Costanza, who has the rank of prince and who has now reached the end of the line because of the cancer that's killing him. He's my godfather. It was he who introduced me into the secret world of the hooded men and the black rose. It was also he who ordered the murder of Madalena after she had seen him with his face uncovered during a ceremony. But it's all too complex to explain in detail. I'll only tell you that they intend to destroy the Bartolotti family, which is why the killing was carried out on their property. A word of advice: look into the past of that family and leave the Black Rose alone. It will never die.

Farewell!

Leonardo Berghoff

PS. I entrust Ingrid Berghoff to you. She is the German woman who brought me up until the age of eighteen and

gave me her surname. She is almost eighty years old and is in
a serious condition at the hospital in Starnberg. She was the
lover of Senator Costanza, the close friend of that pig
Alvise.

I should have poisoned her, but at this point she's no
longer a danger to me . . .

Ferrara gave the letter back to Rizzo, muttering Sergi's name
several times.

Then: 'Leave the Black Rose alone. It will never die.'

And his eyes, which had become watery, met Rizzo's.

They looked at each other for a long time, while those last
words still echoed in Ferrara's mind.

It will never die.

Acknowledgements

I wish to thank Daniela and Luigi Bernabò, my literary agents and friends, Paola and Andrea, my patient editors, as well as my Italian and foreign publishers, for the care and attention they have given my books. Special thanks to my friends Monika and Detlef Glas for showing me, among other things, the wonders of Bavaria and its fairy-tale castles.